PRIMARY COLORS

Anonymus

PRIMARY COLORS
A Novel of Politics

VINTAGE

Published by Vintage 1996

2 4 6 8 10 9 7 5 3 1

First published in Great Britain by
Chatto & Windus Ltd, 1996

Vintage
Random House, 20 Vauxhall Bridge Road,
London SW1V 2SA

Random House Australia (Pty) Limited
20 Alfred Street, Milsons Point, Sydney
New South Wales 2061, Australia

Random House New Zealand Limited
18 Poland Road, Glenfield,
Auckland 10, New Zealand

Random House South Africa (Pty) Limited
PO Box 2263, Rosebank 2121, South Africa

Random House UK Limited Reg. No. 954009

A CIP catalogue record for this book
is available from the British Library

ISBN 0 09 974781 2

Papers used by Random House UK Ltd are natural, recyclable products made from wood grown in sustainable forests. The manufacturing processes conform to the environmental regulations of the country of origin

Printed and bound in Great Britain by
Cox & Wyman, Reading, Berkshire

For my spouse, living proof that flamboyance
and discretion are not mutually exclusive

Men as a whole judge more with their
eyes than with their hands.

—Machiavelli

AUTHOR'S NOTE

Several well-known people—journalists, mostly—make cameo appearances in these pages, but this is a work of fiction and the usual rules apply. None of the other characters are real. None of these events ever happened.

PRIMARY COLORS

I

He was a big fellow, looking seriously pale on the streets of Harlem in deep summer. I am small and not so dark, not very threatening to Caucasians; I do not strut my stuff.

We shook hands. My inability to recall that particular moment more precisely is disappointing: the handshake is the threshold act, the beginning of politics. I've seen him do it two million times now, but I couldn't tell you *how* he does it, the right-handed part of it—the strength, quality, duration of it, the rudiments of pressing the flesh. I can, however, tell you a whole lot about what he does with his other hand. He is a genius with it. He might put it on your elbow, or up by your biceps: these are basic, reflexive moves. He is interested in you. He is honored to meet you. If he gets any higher up your shoulder— if he, say, drapes his left arm over your back, it is somehow less intimate, more casual. He'll share a laugh or a secret then—a light secret, not a real one—flattering you with the illusion of conspiracy. If he doesn't know you all that well and you've just told him something "important," something earnest or emotional, he will lock in and honor you with a two-hander, his left hand overwhelming your wrist and forearm. He'll flash that famous misty look of his. And he will mean it.

Anyway, as I recall it, he gave me a left-hand-just-above-the-elbow plus a vaguely curious "ah, so you're the guy I've been hearing about" look, and a follow-me nod. I didn't have the time, or presence of mind, to send any message back at him. Slow emotional reflexes, I guess. His were lightning. He was six meaningful handshakes down the row before I caught up. And then I fell in, a step or two behind, classic staff position, as if I'd been doing it all my life. (I had, but not for anyone so good.)

We were sweeping up into the library, the librarian in tow, and now he had his big ears on. She was explaining her program and he was in heavy listening mode, the most aggressive listening the world has ever known: aerobic listening. It is an intense, disconcerting phe- nomenon—as if he were hearing quicker than you can get the words out, as if he were sucking the information out of you. When he gives full ear—a rare enough event; he's usually ingesting from two or three sources—his listening becomes the central fact of the conversation. He was doing this now, with the librarian, and she was staggering under it. She missed a step; he reached out, steadied her. She was mid- dle-aged, pushing fifty, hair dyed auburn to blot the gray, unexcep- tional except for her legs, which were shocking, a gift from God. Had he noticed the legs when she almost went down on the stair? I couldn't tell. Howard Ferguson III had insinuated himself next to me, as we nudged up the crowded staircase, his hand squeezing my elbow—Lord, these were touchy fellows—saying: "Glad you changed your mind. Jack's really excited you could do this."

"What are we doing?" I asked. Howard had called and invited me to meet Governor Jack Stanton, who might or might not be running for president. The governor was stopping in New York on his way to do some early, explanatory wandering through New Hampshire. The invitation came with an intriguing address—in Harlem, of all places. (There was no money in Harlem and this was the serious money- bagging stage of the campaign, especially for an obscure Southern governor.) It also came with shameless flattery. "You're legendary," Howard had said in a dusty midwestern voice, cagey and playful. "He wants to lure you out of retirement."

Retirement: I had fled Washington after six years with Congress- man William Larkin. It had been my first job out of school—and I was a victim of his upward mobility, from member to whip to major- ity leader. Too much. I hadn't been ready for power; I'd kind of enjoyed the back benches. It was too soon for me to be someone, the majority leader's guy, the guy you had to get with if you wanted something in or out of this or that. And so, on my thirtieth birthday, an epiphany: "I'm sorry, sir—I need a break," I told the congressman.

"Don't you believe in what we're doing?" he asked.

You mean, counting heads? Lemme outta here. I was going out with a woman named March then; she was great-looking, but she worked for Nader and came equipped with a lack of irony guaranteed to survive the most rigorous crash testing. I found myself having fantasies of working my way through the months: April, May, June. . . . I don't remember what I told her. I told her something. "Henry, isn't this a little young for a midlife crisis?" she asked.

No. I called Philip Noyce at Columbia. I'd known him all my life. He was a colleague of Father's—back when, back before Father left Mother and began his World's Most Obscure Universities Tour. In the event, Philip got me a gig. I taught legislative process. As midlife crises go, it had been a busman's holiday.

Now I thought I might be ready to resume . . . things.

Anyway, I was curious. What was Jack Stanton doing up in Harlem when he should have been down on Wall Street trying to impress the big spenders? Was he trying to impress *me*? I doubted it. More likely, he had invited me along for racial cover. I was, I realized, the only black face in his entourage. Howard Ferguson certainly was about as far as you could get from dark. I noticed a discrete bauble of perspiration moving diagonally down the side of his forehead into his weird Elvis sideburn, as if his sweat were rationed: he was so dry, so thin-lipped austere—and his eyes burned so hard—one imagined that whatever juice he had inside was precious; if he didn't stay lubricated, he might catch fire. Howard was legendary himself, sort of: vestigial, a prairie ghost. He was born to a line of arsonists. His great-grandfather Firefly Ferguson had set the wheat fields ablaze and run for governor from a jail cell. Howard wore Firefly's parched, sandy face, thinning hair parted in the middle—and a pink flowered Liberty tie: I do not take this life, these lawyer clothes seriously, it said. His role in the Stanton operation was elusive—months later I'd still be trying to figure it out. He was a man who never tipped his hand, who never expressed an opinion in a meeting, and yet gave off the sense that he had very powerful convictions, too powerful to be hinted among strangers. He had known the governor forever, since the antiwar days. "You ever been to an adult literacy program?" he asked, then chuckled. "Jack eats this shit up. Says it's like going to church."

So it was. It was a better room than the usual government-issue Formica and cinder block. There were none of the relentlessly cheery posters of books and owls. It was a dark, solemn place—a WPA library. The bookcases were oak and went most of the way up the walls; there was a mural above, a Bentonian, popular-front vision of biplanes buzzing the Statue of Liberty, locomotives rushing through wheat fields, glorious, muscular laborers going to work—a Howard Ferguson dreamscape. (They didn't need hortatory READ BOOKS propaganda back then; there were other struggles.) The class was seated around a large, round oak table. They were what the WPA muralist had in mind: a saintly proletariat.

The librarian, condescending to them in the reflexive, unconsciously insulting manner of public servants everywhere, introduced the visitor: "Governor Jack Stanton, who has been a great friend of continuing education, and is now running for . . ." She tossed a flirtatious look his way.

"Cover," he said.

"Do you want to say a few—"

"No, no—y'all go on ahead," he purred. "Don't mind me."

He took a seat away from the table, deftly respecting the integrity of the class. I sat diagonally across the room from him; I could watch him watching them. Howard stood behind me, leaning against a bookcase. They introduced themselves. They were waitresses, dishwashers and janitors, most in their twenties and thirties, people with night jobs. Each read a little; the women had an easier time of it than the men, who really struggled. And then they said something about their lives. It was very moving. The last to go was Dewayne Smith, who weighed three hundred pounds easy and was a short-order chef. "They just kept passin' me up, y'know?" he said. "Couldn't read a lick, had a . . . learning disbility." He looked over to the librarian to make sure he had said it right.

"Dewayne's dyslexic," she said.

"They just kept a passin' me up—third grade, fourth grade—and I'm like too proud, y'know? It was like no one noticed anyways. I sit in the back, I ain't a mouthy broth—person, I don't cause no trouble, I stick to my own self. So I go on through, *all* the ways through. I graduate elementary school. They send me to Ben Franklin, general studies. They coulda sent me to the Bronx Zoo. No one ever tell me nothin'. No one ever say, 'Dewayne, you can't read—what you gonna do with your sorry ass?' Scuse me." He looked over at the governor, who smiled, urging him on.

"This was twenty years ago," the librarian interjected. "We're better about catching those things now"—as if that canceled out such monumental callousness, the numb stupidity of the system.

"Anyway, graduation come. My momma come. She take the day off from the laundry where she work, puts on her church dress. She don't have a clue nothin's wrong; me neither. I been skatin' through? So we're there and Dr. Dalemberti is callin' out the names and what we did, like 'Sharonna Harris, honors,' or 'Tyrone Kirby, Regents diploma,' and everyone's gotta just stand there on the stage, while they come up one by one. So they get to my name—goin' alphabetical, y'know—and Dr. Dalemberti says, so everyone hear it, 'Dewayne Smith receive a certificate of attendance.' You can hear people buzzin', coupla folks laughin' a little, and I gotta go walk up there, and get this . . . it look just like a diploma, y'know? Same kind of paper—funny, how I'm thinking people won't notice 'cause it's the same kind of paper. But that don't work: everyone know the truth now. And I'm thinkin': Sucker. These folks expect you a fool, they got rid of everyone else can't read, they drop out. And my reward for stickin' around is—I gotta stand there, burnin', and I'm tryin' not to look at anyone, tryin' not to look too stupid, y'know? But feelin' stupid as a rock. The girl come up after me gigglin' a little, still laughin' 'bout me, y'know? She nervous cause she gotta stand next to the idiot. Like it's catchin' or somethin'. And I see Momma out there with her hat on and her purse in her lap. She wearin' her white church gloves. She got her glasses on, and tears comin' down from behind her glasses, like someone hurt her bad, like someone die."

I kind of lost it then. I tried to gulp down the sob, but Dewayne had caught me somewhere deeper, and earlier, than politics. Damn. I shuddered, tears leaked out the side of my eye. And: Do you know how it happens at a moment like that, when you are embarrassed like that, you will look directly—reflexively—at the very person you don't want to see you? I looked over at Jack Stanton. His face was beet-red, his blue eyes glistening and tears were rolling down his cheeks.

The first thought was—relief: relief and amazement, and a sudden, sharp, quite surprising affinity. This was followed, quickly, by a caveat: Weakness? Ed Muskie in the snow in New Hampshire? But that evaporated, because Stanton had launched himself into motion, rubbing his cheeks off with the back of his hands—everyone knew now that he had lost it—standing up, standing over the table, hands on the shoulders of two of the students, leaning over the table toward Dewayne and saying, "I am so very, very deeply grateful that you'd share that with us, Dewayne." It wasn't nearly so bad as the words sound now. He had the courage of his emotions. "And I think it is time we made it impossible—I mean *impossible*—for anyone to get lost in the system like you did. We have to learn to cherish our young people. But most of all, I want to thank you for believing, for having faith—faith that you can overcome the odds and learn and succeed." It was getting a little thick, and he seemed to sense it. He got off the soapbox, kicked back, circled the table over to where Dewayne was; I had him in profile now. "Takes some courage, too. How many y'all tell your friends and family where you're going when you come here?" There were smiles.

"Let me tell you a story," he said. "It's about my uncle Charlie. This happened just after I was born, so I only got it from my momma—but I know it's true. Charlie came home from the war a hero. He had been on Iwo Jima—you know, where they raised the flag? And he had taken out several machine-gun nests of Japs . . . Japanese soldiers, who had a squad of his buddies pinned down. First one with a grenade. Second one by himself, with his rifle and bayonet and bare hands. They found him with a knife in his gut and his hands around an enemy soldier's throat. He had two bullets in him, too."

Dewayne said, "Shit."

"Yeah, that's right," Stanton said, moving clockwise around the table now, like a big cat. "They gave him the Medal of Honor. President Truman did. And then he came home to our little town, Grace Junction. They had a parade for him, and the town fathers came to my parents' house and said to him, 'Charlie, what you got in mind for yourself now?' Charlie said he didn't know. Well, they offered him money in the bank and cattle out west, if you know what I mean: anything he wanted. The mayor said Charlie could have a full scholarship to the state university. The banker said he could understand if Charlie didn't want to go back to school after all he'd been through, so he was offering him a management job, big future, at the bank. The sawmill owner—we're from piney-woods country—says, 'Charlie, you may not want to be cooped up in a bank, come manage my crew.' And you know what? Damned if Charlie didn't turn them all down."

Stanton stopped. He waited. One of the women said, "So what he do?"

"Nothin'. He just lay down on the couch, smoked his Luckies, let himself go. . . . No one could get him off that couch."

"Oh, I got it," said a wiry Hispanic with a pencil-thin mustache. "He got his head fu— ah, mess up. He got one of them post-dramatic things, right?"

"Nope," Stanton said, very calmly. "It was just that, well . . . He couldn't read."

Heads snapped, someone said *What?,* someone whistled, someone said, "No shit."

"He couldn't read, and he was embarrassed, and he didn't want to tell anyone," Stanton said. "He had the courage to win the Congressional Medal of Honor, but he didn't have the strength to do what each of you has done, what—each—of—you—is doing—right— here. He didn't have the courage to admit he needed help, and to find it. So I want you to know that I understand, I appreciate what you are doing here, I *honor* your commitment. And when people ask me, 'Jack Stanton, why are you always spending so much money and so much time and so much effort on adult literacy programs?' I tell them: Because it gives me a chance to see real courage. It inspires me to be stronger. I am so grateful you've let me visit with you today."

I have seen better speakers and heard better speeches, but I don't think I'd ever heard—at least, not till that moment—a speaker who measured his audience so well and connected so precisely. It was an impressive bit of politics. And they were all over him then, clapping his back, shaking his hand, hugging him. He didn't back off, keep his space, the way most pols would; he leaned into them, and seemed to get as much satisfaction from touching them, draping his big arm over their shoulders, as they got from him. He had this beatific, slightly goofy look on. And then Dewayne said, "Wait a minute." The room fell silent. "What about Charlie?"

"Well, it took a while," Stanton said, more conversationally. They were all friends now. "He started hanging 'round the high school when I got up there. He, uh—" Stanton was embarrassed. He was making a decision. He went ahead with it—"Well, I was the manager of the varsity baseball team and Charlie liked to sit with me on the bench, helping out—and that grew into helping out around the gymnasium, and finally they offered him a job when Mr. Krause died."

"Who Mr. Krause? What job he got?"

"Oh, he was the school janitor."

"No shit."

He stayed with them for a time, answering questions, signing autographs. The library lady pitched Stanton about the need for more money—there was a long waiting list of people who wanted to get into that program but had to be turned away. Then they all followed him back downstairs, and out to the car. Howard Ferguson and I trailed the crowd. Howard squeezed my arm gently, just above the elbow, kind of chuckled—a strangled guffaw—and shrugged, as if to say: What can I say?

"How do you know him?" I asked, having to ask something.

"Oh, a long time," he said.

The governor was down on the sidewalk now, chugging through another round of meaningful handshakes. Ferguson and I stood over by the car. "So what do you think?" Howard asked.

I said something enthusiastic, but I really was wondering: Is he expecting me to say something like "Where do I sign up?" Didn't they want to sit down and say, Here's what we're doing and here's what we'd like you to do and what do you think about this issue, or that person, and how do you think someone should run for president of the United States these days?

Stanton came over. Looked at me. So? "Well, that was something," I said.

"I can't believe we can't rustle up enough dough to make this available to anyone who wants it," he said. (What was this going to be—a policy discussion?) "Why didn't you guys fund it better?"

Because my former boss was a weenie. But do you just say that straight off? If you badmouth the old boss, what does that tell the prospective new boss about your loyalty? "Well, it was late, we got trapped in a formula fight," I said and gobbledygooked on about rules and amendments and assorted horseshit, but he didn't listen very long. In fact, he turned away halfway through a sentence—no pretense about just shutting me down—and asked Ferguson, "Where?"

"*Times* editorial board," Howard said laconically. "You're only about a half hour late right now."

Stanton suddenly was red in the face—and I mean the mood had changed with blinding speed: from sunshine to tornado in a blink. "You call them?" he demanded, eyes squinting down. If the answer was no, I was afraid Stanton would deck him.

"Of course," Howard said. "Told them traffic."

Stanton lightened as suddenly as he'd darkened. Clouds scudding on a windy day. "I *love* New York," he said, back to aw-shucks-I'm-just-a-poor-country-governor. "Easiest place in the world to be late."

"But we better roll."

Stanton ducked into the car. Was that it? Weren't they forgetting something? Howard cracked his window, "Can you meet us in our suite up at the Regency, 'bout eleven tonight?"

"Eleven?"

Stanton rolled down his window. "Whatsa matter, Henry," he asked, slyly, conspiratorially, "—you got some action going?"

"No," I said. Boy, did I feel slow. Was he looking for something clever, something sexual? He kept coming at me from places I didn't expect.

"See you, then," Ferguson said as the car rolled away.

Eleven o'clock? Well, it was late. It implied that we were skipping ahead, past the usual formalities. It assumed an intimacy that did not exist, in my mind, yet—but it was flattering, too. It also assumed I was a professional and would understand the rhythms of a campaign, even a larval one. Politicians work—they do their public work, that is—when civilians don't: mealtimes, evenings, weekends. The rest of the time, down time, is spent indoors, in hotel suites, worrying the phones, dialing for dollars, fighting over the next moves, living outside time; there are no weekdays or weekends; there is sleep but not much rest. Sometimes, and always at the oddest hours, you may break free: an afternoon movie, a midnight dinner. And there are those other, fleeting moments when your mind drifts from him, from the podium, and you fix on the father and son tossing a ball out past the back of the crowd, out in the park, and you suddenly realize, Hey, it's Saturday; or you glance out a hotel window and spot an elderly couple walking hand in hand, still alive in each other's mind (as opposed to merely sharing space, waiting it out). The campaign—with all its talk of destiny, crisis and mission—falls away and you remember: Other people just have lives. Their normality can seem a reproach. It hurts your eyes, like walking out of a matinee into bright sunlight. Then it passes. He screws up a line, it's Q&A time, it's time to move.

The suite at the Regency brought all that back. It was generic; it existed outside time. I was, at once, vaguely depressed and entirely comfortable. There was a handful of pols in shirtsleeves, working the phones, hammering laptops, nibbling off platters of fruit and cheese, chugging Diet Cokes. No smoke, no booze anymore. But a haze of ill health all the same; sycophancy frays the nerves, clogs the arteries. I didn't know most of them. There were a couple of bodyguard, trooper types. There were a couple of Handi Wipes with wispy mustaches—statehouse sorts about to be paved over.

And there was Arlen Sporken, a Washington media consultant I knew only by reputation, which was mixed. He was hot right then, as hot as he would ever be, having just won a special election down in the Carolinas with a pro-choice ad that sold the Crackers on the notion that the Founding Fathers fought and died for the right to a d&c. Sporken had a great, fresh effusion of golden farmboy hair, after which it was all downhill, his body dissolving into a shocking wallow of fat. Pols tend toward fat, except for the joggers and jigglers, who burn down like fuses in a campaign. Sporken had a kind face, a pleasant drawl. He was from Mississippi and reeked of the un-ironic liberal fervor common to Southern Baptists who'd had conversion experiences during the civil rights years. He was a booster, an enthusiast—and another toucher, a flagrant one. "Henry Burton, as I live and breathe!" he announced, yanking my hand, then crushing me in a full body hug that culminated in actual backslapping and rib-chucking. "So you're on board."

"Well, I—"

"He thinks you're great. Great! Just great." This was more than your standard white-boy overcompensation in overdrive. "We're gonna win this thing," he was saying now. "Don't you think?"

Since this couldn't possibly be the beginning of a serious conversation about the campaign, I said something harmless like "Well, who else is in?"

"Henry, you really *have* been away. Harris, definitely. Martin, maybe. Luther Charles—well, you know Brother Luther." I did know Luther, mostly as a distant childhood memory; I hadn't seen him in years. But Sporken couldn't possibly have known that: he was assuming that since Luther was a *brother,* I'd have tribal vibes about his political intentions. So I sent him a quasi-disdainful look that said, We don't share vibes on the first date with persons outside the pigment. Arlen—a good liberal—retreated, respecting my racial space. "Uh, the big question is Ozio, of course," he concluded. "You think he's got the cojones to run?"

A mortal dork, this guy. I considered the door. But I wanted to see Stanton again, I guess. "Ozio . . . Don't know him personally," I said. It was one of those conversations you have—usually with civilians—where life imitates the *McLaughlin Group*, where you say the safe, expected things. Political chat. But I strayed a little then, got too close to something real. "If Ozio did go, and put it all together," I asked. "Would you take the two spot?"

"Fuck a duck," said a familiar voice just behind me. "I'll take what I can get."

Stanton had cracked open the door to the bedroom behind me; he was buttoning his shirt over a hairless, pink chest; he was the color of a medium-rare steak just off the grill, steaming a little. I had heard about this. He opened the door wider. "You remember Ms. Baum," he said.

The librarian. I hope I didn't gasp. She was . . . arranging herself. She seemed a bit dazed. She whacked her shoulder on the bedroom door, trying to squeeze past him. "Ow," she yipped. He leaned into her, put his arm on her. "You all right, darlin'?" She stiffened, desperately attempting to maintain the appearance of propriety. He was—well, he was entirely unembarrassed, as if he'd just sneezed, or scratched himself, or yawned, or done any of those semiprivate physical things normal people are willing to do in front of strangers.

"Well, Governor," she said, "it was good to have . . . this . . ."

He saved her, or tried to. "Henry," he said, turning to me. "Don't you think Ms. Baum runs just a great program?"

I said something.

"Thanks so much," she said, moving toward the door. "For . . ."

"You're going to give my best to Irv Gelber, right?"

"Of course, we'll—"

"Take this up with your board. Tell Irv I'll even extend him the privilege of whupping my butt on the golf course." He had moved toward the door, following her. He put his hand on her shoulder, stopping her. He whispered something in her ear. She inhaled, then darted out the door.

"'Bye now," he said, closing the door, chuckling a little. He moved over toward the bar. There were piles of sandwiches, fruit and cheese. He prowled the food; he worried over it. He reached for a sandwich, restrained himself; chose an apple—a perfect red Delicious, like the poisoned one in *Snow White,* and made it disappear. "Ms. Baum is on the regional board of the teachers union," he explained, still chewing.

"I was wondering why you chose that particular library," I said, "in Harlem—"

Arlen Sporken was immediately in my face. "The governor *always* visits adult literacy programs, *wherever* he goes."

Stanton didn't seem too eager to acknowledge the politics of it, either. That part was obvious. It wasn't something you had to talk about. He made it clear, through the slightest of winces, a raised hand, a turn away—something—that this was an invasion of his innocence, a squall line threatening his uncloudy day.

"Well, it was a pretty amazing experience," I tried. What an idiot. And nobody said anything; nobody helped me out.

Stanton peered at me in a kindly way, as if he hoped that I'd know where to take the conversation from there. But I was stuck, clueless, and beginning to sweat. And then, for the first of what would be many, many times, *she* saved me.

The phone. "The missus," a trooper said.

He snagged a sandwich on the way. The receiver seemed tiny in his hand. I noticed his long, graceful fingers. He caressed the phone; it was clear he knew how to work it. "Hi, darlin'," he said. And then she leveled him—the sharp, distant bark was audible where I stood. His eyes narrowed, his brow furrowed. "Oh, listen, honey, I know, I know . . . I'm sorry . . . We got stuck here. But great news. Real progress with the teachers—" His eyes narrowed again. "Tonight? Are you sure? . . . I'm sorry . . . I had no idea—" Then, to one of the statehouse guys: "Charlie, did you know we were supposed to meet the guy from the Portsmouth Democratic Committee tonight?" Charlie shrugged; smiled. He was a thin, taut little man, a jockey. "Goddammit, Charlie—" He shrugged, smiled at Charlie. Then back on the phone, "Tell him I'll come by first thing tomorrow . . . No, no, Susan . . . Please . . . C'mon . . . No, I want to, I want to . . . We'll get right up there. We'll leave now. If you'd just quit poppin' my eardrum, we'd . . . Okay, I'm . . . No, please don't go . . . Stay there. Stay right there . . . Susan?"

He hung up. Shrugged. "We better go," he said. "Where's the plane?"

"Teterboro," one of the troopers said.

"Shit. All the way out there? C'mon. C'mon. We gotta get out of here." There was all sorts of movement now. Papers gathered up. The jockey was in the bedroom, then out, with a suitcase. Stanton snagged another apple. He put his arm around Sporken, "You're doin' what we talked about?"

"Putting it together," he said. "But you know—Washington. They ain't coming along until you show what you can do—"

"Then they'll be pantin' after us like pigs in heat. But let 'em know we know that."

"I hear you," Sporken said. "And, Governor, *I* think you're doin' just great. They're not gonna know what hit 'em."

"See you in DC," Stanton said. "You comin', Henry?"

Coming?

"Look," he said, "We'll talk on the plane. Wait a minute." He dashed into the bathroom. He came out with a bunch of toiletries provided by the hotel. Shampoo. Toothbrush. Comb. "What else you need?" he said.

"I've got classes tomorrow," I said.

"Call in sick—it's summer school," he said. "The kids won't mind."

The jockey was standing next to him now, with the garment bag. "Oh, Henry," he said. "This is my uncle Charlie. You coming?"

He was asleep as soon as we got on the plane. It was a noisy little prop job; any conversation would have been strained, difficult. I tried with Uncle Charlie: "You're the Medal of Honor winner?"

"He say that?"

I nodded.

"Whatever he says," Charlie laughed. "He's the master."

"Are you related to his mom or dad?"

"His dad died."

I knew that. "Did you know him well?"

"Nobody knew him well enough."

It was very late. The plane tracked low over the northeast corridor, between a cottony layer of clouds and an electric map, traces of light, towns and strip malls, country roads. It was like a toy, a model railroad; not quite real. This was all very strange, to say the least. I closed my eyes. I must have slept.

She was standing there, alone in the dark, on the tarmac at Manchester. It was a soft, heavy night, too cloudy for a moon, or perhaps too late. The terminal lights were dim, opalescent in the mist; there was a slight neon buzzing. A minivan stood just beyond the chain-link fence, engine idling, headlights rehearsing a smoky vaudeville of moths and mosquitoes. There was nothing else. We staggered down the stairs; him last.

"Susan Stanton," she said, shaking my hand.

"Henry Burton," I said.

"I know, I met you twenty-five years ago. At your grandfather's, in Oak Bluffs. You were running around in wet underpants. Just out of the sprinkler, I think. Very cute." She rattled this off crisply, an ironic commentary on Susan Stantonhood. I was charmed. Then, without the irony: "Your grandfather was a great man."

Only if you didn't know him, but I just said, "Thank you."

"Jack Stanton could also be a great man," she said, without turning to her husband, "if he weren't such a faithless, thoughtless, disorganized, undisciplined shit."

The governor was off to my side, back a little. I didn't want to look too hard, so I couldn't see the expression on his face. It was, undoubtedly, the furrowed brow, pouty-mouthed, elementary-school-penitent look. He reached out an arm to her, which she swatted away with a file folder.

"First impressions, asshole," she said. "These people don't know you. They don't even know you by reputation. They have United States senators courting them. They are waiting to be swept off their feet by Orlando Ozio, who is the governor of a real state."

"They may be waiting a while for—"

"They don't know that," she snapped. "They don't know shit. The Democratic town leader of Portsmouth only knows that he was supposed to have an after-dinner drink with the governor of a state whose capital he learned in third grade and promptly forgot and never had cause to think about from that day to this, and you never showed. Oh, he was wowed by the missus. Never met a woman so interested in fly-fishing before! Jack, do you realize how incredibly, indescribably, skull-crushingly *boring* fly-fishing is? Do you realize I've now committed to doing this—this *thing* with him? I will fly-fish, with him, because of you. You asshole. You cannot do this to me. You can't. We've only been at this a month, and already you're fucking up in your old fucked-up way. The only shot—the only shot—we have here is perfection. You cannot blow off party leaders. I am not going to let you embarrass—"

I was aware then of a subtle softening of the air. It was eerie, vaguely narcotic. He was . . . whistling. The song was—it was on the tip of my tongue, from before my time—syrupy, mainstream, late-fifties pop.

"Jack," she said sharply, then less so: "Jack—you asshole."

And now he was singing:

> *"Primrose lane*
> *Life's a holiday on*
> *Primrose lane*
> *When I'm walking down that*
> *Primrose lane*
> *W-i-i-i-th you."*

He had a slight, reedy tenor voice with a touch of sandpaper to it; not quite professional quality, but there was a musical intelligence behind it—a humility. He knew not to reach for too much, he toyed with his limitations. It was lovely and utterly insidious. It made her anger seem—transparent, unsubtle, the stunt it was. He was saying: I know your game, too.

Susan turned and began walking toward the minivan. He came up behind her, put his arms around her, snuggling her neck, cupping her breasts. They stood there silently for a moment, swaying slightly to the song he was no longer singing.

"So Henry and I were at this great, great reading program in Harlem today," he was saying as we drove along, crowded together in the minivan—Stanton and the driver up front, me, Susan, Uncle Charlie in the middle, the trooper and a couple of boxes of groceries, mostly munchies it appeared, in the back. "You should have seen those people."

"Was it one of yours or one of mine?" Susan asked him.

"Well, let me think," he said. "The librarian was—well, she was kind of inspirational. It was—"

"Henry," she cut him off. "He'll never tell the truth. You settle it. Here's the deal: Stanton and I have this argument about social programs. He's a sucker for inspirational leaders. He figures you can parse genius, analyze it, break it down and teach others how to do it. My feeling is: Gimme a break. Only God can make a tree. You can't teach inspiration. What you do is come up with a curriculum. Something simple, direct. Something you don't need Mother Teresa to make happen—and that's what you replicate."

"But you can't sell anything if the teacher is a dud," he said. "You've gotta figure out a way to make great teachers. If you can really liberate them, reward them for creativity, they'll make their own programs. Henry, you ever see a curriculum inspire wonder? This is an argument I always win."

"Henry," she interrupted, "tell us about the librarian. *Kind of* inspirational, the governor said?"

"Well, she was . . ." They were, I knew, listening very closely now. It was showtime. "She was a pretty typical library bureaucrat."

"Hah!" Susan Stanton snorted.

"But it didn't matter—she didn't have to be very good—because they wanted it so bad," I continued. Having allowed her the battle, I wasn't about to take sides in the war. "See, your argument is moot when the hunger is there. If everyone wanted to read, or whatever, as much as those folks did today, social policy would be a walk in the park. But you both know that's not where the problem is. It's creating the hunger for nutritious things when all they know is junk food."

"And that's where inspiration comes in," Stanton said.

"Watch out," she said. "He's going to do his Lee Strasberg number on you now."

"Tell me I'm wrong," he said. "They should teach teachers, psychologists, social workers—all the people who do community stuff—like they teach actors, make them aware of their bodies, how to project, how to emote."

"We already have a nation of bad actors," she said.

Okay. It was a set piece, and kind of goofy at that. But it was about policy, not politics—not tactics, not gossip. They cared about it. They went on—not like principals—but like staffers, or perhaps academics. (Susan did teach law at the state university, when she wasn't helping her husband run the state.) They could cite case studies. He had a good one: a professor at the University of Tennessee or someplace had tried the Stella Adler method on half the fourth-grade teachers in Kingsport or somewhere and left the other half as a control group—and found significant improvement in reading scores among the students in the emoted-upon sample. Very goofy, and winning.

And I'd made it through. It was clear that . . . something had just transpired. And I was now part of it, a co-conspirator. I wasn't sure yet that these were people to be trusted. But they were up to something fascinating; their canvas was larger than the tiny brushwork I'd learned in the House. They had a sense of inevitability about them, a sense of entitlement. They didn't flaunt it—it was almost casual; indeed, they were less vain than most politicians. They didn't require any of the usual empty ceremonies of deference and pomposity; they didn't need the reassurance. Their calm, absolutely certain sense of destiny represented a level of audacity well beyond the imaginings of the bulked-up student-body presidents cluttering the Congress. Their ambition was for something beyond public office. It was too breath-taking to be discussed openly; the scope of the project was simply assumed. It was colossal. I found it nervous-making, over the top—and exhilarating. I had grown up in a politics of logic, compromise, and detail. I was ready for a ride.

And so we arrived at a condominium complex on the outskirts of Manchester, one of those nondescript pre-postmodern erections, the residential equivalent of a convenience store. It was now about 4:00 A.M. There were predawn stirrings, early workers starting their cars.

"This is it?" Stanton asked, clearly displeased. "Tell me again, why not a hotel?"

"Money, convenience," said Mitch, the driver. "You can keep clothes here. We can store stuff. We have some privacy."

"I don't give a shit about privacy," Stanton said. "You can't get known in private. I'm here to get known."

He was up the stairs, inside, rousting about, a big man in a small, grim place. There was a Xerox machine in the living room. There were stacks of leaflets, bumper stickers, stick-ons. "This looks like the end of a campaign more than the beginning," he said.

Susan took my arm, nudged me toward the kitchen. Uncle Charlie brushed past with the bags. The governor was circling the TV now. He clicked it on and got snow. "What th—" He switched channels. More snow. Then a local station, a rerun of *Car 54, Where Are You?* Then more snow. "Mitch! Goddammit, Mitch! No cable? You gotta be kidding, man. You can't run for president of the United fucking

States without CNN! Mitch, what was in your head? I'm outta here—This is the worst, two-bit, candy-assed goddamn . . . *Hey!*"

Mrs. Stanton had in one swift, fluid motion reached into her bag, pulled out a set of keys and whipped them—hard—at her husband's head. "Darling," she said, "it's four in the morning. This is not how you want to be introduced to the neighbors."

His reaction was curious. He wasn't angry. "Yeah, well, we're outta here tomorrow," he said, rubbing his cheek. "This place smells like we lost."

I felt faint, woolly-edged, buzzy. It was all just—it was just nuts. But I was there, deep into this thing already, totally sucked in. And she was moving me, pushing me gently, both hands on my back, through the swinging door, into the kitchen. "Tea?" she asked.

The kitchen was white, fluorescent. She pulled two mugs. They were white too. Then, abruptly: "You up for this?"

"For what?"

"Take care of him."

There was no way I could answer that question. But, finally: a job description.

"We're going to win, y'know."

I could have asked, How do you know? It would have been an interesting thing to hear. I wonder about it now, what she would have said. But I was already, by mutual assumption, sort of on staff, and so I merely grunted, "Uh-huh."

She opened a cupboard. It was spiritually bare; instant coffee, a box of White Rose teabags, Fig Newtons. No one lived there. "You take anything?" she asked. "Honey?"

She opened the fridge. It was bottom-heavy. An almost empty top few shelves: a jar of honey, a pint of milk. Down below, maybe fifty Cokes and Diet Cokes, a few stray sixpacks of V-8, ginger ale. The depressing sterility of it made Stanton's pique seem almost visionary. This was a place to work, not sleep.

Susan Stanton didn't seem to notice. She snagged the honey, poured the tea and sat down across from me. She kicked off her shoes, low-heeled pumps. And then, once again, abruptly: "So why did you quit Larkin?"

There was no way to fudge this, not with her. But there were layers of reasons. "It wasn't him," I said.

"He's good—good instincts, usually right, I think," she said. "But too cool, maybe. Does he ever blink? I mean, literally?" She was laughing. It was a nice deep chuckle. "I've never seen him blink. He's got that steady gaze."

"Like a rock."

"Like a lizard," she whooped.

"Yeah," I agreed. "After a while it was all the same. He taught me a lot, but he never surprised me. Not much inspiration there. And it got old, roping the strays."

"Without hope of winning."

"No, it was worse. We always won. It was winning and then not winning. We'd win—and, you know, it was always a hundred tiny deals, things we'd give, and I was always looking for that one vote, the guy who wasn't one of the professional heroes—you know, the smug brothers, the ones who get elected, always from elite districts, because they're 'courageous'—but I was always hoping that one of the sheep would step up and do it for history. Without asking for a lulu—"

"Lulu?"

"New York for artificial sweetener," I said. "And sometimes you'd get one or two. Someone would wake up feeling honorable. Or guilty. Most of the time, there was no percentage in it for them. Why ask for trouble? It was all pretty predictable in any case. We'd win. Then we'd be gutted in the Senate; we'd settle for their version. You know, I got to see Donny O'Brien with his palms raised more times than I'd ever need to. I could *read* his palms by the time it was over. We'd walk through the rotunda to his office, past all the tourists lit up with history—and I'd always be thinking about the chasm between politics and history. But the Lark would just be out there, making himself available to the civilians, into his cybernetic 'Good to see *you*' maneuvers."

Susan laughed. "Yeah, I've seen him do that," she said. "It's like Stanton's mom, working the slot machines in Vegas. Automatic. Once you see something like that, it's tough to get past it. You know what? First time I saw Larkin doing that, governors' conference or something, I had this . . . wicked feeling"—she was giggling now—"that he made a conscious decision to emphasize the 'you' rather than the 'see' because he wanted to seem more . . . what? Natural?" She slapped herself on the forehead. "God. Poor guy."

"Not so poor," I said. "He *is* the majority leader."

"But he wants more, and he'll never understand why he won't get there," she said. "Tell me if I'm wrong, but I'd guess Donny O'Brien is the exact opposite—surprised he got as far as he did, black Irish to the Senate, and then leader? Jeez. Had to be just thrilled to be there, right?"

"Sweet man," I agreed. "And clever. We'd go the office and he'd offer the Lark a Harp. Lark would ask for mineral water. He wouldn't want to say *Perrier* in front of Donny. And, of course, Donny would use that. The tip-off was, we must have gone there a dozen times over the course of a few years, and Donny *always* offered the Harp—just to start him off on the defensive."

"And your guy never took the beer, to see if he'd get a better deal?" Susan asked.

"Amazing," I said. "I *always* wondered about that. He didn't even have to go for a beer."

"Right." She was giddy. "He coulda really rocked Donny's world— asked for a Diet Coke, a 7UP . . . a club sandwich." It was late, but I hadn't expected the irreverence, the humor, the love of the game. She was breathtaking. "So what, then? How did Donny let him down?"

"He'd go up with the palms. 'Lark, this is what we've got. This is what we can do. I owe you one, buddy. What can I say?' " I stopped. I hadn't quite caught the fullness of Donny's Irish grease—he cast a spell, as all the good ones do. "In the end, it didn't mean anything anyway. We'd take it back to our side, renegotiate the lulus, pass the damn thing. And then, as we knew from the start, the White House would veto. And we'd celebrate our great moral victory: we forced a veto."

"That was something," she said.

"Not enough. It was even worse on the stuff that had to pass—the budget."

"So you dropped out," she said. "You gonna drop out on us?"

Very smooth. She was closing the deal.

Okay: "Have I dropped in yet?"

"Say you have."

"Well, I was always curious about how it'd be," I began. "How the whole process—yeah, I guess the country, too—would work with someone who actually cared about . . . Well, y'know, I wonder: It couldn't always have been the way it is now, the feeling of—of blah. Swamp gas. Stagnation. There had to be times when it was better. The other guys had it with Reagan, I guess. But, to me, he was just float-ing with the flow. He didn't try for anything hard. . . ."

"And a good thing, too," she said.

"Yeah, I guess . . . The thing is, I'd kind of like to know how it feels when you're fighting over . . . y'know—historic stuff. I'm not like you. I didn't have Kennedy. I got him from books, from TV. But I can't get enough of him, y'know? Can't stop looking at pictures of him, lis-tening to him speak. I've never heard a president use words like 'des-tiny' or 'sacrifice' and it wasn't bullshit. So: I want to be part of something, a moment, like that. When it's real, when it's history. I . . ." I had let things slip a little bit. That wasn't good. I was interviewing for a job where my primary responsibility would be to not let things slip.

"Goddamn," I said. "My, my, my," I said—just like my father, and just like his father, the Reverend Harvey Burton, the man Susan Stan-ton had praised. Embarrassing, to make this into Black History Month; unprofessional. But I saw: she was with me. It was okay. Still, I had to button it up. "I feel like—a real jerk—even saying that sort of thing," I said. "Maybe we're not living in a time when those kinds of dreams are possible, or even appropriate. But it's late and you asked, and there it is."

"No, you're right," she said. "It's good. History's what we're about, too. What else is there?" Then, "Sleepy?"

She led me into the living room. There was a pillow and a blanket folded on the couch: "Your quarters," she said, patting me on the back, squeezing my arm, drifting off toward the bedroom. I tossed the blanket, lay back on the pillow. It was light now; there were birds, and a piney breeze through the screens. Summer camp. Uncle Charlie came padding through, wiry taut in a sleeveless T-shirt and boxers. And tattoos: "Momma" with a heart on one arm, on the other a sly devil with a pencil-thin mustache—like his—and the words "Made Me Do It."

"Hey," he said. "Coffee?"

II

"Henri, you think it's possible for a black girl to look like Winona?" Richard Jemmons asked.

"Get lost."

"Oh yeah, I forgot. You don't like black girls much."

"Fuck you."

"But then again, there's that Mexican girl in scheduling, Maria Whatsis—she's got the hair and the mouth. So if a Mexican can look like Winona, then maybe . . ."

"Richard, you are diseased." And he was. He was manic, obsessive, very strange-looking, thin as a whippet—his body and all his features were narrow, thin lips, thin nose, dark thinning hair, which made his thick, black-frame eyeglasses seem enormous; everything about him was sharp except his eyes, which were opaque. He never seemed to be looking straight at you, never quite took you in—and that quality, a vehement opacity, defined him. Every conversation was a monologue, more or less. He was an explosive talker, though not always comprehensible—all honks and bleats, mutters and half-swallowed imprecations. He was also, reputedly, the best political strategist in the party. We hadn't seen much evidence of that yet. He wasn't zoned in yet. But he was a trip. He had the eccentricity part of the program down pat. Having seen *Heathers* in a hotel room somewhere, he was on a Winona Ryder jag. He called every woman in the office Winona.

Of all the people we'd taken on that fall—and they were legion (it is amazing how many people start showing up when one of these things gets rolling)––I liked Richard best. He had come down to Mammoth Falls in early October, and spent the weekend riding around with Stanton in the governor's Bronco, on the cell phone to Ohio, where he was in the midst of a hot special election for the Senate. Stanton didn't offer *him* a job, either. They just rode around, the governor listening to country music—and to Richard, working his campaign long-distance. They hit all the hot spots. Fat Willie's Barbecue. The Misty Hill lounge. Uncle Slim's. Aunt Bertha's Soul Shack. Then down to Grace Junction, to Momma's place. Momma, of course, loved Richard. He didn't even say hello; just scooped her up in his arms and said, "How did such a little, bitty woman have such a big ol' redneck sonofabitch of a boy?"

That night, after take-in chicken—Momma never cooked; she ordered—and after Richard stopped using the cell phone, he and the governor sat on the screen porch till three in the morning and held what Richard later called "the Mommathon." They talked family stuff. Family stuff was mostly Momma stuff with the governor, of course. Richard, on the other hand, had more family than he could keep track of—seven brothers and sisters, innumerable cousins, uncles, and aunts; he worshiped them all. His daddy, who was gone now, was a combination justice of the peace, postmaster, store clerk. "Daddy dint say much," Richard would say, "but he said it all." His momma—well, she had been touched by God. She was blind. She was beautiful. She had lost one leg from diabetes, and was in danger of losing another. "And a complete, drop-dead, hold-the-phone, ever-lovin' genius," Richard would say. He couldn't talk about Momma without misting over. He and the governor had several good cries during the Mommathon. At one point, Richard smashed a lawn table out of frustration over his mother's lot; the governor hugged him and sang "You Are My Sunshine," which, he—inevitably—pointed out, was written by another Southern governor and was probably "the most American goddamn song I can think of." They were locked for life after that.

The thing I loved about Richard was, he was overtly race-conscious. I took it as a piece of performance art, a running commentary on the mortal prissiness of most white people.

Most white people do this patronizing number: They never disagree with you, even when you are talking the worst sort of garbage. It is near impossible to have a decent, human conversation with them. They are all so busy trying *not* to say anything offensive—so busy trying to prove they aren't prejudiced—that they freeze up, get all constricted, formal. They never just talk. This may be more true in the political community, where everyone is hyperconscious of perceived offenses and consequences, than it is in real life. But it is hard to be black, and in politics, and not disdain these fools.

There are two subgroups, however, that are tolerable: There are those who are truly color-blind—like Jack and, to a lesser extent, Susan. They will argue with you, yell at you, treat you like a human. And then there are the occasional miracles like Richard Jemmons, who just lay it all out there.

"Lacoste, face it, you are a honky," he would say. He called me Henri Lacoste because I'd gone to Hotchkiss. I was a preppy, an elitist. "Y'all ain't but one-half black—and that's the best part of you. Enables you to intimidate the palefaces, 'specially lib-blabs, and work that voodoo sexual shit with white girls. I'm probably blacker'n you are. I got some slave in me, somewhere. I can feel it."

"Richard, you are the whitest person in America."

"Richard Nixon is the whitest person in America. Although, second thought, maybe not. He's got the rage, right? He's a poor boy, right? Someone's gotta be whiter than Nixon. . . . Ahhhh, whattabout Mondale? Walter Mondale is a fucking albino of the human spirit. Y'knowwhattamean? Can't get much whiter than Norwegian. Though French, Lacoste, is pretty damn close. Too damn close for comfort. Right? You listenin' to me? Right?"

Richard came and went in the early months. He'd pop in for a day or two, then disappear. This was the heavy Winona period and it almost got him into serious trouble. He was particularly obsessed with Jennifer Winona—Jennifer Rogers, one of the press muffins—who really did have the look. He was hitting on her nonstop, but she was very cool; she could handle him. Which made him all the more crazy—Winona, he imagined, would be able to handle him, too.

The day the Ozio business began, he and I were sitting in the little office. This was our first headquarters, a former Olds dealership just down from the state capitol—a big open space, plate-glass windows, with small offices, including my digs, in the back. Richard was in the ratty chair, jiggling, looking over into the big room, not paying much attention to me—I was talking Midwest fund-raising, looking for Ohio money or something—when he spotted Jennifer over at the copy machine. He launched himself in her direction, and I could see him fluttering around her, jabbering, arms windmilling, a spastic Lothario. Everyone else saw it too, but pretended not to notice—everyone knew it was Richard, and Richard was nuts. But he was really on her, and I began to think that maybe I should distract him, pull him back. He was talking about his hotel room. "Got everything, y'know. Got movies. Got room service. Winona, it's like, like . . . paradise. Y'all come back there, we gonna walk the snake."

"The *snake?*" she snorted. "More like a worm, I'll bet. In fact, an enigma: an asshole can't have a penis."

"An enigma? It's a fucking *python*," he shouted. "You don't believe me? You don't believe me?" He was unzipping his pants. I was rushing over toward him, saying, "Hey, hey."

But it was too late. He had it out.

"Hmmm," Jennifer said, not flinching, looking right at it. "I've never seen one that . . . old before."

Richard turned fuchsia. He zipped up and dashed out of there. There were cheers, applause. Jennifer curtsied. I took her arm, walked her back into my office and closed the door. "You okay?" I asked.

She nodded.

"You've got his life in your hands now, you know," I said.

"Don't worry," she said. "I just hope he's worth it."

"Don't we all," I said. "But you're okay?"

She leaned over, took my chin in her hand and kissed me on the cheek. "Very kind of you to ask," she said. Jesus.

At which point, of course, a knock on the door. "Henry, you got a visitor," said Eric, another of the muffins.

"Who?"

"You ain't gonna believe it."

"Cut the shit, Eric. Who—" But I had swung open the door and now I saw: Jimmy Ozio was sitting atop a desk in the middle of the Big Room, taking a very intent look around. He was a big guy, curly hair, handsome in a lurky kind of way. He was wearing a black suit, white shirt, gray tie. We shook hands. His was a cruncher.

"So, what brings you to Mammoth Falls?"

"Business," he said. "Thought I'd stop by to say hi. Nice little operation you got here. Fifteen people?"

"Twenty-three," I said. "Plus eight volunteers. We got some more in New Hampshire."

"The volunteers—kids or old ladies?"

Smart. "Both," I said. (Mostly old ladies, locals with nothing better to do; the kids hadn't found our campaign sufficiently inspiring to drop out of college yet.)

"The boss around?"

"I'll check," I said. I wasn't going to give him shit. "Back in a minute."

I called the governor over at the statehouse. "How important?" Annie Marie asked.

"Code yellow."

"I'll find him, hold on. He ain't doing anything *that* important. Out in the Bronc somewhere. Probably working the cash machine. . . ."

It took a few minutes. Then the familiar crackle, and the governor: "Whut?"

I knew that whut. I was interrupting something. "Sorry, Governor, but Jimmy Ozio just walked in the office. He'd like to see you."

"No shit. Hmmm. What's up, you think?"

"Dunno. Scouting expedition, maybe. If Orlando had anything serious, he'd call, right? He's known for that. So how you want to handle this? Office? Mansion?"

"Dinner, no question. We'll show him around town. Mansion at six. I want you there, too. Tell him, casual. Also, you hear anything from Jerry Rosen lately?"

Rosen was the political writer at *Manhattan* magazine. He was a friendly—and an important—one. If he liked you, and wrote it, it meant New York money . . . usually. But not this year. He liked the governor, and had written it. But the New York money had stayed in New York pockets, because of Ozio. The Wall Street Dems weren't going anywhere until Double O made his move.

"I may have a message in the stack," I said.

"You might want to return that call," Stanton said. Rosen was known to be close to Ozio. "Don't tell him Jimmy's down here, but see what he knows."

I made the dinner arrangements with Jimmy, then called Jerry Rosen.

Jerry said he didn't know shit. But he was wrong. "Basic rule with Double O: All rumors are false," he said. "There is no inside information. Even Jimmy doesn't know what his old man's up to. I talked to Orlando the other day—"

"And?"

"He was off the wall about Stanton. He said, What's he done? That state's last in everything. I said, He knows education. Orlando goes berserk: 'He doesn't know shit about education and he's trying to race-bait on welfare.' "

"He said this on the record?"

"Who ever knows with him? He's on, he's off, he's on and off three times in the same thought," Jerry said. "I'm gonna use it. He'll probably call and scream and call me a superficial fuck, but he'll be happy I used it."

"Why?"

"Keeps him in the game."

"So he's running?"

"Who knows? You figure that he can't go on like this, dicking around—he makes a fool of himself, lives up to his worst stereotype, Oscillating Ozio. But he just can't help himself. His fantasy is a race where he doesn't run and nobody else wins. For what it's worth, I think he's kind of edging toward doing it this time."

"Why?" I asked. "Anything solid?"

Rosen snorted. "Just a feeling. Pride. He's a proud guy. It would be so embarrassing for him to take another run up to it and then back away—start all those Mafia rumors again, give the late-night guys a year's worth of gags. O doesn't like being laughed at . . . which is why he always chickens out in the end. But this time, he's fucked either way: They laugh at him if he backs down. And if he runs—well, he's got to study up on things like what's a 4-H Club and how does it relate to the Future Farmers of America. Because if he gets it wrong, he wants to shoot himself. He drives himself nuts, explodes, takes it out on the press. Anyway, you think Stanton would want to respond to what Ozio said about him, the stuff I'm gonna quote? That's what I was calling you about."

"I'll see," I said. Right. In a million years, he wants to get into a pissing match with Orlando Ozio.

"Look, even if Orlando's in, I think you beat him," Jerry said, and actually sounded like he meant it. "I was up with Stanton in Derry last week, a high school—awesome."

"You ever see Orlando do a high school?" I asked.

"Oh sure, he's terrific. But that's not his problem," Rosen said. "*We* are. He can scream at me. I'm from Brooklyn. I know from screaming. Wait till Orlando has to deal with Americans-of-the-press. Wait till the guy from the Concord *Monitor* gets his first six A.M. screaming phone call, 'You're an assassin, a fucking assassin!' I would say he blows his stack in the first seventy-two hours. His polls peak the first day of the campaign. He begins to slide. He can't handle adversity. It could be very ugly."

"We'll see," I said.

"Or we won't see."

I was at the Mansion about ten minutes early, just in case the governor needed anything. Susan called down from the top of the stairs: "Henry? You're going to want to see the Human Torch. He's in the study."

Richard Jemmons was curled up on the couch, hands pressed between his legs, as if they'd been sucked into his thighs, watching *The Honeymooners* on the big screen. I clicked it off and said, "To the moon, Alice."

"On."

"No."

"Fuck you."

"Fuck me? You stupid redneck sonofabitch. What goes on in that fucked-up head of yours? You never heard of Anita Hill? Man, you are so lucky she's cool."

"I wouldna *done* it if she wasn't cool," he sneered.

"Richard, you will not do that again." It was Susan, in the doorway. "You will not even wink at a muffin. You will not call any person who works for us Winona, even if her name is Winona. If you do, the *best* you can hope for is that we'll can your butt. A more likely scenario is that I'll come after your scrawny little ding-a-ling with a pair of garden shears."

The governor came in. He didn't say anything; he just let Susan handle it. He was wearing a short-sleeved knit shirt—colors of the nineties, purple and teal—jeans and cowboy boots. Both Stantons, in fact, were wearing jeans. The effect was not overwhelming, in either case. In fact, their studied informality seemed particularly lame when Jimmy Ozio came in—still in his black suit, white shirt, gray tie.

"Hey," Jack Stanton said. It was Southern for hi, but with some yelp mixed in, I thought, as Ozio crunched his hand. A campaigning pol's hands are, inevitably, pretty tender from overwork. Jimmy nodded around, once again casing the joint. He saw Richard on the couch. "You're Dick Jemmons?" He said.

"Richard," Richard said, pulling a hand out from between his legs, but still stuck in fetal on the couch. "Yeah."

"Nice work in Jersey last year," Jimmy said. "Orlando thinks you're almost as smart as he is."

Very nice: a light touch, making fun of the old man. Jimmy was a pro. This wasn't going to be easy.

"So, you like barbecue?" the governor asked.

"Hamburgers and hot dogs?" Jimmy's game was elegant: You play Southern, I'll play Northern. We'll see who cuts the shit first.

"We're gonna have to take you out to a real, old-fashioned Southern pit barbecue," the governor said. "What you say, Richard? Wet or dry?"

"The boy takes off that tie, we can take him to Fat Willie's," Richard said. "Ozio, you ever eat pig with your hands?"

"Raw or cooked?"

We drove around, the governor showing the sights. There isn't much to see in Mammoth Falls, but Jack Stanton considered every last bit of it magnificent. He and Susan had Jimmy in the Bronco; I trailed with Richard in my old Honda. "So y'all livin' down here?" he asked.

I wasn't living much of anywhere. I'd spent the first few months with the governor, often just the two of us, traveling the country. It was an apprenticeship. I learned how he worked, and thought. We had entered the race officially in September, but it didn't change the routine much. We did the money thing, mostly—but he didn't get all googly around rich people, the way most pols do; nor did he carp about them behind their backs. Money had no magic for him; the *folks* did. He was lovely with the people, dispensing his meaningful handshakes, listening to their stories; he had a knack—no, it was more than a knack; it was something deeper, more profound and respectful—for making it clear that he had listened to them and understood, and cared. He never left a room—it was small rooms, mostly, those first few months—without knowing everyone's name, and he would *remember* them. Even in New Hampshire, a state that seemed to have a magnetic attraction for chilly, pale, pinched skeptics. Not his crowd, you'd figure. But we moved from living room to living room, coffee to coffee. The governor tilled and mulched slowly, carefully, lovingly; he allowed them their skepticism, encouraged it, joked about it: "I don't want y'all to make up your minds too *soon,* now," he'd say. "Take a look at the field, think about it. You still have a hundred and twenty-three days"—or whatever it was (he always knew)—"before you determine the fate of the republic."

He enjoyed this, and them. And more: He loved what it was about. He loved governance—especially executive governance. (Legislators were a different, somewhat less interesting species.) In two months I'd learned more from him about the public sector—the people's business—than I had in five years with Larkin. We always hit the statehouse, wherever we went—and he never had to ask for directions. He always knew where the governor's office was—sometimes other officials as well. He was ecumenical. He liked them all. It didn't matter if they were Democrats or Republicans. He could tell you what every last governor had done, what their strengths and weaknesses were. The amount of information was staggering—but even more impressive was the energy, and interest, he put into it. A bureaucrat somewhere—in Lansing, in Austin—might tell him a new way to work

Clean Air money, and he'd put the big ears on, and he'd stay and stay, we'd fall hours behind, it didn't matter. He wouldn't leave there until he'd drained the guy.

It would pay off, too. He was a human clearinghouse; he cross-pollinated. One time we were in Montgomery, wandering through the state capitol—a building that had deep, fearful resonances for me, the cradle of the Confederacy, George Wallace's joint—and he said, "Henry, you're freaked, I can feel it. I'm gonna make you feel all shiny and good."

He dragged me down a hallway, to the attorney general's office. "Now, Jim Bob Simmons, he's the boss here—and not a bad fella," he explained, "but I'm gonna show you the real brains of the operation. Hey, Betty," he said to the receptionist, a drab white woman with great butterfly eyeglasses, for whom the blush of youth had faded much too soon. "Your momma back on her feet again?"

"You bet, Governor," she said, matter-of-fact, as if governors were always stopping by to ask about her mother. "But the chemotherapy was a bitch."

Stanton stopped, squatted down next to the woman, took her hand. "But she's clear now?"

"So they say."

"Ain't that the truth," he said, snagging a couple of Fig Newtons from her half-opened top drawer. "You never know. She a church-goin' woman?"

"Every Sunday."

"You go with her?"

Betty hesitated. Stanton took her hand. "Look, honey, you might think about that—goin' with her. Specially now. You can ask your husband to take the kids— Ray, right?"

She nodded, and now began to tear up. "He's got so much, Governor—long-haulin'. He comes in Saturday night, he's just dead."

"Yeah, I guess," Stanton said, pulling her closer and giving a gentle peck on the side of her forehead. "But you think about it. Mean a lot to your momma. Maybe you take the kids, put them in Sunday school, or with a friend, or somethin'. . . . So where's my man? He's gotta be here, right? He ain't off dove-huntin' or anything?"

"I just buzzed him," Betty said, and a tall, thin black man came through the door. Stanton stood up, brightened, and threw his arms around him.

"You coulda called," the black man said.

"Coulda, shoulda, woulda—just passin' through, Billy," he said. "This is Henry Burton, my new drone. Henry, this is William J. Johnson, deputy attorney general of the state of Alabama, a great American but a semiretard when it came to Torts."

"Pleased to meet you," Johnson said, his enormous hand swallowing mine. "What the governor neglected to tell you was that my notes got him through Contracts the year he decided to manage a hippie runnin' for Senate down here, 'stead of hangin' out and being a student like a normal person."

"He wasn't a hippie," Stanton said. "Just antiwar."

"Last I heard, Jack, he was livin' on a farm in northern California, makin' goddamn furniture."

"You *seen* the stuff?" Stanton said. "It is awesome great. We're sleepin' under his headboard, at the Mansion."

"C'mon back, you fool," Johnson said, throwing an arm over Stanton's shoulder.

It was a small office, piled with reports and lawbooks, diplomas on the wall, pictures of Bill Johnson elegant in midair, driving the lane against Michigan in the NCAAs—and another picture of Johnson, in an enormous Afro, with Jack Stanton, his face camouflaged by what appeared to be a costume mustache, sitting side by side on a couch, deep in what seemed a very serious conversation. It was a surprisingly intimate photograph for a politician's wall—usually, you don't want to risk much beyond your children's orthodontia and handshakes with people more famous than you—and it moved me. "Law school," Johnson explained, noticing my interest. "What were we arguing about, Jack? Sending the North Vietnamese guns or bandages?"

"Naww, you were pissed off at me for asking your sister out," Stanton said.

"Susan was pissed off at you 'bout that," Johnson replied. "I thought Cyrilla'd teach you some manners, 'specially 'bout not eating off other folks' plates. You remember what we really were talking about?"

Stanton nodded. "What we always talked about: white folks. Dr. King had just died—"

"No, it was months later—it was Bobby," Johnson said. "We were in finals. You were about to go off to work for him. Remember, you were trying to get Professor Screechy—whatsisname . . ."

"Markowitz."

"Yeah, Markowitz—to reschedule torts, or let you take it long-distance, so you could be out there on primary night?"

"Yeah, I remember," Stanton said softly.

"You figured you would've spotted Sirhan."

"And *you* were ready to pick up a gun, or somethin'."

"Right," Johnson said, turning to me. "This asshole talked me out of it. I was ready to walk out of law school. I mean, what was law? Who gave a shit about law with all our guys gettin' capped? But he said we had to stick with it, stick with the program. I had to think about my responsibility to the kids, the message I'd be sending if I walked. 'A lot of people would like to believe a black ballplayer can't make it through Harvard Law,' he said. 'You're givin' them aid and comfort if you don't.' Right, Jack? And look where it got me," he said, spreading his arms and nearly touching the two side walls, "—the lap of luxury, right?"

"You wouldn't trade it for a white-shoe partnership if your life depended on it," Stanton said.

"If my wife depended on it?" Johnson laughed. "Lucky she don't depend on my measly bucks—she's makin' a fortune"—he glanced over at me—"teaching elementary school." He reached into a small refrigerator and tossed the governor a Diet Dr Pepper. He nodded toward me, I gave him the high sign and he tossed me one. They talked wives. They talked shop.

"You gonna go for it, now Jim Bob's lookin' to move up?" Stanton asked.

"Can't—it's still Alabama," Johnson said. "Might if Jim Bob or the governor endorsed me. But they're too cute for that. Why risk a single, skinny-assed redneck vote?"

"Uh-huh, uh-*huh*," Stanton nodded, then got serious. "Now listen, Billy. I know you got a family to support, can't do it now—but I want you to think about coming on with me y'hear? I need you, man. I make it, you can start house-shopping in Arlington, okay?"

"Vice president's staff don't pay too good, I hear," Johnson said.

"O ye of little faith," Stanton said. "You didn't think I could pass Contracts either."

"Not without going to class."

"But I did, I seem to recall," Stanton said. "Now look, tell me 'bout my favorite program. If I'm gonna try it, you'd better have made it happen." He turned to me: "Dr. Johnson over here has been lifting driver licenses off of kids who are truant in three counties for the past year."

"Attendance up twenty percent," Johnson said. "Dropout rate down ten percent."

Stanton whistled. "Now aren't you glad I talked you out of pickin' up the gun?"

The point is: a week later we were up in New Hampshire, talking to a small group of state legislators in some bare, pathetic law office conference room in Concord—a woman from North Conway brings up youth problems, the French Canadian kids dropping out of high school—and Stanton says, "Look, you gotta call William Johnson, friend of mine, deputy attorney general down in Alabama. He's got this program." Afterward, Delia Schubert, a rep from the Seacoast—middle-aged, standard-issue enviro type comes up, aflutter and says, "I've met your boss twice and both times he taught me something. Is he always like that?"

Yes he was, and she was on board. We were picking up a sprinkling of locals like that, very retail. Stanton was gaining strength, on the merits, from people who knew better, who knew their best shot was to hang out, stay uncommitted, wait for Ozio—they could always come over to us if Orlando passed on the race or stumbled. But they just couldn't help themselves. He was so good they just couldn't wait. I was very proud to be working for him.

So we did the country. He never talked all that much about the ultimate prize—it was almost, at times, as if we were running for governor of America—largely because the big show hadn't really begun yet. Stanton figured (correctly, as it turned out) the campaign wouldn't begin until Ozio made up his mind or the New Year, whichever came first. There was no way of knowing what it would be like, the shape and intensity of the thing, or what would matter. He understood that. He'd watch the opponents, and potential opponents, very carefully. He wasn't impressed. Three senators—two active, one former—had announced at that point. The most plausible of them was Charlie Martin, a Vietnam war hero and another boomer. Stanton liked him but didn't take him very seriously: Charlie had just decided, spur of the moment, to run. He hadn't thought it through. "He's a résumé searchin' for a reason," Stanton said. A couple of weeks after he declared, Martin called the governor and said, "Hey, Jack, man, is this a trip? Can you believe we're really doing it?" Stanton had said something expected, like Yeah, it's wild, running for president of the United States, but he was disdainful when he hung up. "A war hero and he doesn't have the discipline to do this thing straight on," he said. "No footprints, Henry. None of these boys are leaving any footprints."

Nor did he, in his way. He taught me everything, told me nothing. Gradually, I came to see how he devoured every aspect of public life—nuances, and hints of nuance, that only he knew existed. It was, I imagine, something like the way a hawk sees the ground—every insect, every blade of grass is distinct, yet kept in perspective. I came to know how he'd react to any new situation; I learned to read his moods, when to talk and when not. I became inured to personal details, his chronic heartburn, his allergies. I became his Maalox bearer. I saw him angry, and thrilled, and frustrated, and depressed. I learned what sort of information he needed immediately—we had little cards I'd put in front of him—and which I could hold back until we had a break. There was intense familiarity, but no intimacy. He never talked about anything personal, about Susan, about their son, Jackie, about his Bronco wanderings, about his childhood—never really talked about them, beyond the public storehouse of stories told and reported. He was incredibly undisciplined about time, and making decisions, and figuring out who should do what on staff, but there was a strict precision about self-revelation. He was always in control.

Lately, as we began to build a staff, he'd been leaving me back at headquarters more often. The training was over. He trusted me now

to see things the way he would, to get things ready for the show. I understood the motivation but still suffered staffer pangs: Where he was
was where it was. I wanted to be there.

Mammoth Falls didn't help. It drifted along in black and white, and
I—neither and both—had trouble with the vibes and assumptions as
I wandered about. The vibes were quieter, more civil, but, in a way,
clearer than those I was accustomed to up north. One night I had a
burger at a fern bar in a mall on the white side of town. The cineplex
there was the only place in the area you could see a foreign film, inevitably broad French or Italian comedies (it was *Cinema Paradiso* that
night, I think—not bad), never anything heavy or dark or deep or significant. Anyway, the waitress gave me a look and asked, "Are you
from around here?" Meaning: You mustn't be, because if you were,
you wouldn't be here. Normally, that sort of thing wouldn't bother
me. It is barely worth remembering. But I was alone, in a strange—
very out of the way—place, a place where I got *The Washington Post*
by fax each day (and the thin, unsatisfying national edition of the
Times). I was constantly, acutely aware of my skin, and both ways: the
way others saw it and the way *it* experienced the physical world. I was
more conscious of everything. Humidity made me sluggish and
mushy. Air conditioning hurt. So I pretty much kept to the campaign,
and to myself. I ran every evening, three miles, down one side of the
river and back the other. I lived in a sterile apartment very much like
that first one we'd rented, and discarded, in Manchester. I read novels,
early Doris Lessing (she was, I imagine, very sexy in Africa). I had
muffin fantasies.

"Wonder what he's sayin' up there," Richard said, as we trailed the
governor and young Ozio in the Bronco.

"Nothing Jimmy can take to the bank."

Richard laughed, "He's a peach. No question."

"You ever had one so good?" I asked.

"Dunno how good he is yet," Richard said. "What's more, *he* don't
know how good he is yet."

"He's got a suspicion."

"*She's* got a suspicion."

I imagined the governor singing one of his favorites: " 'We cain't go on together, with suspicious mi-inds . . .' "

Fat Willie's was a trailer with a long plastic awning and picnic tables spread out around it. It reeked of smoke and carcinogens. Fat Willie was . . . as advertised: a big, sweaty black man—former all-state tackle for Mammoth Falls Central High—wrapped in a long white, sauce-daubed apron. He brightened immediately when he saw Stanton. "Hey, Gov! . . . Hey, Amalee, the Gov's here," he said to his wife, who was not insubstantial herself. Stanton, oblivious to the sauce, wrapped Willie in a full frontal, then wheeled to throw an arm over Amalee. He stood there between them, grinning his "aw-shucks, proud to be a country boy" grin; it was pure joy. There was an easy familiarity to this: it happened every time we came. Once, several months earlier, I'd sat—awestruck—as the governor spent an hour sitting at one of the back tables, consoling Willie over the death of his mother. "How's business, Will?" he said now, squeezing the big man. "You got your mojo workin' tonight?"

"Ain't no end to it, Gov," Willie turned his head. "Hey, honey, where's Loretta? Hey, Lo—Gov's here!"

Loretta was their daughter, the sort of girl who was destined for obesity—you could see it coming in her upper arms, her thighs—but, for the moment, deeply, adolescently luscious. She flashed Stanton a look, then tried to hide it. Susan gave her a hug, "Hi, honey, how's it goin'? School okay? We've missed you—but I guess your mom and dad keep you busy here, not much time for sitting."

"Yes'm," Loretta said dully.

The governor—a stone Pavlovian when it came to pork—negotiated the meal with Willie. "Now, I want you to fix all these folks up *right,* y'hear? And send me a double."

We moved out to a back table, away from the sharp halogens Willie used to illuminate the ordering window. The night was a touch chilly; Willie hadn't put up his winter plastic yet. But he pulled out a space heater and hooked it up next to Susan, creating a viral undulation, electric heat and November breezes. When the food came, the governor inhaled his, then looked up shocked—and not undelighted—that the rest of us were still working, which left the possibility that more was to be had. He kept his eye on Susan's plate, then—at the instant she crumpled her last paper napkin—swiped the leftovers. He snagged my Texas toast when he thought no one was looking (he was wrong; Jimmy was). I was, for once, disappointed in him. This wasn't good.

Afterward, Jimmy lit a cigarette, a Parliament actually—a brand I thought no longer existed; Susan grimaced (Jimmy caught that, too). The governor had kept up a steady patter throughout, pork and football and Mammoth Falls—nothing remotely close to the business at hand. It was Ozio's hand to play.

"So," Jimmy said finally, "Orlando's been watching you move around the country. He's noticed that every time you go to New Hampshire, you make connections through Chicago. You stop there, see the mayor, get to know the city. That's very good, but not so good for us. It's too bad our primary is a month after Illinois. You'll never get to know us that way . . . until it's too late, maybe. You should get to know us a little better. The governor certainly thinks so. He was hoping the next time you pass our way, you'd stop in, spend a little time, get to know us better."

We'd been stopping in New York as often as Chicago, batting our heads against Wall Street, but Stanton didn't say so. He was obeisant; it was nauseating. "Absolutely," he said. "We will absolutely do that. I mean, I've been really wanting to . . . consult with your—with Governor Ozio."

"He knows a lot," Jimmy said.

Richard rolled his eyes. (Jimmy missed that.)

"Henry, you got the book?" the governor asked. The book. The book was in the car. I got the book.

"Next Tuesday we'll be up there," I said.

"Orlando is usually in the city only on Mondays and Thursdays," Jimmy said.

"Albany's on the way to New Hampshire," the governor said. Nice.

"Let me check with him," Jimmy said. "Anyone got a phone?"

Richard and I both did; so did Susan. We produced them simultaneously, a bit too enthusiastically. Ozio took Susan's and dialed a number; he reached his father immediately. "Yeah . . . Right now . . . No, they took me to a restaurant," Jimmy said. "Listen, Governor Stanton's going to be in the city on Tuesday, but he says he's willing to stop in Albany on the way to New Hampshire. . . . Uh-huh, uh-huh." Jimmy looked over to me: "He wants to know what you're doing in the city on Tuesday."

I glanced at Stanton: Tell them how much? He glanced at me: Some, but not all that much. I gave Jimmy the public stuff. Lunch with the Council of Jewish Organizations. An afternoon speech at the executive council of the Bar Association. A drop-by later at a teachers' union cocktail party. Jimmy relayed these to his father. "He wants to know where the cocktail party is," Jimmy said.

"Sheraton City Center."

"Uh-huh, uh-huh. . . . All right, I'll ask him," Jimmy said. "He says he'll be speaking at the teachers' dinner so he'll be at the Sheraton too. We can meet there. Now he wants to speak to you," he said passing the phone to Stanton.

"Yeah. . . . I do. . . . Naw, I guess I'm with the Bulls these days— they got one or two of our boys up playing there. . . . Well, that's hard to say. . . . I like 'em both. . . . You've got a fine son here. . . . I will. . . . Look forward to visitin' with you next week. . . . Right. Thanks. 'Bye."

Stanton handed me the phone. "The governor wanted to know," he said, "which I like better: the three-point shot line in college basketball, or the pros."

He was, clearly, thermonuclear pissed. My only hope was that it would wear off on the drive home. I had fucked up. I knew it. I knew, too, a preemptive apology wouldn't work. He had to let it blow.

"Fuck *all,* Henry—fuck all," he began, when we were back at the Mansion, having dropped Richard and Jimmy off at the hotel. "You don't know fuck-all about briefing me . . . You make me look like a fucking amateur, a rube-ass, barefoot, dipshit, third-rate, southern-fried piece of shit alderman. You couldn't tell me? You couldn't look it up in the fucking book before we took the kid out? You didn't know we were playing the same teachers' conference as Ozio? What the fuck kind of operation we got here, Henry? How do we get scheduled for hors d'oeuvres when he gets the main course, anyway? I'm Ozio's fucking warm-up act. And don't think he didn't know that. But, somehow, *we* didn't know that. Henry, there is no way we win this thing—we even compete—if we don't know shit like that. Now we're committed, we go there, we meet—his turf, his show—

and he's top dog. Amateur fucking hour. Jimmy's probably on the phone right now, tellin' him he ain't got anything to worry about down here."

"So what's wrong with that?" Susan asked.

"What's wrong with it is, he gets more time to dick around," Stanton said. "We're putting no pressure on him. He's in no rush. All that money stays tied up. The press keeps sniffing around *his* governor's mansion. He's the story."

"That would be the case," Susan said, looking over at me, "even if Henry hadn't screwed up." So she was pissed, too.

"Henry, you've got to get on your bicycle, man," Stanton said, the storm passing. "Before I walk into that room next Tuesday, I've got to have a better idea what to expect than I did tonight. Okay?"

I understood, but couldn't do much about it. I called Jerry Rosen the next morning.

"Doesn't sound good," he said. "Orlando calls for a meeting only if he wants to fuck with you. The people he likes, he talks to on the phone."

"So what'll he do?"

"Your guess is as good as mine." Rosen said. "He talks to me on the phone."

Thanks, I knew that. I called Howard Ferguson III, who wasn't much better. He laughed a dry little laugh. "Oh, Orlando's just trying to fuck with you," he said. "He's a bully. He wants to see how much he can mess with your mind. Just don't let him."

"Easy for you to say."

"You can't handle Orlando," Howard said, "how you gonna handle the Republicans?"

There was no campaign buzz in Orlando Ozio's suite at the Sheraton, no sense of urgency—but a powerful, primordial feeling of turf. Ozio was known for being a one-man show. He wasn't big on entourage, and the living room of the suite was empty, except for a press guy and Armand Chirico, Ozio's old law partner. On our side, it was me and the governor; Uncle Charlie and Tommy the Trooper were waiting downstairs.

Chirico knocked softly on the bedroom door, then opened it a crack and simply nodded; he turned and gestured us in, like a head-waiter. Ozio was in shirtsleeves, in the shadows. The room was dark; he had only the desk lamp on, and the television. He gave the impression of being a nocturnal creature, and he was larger than I expected him to be, with powerful shoulders, neck and hands. He'd been a pretty fair middleweight boxer until his cheek was crushed in his seventh professional bout. He was watching the local news. The sports was on. He went straight for what he thought was Jack Stanton's jugular: "You ever play any sports, Jack?"

"Golf," Stanton said, knowing Ozio meant competitive sports.

"My father used to say that golf was the most capitalist sport—it used more land for less reason than any other," Ozio said, and laughed gently. "Papa . . . But he came from the old country. He had resentments, along with his dreams. You want some fruit, a sandwich? A Diet Coke?" Stanton refused the food, took the Coke. "Come, sit."

So they sat across from each other, in the darkened bedroom. We, staff, stood at a distance, on the other side of the bed. It was odd, uncomfortable; I felt like a servant. Ozio was into family history now. His father, his mother. The store. Brooklyn. It was impersonal, a recitation. Nothing much was happening, so far as I could see. Then: "How many people you got in your state, Jack?" Ozio asked. "We've got two point three million in Brooklyn alone."

"Brooklyn is pretty remarkable—you've got a little bit of everything there," Stanton said, vacantly. Then, hoping to ingratiate, he began to talk about a jobs program we had visited in Bed-Stuy, and how much he admired it.

"You've been there?" Ozio asked, surprised and a little disturbed. "You should tell us when you're planning to come and see these things—we'll arrange it for you."

Stanton nodded, not quite agreeing to have Ozio control his movements in the state, and went off on a little discourse about jobs programs. He talked about one of his proposals—a national computer system, a way of linking everything together, a way to determine which jobs were available, which training programs got results. "We *did* that already," Ozio said abruptly. "We've got that in this state. Armand, get the governor in touch with Herman Gonzalez—he'll tell you all about how we did it here."

"You've done it statewide?" Stanton asked. "I knew you had that pilot program up in Buffalo."

"That's what I mean," Ozio said. "Buffalo. . . ." Then, "So, how do you see this campaign, Jack?"

Stanton was beginning to feel more confident. He talked about the campaign: The president was riding high, but something was happening out there—the people felt neglected, worried. "The world's getting to be a pretty scary place for them," he said.

"You don't want to play to those fears," Ozio said. "Any jackass can knock down a barn."

"But you do have to acknowledge them," Stanton said. "I think we have to understand why we've been losing elections."

"And why is that?" Ozio asked. He could have had Jack Stanton for dinner then, but he didn't wait for an answer. He barged: "I'll tell you why—because we get defensive. We're ashamed of who we are. We try to be like the other guys—and the people know that. They get a choice between a pale copy and the real thing, they'll choose the real thing."

It was boilerplate. It went on. Ozio gave a stump speech. He was a powerful big-hall speaker; the histrionics didn't work so well in a small room. Stanton sat through it politely. Finally, Ozio said, "Well. That's it. Gotta go downstairs. Thanks for stopping by. I think you've got something, Jack. A nice quality. People like you. I think you have a big future. I wrote that in my diary the other day, after I saw you on C-SPAN. Talking to kids somewhere. You're smart, you cut a nice figure. I can see you on the ticket—maybe even this year. I want you to keep in touch. I can help you. Sometimes I think I should quit this business and open a consulting shop with Jimmy—most of these consultants are ice-skaters, right? They charge an arm and a leg, and then take thirty percent of production costs on top of that. Can you imagine? Highway robbery."

He was moving us toward the larger, lighted outer room. He grew smaller in the light; he seemed older. "You come by again, I'll take you to the old neighborhood. We'll go to Gargiulo's in Coney Island. You call in advance, they'll cook a whole baby pig. I understand you enjoy a good meal."

So that was it? Had anything happened?

Apparently so. We found out two days later, on Thursday, in New Hampshire. We were in the Stanton Van, heading from Lebanon toward Hanover—a chill, slate-gray day, dead leaves roiling the highway. I got beeped, the press-urgent line from Mammoth Falls. "Dick Lawrence from the *WSJ* says you better get in touch right now," Jennifer Rogers said. "They want to go with something in 'Washington Wire' tomorrow."

I called Lawrence. "Hi," I said.

"You meet with Ozio?" He asked.

"Why?"

The call broke up. Before I called back, I told Stanton: "Governor, it's the *Journal*. They know we met with Ozio . . ."

"So?" he asked, perturbed. He was riding up front, working a stack of paper, singing along with Reba McEntire.

"I don't know." But I knew. I knew it wasn't good. I called back. "Dick. Hi, it's Henry Burton. Sorry. We're in the van."

"You meet with Ozio?"

"Why?"

"We hear you met in a New York hotel room and hit it off so well that Stanton said he'd be willing to accept the two spot if Ozio got in."

"Get out of here."

"That's your response?"

The phone crackled a little, so I took the opportunity to hang up. "Governor, we've got a problem," I said in a way that Stanton immediately took for serious. (It was worse than serious; I was already in a cold sweat.) He turned off the Reba. Turned to face me.

"Okay, Henry," he said.

"Governor, *The Wall Street Journal* knows we met with Ozio. They think you told Ozio you'd be willing to take the two spot if he got in."

"That mother . . . fucker," he said slowly, stunned—awestruck. It was so brazen. "Pull over. *Now!*"

We pulled over, skidding a little on the gravel shoulder. "Goddammit, Mitch, don't kill us—just pull the damn thing over," Stanton said, jumping out. I followed him. "How much time we got?" he asked.

"An hour or so. Maybe less."

"Yeah, they'll say we missed their deadline. You think a flat denial is good enough?" he asked, knowing it wasn't. "This had to come directly from Ozio. You can just hear him talking about what a comer Jack Stanton is, what a rising star, how well the meeting had gone. *Really, Governor?* 'Well, Dick, since you ask.' " This was something new. Stanton was doing both sides of the conversation, including a reasonable—if bilious—Ozio impression. " 'I was explaining to Governor Stanton about the New American Community, my program for giving all Americans the sense of possibility that mom and dad had when they came here. We started trading ideas. There was real affection, mutual respect, a very good—a natural—working relationship, and Governor Stanton says the two of us would make a great team, a great ticket. And you know, it's not such a bad idea. A natural combination—North and South.' *You mean, Governor Ozio, you'd take him?* 'Well, Richard, if you were in that position, you'd have to think about it very seriously, now, wouldn't you?' "

"You really think so?" I asked.

"He's sucking the oxygen out of this campaign," Stanton said. "He's suffocating me. You know who reads *The Wall Street Journal?* People who aren't going to take a flyer on some yahoo fucking governor who says he's running for president but spends his off-hours sucking Orlando Ozio's toenails. Call the *Journal* guy, Henry, and give me the phone."

I did. "Hey, Dick, it's Jack Stanton—howyadoon?" Stanton said. "Yeah, we're stopped, side of the road, make sure we don't get cut off again. About this thing . . . Yeah, I think Governor Ozio may have misinterpreted it some. . . . Yeah, we did meet. We were both speaking at a teachers' thing. So we took the opportunity to visit. It was a real good visit. We talked 'bout what a great chance the party had this year, how there were a number of us who could give the president a hard time—y'know, especially on the economic issue. I mean, when was the last time you heard him say anything about jobs? That's what people up here in New Hampshire want to hear him talk about." Stanton had to attempt the pro forma detour onto his stump speech. Lawrence, a good reporter, didn't let him get very far. "Yeah, well no, it didn't quite happen that way. . . . No, I said it was important for us all to play this thing straight, have a good discussion of the issues—and then unite together behind whoever the nominee was."

Stanton's eyes were getting narrower, his face turning red. He kept his voice calm, though. "Well now, Dick, I just don't remember that coming up. . . . It's premature to even think about that. First, he has to get into this thing and see if he can beat a few of us. And let me tell you, it'd be a good thing for the party if he did come in. I'd welcome it. Look, it was a very good meeting, but this is just a misunderstanding. No big deal. Okay. Thanks. See you up here. 'Bye."

Stanton closed the phone and heaved it deep into the forest. "Get Susan," he said. "Richard, Arlen, Fergie, Lee, Arthur Kopp. Who else? Get them up here."

Yeah, except I needed a phone for that. I started into the forest. "Henry," he said, exasperated, "forget about that. Mitch, can you get us to a Dunkin' Donuts?"

We met at midnight that Saturday, in Stanton's suite at the Holiday Inn in Manchester. Jack and Susan sat next to each other on the couch, the governor positioned so that he could keep an eye on a late-night football game from the coast. "Whatcha got there, chief?" Richard Jemmons asked, "Mormons versus Africans?"

He was close. "Utah State versus San Diego State," Stanton said. He took his college football very seriously. "You ever see this tailback they got at San Diego?"

Richard stretched himself out on the floor over by the wet bar. Everyone else was in those ugly, low-backed Holiday Inn "comfortable" chairs, except for Howard Ferguson, who had pulled the desk chair over and was leaning forward, dangling copies of *Manhattan* magazine and *The Wall Street Journal*—Jerry Rosen's column with Ozio's attack on Stanton, and the "Washington Wire" item—over the coffee table. Howard ran the show: "So: Orlando Ozio," he said, playing with the alliteration, making the whole thing seem trivial. He was wearing a wrinkled gray suit and burgundy cable-stitch pullover, with his trademark Liberty flower-print tie loosened a bit, as if he'd just come from the office. He was a very cool customer. "Anyone have any brilliant suggestions?"

"Take him on," said Arthur Kopp immediately, and to no one's surprise. Arthur was the founder and director of Moderate Democrats of America. He was short, chesty and brush-cut; he went through life with the bearing and subtlety of a noncommissioned officer from the Deep South, a corporal perhaps—a brilliant piece of theater on his part, since he was a rabbi's son from Minneapolis. No one liked him much, but MoDems had been a useful podium for the governor—he always gave a good speech at their national conference and made a splash with the national media. Kopp's presence now was a subtle, interesting call: he wasn't part of the inner circle—he wasn't a Stanton kind of guy; the chemistry wasn't there (with Susan, especially, who worked overtime to steer clear of him)—but if it was going to be war with Ozio, we'd need to mobilize the moderates in the party. Of course, if it didn't turn out to be war with Ozio, Kopp would be faded back into the chorus.

Stanton was quietly obsessed about whether it would be better or worse, long-term, to run against Ozio. "Figure it this way," he'd said on one of our small-plane trips that fall. "If Ozio's in, we run straight up the middle—which makes it easier in the general election, if we beat him. And if we beat him, we'd be a monster, a giant killer—right, Henry? 'Course, we may not beat him. Though if we ran up the middle, and lost, he'd almost have to pick us for number two. 'Course, if he ever did pick us for number two, and we had the misfortune of winning, I'd spend the next four years pullin' stilettos out my back. I mean, whut's the word for pincushion in Italian?"

The question was modulation. How sharply to distinguish yourself from Ozio, how tough to run. These were issues that did not dent Arthur Kopp's consciousness. "This is a contest between the future and the past of this party, and Ozio ain't the future," he said. "If you take him on now, you can raise your profile, define yourself as the anti-Ozio, separate yourself from the crowd."

"You don't want to define yourself as *too* anti-Ozio," Arlen Sporken jumped in, the anti-Kopp. Sporken—Mr. Crisco, Richard called him—would have been loath to draw too sharp a distinction even if his media consulting firm didn't represent some of the deepest, stiffest old-left interests in the party (who doubtless figured his all-American blond hair and soft Mississippi drawl gave them public cover, made them seem Middle American). "Remember, you're gonna want to have Democrats voting for you in these primaries. You're gonna want to lead this whole party, not just MoDems."

"But you can't just let him take you apart like this," Kopp came back. "First, he cuts you up in Rosen's column. Then he has you beggin' him for a place on the ticket in the *Journal*."

"He's makin' me look like a wuss," Stanton agreed. "How's this playin' with the New York money, Fergie?"

"He may be overplaying his hand," Howard Ferguson replied. "I mean, why's he so interested in cutting *you* up? Makes you look a little stronger."

"You'd look stronger still if you took him on," said Arthur Kopp, relentless, artless, obnoxious. "You can make this thing into a two-man race right now. You take Orlando Ozio on and you'll see the world open up to you—the media, the money guys. I called Bill Price in Chicago, Len Sewell out in California—they're looking at you and Charlie Martin, they're waitin' to see who's going to come out of the gate as the real New Democrat. There are—"

"No, no," the governor was shouting, "—throw it, *throw it*. Shit! You see that? You were saying?"

"The money guys don't vote in primaries," Sporken said. The governor's football interruption had worked, subtly, against Kopp, whose passion for MoDem money was clashing, spiritually, with the governor's African rooting interests. It was one of Stanton's more endearing qualities: he always, reflexively, pulled for the brothers. "Governor," Sporken continued, "you've spent all this time working the teachers, the geezers, the party's natural base—they like you, but they love Ozio. You don't want to risk that. You've *got* the Mods, you need to solidify the base. And what if Ozio doesn't get in? You want to get into a pissing match with him now, when you may need him later?"

Kopp and Sporken went on, fiercely: two unsubtle fat boys, whipping each other, while the rest of us watched them the way the governor watched sports—following it, but not too closely, waiting for the next thing to happen. Sporken, I realized, was getting the worst of it, hurting himself merely by engaging Kopp, marginalizing himself—becoming a spokesman for one wing of the party, just as Kopp was. In a situation like this, you wanted someone with perspective as your media guy, someone who could make a case without *becoming* it: the inner circle had to transcend all arguments. I realized then, with some relief, that Sporken might not have all the wheels and gears necessary for his role. He might have to be . . . augmented, or paved over, before it was done. (I had a sudden, slightly orgasmic tingle: Was this the way Stanton was seeing it? Was I really beginning to think like him?)

I looked over at Richard. He had snagged some couch pillows and was lying flat out, head on the pillows, arms crossed behind his head, deeply into his opaque mode, eyes closed behind his thick glasses. He hated them both, of course—Sporken and Kopp. He hated Sporken's buttery glad-handing; he hated Kopp's lack of irony and grace. At that moment he probably was hating Kopp a bit more, because he knew he was going to have to agree with him, and he couldn't stand the idea of having to side with anyone so unsubtle.

Howard Ferguson was sitting back, a slight smile on his face, not doing all that much to control this, perhaps figuring—although you could never really be sure with Howard—that if Sporken and Kopp killed each other off, we'd be rid of both. The governor hadn't raised any objections. (It was a pretty good football game.) But it was getting late and nothing was happening. Susan, finally, took the next step: "You with us, Richard?" She asked. "Or is it past your bedtime?"

"Ma'am?" Richard asked, raising an eyebrow.

"Your thoughts, Richard?"

"Pollster!" Richard said, up on an elbow, addressing Leon Birnbaum, who had been sitting quietly, a thick looseleaf on his lap. Birnbaum was a little guy with curly blond hair; he had worked on Stanton campaigns for a decade and was absolutely crucial. Leon visited the Mansion from time to time and would sit with the governor late into the night, going through the cross-tabs, road-testing phrases (rather than ideas), showing him what worked and what didn't. Everything Leon said in these late-night sessions seemed insidious, conspiratorial. He spoke soft, barely audible deep Bronx: "See—'responsibility' is great when you're talkin' about welfare. 'Fair share'—awesome. Great for fat cats, too. Works both ways: Rich-and-poor! '*Do* their fair share.' '*Give* their fair share.' Same difference, y'know? You match 'em up: righteous us against piggy them. Rich-and-poor! See? You don't need to get too specific. The folks will extrapolate—'responsibility' sounds both tough and moral, without being primitive, y'know? Y'see?" He'd giggle: heh-heh, heh-heh. "You want to use *value* words. You connect midbrain, subcortical—you want to hit them down under, in their lizard brains, access their personal reptiles . . . heh-heh . . . where they don't think—where they just, y'know, react—with *value* words." Stanton loved that stuff. Leon was another one who was a lot more talkative one-on-one with the governor than in groups. In fact, this was the first time I'd seen him in a group and he hadn't said anything yet.

"What say you, pollster?" Richard asked.

"'Bout what?"

"We are where in New Hampshire?"

"Four." Leon smiled devilishly. He sensed where Richard was going.

"And Governor Ozio?"

"Twenty-eight, heh-heh, heh-heh."

"And Governor Ozio is willing to acknowledge our presence in this race? He has to be the stupidest fucking Eye-talian since Richard Burton fell for Cleopatra." Richard crossed his arms behind his head again and closed his eyes.

"Meaning what, Richard?" Susan asked.

"Meaning you take him on," Kopp said. "You define this thing right now."

"But you have to do it carefully," Sporken said, folding his hand.

"Hold the fucking mayo, Arlen," Richard said.

"Well, how *would* you do it, Richard?" Susan asked.

"Drop something into a speech. Make sure Rosen and a few others—that slug at the *Post,* what'shername—know it's comin'. Doesn't have to be huge. Just get Ozio's attention, let him know we came to play. Let the scorps know the governor's got some hide on him, too." Richard called reporters scorpions—scorps for short. "Let's see where Ozio wants to take this. I'm kinda gettin' bored waitin' for that sad-assed old dog to make his intentions known."

"And if he escalates?" Sporken asked.

"He's even stupider than I think he is," Richard said. "He tells America he's more concerned about a governor no one ever heard of than he is about the fucking president of the United States."

"Henry?" It was the governor. "You have any thoughts about where and when?"

So it was done.

We tried to make it as classy as possible. The University of New Hampshire. A student forum on the future of the welfare state. We'd stick in the knife between points five and six, go straight at Ozio's New American Community. The governor would say, "There are those, including some who contemplate entering this race [We gave Stanton the option of adding, "and contemplate, and contemplate . . ."] who believe you can have a new American spirit of community but have it without an equal sense of responsibility, without asking the same standard of moral behavior from the less fortunate that we demand of each other—and which we should demand of the wealthiest Americans as well, I might add. It is simply *misguided* not to demand that each of us do our fair share. It is as patronizing as our opponents who say—well, usually they don't have the courage to say it, they merely imply—that it's useless to help the poor, there's nothing we can do for them."

Kopp was furious. His reptile brain was apparently less subtle than the ones Leon connected with in focus groups. "That's *all* you're gonna do?" He stormed. "Why not throw down the gauntlet? Make it clear that this election is going to be a contest between the future and the past of the Democratic—"

"Because it isn't, Arthur," I said. "The primaries may turn out to be. But the election is between us and the Republicans."

"You're sounding like that jerk Sporken."

"This is what we're doing, Arthur."

We set up an open phone line from the microphone at UNH to anyone who wanted to hear it. We told Jerry Rosen, and several other New York types, that Stanton was going to have something interesting to say about Ozio. We told some of the Washington scorps they might want to listen in, too—though we weren't too specific on the Ozio part of the program. "You want me to listen to a welfare reform speech on the telephone?" A. P. Caulley of *The New York Times* asked. He was smart, but better known for oenophilia than initiative. "Do you think this election is going to be *about* welfare reform?"

"Well, that's part of it," I said. "The folks seem interested. What do you think it's going to be about?"

"What it's always about," he said. "Sex and violence."

And he was right: this was about violence.

Stanton didn't say very much as we rode the van to Durham. He didn't even play any music. He flipped through the cards for the speech, noodling with this and that, crossing out and overwriting with his felt-tip. I couldn't tell what, if anything, he was doing to the Ozio card. And then he did something odd. He asked me something personal: "Henry, what are you doing for Thanksgiving?"

It was two days away. We were heading back to Mammoth Falls right after the speech. I had thought about visiting Mother and her new husband, Arnie Nadouyan, in Bel Air—a Hollywood Thanksgiving: turkey and sprouts by the pool, starlets and equipment. (Arnie always had the latest in clients and electronics.) But I hadn't thought very hard about it, and now it was too late to make reservations. I'd figured I'd see what the muffins were doing.

"Would you be able to join Susan, Jackie and me at the Mansion?" he asked.

"Absolutely," I said.

"You know," he said, suddenly deepening his voice and giving me his most intense look, "we've kinda come to think of you as family."

"Yuh," I said, swallowing hard, hoping to gain control of my voice. "It would mean a lot to me, Governor."

And then we were there, at UNH.

And he whiffed on it.

He skipped the Ozio card. He didn't mention Ozio at all. He delivered a standard welfare reform speech—badly. The kids snoozed. I paced the back of the hall, feeling dog-tired and slightly sick. Stanton did rally during the Q&A. He was absolutely brilliant on a question that came out of nowhere, about the similarities between the black underclass and the Irish underclass of the nineteenth century. His belated virtuosity pissed me off.

I hadn't felt strongly about nuking Ozio. It was an irksome situation—the governor was, clearly, irked and that had to be respected—but it seemed a preseason game nonetheless, one of those peripheral dustups you get all tangled up in early on, before the real campaign begins. Some candidacies get lost in these distractions; others use them as a road test, a way to keep everybody occupied, see how the team reacts to stress, see what the pecking order will be; others ignore them completely. Usually they don't count for much. But we had decided to take it public. We had made the decision, told selected scorps (who would, no doubt, get the word back to Ozio). We had planned the thing, and then whiffed on it. It was not good. It smelled of weakness.

Stanton knew it. He rushed out of there, stinting his usual ration of meaningful handshakes. He almost always took special pains with college kids, desperate to lure them aboard—the social and ideological dynamic of the Eugene McCarthy campaign was written into the fiber of his being: his candidacy wouldn't have legitimacy unless the kids were on board. But he wasn't seeing them that day; they were a blur. He got into the van. He didn't turn around. He said, staring straight ahead: "I didn't want the first thing they heard about me to be negative," he said. "I didn't want to give Ozio the power to make *me* the sonofabitch."

He plugged *Ray Charles Sings Country and Western* (Volume One) into the tape deck. He worked a stack of paper.

Thanksgiving dinner was for two hundred, mostly residents of Mammoth Falls's homeless and battered women's shelters. A tent was pitched on the back lawn of the Mansion. We served. That morning, the governor and Jackie had gone out in the Bronco, trailed by a panel truck from a local market with Uncle Charlie riding shotgun, delivering turkeys to the homebound. He returned about noon, glowing, as if he'd just made love. He and Jackie tossed a football on the front lawn, waiting for the guests to arrive; neither was an athlete—but both were enthusiastic.

Jackie had, somehow, come out normal. He didn't sulk or strut, like most politicians' kids. He went to public school. He liked computers. He seemed entirely unaffected by the passions and ambitions that swirled through the household. Indeed, he was an anchor—a reminder, for both Stantons, that there was a normal world out there, where the greatest looming issues were the embarrassment of orthodontia and the need to stay awake through *A Tale of Two Cities*.

There was nothing strained or showy about their relationship with their son; the affection was deep, comfortable and unadorned. At times, when things got really bad, when I wondered how I'd gotten mixed up in such a thing, when I had to list the reasons, the image of the three of them chattering over a board game or just sitting together on the couch in the study watching a video would be the first thing that came to mind. It was the best evidence I could marshal that these were actual human beings. That the governor's egregious empathizing wasn't just for public consumption, but had some basis in his own life. That he lived a life beyond strategy.

I was, in truth, having some doubts about the entire Stanton enterprise that Thanksgiving. I had defended the governor on the phone with Richard after the Ozio whiff. "He had his reasons," I said. "He may be right."

"Or he may be a chickenshit," Richard said. "My perfect candidate, my wet dream, is warm and strong, fucking warm without being squishy-shit and quiet, Clint Eastwood strong. Don't need a rocket scientist to figure that one out. Always wonder why more of these overgrown student-body presidents don't get it. Our boy's got the warm part knocked. I'd be feeling just a little bit more comfortable about this if we had some sense of the *strong*."

"I saw him in that room with Ozio," I said. "He was fine. He didn't get pushed around."

"Maybe." Richard was bored. "Where are you, anyway? Pit Falls? You bakin' any muffins?" Then, "Henri, look—don't worry 'bout it. We're in this now. It works or it don't. It don't work, you got a gig with me. You got the makins of a serious rainmaker, Henri—bring me all the black caucus business. You'd be a monster with suburban housewife candidates, too, I'd reckon. We'll make a fortune. But, Henry"—his voice turned serious—"you don't need to go getting TB on me now, y'hear? It ain't worth it. Life goes on."

TB: True Believerism. It was part of the code, consultant duende. It was what separated the men from the boys, staff from pols, servants from operators. You wanted to keep perspective. You wanted to see the horse as a horse and not Pegasus. But I couldn't. I remembered Stanton, glowing, coming back from delivering the Thanksgiving turkeys, his arm draped over little Jackie—and I knew it was hopeless. I was caught up in this thing. I had no perspective. I was a staffer in my soul. Different code.

Later, after we'd fed the multitudes—Jack, Susan, Momma, Uncle Charlie, several state commissioners and I made for a very high-profile cafeteria line (and it looked real good on the evening news that night)—after the governor had led the homeless, the meek and the halt in a sing-along, after he had repaired to the study with Jackie to watch Texas play A&M, Susan snagged me at the door.

"You're down," she said.

"I'm okay."

"Come here—talk," she said. Momma and Uncle Charlie were sitting in rockers on the broad front porch, Momma yammering about this and that, smoking one of her too-long-to-be-reals; Charlie, perpetually bemused, comforted her with an occasional "Uh-huh" or "Ain't that the truth." Momma shot Susan a glance as we came out, just about missing a beat in her Grace Junction elegy, then continuing on—relieved—as it became clear we weren't going to join them. We took two rockers on the other side of the porch.

"You're down," Susan said again. "Ozio's got you down."

"He outthought us," I said. "He made us look slow."

"We *are* slow," she said. "And anyway, you can never be fast enough for Ozio."

"You think he's that good?"

She laughed. "Nawwww," she reached over, tousled my hair like I was a little kid. "You don't get this, Henry? Ozio says it all the time, the line he stole from Sam Rayburn—'Any jackass can knock down a barn.' That's all *he* ever does, sitting up there, leaking lies to this one and that one, taking potshots. And Jack has always been vulnerable to that, 'cause he's a believer."

"That could be a problem," I said, stupidly.

She ignored me, and went on. "You should have seen him back in the war days. Ol' Jack seemed like a real wimp back then. You always had the guys who got up there and called the president a baby-killer—it was real easy to be extreme. You were more credible if you were extreme. Jack wouldn't play that. The radicals made fun of him.

He kept his hair relatively short, for those days. He wore a jacket and tie. When we were in law school, he was always down in Washington working, working the state delegation, trying to get them to oppose the war.

"I'll never forget. There was a senator, real redneck hardball jerk, LaMott Dawson. Always going on about the 'commonists.' He found commonists all over the place, in Washington—and especially back home, especially when he was running for reelection. LaMott came from a little town northwest of Grace Junction named Anderson or Henderson—something like that. And a boy from there died. Now Jack had this thing—it was a grisly, self-flagellating kind of thing—but he'd always go visit the families of the people in the state who lost boys. I mean, he was just in school, right? What business did he have? No one else but Jack could get away with this. The obvious question would be 'Why ain't you over there in 'Nam, sonny?' And Jack would have to answer, seriously, 'Trick knee, ma'am.' He was *so* embarrassed about that—don't know what he hated more, the war or his excuse for getting out of it. But he'd go as often as he could, visiting the families. And he'd always find a way to get through to them, to comfort them. And the hard work paid off. He caught a break—up in Henderson, of all places, LaMott's hometown. He found Mrs. Ida Willie West, who said she had half a mind to go up to Washington and tell them what a waste she thought this whole business was.

"Well, Jack supplied the *other* half a mind. He raised the money from some antiwar sources. He brought her up to LaMott, who didn't want any part of Jack, of course. Everyone knew what Jack was about. But Ida Willie wouldn't go in to see him without Jack, and Jack told Sherman Presley—you know that sonofabitch was working for LaMott back then—that it would be unfortunate if the Mammoth Falls *News-Tribune* found out that Senator Dawson was refusing to meet a Gold Star Mother who wanted to meet with him. So they met. And Ida Willie just came out and asked, 'Why'd my boy die?' And LaMott goes on about commonists. And Ida Willie said, 'Now, LaMott, didn't we always take care of you?' And she talked about all the things the community had done to get LaMott ahead over the years—you know, they spot the smart ones like Jack and

LaMott, and, in a lot of towns, they'd only get to college—good Eastern schools—because the Rotary took up a collection and they called it a scholarship fund.

"Anyway, Ida Willie West. She reminded LaMott of every bake sale and scholarship drive the town ever did for him, and she said, 'We took care of you. And now I come to ask you why my boy died, and you trot out that same bull-rinky about commonists you always trot out at election time. This is more important than an election, LaMott. My boy's dead. Now, why'd he die?' LaMott didn't have shit to say for himself. And Jack—our Jack—let him stew in it for a moment, and then he *bailed him out*. Can you imagine? He said, 'Now, Mrs. West, you know public officials like Senator Dawson have a lot of tough decisions to make. They have to try to look at the big picture, as well as the individual lives. And sometimes they get lost in the big picture. Maybe it's come time for the senator to reconsider his position on the war. You know he wouldn't want to feel responsible for any more boys like yours dying. Isn't that right, Senator?' Well, of course, LaMott was too proud to change right then and there. He promised to *consider* it. And give him credit: within a month, he was out on the floor, making a speech. It was a tough thing to do if you were from the South back then, unless you were an intellect like Fulbright. And, believe me, LaMott Dawson was no genius. But he turned around. We had his vote after that. And Jack did it."

It had turned dark and colder. A light breeze rattled the last of the brown leaves lingering in the seasonal trees. "So how'd you get me started on that?" she asked.

"Ozio."

"A grown boy," she said. "A yakker. He isn't half the man Jack Stanton is. So, Henry, don't be a jerk about this. Jack knew what he was doing."

"Why'd he let us get out there, public and all?"

"'Cause sometimes"—she laughed—"it takes a while for Jack to know what he's doing. But don't worry about this."

"We look bad with the scorps."

"When it starts, it won't mean anything."

"When will it, you think—start?"

"When Ozio decides."

"What do you think?"

"Oh, he won't go," she said. "And it's too bad."

"Why?" I asked.

Susan stood, ready to go back in. "Because," she said, "I would just love to have had the opportunity to crush that scumbag."

III

Thirty of us were in the back room at Slim's after the final New Hampshire war party, the weekend between Christmas and New Year's. The campaign was down; the Stantons were off in Florida. "Well, we sure as hell planned the shit out of the next few months," Richard muttered. "Except for the woman thing."

"WHAT woman thing?" Lucille Kauffman asked, too loud, too sharp; the entire table went quiet. Lucille was an old Susan friend with a disconcerting sense of ownership about the campaign. She assumed herself part of the inner circle, and the Stantons never said otherwise, and so she was—when she was around. Most of the time she was lawyering in New York. She kibitzed by phone. Tiny things: She didn't like Jack's ties. She didn't like the color of the campaign posters. And larger things: the staff was stupid; disloyal; uncomprehending. She was an antic conspirer; she was out for blood. She wanted a friend of hers, Laurene Robinson, hired as press secretary. She wanted Sporken replaced. (We wouldn't have minded that.) She threatened to take a leave and join the campaign full time. All Mammoth Falls quaked at the thought.

Richard would have despised her even if she weren't dowdy and awful, even if she didn't always wear power suits and running shoes and Gloria Steinem aviators, even if she wasn't always rousting around in her purse for her compact, fussing with her hair, pulling out lipstick and applying it in the most ridiculous manner, squeezing her puckered lips around it, rolling it once, twice, then saying—always—"There!" No, even if she'd been benign, Richard would have hated her because she was an amateur. "Lord save me from friends and amateurs," he would say.

This was a basic Stanton problem. He had been collecting friends since kindergarten, with the *intention* of bringing them on board when it was showtime. Some were very good; others were okay; others, long defeated by the world, were testaments to the utter unpredictability of life—knowing Jack Stanton "back when" was the most notable thing they had ever done with themselves. Lucille was in a category all her own. She was awful beyond imagining. She was one of those people with no sense of human spatial dynamics—always a step too close—and no sense of propriety. She would say whatever came to mind: the mere fact that she had thought it made it significant, she believed. Indeed, the campaign had exacerbated this: Since she was Susan's best friend from college—since she knew Susan better than anyone—people actually *acted* as if the things she said were important.

She was very dangerous. She scared me to death. She raised questions about Susan I didn't want to consider.

"What woman thing?" she asked Richard. "You put ketchup on your steak? God."

She was picking at a salad. Everyone else was eating steak—which was, indeed, the only dish on the menu at Slim's. Obscene, steaming piles of beef were stacked on platters along the tables, interspersed with piles of fried onions and potatoes. It was all very excessive and primal. "This ain't Noo Yawk, honey"—Richard dismissed her. "You gonna play politics in America, you can't be put off by the customs of the natives. Americans eat steak with sauce." Then, to me: "Say a woman comes forward and says—"

"Bullshit!" Lucille said. "It's not going to happen."

"Maybe someone classy," Richard went on, "like a Democratic Party activist."

"No!"

"Someone he popped at the 1984 convention."

"Never!"

"Right," Richard said. "I don't think so either. I'm just trying to figure out how it would work. You gotta figure he ain't gonna get trapped, like Hart. He knows the rules. Some bimbo from a former life comes forward, and we just say—Bullshit."

"Bullshit is right," Lucille said. "I don't know why you're even talking about this."

Interesting. Lucille seemed frightened. She averted her eyes when I looked at her instead of staring back and saying, "What? What?" as she normally would. What was it? Did she know something? Or was it, perhaps, that she so completely imagined herself the voice of Susan Stanton in the campaign that she was reacting now as she imagined Susan might?

The other thing was: I felt the same way. This was something I didn't really want to think about. But that, I knew, was bad staff work: Richard was doing his job—and, as always, saying aloud something we all thought about but were too embarrassed to say. We had just finished two days of meetings, going through the calendar, coordinating it all—paid media, fund-raising, debate schedule. We had spent an entire afternoon meticulously figuring out the opposition—not just our three opponents, but the media as well. Brad Lieberman, a gift from the mayor of Chicago, had made the trains run on time—a brisk coordination of schedule, fund-raising, advertising, message. Brad had made it all seem controllable, a rational process, and everyone was feeling very up.

The money had been rolling in since Ozio folded his hand. He had gone out in a lather, furiously, defensively, ridiculously, trying to make up his mind until the New Hampshire deadline passed, then announcing that his state's perpetual urban crisis prevented him from running, for the moment, but that he might reconsider later, if none of the candidates addressed the issues raised by his blather about the need for a New American Community. It was a total flameout. *Manhattan* magazine ran an Ozio cover with the headline "Zero for O.O." Wall Street cracked open like a piñata; we'd been pulling in bundles from the big houses, pledges averaging $175,000 per day for the past two weeks. And so, this dinner, all of us arrayed at two long tables in the back room at Slim's, had a celebratory air: We were about to launch ourselves into battle—and we had the hot candidate.

The last few weeks in New Hampshire had been very encouraging; Stanton had been awesome on the stump; we were picking up endorsements from key activists. The word was spreading. Various bigfeet from the papers, even some columnists, were beginning to come out—Ozio's departure meant that it was time for them to pay attention to the rest of the field. They'd been impressed by Stanton, for the most part. We were, suddenly, plausible in New York and Washington—the days when Jack Stanton was seen as a possible vice president were over. We would have forty-eight hours off now— New Year's Eve and New Year's Day—and then the war would begin. And we were up for it.

"I'm talking about this," Richard said, relentless, unable to give up the woman thing, "because all that planning ain't gonna be worth shit when it happens. Because if we can't know what it's *gonna* be, we gotta sense what it *might* be. And you know it's gonna be something. Right, Henri?"

I didn't know. I was glad the conversation had contracted again— somehow—after Lucille's initial outburst. There was laughter down the other end of the table, Lieberman telling Chicago stories. Richard was freight-training, somewhere between a whisper and a mumble, swallowing half of it; I was sitting next to him and it was hard to keep up. He was rattling through the possibilities.

"Say a woman, a plausible woman, comes forward—but, then, you figure, if she's plausible, why'd she come forward? Act of coming out undercuts her credibility, y'knowhattamean? And why? Revenge? Politics? Money? Money, we're okay. Money, she has no credibility. 'Less she comes in quiet, hits on Stanton quiet—and he, jerk, pays off."

"*Richard!*" Lucille again.

"Outta guilt or somethin'. But that ain't a problem. The problem is a serious woman comes forward. But a serious woman, by definition, wouldn't. 'Less . . . Y'think he ever porked a Republican? But even with that, say he was doing a serious Republican woman and she comes out."

"It's not pos—"

"Shut up, Lucille," he said. "Y'think, maybe, we can just *admit* it— I mean, if it's someone plausible? Say, yeah, it happened, the flesh is weak, the sexual revolution. Didn't everyone fuck up sometime, the last twenty-five years?"

"Richard, I don't want to—"

"Lucille, why cain't you be true?"

"It's Maybelline." Another county heard from: Daisy Green, Sporken's junior partner. She was sitting next to Lucille (on assignment from Sporken, no doubt—he knew Lucille was looking to coup him).

"Saywhut?"

" 'Maybelline, why can't you be true?' You're mixing it up with B. B. King's guitar. That's Lucille," Daisy said. She was mortally thin and poky. She had the look of someone who'd spent far too much time indoors—which she did, cutting and mixing spots for Sporken. She was wearing a hooded sweatshirt with nothing written on it, and jeans. She was very New York; outer boroughs, clearly. Her mother's generation, it might have been CCNY or Hunter, and left-wing politics. She was more polished—Ivy League, probably—but still, a touch of the accent, a roughness: she hadn't worked overtime assimilating. She smoked cigarettes.

"Who givesa fuck?" Richard said.

"Just if you're gonna be *authentic,* Richard."

"Awww." But she had managed to move him off the woman stuff—a move she may have immediately regretted.

"Hey, are you *sure* about no plaid?" Lucille asked, turning on Daisy now. "You know, Pendleton? It's New Hampshire. He looks stiff in the suit."

"He's running for president. We shot the ad with him sitting on the desk, instead of behind it—that's informal enough."

"You want to get their attention," Lucille said. "You don't want him to look like just another politician. You want something like Gary Hart with the ax."

"Right—that's exactly what we want," Daisy snorted. "How about this for a tag line: Jack Stanton—A Gary Hart Democrat." Very nice: she wasn't intimidated by Lucille. "Every other fucking politician in the race is wearing a plaid shirt, or a ski outfit or some fucking thing. People understand bullshit this year. We have to establish: no bullshit."

"Harris did skiing," Lucille said. "Nobody thinks he's a bullshitter."

"He had a heart attack. He needs to establish he's still alive."

"You have to smoke those things? You'll have a heart attack yourself."

That stopped Daisy.

"You don't want to do that in public, either," Lucille said, pressing her advantage. "We don't want people to think Jack Stanton's people are—*smokers,* right? I mean, if they can't run their own lives, how do they run the country?"

"Like five-hundred-dollars-an-hour New York fucking lawyers," Richard said. "Whaddya do for five hundred dollars an hour, Lucille? And who do you do it to?"

"Very funny. You're another one: we really want the public to see Jack Stanton has some hillbilly who looks like he was sired during the love scene from *Deliverance* running his campaign."

Daisy cracked up: "Not bad, Lucille." But I was worried. Lucille was *so* awful, so clunky—why did Susan keep her around?

Someone was tapping a glass. It was Sporken. "I want to propose a toast—"

"Make me puke," Richard muttered.

"—to the New Year, the year we change America," Sporken said, "and to the team—this great, great team—that will make it happen."

There were whoops and cheers. I looked around the room and wondered about the team. Daisy caught me looking, saw what I was seeing.

It rained that night, and froze. Mammoth Falls was a mess; jagged, angry icicles hung from power lines and tree limbs, the streets were skiddy, terrible. The morning news led with an eight-car pileup on the interstate. The airport was closed. I walked to the office; no one was there and the lock was frozen. It was an odd cold, not bitter-sharp like up North; at first it hadn't felt so bad, but now my ears were tingling and I wondered what to do. There would be a trooper on duty, and probably Annie Marie, at the statehouse, up the hill from the campaign office. I needed to call the Stantons at Marco Island, just to check in, give an update on the New Hampshire meetings. I had my phone, but I didn't want to stand outside, shifting around, having to take notes, and who knows what else, in the cold. I felt paralyzed, depressed, vapor-locked. I had to go to the bathroom. I started up the hill toward the statehouse, slipped and fell—hard—on my butt, and then I did it again, trying to get up. I rolled over onto the crunchy ice in the island between the sidewalk and street. The traction was better there—not bad, in fact, crunching up the hill—but it was raining again now, and harder, too. I put up my umbrella, a gust yanked it out of my hand. It bounced down the hill and I decided not to chase it.

The trooper at the door was new, didn't know me and was suspicious. "Just call the governor's office and tell them Henry Burton's here," I said.

"You don't have a staff pass?"

"I'm not on the gubernatorial staff," I said, a little too huffily. "I'm on the campaign staff. Please call the office. It's extension 3258."

"Hold your horses, there, young fella," he said. "I'll call the damn gu-ber-na-TOR-ial office."

The gubernatorial office was humming. Stanton was on the phone with Annie Marie, directing the ice storm. "Henry just came in," she said, then handed the phone to me: "He wants you."

"Henry, all's well?"

"Seems so. You want me to go through what we did?"

"No, I know. I checked with Richard and Lieberman. Here's the deal: I want to do LA."

"You sure, sir? It takes us out of New Hampshire two weeks before the primary."

"It's money, Henry. And warm weather. We're doing fine. At least, it looks like we are. You hear Leon's numbers? Shit. But, then, it's early. We got a lifetime between here and the election, all the time in the world to fuck up. You think it's okay? You think there's something we're not doing?"

"I can't think of—"

"Listen, here's what I want," He said, cutting me off. I still wasn't quite used to that. He never really wanted an answer when he asked how he was doing, just reassurance—and he would settle for anything, even Sporken's inevitable, transparent "Great, great, just great, Governor." It was banal, unworthy; I couldn't get used to it. "I want a conference call with the Gang of Five—let's try Wednesday, morning sometime, after whatever breakfasts we have." He began to laugh. "You hear what Richard is calling the Gang? The Elders of Zion? We can't let that out." He laughed again. The Gang were his economic advisers. "But tell them we gotta figure out how far on health. Charlie Martin's gonna hammer us on that. And tell Rosenbaum that I'm still waiting on his tax cut numbers." David Rosenbaum was the policy-staff numbers sherpa. "And listen, tell Annie M. I want the names and home phones of every family involved in that bender on the interstate, right? So what you doin' tonight, Henri?" He was doing the Henri bit now. "Muffin hunting, or just stay at home and crack open a bottle of Chablis?"

"I'll go to the staff party," I said, affecting a slight pissed-off chill. "You know we opened it up to the public, trying to get the kids in town someplace safe for New Year's."

"Great idea. Who did that?"

"Jennifer, Eric. I don't know. They're very good."

"You, too, my man," he said, picking up on my mood. "Henry, listen careful now. Two things. One, I want you to get your ass out of that office and kick back today, y'hear? Rest. Have some fun. Do something for yourself, y'know? Then you come out and meet me in Manchester on Tuesday. I want to start this thing with you there. The other thing is this. Susan and I were talking: You're the best goddamn thing happened to us this year. Happy New Year, and thank you. I know what you do, and how you feel, and how hard you work. I'm honored by it. Honored. You hear? Now listen, this is very important: Do you think it's at all possible for you to get yourself laid tonight?" He was laughing. "I'm serious. I don't want you too horny to think straight, okay?"

"Yes sir," I said. "You have a happy New Year too. And thank you."

"And tell Annie M. I want those phone numbers, right? And—we're doin' okay, dontchathink?"

"Just fine," I said.

I went back into the governor's private office to call Mother in LA, and found Daisy Green was sitting there, tiny, behind Stanton's big desk, oversize horn-rims on, studying Leon's cross-tabs, smoking a Marlboro. "Hey," she said, "this stuff is un-fucking-believable. You see how we're doing with World War Two veterans? They don't give one half of a shit about Vietnam. They love him."

"You shouldn't smoke in here," I said. "He'll walk in three weeks from now and choke to death."

Daisy stubbed it out. "You see the focus groups?" she said. "I'm a little worried about the tax cutting. They're onto it. This is going to be a very cool year, I think. They're *thinkin'*, y'know? They're into it. They're ready for us. It's amazing none of the big Dems went, but, then, they're Dems, right?"

"What are you doing here, anyway?" I asked, but not harshly.

"Ice storm," she said, closing Leon's binder, shoving the horn-rims up her forehead. "We're *all* still here. I had to get out of the hotel. They're all down pacing the lobby, hating each other—Arlen, Jemmons, Lucille. It's the most awkward fucking thing. Didn't want to babysit any of them. Richard's jiggling around, wanting to get in my pants again. 'Got a wet bar in my suite, Daisy Mae, got movies, it's lahk—*pair*-ah-dahse.' I told him to go hit on Lucille—'You could save her life,' I said. Richard—" She was laughing now, belly-laughing— she couldn't get it out. "—Richard . . . Richard says, 'Lucille? I could neither *achieve* nor *sustain* with that woman.' Never heard that one before. Meanwhile, Arlen's trying to charm the shit out of Lucille. He's all over her. He's eating breakfast. She comes down, *pointedly* picks another table. He gets up, moves his runny, yucky, half-eaten eggs to her table. She says, 'Eggs, Sporken? Cholesterol.' Yikes. That woman is like a figment of George Romero's imagination."

"Who?"

"The zombie movie hack. Brilliant hack."

"Oh." I looked at her, and couldn't resist the obvious—her candor demanded it. "Again? Get into your pants again?"

"Richard?" She laughed. "Last year in Atlantic City. He was so nutty Election Day, had to do something to calm him down. We'd been through it by then, he'd brought that suckball—talk about zombies—he'd brought that suckball zombie prick, Jeff Millar, all the way back, and then the asshole choked in the last debate. But the debate is on against a gazillion points, y'know? Like *Roseanne* and *Sex Lives of the Rich and Famous*—so maybe no one was watching. Anyway, we're really sweating the last twenty-four hours. We get the final tracking at midnight, and we're holding. We're both so relieved that—well, you know how it is in campaigns: indifferent sex, great companionship."

I had stretched out on the leather couch below the giant photograph of the state university football stadium, filled to capacity with people dressed in orange, two tiny teams on the field. It seemed an entirely bizarre artifact; but, then, the governor's office was filled with bad local crafts—cutesy, calico, primitive stuff. "So," she continued. "I'm stuck here. I'm not going back to those lunatics at that hotel. You wanta catcha movie?"

"This is America," I said. "No movies in town. You have to mall it."

"Any video stores downtown?" She was up, rousting about the governor's closet for a phone book, then gone to the outer office and back, flipping through the yellow pages. "Got a couple nearby. Look, let's see if they're open, you got a VCR at your place, right? We can hang out—"

"No, I have things—"

"Oh come *on,* Henry. Let's lose a couple of hours, huh? It's New Year's Eve. We're out here in America. You don't have a date or anything?"

I shook my head no before I thought about it. She wasn't going to let it go. "Okay," I said. "But let me make a phone call first."

"Personal, huh?" She caught everything. "Okay. You do that. I'll go outside, call around these stores, see who's open."

I made the call. Told Mother I'd be out there with the governor in early February, and that she and Arnie should buy tickets for the fundraiser. Arnie got on. He and I had never had a tense step-relationship. For one thing, we'd never lived in the same house—I was pretty much grown before he turned up; for another, he had the genius salesman's gift, which was no gift, just an easy, inherent kindness. "So I'm gonna waste my money on Stanton?" he said. "They say he fucks around."

"He's a good man, Arnie. You'd like him."

"I didn't say fucking around is a *bad* thing. I think it's a good thing. It's basic. Like your position on abortion or something. You want a guy who's got juice, right? A human being." Good old Arnie: never disagreeable. "You should only work for guys who fuck around, Henry."

. . .

It had stopped raining. The storm had broken apart in the sky; heavy clouds were interspersed with sharp patches of deep blue. The sun was in and out. Daisy looked profoundly unglamorous, the hood of her nondescript sweatshirt up from under a blue down jacket, covering her mouth and eyebrows; only dark eyes and her stubby nose, quickly pink in the cold, showed. It was suddenly warmer whenever the sun poked through. "The planes may be going soon," I said hopefully.

"Third Street, you assume would be three streets from the capitol, right?" she said.

Right. "I know this store," I said. "They only have garbage."

"Good," she said.

"Good?"

"Well, what do you want, Henry? *Boudu Saved from Drowning*? Let's see something great and crappy and kinetic."

"You pick it, then," I said. The store was a combination smoke shop, newsstand and videos. I checked out the magazines, which included every known wrestling, muscle-building, heavy metal and biker title, a garish and oily rack. Daisy was back in a flash. "We're in luck—look what I got."

"*The Abyss*? You're kidding, right?"

"James Cameron," she explained. "Awesome director. I live for his next movie. You see *Aliens*? You got any food at your place?"

We bought sandwiches at Subway. My apartment wasn't far, down by the river. "This is unreal," she said, as we went up the stairs, past the tricycle, big wheel and baby carriage on the lower landing. "Very exotic, living in Mammoth Falls, in a building with families. And just *look* at this place," she shrieked as I opened the door. She was laughing. "This is fabulous, fan-tastic, Henry!"

"Just your basic efficiency—"

"Efficiency doesn't begin to cover it—maid service, Henry? Or do you do this?"

"I—"

"Excuse me, but I've got to see the fridge. The fridge is very important." She leaped across the room, opened the door, whooped and doubled over. "Henry, too much, too much." I looked and saw what she saw: Yogurt, neatly, top row. Perrier, neatly, second row. Paul New-man's marinara sauce, a half gallon of orange juice, various condi-ments in the door. "Henry," she said, "no half-eaten pizza? No Diet Coke? No beer?"

"Sorry. I usually just eat breakfast here."

"Yogurt? No Cocoa Krispies or anything interesting?" She closed the fridge and wandered over to the windows, inspected the books on the ledge. "Novels?" she asked.

"Escape."

"You escape with Doris Lessing and Thomas Mann?"

"Different strokes," I said, lamely.

We ate the sandwiches. She wanted to smoke a cigarette afterward; I got a saucer from the cupboard, tried not to seem too fussy. Then a logistical problem: the television was at the foot of the bed. The couch and easy chairs were diagonally across the room, over by the light—and a nice view of the river. I toyed with the idea of turning the television around, to face the couch across the room, but it seemed—fussy. Daisy, who continued, uncannily, reading my mind, said, "The bed, Henry? You've set the scene for a seduction."

She whipped off her sweatshirt. She had a Princeton T-shirt on un-derneath and no bra—but not much need for one. She seemed smaller, younger and tiny, without the sweatshirt. "Okay, okay. I'm practically a guy . . . up top," she said. She did have a nice—pert, sexy in a businesslike way—bottom.

"Okay," I said. *"The Abyss."*

It took place underwater, and was sort of spiritual. I fell asleep.

It was dark when I opened my eyes. The movie was over, and I sensed that she'd been sleeping too. Her head was under my chin; her hand was on my stomach, warm and soft, unbuttoning and moving slightly now, stroking. It was odd: her hair smelled of cigarettes, but her mouth didn't when she tilted her head up toward me. It was a thoughtful kiss, not pushy; nice. Everything proceeded apace. The clothes were shed effortlessly, without tugging or elbows. She was wiry, spidery, twined all over me—but there was no embarrassment here, no awkwardness; she was neither too active nor passive, she con-tinued to read me. It was, in fact, very—pleasant. It was thoughtful, intelligent. Until it stopped, rather too abruptly. My fault. "Sorry," I said. "Campaign sex."

"But great companionship," she said, kissed me and snuggled under my arm. "Jesus, Henry—Leon's numbers do look fabulous, don't they?"

It seems hard to believe now, but we were geniuses for two weeks. We were rolling. The crowds were good in New Hampshire; the money was good; the press was good. The opposition was lovely. Charlie Martin, the hippie Vietnam vet, still couldn't believe he was running for president and had difficulty remembering what his message was from day to day; his biggest news cycle came when he started a snow-ball fight and caught Barbara Walters in the back of the head as she was heading out of the Wayfarer. She was very cool. She turned, put her hands on her hips and shook her head, about to scold him—but her frown slowly dissolved into a knowing, sardonic grin. He was a child. Nothing needed to be said. Good-bye, Charlie.

Barton Nilson, a senior senator and former governor of Wisconsin, was going nowhere as a prairie populist—he was traveling the state in an RV, camping out instead of staying at hotels, and offering Franklin Roosevelt's jobs program (forestry, road-building) to out-of-work computer jockeys. He seemed ancient at sixty-two—slower, less hungry; it was a valedictory campaign. He had a great head of hair—silver, parted in the middle: perfect prairie-populist hair. He gave grand, juicy speeches in a voice made for crystal radio sets—a dry, crackly, distant, American voice. It was like running against a museum. We were ignoring him, hoping he'd go away before we hit the big midwestern primaries. He showed no signs of disappointing us.

And then there was Lawrence Harris, who wasn't considered a serious candidate after three heart operations, but he was the most interesting and formidable of the lot. He was a favorite son, with a farm up near Lebanon. He'd settled there after two distinguished terms in the U.S. Senate and two heart attacks. "I am running as a classroom exercise," he said, and it was true: students from his poli sci and political process classes at Dartmouth were staffing the campaign. They had formulated ideal, nonfudge positions on all the issues. The students were making cute commercials, too—in one, the ski-run ad, the candidate creaked down some moguls, pulled up to the camera position and said, "Ahhh, gravity—such a *delightful* natural force! The world is full of wonders. Natural forces we can use, more profitably, to our advantage. The wind, the sun are clean and safe. We need to tax dirt, save the earth, balance the budget, serve our grandchildren," at which point a horde of children raced into his arms, knocking him over on his skis. Not bad.

Richard called Harris a Neo-Martian, since none of his positions were vaguely plausible in the real world, but he did cause problems, mind-game problems, especially for Stanton, who'd always been the most serious policy guy in every campaign he'd contested. The governor hated the idea that someone else might be the darling of the National Public Radio crowd. "Y'all can't be seriously worried?" Richard said to him as we skidded along route 101 one day on our way to the seacoast, where Stanton was scheduled to pull balls at an Indian bingo parlor. The governor was up front, Richard was in the backseat leaning very far forward, trying to get as close to Stanton's ear as possible. "Folks up here don't mess around. They think it's their patriotic duty to choose a president for all the rest of us pathetic redneck shitheels. They ain't gonna waste a vote on ol' Natural Forces. They're just gonna use him to make you work a little harder—which ain't a bad idea. You can't let up. You're coasting."

"But he's making me look bad on the tax cut," Stanton said.

"Bad where?" Richard asked. "Oh! I know: Doo-doo-doo-dahhh, doo-doo-doo-dahhh," he said, viciously parodying the theme song for *All Things Considered,* making it sound idiotic. He was out of the backseat now, on his knees, squeezed between Stanton and Mitch, the driver. I reached over, fingers scraping the tan leather sleeve of the high school letter jacket Richard still wore, and tried to tug him back. No luck; Richard was into hyper-Richard. "Leon has this whole thing breaking our way—you are running even with Harris in Hanover, for Chrissake—and you are worried about the fucking Nina Totenberg vote? You wanna worry? Worry about somethin' real. Worry about the asshole from the *Times* who hates your butt because you went north to college and he went to UNC-Charlotte. Worry about the Republicans, who will soon know every time you pulled your pud. Worry about the woodwork, and which slime-bucket crawls out of it first. Forget Natural Forces. A fart is a natural force."

Richard remained crazed about the woodwork, which hurt him a bit with Stanton: the governor was able to slot it, dismiss it as another of Richard's obsessions. He tended to do that. He had everybody slotted, and could handicap their advice accordingly. I didn't mind when Sporken and Kopp, or the Gang of Five (each of whom had a brilliant, utterly impolitic silver bullet) rutted themselves in their self-aggrandizing tangles, but I didn't like Richard falling into the same trap. He needed to stay credible with Stanton.

Luckily, he wasn't around—physically around—much. He came up twice for debate prep. But he was driving me nuts on the phone. Five, six times a day. Always: "Y'hear anything?" No. You? "Happy Davis says the LA *Times* snoopin' round somethin'. She thinks it's drugs. Whatcha think—a woman?"

"Happy Davis is a gossip columnist."

"So? Look, Henri, we're flyin' blind. We don't know shit about this guy. We need to hire someone. Oppo our own self. This is fuckin' crazy for us to be sittin' around, scratchin' our balls, so much at stake."

He had a point. But no one had the guts to approach Stanton on it—least of all, Richard. He would call me at the office, page me on the road. The eightieth time or so, I returned his page from a high school gymnasium in Nashua. Stanton was just finishing up a town meeting—awesome as always on the Q&A, moving up the aisle aglow, conferring meaningful handshakes on the multitudes—and I said to Richard, "Goddammit, tell him yourself," and handed the phone to the governor.

"You're nuts, Richard," Stanton said, laughing. "The Cowboys are gonna beat the spread." He handed the phone back to me.

"Thanks for joining us," I said to Richard, "for this week's edition of campaign profiles in courage."

"We're gonna get fucked, Henry, and it's going to be our own damn fault."

I was worried too: It was all too good too soon. We roared into the first debate, a month to the day before the February 17 primary. It was held in a converted knitting mill, the new home of a local TV station, in a large room with the feel of a SoHo loft, smelling of plaster and polyethylene. There was to be a live audience, equally divided between civilians and half the known political world—it was the first great tribal event of the season for the scorps, the first chance for the heavy hitters to see us in action.

It was a strange scene. No individual greenrooms before the show: the four candidates were thrown together with their wives and seconds, a coffee urn and chocolate chip cookies in a bare room with newly painted white walls. Stanton overwhelmed the room, or so it seemed. He created his own dysfunctional family—Charlie Martin was his raffish, goofy younger brother; Bart Nilson was dad. But Lawrence Harris wasn't playing: he sat off to the side, checking his notes and carrying a copy of *Scientific American* with "The Promise of Desalinization" on the cover. He drove Stanton crazy, standing off like that—the governor kept glancing over at him and, I could swear, ever more egregiously chatting up and charming the others. He was eared into Nilson bigtime; he loved the old coot, loved listening to his stories. "Henry, c'mere," he said. "Senator Nilson was just telling me about the time Hubert Humphrey tried to get Eisenhower to move on civil rights, back in the fifties. Senator, this is Henry Burton—you know, the Reverend Harvey Burton's grandson." He could be an absolutely shameless asshole when it suited him.

"Really?" Nilson asked—shocked, suddenly ashen. "I marched with your grandfather. I was there when he was . . ."

Shot. But Bart Nilson was too proper to go on. His eyes filmed over—Stanton's too, I was certain, without looking. "We've got to keep that spirit alive, don't we?" Nilson said, touching my arm. "We got pretty close there for a while, Henry. Pretty close to makin' it happen."

"Yes sir," I said.

"We'll make it work again, Senator," Stanton said, fixing him very close. "One of us is gonna do it," he said, with a certainty that almost caused Bart Nilson—who knew it wasn't going to be him—to recoil. "You see how the folks are, right? You can feel them—hungry for something, worried. I don't think the Republicans understand that yet."

"Republicans never understand that," Charlie Martin said, laughing. "The only thing they want to do is scare the shit out of 'em. But, hey, Jack, I love hearin' you talk that sixties shit. The idealism! The Movement! The *sex*. I'll bet you got laid four hundred times while I was getting my butt shot off." Stanton quickly glanced over at plain, dowdy Elizabeth Nilson, standing just to their left, alone at the coffee urn. Charlie caught the look, shrugged, mouthed: "Sor-ry." (Susan and Martha Harris, who'd never be mistaken for anything other than the women's studies professor she was, were engaged in deep, animated conversation across the room—Susan, it seemed, was having better success penetrating the Harris Curtain than the governor, but, then, she came from their class.)

"Hey, Jack, I have this great idea—let's mess with Harris's mind," Martin said. "When they ask us about taxes, and he trots out his Natural Forces fee, or whatever he's calling it, let's say it's not enough. I'll say, Double it! Then you can say, 'No, higher.' Bart can say, 'Maybe we should tax *un*natural forces, too.' "

"Gee, Charlie," Stanton said. "That would just be stone hilarious, wouldn't it? I'm sure the Republicans would love it to death."

"I guess," Martin agreed wistfully. "And some of our folks are so fucked up righteous, they'd probably think we weren't kidding. But it would be nice to strafe Larry a little. He didn't used to be so saintly when we were freshmen together. I didn't know when you have a heart attack they stick a cork up your ass." Then: "Hey, Jack, speaking of righteous, what did *you* have to promise Harriet Evergreen? She wanted me to agree that every piece of paper my administration used would be recycled."

Harriet Everton was the leading enviro-lunatic in New Hampshire. She had been giving Stanton grief about the huge pig-processing operations down home, and the clear-cutting he'd allowed in the piney woods. So he'd taken the pledge on recycling to shut her up, and was beginning to redden a bit now (and Charlie Martin saw it).

"She was all over me about a vote I made on acid rain eighteen years ago," Bart Nilson said.

"So you caved, Jack?" Charlie Martin pressed. Happily, though, someone said, "Gentlemen," and it was time to roll.

The debate started out a breeze. Stanton seemed very cool, presidential—and, to everyone's amazement, out of the line of fire. It wasn't hard. The others were murdering themselves. Charlie Martin tried to

explain his very elaborate health-care scheme and got so bollixed up
that he threw up his hands and said, "Well, this thing makes a lot more
sense on paper than it does when anyone *talks* about it. But you know,
we do this, and our national energy level will just, just . . . explode!"

Then Nilson and Harris got on each other. Nilson went into his
usual stump number about how we ought to spend a lot more money
helping folks off welfare: "Give 'em a ladder, not a safety net."

And Harris, incredibly, went after him. "How can we serve our
grandchildren if we're spending all this money providing pickaxes to
people who need to be computer-literate?"

"You think the folks'll be willing to pay your dollar-a-gallon gasoline tax and get nothin' back except owin' ourselves less money on
the national debt?" Nilson said, truly angry. Harris's bloodless aloof-
ness promised a Democratic Party very different from the blue-collar,
lunch-pail outfit Bart Nilson had signed on with.

"It's not a gasoline tax," Harris said, with enough condescension to
start Charlie Martin giggling. "It's a Virgin Sources Usage fee. And a
lower deficit will mean—"

"A better life for your bond-holding fat cats," Nilson shot back.

The wise thing for Stanton to do would have been to stay down,
let them kill each other. But he jumped in ("No! No!" Daisy Green
whispered, squeezing my hand hard), acting on a deeper need than
political expediency, the need to be a peacemaker—and to ingratiate
himself with Lawrence Harris. "Not just the bondholders, Governor
Nilson," he said. "Working families will have lower mortgage rates,
small businesses will be able to borrow money on better terms and
compete in the world. A modest but steady reduction in the deficit
will be good for all of us."

Okay. Not bad. But shut up. But no: "Of course, Governor Nilson
does have a point. We do need to provide jobs for those who need—"

"Hey, Jack," It was Charlie Martin. "What, if anything, are you
against?"

There was laughter in the hall. Not a lot. But laughter.

"I am against doing nothing while people are suffering." Stanton
was furious. "I am against the style of government that says, Wait—
things'll get better. Just wait. I am against that kind of patience. I am
impatient when it comes to the people you and I—all of us—have seen

up here, the folks who worked hard all their lives, did what they were supposed to do and suddenly the bottom drops out. You've seen their eyes, you've heard their stories, Senator Martin. Are you saying we should do nothing to help?"

"Well, of course not," Martin began and then stumbled through a convoluted acquiescence. He was toast.

We dashed to the spin room, another loftlike contrivance one floor down, with rows of long tables and a press podium. Me, Sporken and Laurene Robinson triangulated and began working the room. (Lucille Kauffman had had her way; Laurene, a tall and smooth young black woman, was now press secretary—and not bad, I had to admit.) We were very cool. It was a good night. It was fine. A good, substantive debate on all sides. We were satisfied. Even Sporken knew enough not to launch a "Great! Great!" barrage. Losers spin; winners grin.

"But didn't Senator Martin have a point?" asked Felicia Aulder, a real pain in the butt from the New York *Daily News*. She hated us for some reason. She loved Charlie Martin—or, rather, she loved Charlie's pollster Bentley Benson, who fed her all sorts of chow for her "D.C. Wash" column and was quietly, we knew, plying her with "woman trouble" rumors. "What *is* Governor Stanton against?"

"I think the governor explained that," I said.

"They were laughing at him," she pressed.

I looked away, and caught Laurene's eye. Something was wrong. She needed help. The question was, how to get over to her side of the room without bringing along my swarm of scorps—especially Felicia. "Listen," I said, "gotta go—" and I headed toward the door—with Jerry Rosen tagging along after me, a puppy in love, his arm around my shoulders, whispering in my ear, "Awesome, awesome. You're gonna wrap up the nomination by Valentine's Day."

I went out the door. Waited one, two, three, four, five. Then back in, over to Laurene's side. Everything seemed fine at first. Then a tall, gaunt, pockmarked fellow approached me, "Mr. Burton, maybe *you* can help me?"

I looked at Laurene and saw that this was the problem.

"I can try," I said. The other scorps were still pummeling Laurene—tactics, advertising plans, fund-raising, bullshit. They didn't know this guy. He wasn't one of the regulars.

"Was Governor Stanton ever arrested during the Vietnam war?" he asked.

"I don't know," I said. "I can ask him and get back to you."

"All right," he said, too calmly. He knew what he was doing, and he had something. He handed me a card: Marcus Silver, *Los Angeles Times*.

"You're covering the campaign?" I asked, hating to have to show any sort of interest or concern, but needing to know.

"Not really," he said. "Special projects."

As I feared.

"Okay, I'll get back to you."

But he got to Stanton first. It was about fifteen minutes later. I'd gone down to meet the governor in the holding room. He was there with Susan and Uncle Charlie—and in a foul mood. "Let's go, let's go, let's go, let's go."

"What about Laurene and Sporken?"

"What about them? Let's go."

And we were moving, down in the stuffed, sweaty elevator out into the sharp, clear, very cold night, sweat and chill and confusion, television lights and shouts of "Governor . . . Governor . . ."

We moved toward the van, past the lights and into a bitter cold and darkness. The ground was slick. We were near the van, and there was Marcus Silver. "Governor," he said, very calmly, and, again, his calm penetrated the frenzy like a knife. Stanton stopped.

"Governor," I said, trying to push him along.

"Governor," Marcus Silver said, holding him.

"Yes?"

"Were you ever arrested in a Vietnam-war protest?"

"No," Stanton said.

"Are you sure?" He *did* have something.

"I participated in protests. Everyone knows that."

"But you weren't arrested on August 16, 1968, in Chicago—during a radical protest that took place before the Democratic convention called the 'Lock Up Your Daughters, We're Comin' to Town' March, led by Abbie Hoffman?"

"I was detained and released," Stanton said. He was cool. He didn't seem at all perturbed. "It was all a big mistake. The record was supposed to be expunged."

"So you weren't arrested for civil disturbance and destruction of property?"

"No, I was in Chicago a few days early, visiting friends—I was thinking about applying to the University of Chicago law school. I happened to get caught up in the protest. It was a mistake. They released me. That's all." He got into the van.

"Do you remember how you got released?" Silver asked.

"No," Stanton said dismissively. "They released a lot of us. They must have realized it was a mistake. It was a long time ago."

I was totally freaked. Stanton seemed calm. Susan seemed calm. He had been pissed before; now he was calm. We were in the van, and it was ultra-warm again, and I was sweating. Still cold—my feet were frozen—but sweating. "Governor," I asked as we drove off, "is there anything else we should know about Chicago?"

"No," he said. Then to Susan, "Can you believe that Charlie Martin?"

"You handled it," she said.

"But they were laughing at me," he said, and he sounded . . . frightened. "It was okay, right? It *was* okay?"

"You did fine," she said, ending it.

I knocked on Daisy's door. She opened it—smiled, surprised—then she saw. "What's wrong?"

"Gotta call Richard."

"What's wrong?" I didn't answer. The room was softly lit, just the bedside light; it almost seemed cozy. I went over to the phone by the desk and began to dial. She came up from behind, put her arms around me—and it felt so good, so good. I stopped dialing. "Henry, you're soaked," she said. "What's wrong?"

I detached her, gently. I switched on the desk light, dialed again. "Pick up the other line," I said. She went over to the bed, sat down. Ringing. Ringing. I lost track for a moment, drifted, read the late-night pizza delivery card, forgot who I was calling. Amazing how far away you can go in an instant.

"Yeah?" Richard answered.

"Richard," I said, "We're fucked."

"Yeah?"

"Or we may be fucked—I'm not sure. Stanton didn't seem worried and Susan was cool, but it doesn't look—"

"Henry," he said. "Shut the fuck up and talk to me."

"Guy from the LA *Times,* investigative type—"

"The drug thing? Shit."

"*It's not the fucking drug thing, it's the fucking war thing,*" I screamed. I was, I realized, totally out of control. I had to pull it back. This was nothing—this was just the beginning. I had to pull it back.

I told the story.

"And he's going with it?" Richard said.

"Sounds like it," I said. "What's today? Friday. Then Sunday, I'd guess."

"And that's all there is?"

"I don't know. I don't know. I don't think so—I had this feeling, y'know? I think there's more."

"But we don't know," Richard said. "We don't know shit. See? See? Didn't I call it? I been telling you this, Henri, I been saying it— since when? Since Jehoshaphat was a monkey. We gotta get someone to check out this shit. We gotta talk to him about this. We can't fucking fly blind like this. They're all gonna be comin' after us now. I mean, 'dja see any *other* president up there on the stage tonight? We're it, man. We're the ball game. They're gonna want a piece of us, y'knowhattamean? Every fucking flea that ever nipped his ass is gonna want a piece of this. We gotta talk to him. Get someone on flea patrol, y'knowhattamean? And we need it now: Yesterfuckingday. We got no other option."

"Yeah, but who goes to him?"

"You. You're the body man and the mind man. You're it."

I couldn't. "I can't," I said.

"Then you gonna freeze your butt off this next month, watching our boy go down like the *Titanic.* And then you gonna be unemployed, and disgraced, and I won't even be able to hire you to handle the Nee-groes and suburban women. You're it. We got no other option."

"Yes we do," Daisy said. "We can talk to her."

"*We can't talk to her.* Are you out of your fucking mind? What are you gonna say? 'Listen, Mrs. Stanton, we gotta hire some sleazy fucking dick-ass gumshoe to find out who all the governor's been plugging?' Listen, Daisy. Get real."

"We've got a better shot with her than him," Daisy said. "Think about it. And we don't put it to her that way. Only *you* would do it that way. Remember, it's not sex now—it's the war. That makes it easier. It gives us an opening."

"She's got a point," I said.

"Awwwww. Can you believe he got arrested at a 'Lock Up Your Daughters' demonstration?" He laughed. "Perfect, huh?"

"Richard, get on a plane—first thing," I said. "You and me . . . and Daisy." I glanced over at her. She smiled. "We've got Susan patrol tomorrow. And Richard, your gossip columnist at the LA *Times*—Honey, is it?"

"Happy Davis."

"Call her."

"No. Seem worried."

"I suppose," I said.

"Henri, face it. We're flying fucking blind."

We put down the phones. Daisy came across the room, put her arms around me, snuggled. She tilted her face in toward mine, put her mouth on mine. There was a tenderness to this, an intimacy—really strange. I pulled back, looked at her and at the room—and laughed. I was suddenly giddy.

"So?" she asked. "So?"

"Look at this place," I said. "You're neat, too."

"Fuck you. I just got here."

"No, no," I said. "You hung up your coat. It's in the closet. You did, didn't you? Of course you did. I bet you even *unpacked*." I went over to the bureau, opened the drawers. "Uh-huh, uh-huh, I see." T-shirts on left, neatly stacked. Sweatshirts on right, neatly stacked. Underwear, drawer below. The sight of the underwear reminded me and I turned to her. She was there, but pulled back as I moved toward her.

"Paper," she said. "Clothes are easy. Paper is hard. Faxes." I was nibbling her neck. "I mean, what do you do with faxes?"

A knock on the door. It was Jack Stanton. He didn't give me time to wonder why he was knocking on Daisy's door at one in the morning, and he didn't seem to wonder why I was there. He just started talking. "The Martin thing is no good," he said. "It's gonna come back. That motherfucker doesn't have a single idea, all he's got is grenades. He's a kamikaze—he can only do me harm. The war really hurts, don't you think? It hurts in ways I never realized. Dammit, damn *me*. Charlie can get away with things I never could, because of that. He can be loose in a way I never can, and confident. I've always got to be on the lookout, thinking about that—you can get blindsided in one of these things. I make one false move, and he can make me seem like a chickenshit." He sat down on the bed. He didn't seem to see us. He was wearing a nylon jogging suit.

"You were presidential," Daisy said. "He wasn't."

"You think so? No kiddin'?" He fixed Daisy with paralytic intensity, sucking air out of the room. She nodded and he relented. "See, but it's not just him—the damn tax cut is killing me, too," he said, to her. He had said this to me a hundred times already. "Martin's setting me up for Harris. It's really him. He's Mr. Integrity. You think we should bag the tax cut?" He wasn't asking a question. "I never wanted that fucking tax cut. A children's exemption. We coulda got by with that."

I didn't dare look at Daisy. I wasn't looking at the governor, either. I was looking at the floor.

He went on. He went through the entire debate. He went through each of his answers. And then: "It's so unfair. So goddamn unfair, don't you think? You work so hard. . . . You know, I had it figured. I knew what could be done, could be said, how far you could go—and then this . . . professor. He makes me look a like a phony. A politician. He's got nothin' to lose, nowhere to go. He's not even trying. He's just there to hurt me. Did you see what he did to me on the environmental-tax thing? Made me seem like a bureaucrat, a regulator. You see what this is about, don't you? As if he'd get eight votes in the Senate for that fucking tax of his. I mean, how do we handle this?"

He paused. Did he want a strategy? I began, "Maybe we could—"

"See, the thing is, if you're not gonna go with a tax, you have to go with CAFE standards." He began to explain the history and intricacies of auto emission standards. He seemed to have lost all sense of time, of parameters, of the natural arc of conversation. "You can't go too far with CAFE standards because of Michigan. We've gotta think about Michigan—and he couldn't care less. He doesn't expect to be around for Michigan. His semester ends with New Hampshire."

It went on like that. I had seen him wend his way through a complicated situation before, talking like this, talking for hours. But that was just the two of us, on the road; he was teaching me, I thought, showing me how his mind worked. It was an odd thing, a tic, compulsive in a way—and certainly intense—but not *pathetic*. This was, sort of. It was needy, in a frightening way. Weird. Daisy fell asleep on her bed, and Jack Stanton was still talking. But he hadn't been talking to her, and he hadn't been talking to me—and while he did talk about the war, he never mentioned Chicago.

Saturday, it was as if the strange scene in Daisy's room had never happened. We were still flying. The sun was shining. The papers all gave us the debate. He seemed presidential, they said. The Charlie Martin episode played our way: Stanton's response seemed forceful in print. Nobody—except *The Washington Post*—mentioned the laughter that preceded it (which had Stanton worried—the *Post* was always a beat ahead of the others when it came to nuance and minutiae). We were moving north from Concord, up the spine of the state toward Conway, and everything felt good and clean—blinding sun on snow, sharp cold, a slight breeze sending a fine spray of ice crystals into the air. We were doing a lunch thing—volunteer firemen's club at a church in Franklin—and I noticed that it was really getting crowded now back in the scorp zone. The reporters seemed dazed, balloony in their down jackets, an obscure clerical sect—they dressed up in Washington, but campaign scorpwear was less formal. They looked overloaded, distracted and clumsy, lugging satchels of paper and laptops about. They were easy to class.

"How many we got?" I asked Laurene.

"Twenty," she said. "They're really jammed into the vans, too. Had to blow off that woman from Phoenix, and a few others who didn't sign up until after the debate."

"You think we need a bus?"

"Maybe. But the immediate problem is, a lot of them want to go back to Manchester after Laconia. They don't want to go all the way up to Conway. The guy from the *Chicago Trib* is really pissed. He didn't know Stanton was *flying* back to Manchester—and *none* of them are too happy about the three-hour drive on a Saturday night. We don't have any seats on the plane, do we?"

"Absolutely not," I said. "But let's peel off one of the vans after Laconia for the ones who don't want to do Conway. You stay with the other one, keep them as happy as you can."

"Gee, thanks," she said. Laurene was cool, a real pro. She didn't feel the need to do the "Hey, bro—ain't these white debbils fucked *up!*" routine with me. Our thing—Laurene's and mine, I realized—was that we were above all that defensive shit. We were very uptown. "Who knows this place?" Laurene asked. "Maybe we can find a cute inn or something, land them there for dinner on the way back. But, Henry, we gotta start thinking this through better. We need someone who thinks scorp logistics days ahead, y'know?"

We continued north. It was like that all day. Normal. We brought local activists, one by one, into the van. We had Barry Gaultier, the minority leader of the state assembly and a real power, riding with us all the way. Barry was on the cusp of an endorsement, but he wanted us to guarantee him a job with the campaign after the primary. We were doing well enough that we didn't have to promise shit. We wanted Barry to see that. He was a former insurance salesman, had the terminal gray look. And you could almost see him troping closer and closer to Stanton with each stop. I hated this part of it—reminded me of the crap I had to do with Larkin: stroking, stroking, promising, praising. But, then, Barry Gaultier *was* a legislator. Stanton was right about that: they were a lesser breed.

Laconia: a town meeting in the high school gym. There were some empty seats, the first the governor had seen in a week or so—advance had miscalculated. Daylight was waning in the narrow windows at the top of the bleachers, cold and blue-gray. Several of the scorps stayed outside, in an echoey pea-green tile lobby with the unpolished trophies and faded ribbons in glass display cases, working their cellulars, calling the desk, seeing if they could blow off Conway—it would be right on deadline. The wires, looking particularly glum, knew they couldn't. They'd be coming with us all the way—and driving back all the way, while we flew. Bad staff work.

"Henry, you gotta fix this shit up," said Tommy Aldrenio from the Philadelphia paper. "You let the schedule drift, you don't think about filing time. This is the big step up now—you gonna step up and be real or is this gonna be a bush-league operation?"

"We're real, Tommy," I said. "You wrote it today."

"You're real by default," he said. "You're running against dogmeat. The big leagues gonna be harder than this. Don't get cocky."

"We'll work on it, Tommy," I said. "What's everybody writing?"

"They're writing you," he said. "They hear *Time* has a Stanton cover coming Monday. They want to beat the call."

"No shit," I said. I had completely forgotten about *Time*. They'd been along, earlier in the week. They'd had two editors, their beat man and a bigfoot interviewing Stanton in a ratty Concord motel room on Tuesday. They'd shot him—forty-five minutes out of our schedule—on Wednesday. They'd said "maybe" a cover. It was either us or a new book about pet psychology. I assumed the latter, as the folks from *Time* seemed to, and then I'd let it slip—the debate, the guy from the LA *Times,* a hundred other worries. I do not absorb the possibility of good news very well, I guess.

"Excuse me," I said to Tommy, and I went to the principal's office and used the phone to call Brad Lieberman, who had moved his operation to the Manchester storefront.

"You hear anything about *Time*?"

"You hear anything about *Time*?" Brad shouted to the room. Then: "Richard just got in. Hold on. Spork? Yeah? No shit. Spork has a kid over there, a researcher—did some summer stuff for him. He'll call over. Wait."

"Meanwhile, Brad—we need to get our scorp act together. They're tolerating us now because we're throwing heat and it's early. But we gotta get someone thinking strategically about this. We gotta think about buses, and planes—how many you need before we get a plane?"

"We went through this in the war party, Henry," he said. "No plane until after New Hampshire. We don't do a big plane until we get the Service. Anyway, you don't need a fucking plane in New Hampshire."

"Yeah, but we've got that Southern swing week after next, and—"

"Yeah." He was listening to someone talking. Then he said to me: "*Time*'s closed already? No shit. Gotta be someone there. Spork's trying his guy at home."

We talked logistics some more. You can talk logistics forever and never talk logistics enough. Finally, Brad said, "Hold on," and then, really excited: "Spork found him at home. He's shootin' me a thumbs-up. He's jumpin' his fat ass up and down. We're *happening*, Henry! It's on."

I raced out of the room. Slowed down. Past the scorps in the lobby, into the gym, where Stanton was talking about shoe imports and the room was feeling kind of drowsy. I moved into his line of sight, locked in, gave him a cut sign. He went on. He took another question, about early education. Shit. That would be good for another ten minutes—and it was. As he wound down I said, pretty loud: "Last question, Governor."

"We'll just take one or two more," he said. I rolled my eyes, so only he could see. He flashed me a smile: Let me work, he was saying. He had this sense about these things. He knew how and when an audience felt tapped out, listened to.

I went back out into the lobby. I called Manchester, asked for Richard. "Great, huh?" I said.

"You forget what I'm doing here, Henri?"

"We're on the cover of *Time,* man."

"Does he know yet?"

"No, he's in mega-explain mode. Doing shoe imports. Can't shut him up."

"Henri, we can't fuck this other thing up. We're *gonna* fuck it up—but we can't. Y'knowhattamean? We gotta get Susan on board. Hate to admit, ol' Daisy Mae got it right."

Stanton was moving now. There was a shuffle from inside, the doors swung open, doors opening and closing, stuffy air from inside, cold air from outside. I moved toward Stanton, found my place near his elbow, watched the handshakes. An elderly woman hugged him. "You remind me of Kennedy," she said breathlessly. "He was here. I saw him. He was thinner than you—but you're just as cute."

We moved him toward the van, into the van. Barry Gaultier was still with us—good. This news should do it. There was a knocking on the window. It was Bob O'Connell, from *The Washington Post*. He wanted to ask a question, he was moving along with the van as we were beginning to roll. "Hold it," I said, but Mitch was already moving and O'Connell had given up, with a very pissed-off look. What was that?

Anyway: "Governor, you're on the cover of *Time* magazine this Monday."

Stanton turned, looked at me—and then at Barry Gaultier. "What's the cover line?" he asked.

Shit. I didn't know. I could see he was pissed. But—saved by Barry Gaultier. (No time for temper now.) "Whatd'ya think, Barry?" Stanton asked. "Not bad, huh? This thing's got some flame under it now."

"Not bad at all," Barry said, fumbling—looking for his next move.

"Now, I know you've been thinking long and hard about this," Stanton said, fixing Barry Gaultier with an intensity that the poor man probably had never experienced before in his life. Stanton seemed to expand in the van—and he seemed to have turned fully from the front seat, turned to face Gaultier directly. It was an amazing thing. I couldn't imagine what he'd done to his body. The air wasn't moving. There was no sound from outside. No wind. "And I know," Stanton continued, "that your endorsement means a lot—it's your word of honor, it's your bond—and that it would mean the world to me here in New Hampshire. You have it in your power to make the next president of the United States, and I know you don't take it lightly. I don't take it lightly. Everyone knows the respect that people have for you here. But listen, Barry: We are going to do great things. We are going to make history. You want to be part of that. You want to be part of it now—and next year in Washington, after we win. We'll make a place for you, an important place. I'm not the sort who forgets who brung him to the dance. We take care of our friends, Barry. You know what that means, right?"

"Right, but—"

"A title. There's the matter of a title. How does strategic coordinator sound?"

"Great. It couldn't sound better. Of the whole campaign?" Gaultier asked.

"Strategic coordinator for the New England region."

"Ahhh." Barry almost choked.

"You'll be in on the highest councils of this effort," Jack Stanton said. "You'll be a part of the team."

I had been holding my breath, I realized. I exhaled.

And then inhaled again, sharply, at Conway. Rob Quiston of AP, a solid guy—a straight shooter, no bullshit, no games—opened the van door for Stanton and said, "Governor, we're going to need a reaction from you on this."

I jumped out behind him. Barry Gaultier was behind me.

"The *Los Angeles Times* is reporting that you were arrested in a radical demonstration before the Democratic National Convention in Chicago in 1968."

"Yes, I know," Stanton said. "It was a mistake. I was detained, not arrested."

"And that you called a United States senator to get you out of jail."

"I . . . I don't . . ."

"And that he persuaded the mayor of Chicago to have your record expunged—"

"Well, I don't know about that part."

I noticed the movement had stopped behind me. Barry Gaultier wasn't getting out of the van.

"This is bullshit," Susan said. "It's just bullshit. Jack wasn't a radical."

"It don' look great, ma'am," Richard said.

"Yeah, but it's not important. People don't care about this kind of thing."

It was late Sunday morning. Brunch in the Stanton suite at the downtown Holiday Inn in Manchester. There was a good-sized dining room table in this one. We had shoved stacks of newspapers and briefing papers down one end of the table. There were bagels and Danish pastries, and a platter of sorry-looking scrambled eggs and

cardboard bacon that no one touched, except Daisy, who broke off
and nibbled tiny pieces of it. Lucille Kauffman, who was there when
we arrived—much to our dismay—carefully monitored everything
everyone was eating. The governor was off, working churches.

"They might care about it," I said. "It's early. We don't know what
they care about yet, for sure."

"Nobody cares about this stuff except the press," Lucille said. "It's
microscopic, meaningless. They're pigs and we should never forget
that. Treat them like the pigs they are. I know you like them, Henry—
and I know they've . . . mythologized you, Richard. But they're scum.
They're the enemy—they're what's standing between us and victory."

Was this necessary? Everyone in the room knew who the scorps
were and what they did. Lucille was performing for Susan, it seemed.
I found myself wanting to be able to look at Daisy: to see her eyes, to
feel her reaction, but she was sitting next to me, down the table from
Susan, who was at the head. Richard and Lucille sat across from us, in
front of the plate-glass balcony window. Cold, windy Manchester was
behind and below them. I wanted to get up, take a look at it, see if
there were any clues out there.

"Okay, Lucille, let's say you're right," Richard said, his eyes opaque
behind thick lenses. He was being careful. "They are scum. They are
shitbird reptiles." Then he had a thought and became Richard again,
up like a shot and pacing around the table: "Say you're out in the
woods, takin' a shit, and a wild boar comes chargin' at you. Do you
pull up your pants and run? Or do you try to pull up your pants and
grab those doves you just shot, and then try to run, all at the same
time? You forget the fucking *doves,* right?" He began to giggle, and
swallow his words. He was all tangled up in it now and, incredibly, he
wouldn't give up. He was a stubborn sonofabitch: it got worse. He
seemed to be imploring Susan. "You pull up your pants and run.
Y'knowhattamean? You'd grab your gun before you took the goddamn doves. And you'd pull up your pants rather'n shoot the boar,
'cause you don' have time to aim *and* button your fly. And, if you
miss, you don't want to die with your dick hangin' out. So, hah, hah,
yeah. I guess that's right. Y'might even *leave* your gun if the boar's
runnin' fast enough. Y'knowhattamean? Might even forget your gun
and save your ass."

"Richard," Lucille said. "I can assure you that none of us has a clue what you're talking about."

"You leave the doves for the boar," he said. "You gotta feed the beast."

"I think what Richard is saying," Daisy said, "is that this is the game we have—it's the only game in town—and we're not in complete control of the rules. There are other players. We have to think about them, and react to them."

"That's what *I* was saying," Lucille said. "He was killing birds and taking a—"

"Daisy," Susan said, cutting Lucille off. "So what do we do? How would you deal with them?"

"I have to go to the ladies' room," Lucille announced.

Richard stirred, about to say something, thought better of it. He let Daisy take the lead. He had sensed she could talk to Susan better than either of us could—and she was doing it, with a quiet confidence.

"We need to beat them at their own game," Daisy said. "We need to know more than they do, and anticipate what they're up to. We need to be prepared when a story like this one turns up, be able to strike back—with the truth."

"How can you know what kind of garbage they're going to come up with?" Susan asked, cutting to the chase.

"Well," Daisy said, "We have to— We need an operation to do research. Y'know? We need someone who can—"

"Investigate ourselves?" Susan asked. She seemed to settle in her chair. She knew what it was about now. "*Our* lives?"

Lucille came back. She walked into the silence but had no sense of it—remarkable: a woman without intuition or antennae. "This is all ridiculous," she said. "We don't play *their* game. We're playing the people's game. We say to them: The media and the Republicans want the election to be about trash. We want it to be about your future. People will understand. They won't swallow this hogwash. We don't shoot *doves* in this campaign, Richard. We protect them."

It was a standoff. I looked at Richard. He was considering jumping out the window. I couldn't see Daisy, didn't want to look directly at Susan. She knew this. "Henry," she said. "You agree with Daisy?"

I nodded. "We can't assume—" I began, and then I was paged. I checked it: Laurene on the utterly urgent line. "I think I have to take this," I said.

Susan—briefly, fleetingly—flashed fear. She had imagined the worst possible news about her husband; she lived with that, I realized. It was understandable, but awful. I felt awful for her. But she quickly covered the fear with something less intense: concern. "Go ahead. Who is it?"

"Laurene," I said.

"Isn't she terrific?" Lucille said as I dialed.

"Henry, this is insane," Laurene said. "We got twenty camera crews out here, more scorps than you can shake a stick at. They're waiting for him to come out of church. What do we do?"

"Hold on," I said, then explained the situation to Susan and the rest.

"Animals," Lucille said. "It's *Sunday*."

Susan shushed her: "Henry?"

"Laurene, you've got Mitch there?" I said. She said Uh-huh. "He's wearing a tie?" Uh-huh. "Send him into the church with a note for the governor. Say this in the note: 'Swarm outside. Will need react on LA *Times* story. Remember it's Sunday.' Okay? And listen: Stay very cool and friendly, unconcerned. Pity them for being such lowlife jerks that they have to cover this piece of shit nothing of a story on a Sunday. Act like it's nothing, okay? Then call me back when it's done."

I hung up. Susan seemed shaken, Lucille impervious. "See, Henry," she said. "when it comes right down to it, you feel the same way about them as the rest of us do."

"Oh come on, Lucille," I said, figuring: Fuck it. "It's apples and oranges. You don't need to love them to know how they think, what they need. It's not about protecting doves, it's about feeding time. We've got to be able to control when it's dinnertime and what's on the platter."

"We're flying *blind* here," Richard blurted. "We need to know *everyth*—"

Susan started. Everyone saw it.

"Okay," she said, slowly. "We'll do it. I'll tell the governor. But we will control it. I want Libby Holden to do it. It has to be someone who knows us, someone we trust."

"Is she out of the hospital?" Lucille asked. Susan nodded.

"Is she, y'know, *okay* now?" Lucille asked. Susan nodded.

Richard looked at me. I shrugged. I had heard of Olivia Holden. She had been Jack Stanton's chief of staff, but she'd quit suddenly in a dramatic, tearful—and utterly incoherent—press conference several years back; and then disappeared.

Each of us had just found out where she had gone. And Susan had just placed the campaign in her hands.

IV

Olivia Holden was wearing, I swear, a tan down vest, an orange-and-green tie-dyed muumuu and an Aussie outback hat. She was enormous, with fierce, piercing blue eyes, hair turning gray, skin that was waxy pale and translucent in a sickly way. She was lugging a large leather satchel. Everything stopped—even the phones seemed to stop ringing—when she marched into the Mammoth Falls headquarters two days after the New Hampshire church debacle. The office staff was somewhat depleted; most of the troops were up in Manchester. There were volunteers working the phones, plus some new staffers—people I didn't know, hired by Brad Lieberman—and a few of the old muffins. The Olds dealership felt open, airy; all Mammoth Falls did, after New Hampshire. The world seemed a quieter place. Except for Olivia.

"I'm HERE," she announced. "Who's talking to me?"

I was. Lucille—who had made herself more of a presence in the campaign now—and Brad Lieberman were joining me.

"Henry Burton," I said.

"Ah-HAH," she said, not introducing herself.

"Brad Lieberman."

"Ah-HAH."

"Hello, Lib," Lucille said.

"Shit for brains!" Libby greeted her. "You learned how to watch your mouth? Remember the geezers? Remember the geezers? I will not let you fuck up this campaign like Florida! I WILL NOT LET IT HAPPEN!"

"That was twenty years ago," said Lucille—a new, diffident Lucille. Olivia Holden had done her first good deed.

"I was thinner then," Libby said, turning to me suddenly, putting her face too close to mine, blue eyes flaming. "I had a waist. Truly, I did. WHERE IS THIS HAPPENING?"

In my office, which seemed too small to contain this . . . whatever. Brad brought in some chairs. Libby didn't use one; she sort of half perched herself on my desk—she couldn't get up all the way—facing out. Which meant her back was to me. Which meant I had to move. And so I did, around to the other side of my desk. The three of us faced her in a semicircle now. It was clear who was running this meeting.

"You will give me WHAT resources?"

"What do you need?" I asked.

"WhatdoIneed, whatdoIneed, what *do I need*? NOT HERE. We do this someplace else. I will take a house. I know the house. Nice little house, north of the capitol. It has the sweetest little rose garden—*call Becky Raymond, 6734982*—tell her the governor will require the house for his presidential campaign. She'll know what you mean. It's her house. Now, staff: THAT one. The one who looks like Winona Ryder—mmmm, absolutely gorgeous." She pointed to Jennifer, the media muffin, working the phones, dark hair down over her eyes. "Is she smart?"

"She's smart," I said, fearing—briefly—for her safety (then remembering how easily she'd handled Richard during his Winona period).

"TOUGH?"

"Eats nails," Brad said.

"NAILS? Hoo-HAH! One other. A quiet little pussy boy. A fetcher, a scanner. Good eyes. Let me look." She walked to the doorway, looked over the various muffins: "THAT ONE." She pointed to Terry Hickman, a soft, scraggly mountain boy who had wandered down from the state university—"Takin' a breather," he had said—and was working on scheduling. He played the guitar and banjo, entertained the troops. I hated to pull him out of the office. He was good for morale.

"If it's okay, I'd like to keep him here."

"NO WAY," Libby said, in my face again. "We do this RIGHT or not at all, *yagotme*? Don't fuck with me, Henry."

"I'm not fucking with you. We want this to happen, but we've got a lot of other things going on here."

"All right, all right, *alllll right!*" she said. Phew. "Then, THAT one," she said, pointing to a kid in fund-raising I didn't know. I turned to Brad, who knew everyone.

"Peter Goldsmith," he said. "Good choice. Quiet, hardworking."

"But can he read *smart*?" Libby asked.

"In three languages," Brad said.

"Okay, I want them as soon as we're done," Libby said. "Now, Chicago. I need Chicago. What gives?"

"Brad used to work for the mayor," I said. "He's been handling that."

"The MAYOR? THAT FUCKING FOOL? We HATE the mayor—the other one, the real one. His father. That's why we're neck-deep in shit in this country, because of people like that. That's why . . . So? So, where is it?"

"This mayor is working with us," said Brad. "There have been seventeen media requests to check through the arrest records of everyone involved. We've slowed down the process, but we're not going to be able to stop it."

"Why *stop* it?" Libby said. "YOU DON'T KNOW ANYTHING, do you?"

"What do you mean?" I asked.

"Jack's right," she said. "It was a mistake. It was YOUR BOYFRIEND," she said, pointing at Lucille.

"Not till later," Lucille said. "I wasn't there."

"But you must know about it, right? Right?" Libby had moved into a snarly whisper now. "After grinding your scrawny little pushy-assed body, sweating, juicing, heaving with Mr. Howard Ferguson, you never whispered sweet nothings, past histories, conspiracies? You never talked? No postgame analysis? Never?"

"Libby, you're fucking out of your mind," Lucille said.

"RIGHT! WE KNOW THAT!" Libby said. "What we don't know is what you know about Chicago."

"Nothing."

"Well, *I* know."

"What," I asked, "do you know?"

"That Jack went along to stop Ol' Firefly from doing something crazy, that's what! Ol' Firefly never had the chance to do something crazy—at least I don't think so. The pigs nailed them before"—she turned to Brad—"your fucking ex-employer's father's fucking storm troopers. If you were there, if you were there, you—can—never—for-get—what it SOUNDED like."

"But he called Senator Dawson?"

"OF COURSE HE DID! What would you do? He was only trying to save his friend—his ollll' college buddy, ol' Pinky Penis Ferguson—from doing something stupid. He put his future on the line FOR A FRIEND! Would you do that, Henry Burton? Huh? So, of course, he called LaMott Dawson—and, of course, that shitheel Sherman Presley would use that information now to try to take Our Jackie out."

"Sherman Presley?" I said. Of course: how stupid that we hadn't figured it out.

"Boy, are YOU lame!" Libby said. "Anyone with any brains would just *assume* Sherm the Worm. Susan knew it right away."

But she didn't tell anyone. "Why does Sherman Presley have it in for the governor?" I asked.

"Why does anyone have it in for anyone?" Libby said, almost sanely. "Jealousy. Jackie stole his boy—the good senator. LaMott just simply fell in love with Jack. And then, the whole thing with Beasley Arnold happened. You know about that, right?"

I didn't. "Tell me," I said.

"Life's too short and we've got scum to trash," she said. "Like that shitbird Cashmere McLeod." Libby read my face: "Boy, you really don't know shit, do you?"

"You mean Susan's hairdresser?" Lucille said.

"And Jack's porkpie," Libby said. I felt dizzy. "Oh, for Chrissake, Henry, you never heard Tommy the Trooper saying the governor was goin' out to work the cash machine? What use did Jack Stanton ever have for money?"

The cash machine. I had seen Jack Stanton from Washington down; Libby Holden, clearly, knew him from Mammoth Falls up. It was strange, vertiginous—the same Jack Stanton but a different world, a world that I'd not thought about much. I knew some of the Mammoth Falls friends and backers. They seemed the usual boosters—a few like Dwayne Forrest, the Hero Feed king, were national players. The rest were lawyers, squinny-eyed local adepts. I knew that Sherman Presley was a serious lawyer in town, the former head of the local power authority—and, of course, Senator Lamott Dawson's former legislative assistant; I knew he didn't have much use for Jack Stanton. But who cared? That was Mammoth Falls; we were leaving that behind. I hadn't really thought about Mammoth Falls's ability to reach out and pull us back. And Cashmere McLeod: Richard would truly enjoy that one, after all his elaborate war-gaming, after all his scenarios. Susan's hairdresser. I noticed that Lucille Kauffman hadn't said a word. I tried to think about this as Richard would: "So what about Cashmere McLeod? What can she do to us?"

"She can sell her story to the *National Flash* for a hundred and seventy-five thousand minus the ten percent she's giving to that slime-sucking, down-on-his-luck, shit-on-his-shoes, night-school *attorney*—attorney, HAH!—Randy Culligan, who's agenting the deal for her," Libby said. She was awesome.

"You know this?" I asked.

"No, I IMAGINED IT IN THE BOOBY HATCH!" Libby said.

"How long, how intense?" I asked.

"Let me see," Libby Holden said, suddenly falling to her knees on the floor with a splat—eliciting a gasp from Lucille and, I think, me—and then bending over her leather satchel, rummaging through it. "Lemmesee, lemmesee. 1989, maybe, 1988? Ah-HAH! Here." She pulled out a cheap black vinyl-covered datebook, flipped through the pages: "He drove her home from the Mansion April 12, 1989. He stopped at her house. He stayed for an hour. Hoo-HAH! Ya suppose they were playing CLUE?"

"It's bullshit," Lucille said, finally.

"In your dreams, sweetheart."

"She can't hurt us," Lucille said. "She's *selling* a story. She has no proof. She has no credibility. It's bullshit."

"It's a leading indicator," Libby said, still on her knees on the floor. "Our Jackie has done some pretty stupid things in his life. He's poked his pecker in some sorry trash bins. We gotta stop *them* before they stop us. We gotta CRUSH'EM, then sweep 'em up. From now on, you can call me—THE DUSTBUSTER!" She smiled, wickedly, crazily, then leaned over and took my chin in her hands and stared me very close in the face. "You know, honeychile, I'm stronger than dirt."

Yeah, no kidding. But I was numb. The shape, texture, dimensions of the campaign had suddenly changed. It was a different landscape now, though still familiar, which made it sort of creepy. The Chicago story sounded about right—and so did Cashmere McLeod (I had to admit). I wanted to set up Libby in a nice quiet room—padded, perhaps—with a pile of her favorite food (ribs with wet sauce, I later learned) and have her tell me the whole story, from the beginning. Slowly, comfortably, coherently. Richard had said it, again and again: we were flying blind. But I'd never quite believed it. I figured I knew Jack Stanton, at least the important things about him. I knew what sort of man he was. I knew his weaknesses. I'd known the shape—if not the extent—of his problems from the first day I'd met him. I'd placed that information in my own, desperately hopeful, context: he wasn't perfect, but he was the most talented natural politician I'd ever seen—and his heart was in the right place. Signing on had been a risk but not a very difficult decision. The strengths so clearly outweighed the weaknesses. I couldn't not.

So Libby was, oddly, reassuring. She had come to a similar conclusion, with much better information than mine. She knew the stories; she was the Stanton family griot, but, I soon learned, that was the extent of it. She brought no analysis to the table. She wouldn't be able to tell me *why*. (We would all have to come to our own conclusions about that.) She had affixed herself to the Stantons early on, out of a primal sort of attraction. There had been no calculation involved. It reminded me of what Hector Alvarado, a back-bencher from Los Angeles used to say, back in my nose-counting days, about Louis Parsons, a mortal yellow-dog redneck from Mississippi. The two had nothing in common but had become very tight, constant phone pals. "The animal in me," Hector would say, "gets off on the animal in him." Wasn't that how all of us made up our minds about these strange public people? Wasn't the staffer's passion, ultimately, visceral rather than ideological? Libby's insanity was an extrapolation, I realized, of my own propensities. That realization did not please me, but—for the moment—I could live with it.

I conferenced Richard and Daisy at about midnight that night. I was at home—it *was* sort of home now; more than New Hampshire was, at least—lying back on the bed, watching CNN with the sound off. "Richard, I met your dream woman," I said.

"The *fuckee*? Who is it?"

"Oh, I found out about that too," I said. "But I was referring to—the *Dustbuster*!"

I told them about Libby. I told them the campaign had acquired a manic, six-foot, 250-pound lesbian who knew where all the bodies were buried and could shut up Lucille.

"So Lucille and Howard?" Daisy said. "Wow. It's like birds fucking. You just can't picture—"

"But it all fits: Howard as the rad, Jack going along to the protest, trying to pull him back," I said.

"*Who cares about twenty years ago? Who's the fucking fuckee?*" Richard said.

"Her name is—Cashmere McLeod. She's Susan's hairdresser."

I could hear Daisy laughing. Richard wasn't: "What she look like? She a piece of ass? She plausible?"

"Don't know," I said. In truth, as soon as I'd heard the name, I'd imagined the rest of the package so immediately and so totally that I wasn't even curious.

"Farrah Fawcett in *Charlie's Angels*," said Daisy. "I'd stake my life on it. Farrah Fawcett—with a blanker look and maybe twenty, thirty pounds more beef on her."

"No shit: Susan's hairdresser?" Richard said. "And she's coming out?"

"For one hundred seventy-five thousand dollars—to one of the supermarket sheets," I said.

"We can't bid any higher than that?" Richard asked.

"Do we want to?"

"We don't have to," Daisy said. "This is a joke. We're all laughing."

"We ain't gonna be laughing when the rest of the world—all the fuckees all over the globe, the talented ten thousand, discover there's money to be made off Jack Stanton," Richard said. "So when is this happening?"

"Dunno," I said. "Soon, I guess. The deal's done."

"The Stantons know?"

"Dunno."

"Who's gonna spring it on them," Richard said. "Shall we take *this* one to Susan, Daisy?"

"She knows," Daisy said softly, in a manner that made it clear she had gotten it from the horse's mouth.

"And?" I asked.

"And what?" Daisy asked.

"And is she pissed? Is she packing? Is there gonna be a divorce?" Richard was just getting revved up. "And how long has she known? Did she just find out? Did you tell her? Did she always know? Did she just put up with it? Does she like to watch? Y'knowhattamean? Did Cashmere service both Stantons simultaneously? Sequentially? A rinse and a rim job? What the fuck are we dealing with here?"

"I don't know," Daisy said.

"But you know she knows?"

"Yes."

This was something new: Daisy—universally revered for her transparency and candor—oblique.

We let that sit for a moment and talked about the last two days. ABC had led with us—good *Time*, bad times—the magazine cover and the mob scene in New Hampshire. The other two networks had led with something about cholesterol or cancer: something from out of our world.

"I looked through the New Hampshire tape," Daisy said. "It's bad. The worst part of it is him. If what Libby says is true, he doesn't have all that much to be defensive about, except the appearance problem, calling the senator and all."

"Just being there is a fucking problem," Richard said. "Especially given what we now know: *Lock Up Your Hairdressers, We're Comin' to Town!*"

"Yeah, undoubtedly," Daisy said. "But he makes it worse by seeming so damn guilty about it. Watch his body language. Look at his chin, down, in, like he was about to be arrested."

"May happen before we're done," Richard said.

"Look, Richard," Daisy said, steely suddenly. "You haven't been sentenced to this campaign. You think he's guilty? Quit. You think it's hopeless? Book."

"I just wish we knew what the fuck we're dealing with."

"Daisy's right," I said. "We know what we're dealing with tomorrow. We're going back to New Hampshire. We're probably going into the Cashmere McLeod story. The immediate thing is to get him to stop acting like an ax-murderer. He didn't do anything wrong in Chicago. Cashmere McLeod is telling a story for money. If Susan isn't concerned—Daisy?—then the governor shouldn't be."

"She's not concerned," Daisy said.

"Then he should act pissed," Richard said.

"But not too pissed," I said. "He's running for president. It's more 'Well, we expected this kind of crap to happen. It's too bad, but we don't take it seriously.' "

"Yeah, but he doesn't have to say that," Daisy said. "He just knows it—right, Henry?"

"Right."

"And you're going with him? You'll work this on the plane?"

"I'll try," I said.

We hung up. I immediately called Daisy back. "She called you?" I asked. "What's going on?"

My call-waiting clicked. "That'll be Richard," Daisy said. "You talk to him."

Right. "What the fuck's going on with Daisy?" he asked. "What is it—we got the boys' team and the girls' team in this campaign?"

"I don't know," I said. "I'm kind of blown away by the whole thing. I gotta be up in three hours for Manchester. We'll just have to see."

"Listen," Richard said. "He's gotta find a way to get it out that, this ain't nothing—ain't nearly as frightening as things that happen to real people, losin' your job, gettin' foreclosed. We can turn it to our advantage, y'know? Shit happens. He's calm in a shitstorm. Use that in our ads, y'know? Jack Stanton: A Man You Can Trust in a Shitstorm." He was giggling now. "Y'knowhattamean?"

I wanted to say, But what if they don't want a candidate who seems to carry his own portable shitstorm along with him? But I didn't want to break Richard's mood: he had made his own little visceral decision. He was on board. He was sticking. We were stuck with this thing.

"Henry, they are going to kill me with trash," Stanton said the next morning, his face blotchy and reddening, about to blow. "We gotta stop this."

He looked at me as if it were an assignment: Stop this. Turn back the tide. He looked awful, as if he'd been up all night. He had a cup of coffee in one hand and a doughnut in the other. He inhaled the doughnut. Two bites. Reached for another from the box, which was vibrating on the fold-down table between us as the plane rattled down the runway. Gone. A third.

"Sir, we were talking . . ." He looked as if he were about to pounce on me, devour me like a doughnut, but he didn't say anything. "Daisy watched the tape of what happened outside the church."

"Sunday morning. Outside a church. Can you imagine? I'm trying to do something, and all they care about is this crap."

"Anyway, Daisy's feeling was that you, uh, looked guilty," I said, then, realizing that I had laid it on her, quickly added: "Richard and I think she's right. Libby says there's nothing there."

His head was down. "I am guilty. It's my fault. It's my own god-damn fault."

What was? No matter. "Listen, sir. We're gonna win this. We have to get over this rough patch. You can't be defensive. You didn't do anything wrong. Richard says at some point you should toss in that the hits you're taking are nothing compared to what average folks are going through." He looked up. I had his attention now. "Gotta be the right spot. Not as soon as we get off the plane. But keep it in your mind. Keep the folks in your mind."

"It is about them, isn't it?" he said, brightening. "You're a good man, Henry. By the way, you see what Charlie Martin said about Chicago?"

"What?"

"He said the only thing he held against the war protesters was all the fun they had." Stanton laughed. "He said we were right about the damn war. Can you imagine? I could grow to love Charlie Martin."

Actually, we were wrong about New Hampshire. It had stopped being about the folks; it was now about the scorps. That was the new reality, and it sucked—but there it was. We still went about, covering the same bases, going to coffees and town meetings, to the seacoast and the southern tier of Boston suburbs. The same questions were asked; he was still fabulous with civilians, still seemed able to connect and win them over. But the real campaign was what happened *between* those events now. It was about whatever Jack Stanton chose to say in response to the fusillade from the sullen throng that began to follow us around; it was about the logistics of ferrying these people—who had suddenly materialized from nowhere, gulls following a garbage barge—from place to place, and providing the facilities, mult-boxes and risers and all the rest, so that they could hound us and pound us and send the message forth: The unexpected front-runner was, suddenly, "in trouble." We had been presumed victorious and were now presumed comatose before most Americans even heard of us.

Internally, the campaign was a never-ending series of frenzied phone calls. Immediately, there was news that the Cashmere story would break on Thursday, and we had to figure out how to handle that. Chicago suddenly faded as a story—there was no paper trail, no way to prove that Stanton had gotten Senator Dawson to make the call, no place for the press to go with it. It didn't fade entirely, of course: it became part of a litany, part of the governor's portable shitstorm.

I never actually got to see Jack Stanton speak anymore; none of us did. I worked the phone in the back of the room, talking to bigfoot scorps back in Washington and New York. Telling them: "The campaign isn't about this garbage. You should come up and see what the folks really care about." (And hoping they wouldn't take me up on it.) The tangled skein of phone calls—I'd call Richard, Richard would call Leon, Leon would call Daisy (who was, rapidly, replacing Arlen as the person we called on media stuff), Daisy would call me— would continue long after the day was done, building to a climax at midnight, when we'd conference for several hours. And then between two and three, after that call, I'd deal with the governor, who prowled the halls of the Hampton Inn, where we'd planted ourselves in Manchester.

Often I'd find him across the frigid, brutally plowed parking lot, at the Dunkin' Donuts. A crippled kid worked the overnight shift and Stanton had latched onto him earlier in the month. Now he was there most nights—the combination of sugar and sympathy was overpowering. He had made Danny Scanlon his lodestar. Danny was what the election was all about. He had a shriveled leg, slurred speech, and who knew what else, but he was endlessly cheerful, always had a lopsided smile for the governor. He worked hard and never complained; he served apple fritters, hot out of the oven, and deserved a better country—and that was what this election *had* to be about. He and the governor would talk sports, college hoops (it was that time of year). Stanton would try things out on him—political riffs. If it worked with Danny, it was good. Sometimes, when we'd be walking out of a town meeting, about to be set upon by the scorps yet again, the governor would say to me, "We gotta keep it together now for Danny. That's what this is about."

For Henry Burton, the election was about rousting Jack Stanton from Dunkin' Donuts at two in the morning and talking him down for an hour, then fidgeting through a couple of hours of fretful sleep, then getting up at six. And then the scorps. We had hired—immediately, after the church debacle—a press deputy for Laurene: Marty Muscavich, an ancient, who had worked New Hampshire primaries for various Kennedys and knew the shape and feel of the place, and had been through too much to be flustered—even by the cataclysmic zoo that we soon became. The Chicago arrest had made our candidate a national story; Cashmere would make us a national scandal. Our opponents were still wandering about New Hampshire in a van or two; we had press buses now. We had to change a lot of things. A new class of journalists appeared that week: the snuff specialists, there to watch us writhe and die. People who did not have the vaguest clue of who Jack Stanton was or what he stood for suddenly were following us around with a simple assignment: Get it on tape if he breaks down, watch if he loses his temper or cries.

We moved into all this so quickly that it was difficult to comprehend. It was as if we were being borne, actually propelled, through our schedule by a lunatic tide—we were *sucked* out of high school auditoriums, Kiwanis club luncheons, all the other stations of the cross, sucked into this narrow vortex, a combination of gauntlet and undertow. He would be smiling, waving, denying—but moving faster than in the old days, when he could linger and bestow meaningful handshakes; if he stopped now, they were all over him. So we whooshed through the vacuum tube, propelled by media force, and no longer in control of the pace of the campaign.

It reminded me of a time at the beach when I was very young. I was with my father; it must have been the ocean side of the Vineyard. He had me in the waves; he was behind me, holding me by the shoulders, walking me—pushing me—out, deeper, chuckling, "C'mon, boy, don't be afraid." Calm, casual, sort of mocking—as if my fear were a silly thing, a kid thing. But the waves that capped his knees crashed my chest; to me they were scary, brute explosions, a buckshot of sand and shell fragments. And then, from nowhere, a much larger one came, and he lost his hold on me, and I was picked up and tossed backward, overwhelmed by green water and tumultuous silence. It was suddenly, eerily, not noisy. I was spun about, gulping, then thrown backward and washed up in a shallower place, behind my father. He had assumed I'd been carried out to sea, and he lunged out deeper, hunched over, searching for me, terrified. He turned toward shore to call for help, eyes huge, mouth agape—and saw me, and dived for me, scooping me up in his arms. His panic allowed me to cry; I'd been too stunned before that. "Oh, God, Henry, I'm sorry, I'm so sorry, I'm sorry." He held me out, looked at me: "Are you okay? Forgive me. Okay? Okay? All right now." And then, when I'd calmed, "Good thing you're your mama's child," he said. "A full-blooded nigger probably would've drowned."

And now I felt I was back inside that wave, hurtling backward, overwhelmed and disoriented but in a noiseless world: the story had broken, it was real—there was a woman—but it wasn't quite real yet either. We hadn't seen the woman, except for pictures, which were sort of hilarious: truck-stop pinups. Daisy had been wrong. This woman would have given her soul to look like Farrah Fawcett with thirty pounds. She had dark, curly hair—a bit of Loretta Lynn—and a pug nose, and lips that seemed cartoony. Curled, snarly lips, as if she had bitten into a lemon while having an orgasm. She had breasts, that was clear enough. But the rest of her body remained a mystery, as did the quality of her mind. On Thursday the *National Flash* issued a press release and started distributing advance copies: the thing would be smeared across checkout lines all over the country on Monday. On Friday we were the talk of the New York tabloids—the *Post*'s headline: READY CASH; the *Daily News:* THE HAPPY HAIRDRESSER—which meant we'd soon become the stuff of Eyewitless News everywhere. But the classier media, the big city papers and the networks, had taken a pass. Their silence added to the weirdness. We did not know where this would take us yet.

On Friday morning, Stanton was out on the stump; we were back at the hotel—Susan, Richard, Daisy, Sporken, Howard Ferguson, Lucille, Leon and Marty Muscavich, whom we'd asked to sit in with the core group because he seemed an adult, and we needed a few of those. There was a lot of business. There would be a debate that night. And Koppel wanted someone for *Nightline.* And we had to decide, finally, how we were going to deal with Cashmere McLeod. *60 Minutes* wanted us for Sunday night, after the Super Bowl; Brinkley wanted us for Sunday morning. The decision to do one, the other, both, neither, had fractured us. Everyone had a theory. (Except me: not only did I not have a clue, I was in heavy denial mode—I didn't want any of this to be happening.)

The Stanton suite, where we met, was something of a mess now. The whole sixth floor of the Hampton Inn, where we had camped out, was beginning to take on the musky odor—sweat, dirty laundry, stale pizza—of a college dorm. We each had our rooms. There were piles of garbage everywhere—newspapers, faxes, campaign literature, street signs, empty Diet Cokes, half-eaten sandwiches, empty Dunkin' Donuts boxes, spoiled fruit. There was an actual campaign office in downtown Manchester; but more and more, as we hunkered down, the sixth floor became the nerve center of the campaign. Brad had moved in Xerox machines, faxes and computers. There was a press office; there were muffins—and bustle. I was relieved by the bustle: we still seemed a normal campaign.

Susan floated above the mayhem. When we met that Friday morning, she sat at the head of the table in the suite, carefully put together in a blue Armani blazer and gray slacks, with a very cool lime silk blouse, drinking tea. Her hair was gathered, severely, under a hairband. Her eyes were clear, the least bloodshot of anyone's in the room; she was wearing mascara—and lipstick. She was making a statement. The rest of us were a mess. "Leon, when do you think we'll have some sense of how this is playing?" Susan asked.

"Well, we know this much already: We were moving and Chicago stopped us. We didn't lose anything, but we stalled out at thirty-five. No one else is moving either." Leon was sitting but moving; his leg was jiggling, which caused his tight blond curls to shudder slightly—a human hummingbird. "It's as if this whole thing is frozen. The folks want to see what happens next. Now, I'm sure a lot of the others will be in the field tonight, but I'm gonna hold off. Friday nights are lousy."

"But won't this be different," Susan asked, "with the debate and all?"

"Let the debate settle in," Leon said. "Immediate reactions don't mean much there, either."

"But we gotta have some sense of where it's goin'," Richard said. He was jiggling, too. Then he was up and pacing. "And we gotta start preparing for what happens if we start to lose ground. Like what do we put on the air? Do we confront this stuff directly? Y'know they mighta given him Chicago—twenty-five years ago and all—and they mighta given him Cashmere, she's sellin' a story, right? But the two, right on top of each other. Y'knowhattamean? Y'know, do we really want a former revolutionary who messes around with hairdr—"

Richard stopped in his tracks. All eyes turned to Susan, who was flushed and furious. She launched herself into Richard's face: *"He didn't fuck Cashmere McLeod,"* she said with a vehemence that was impenetrable and startling. The room was silent. Susan was standing, leaning, hands planted on the table, staring us down; no one, so far as I could see, had the courage to stare back. "If you can't handle that simple fact, you can leave right now," she said.

No one knew what to say. I didn't know what to think, and I didn't dare look around the table—not even just across it, at Daisy—because I was afraid that it would convey something less than total devotion. "All right, then," Susan said. "Let us think this through."

So much for that: there would be no debate on how we'd "handle" Cashmere McLeod. The campaign would proceed under the assumption that the story was trash. The official posture would be outrage: who could take such garbage, sold to a supermarket sheet for money, seriously? "Who has thoughts about Sunday?" Susan asked.

"You do *Sixty Minutes*, you have a national audience," Arlen said. I looked at Daisy now: she was deferring to her boss, but she had her doubts. She glanced back at me: it was an I-need-a-hug glance. She had a wad of Kleenex in her hand; her nose was red and running; her eyes were watery, feverish; she coughed. Sporken continued, bubbly: "You and the governor will be able to put this thing down, show who you are, what this campaign is really all about, and you'll do it before the largest possible audience."

"They gonna let you show what this campaign's all about?" Richard asked. "Who's been dealing with them?"

"Howard?" Susan asked.

"They will give you twenty minutes, immediately after the postgame Super Bowl show," Howard said dryly, precisely. "It will be Lesley Stahl or Steve Kroft. They didn't even propose Wallace—I guess they figured we'd never say yes. I said you'd only be interested if you and the governor could talk about the real issues in the campaign, why you're running. We didn't want the piece to be a high-toned *National Flash*. They said they understood that."

"This would be live?" Marty Muscavich asked.

"I don't know," Howard said.

"Does it matter?" Susan asked.

"Of course," Muscavich said. He had a kindly, rubbery face, dominated by a large mouth with thick lips. His hair was white, what was left of it. I remembered seeing pictures of him, from the sixties—black and whites, White House photos; he was never one of the group in the Oval Office, but you'd see him in the campaign shots, one of the bright young men in thin, dark, loosened ties and slope-shouldered Ivy League suits surrounding the young president as he made his way through a crowd. He'd never been a real player, but he'd been there. And now he was here, with us, wearing a dullish paisley tie and a PT-109 tie clasp. (He was the only man in the room wearing a tie, I realized.) "If it's live, you can control it better," he said. "You can tell your story, use the tension of the moment to embarrass whoever's interviewing you. Y'know: Why on earth is a nice fella like you so interested in this trash? Why would you dignify such accusations? This is a presidential campaign; let's talk about the economy. If you pretape, they have control: even if you get the upper hand on their interviewer, the audience will never know that. Your great moments'll wind up on the cutting-room floor."

"I don't know why we have to do any of this," Lucille said.

Marty ignored her and went on: "There's a famous story about Menachem Begin and *Sixty Minutes.* Who knows? It might even be true. Anyway, Mike Wallace—I think it was Wallace—wants to interview Begin. He calls up and flatters him, and says he'll need two hours to do the interview. 'Two hours, Mr. Wallace?' Begin says. 'You are going to use two hours of Menachem Begin on American television?' Wallace said no. They would edit the piece down to eighteen minutes. 'Then, Mr. Wallace, I will give you eighteen minutes,' Begin said."

"Howard, why don't you go into the other room and call them?" Susan said. "We'll talk about *Nightline.*"

"Do we have to do it?" Lucille asked. "And why do we have to do it *tonight*? Why can't Koppel wait till Monday or something? It's gonna step all over the debate."

"We *asked* the Stanton campaign to par-ti-ci-ate in this broadcast," Richard said, doing an awful Ted Koppel, "but they refused. So they must be guilty as fucking sin, right?"

"So we just have to take it?" Lucille pressed. "They're going to dignify this garbage, treat it like a real story—and we have to go along with that?"

"They say it's a show about how the media handles these sorts of stories," I said.

The room dissolved in laughter. "Hey, why'n'tcha call Koppel back"—Richard was giggling—"'n tell'im we're up for a show about how fucking *Nightline* finesses sexy stories it doesn't want to acknowledge? *I'll* get on for that."

"Oh, *that* would give us real credibility," Lucille said. "The Stanton campaign will be represented tonight by a hyperactive redneck from outer space."

"You'd do well yourself," Richard said, and was about to say something fabulous about Lucille and sex when he remembered Susan was in the room, and shut down.

"Well, who do we put on?" Susan asked.

"How 'bout Henry?" Lucille said.

"Not bad," Richard said. "He can Mau-Mau Ted with race voodoo and erudition."

"Henry's too young," Susan said. I was sort of stunned, and yet relieved. I was being talked about as if I were a commodity, as if I weren't there—but I was more than happy to be rejected for this particular assignment. "We need someone more authoritative. Marty?" she asked. Susan had, suddenly, fallen in love with Marty.

"Who am I?" he asked. "You need someone who's been associated with the campaign."

"Who the fuck *knows* who's been associated with the campaign?" Richard asked.

"The people who watch *Nightline*," Marty said. "It's a New York–Washington show. They want to see what kind of face you're going to show the public when times get tough, and they also want to see some continuity. If you change horses now, they'll think we're panicking."

"Aren't we overthinking this a little?" Leon asked.

"No," Daisy said. "Our public face is absolutely crucial, especially now. We need someone who's calm, confident—and someone who looks like a regulation American: I nominate Arlen."

Oh, Daisy: browning the boss. But she had a point. As I looked around the room, I realized that, as a campaign, we were short on regulation Americans. As if to prove my point, Howard returned then, sere and hawklike and intense. If you put him or Richard, or Lucille, or Libby on the air, or, better still, all four of them together, you would have the College Bowl team from Bedlam State. I started to smile at the notion of them, there together: the Stanton campaign electro-shock troops—then saw that Daisy thought I was laughing at her. She froze me with her eyes, then seized up into a fit of tight, angry cough-ing. Poor girl.

"I think Daisy's got a—" I began, but Susan wanted to know about *60 Minutes*. (Daisy acknowledged my apology with a nod, wiping a cough-induced tear from her eye.)

"Tape," Howard said.

"You asked for live?" Susan asked.

"Of course, but they gave me some technical gobbledygook that was impossible to understand."

"You said live was the only way we'd do it?"

"I implied it. I didn't want to close any doors."

"Do we really need this?" Lucille asked again. "Is this how you want to be introduced to the American public? Those are going to be real people—American people—not just primary voters out there watching. They're not thinking about politics yet, and suddenly you get this governor from a state no one ever heard of, denying a super-market tabloid story on *Sixty Minutes* right after the Super Bowl. Doesn't that look just a little bit defensive? If Leon is right, and we don't know how the folks are reacting to this thing, why should we put everything on the line? People may turn out to be *sane* about this. They may just think it's trash. You never know."

A reasonable point from Lucille. Wonder of wonders. "But we do need to do something," I said, "or else they're going to say we're ducking it. We should make some sort of stand. The *Times* or the *Post* maybe?"

"Don't have any more control over those fuckers than we do CBS," Richard said. "I say Brinkley."

"What's the story with Brinkley?" Susan asked.

"They were going to do the president's trip to Japan," I said, "but they said they'd give us twenty minutes at the top, before the Jack Smith set-up piece. We can do it from here. But I don't know. You want to contrast our problems with the president being presidential for a change?"

"It's not the president they're having on, is it?" Arlen asked.

No, of course not. The secretary of state. "Then no one's going to notice," Richard said. "Soon as we're off, half of Washington's gonna pick up the phone and start callin' around to the other half—How'd he do, how'd he do? Y'knowwhattamean?" True enough. I wasn't having a very good meeting here.

"Who does the interviewing?" Susan asked.

"The usual," I said.

"Cokie?" She asked.

"I'd guess," I said.

"Then it's gotta be both of us."

Lucille looked up sharply at Susan. "You . . ."

Susan met her glance—calmly, firmly, completely under control. Well, of course it had to be both of them. I had assumed it would be both of them. But up till that moment I hadn't realized how absolutely crucial Susan's presence was going to be. She would be watched as closely as the governor. She would have to strike the right chord— vehement, but not too defensive. I wondered what she *really* thought about all this; I realized I didn't have a clue, not a scintilla of an inkling. I was feeling out of it, removed from them for the first time since I'd signed on.

One thing was clear. Susan had—suddenly, and not very subtly— taken charge. *She* had decided how we'd respond to the Cashmere situation (and that there wouldn't be any internal debate about it). *She* would make the final call on who did *Nightline*. *She* was, obviously, tilting toward Brinkley and away from *60 Minutes*. She had always been a powerful force in the campaign, of course, but Cashmere had made her indispensable. "Henry, where's Jack?" she asked, emotionless. "You want to take this to him before we firm it up? Now, let's move on to the debate."

The debate was strange, otherworldly. Charlie Martin hit us for not being specific enough on health care; Lawrence Harris hit us for proposing a tax cut, given the enormous budget deficit; Bart Nilson hit us for not proposing more government jobs to ease unemployment. None of them talked about Chicago or Cashmere. It was as if there were two campaigns going on: the legitimate one, the campaign being covered by the prestige papers and the television networks (none of whom had touched Cashmere yet)—which our opponents were still honoring—and the trashball one, the tabloid morass that had become *our* reality. There was overlap, but it was oblique: the other candidates' energy level was up a notch, their excitement over our difficulties was palpable, but it remained discreet. That was smart. (It was interesting how even mediocre politicians reflexively found their way to the elemental rules of the game—in this case: Never attack an opponent when he is in the process of killing himself.) So they remained determinedly high-toned. They stayed clear of the sewage, fearing that some might splash back on them. But heightened ambition was in the air, sharp and obvious, like English Leather, and you could see the three of them puffing themselves up, trying to appear presidential, auditioning to replace us—if and when we went down.

Not even Harris, Mr. Classroom Exercise, was immune. His poll numbers had drifted down as ours moved up, but he remained respectable (about 20 percent); we assumed that he was serving as a familiar parking place while the New Hampshire Democrats watched the show and waited to see if we'd prove worthy. Now, though, you could see the first, faint glimmerings of aspiration. I imagined him shaving that morning, the thought drifting idly from deep brain to frontal lobe: Hmmm. If Stanton went down, who else would there be? His challenge had been deft, playful in the past. But now there was an edge to his skepticism when he came after us in the debate. And he used an interesting word: "moral." "It just isn't moral to play with our children's future," he said. It was used in passing, no special emphasis, but I saw Jack Stanton flinch. His head was down—he was taking notes—but he caught a breath and his shoulders tightened. Did anyone else notice?

We'd figured Harris wasn't just playing the game for fun. He was looking for work. The campaign was his application for the position of elder statesman. He would push us, push his ideas, win plaudits from the pundits, then warmly endorse us when it was over. And hope for—what? Treasury secretary? Something. That still might be his game, but the use of that one word—"moral"—seemed a scouting expedition, an exploration of the next level up. The purpose was mostly *self*-exploratory, I guessed. He wanted to see how it might feel, coming after us, being a player. He wanted to feel the adrenaline rush; he wanted—literally—to feel it in his damaged heart, to see if he could handle it. The moment came and went too quickly, and I was too intent on my candidate, to read the reaction. But I took a certain satisfaction from having caught this nuance. This was, if you could stand back from it, a wonderfully intricate game.

Afterward, the spin room was eerie. There wasn't as much attention directed toward us as there'd been in the past. It was a barely notice-able diminution, but I sensed that the first rush of scorps—the heavy hitters—was toward the other candidates. This made sense. The other candidates hadn't been paid much attention for the last forty-eight hours. The scorps had been on our case, and this was the first oppor-tunity to probe the other camps for Cashmere "react." Clearly, they weren't too interested in the debate. You could just sense it in the room. They had heard our react all day—the outraged stonewall—and figured that the news, if there was to be any, would come from the other candidates. I was kind of curious about that, too: Had any of the others made a decision to have a spokesman let something slip, move the story just a little bit closer to the center of the campaign? Again, the strange meteorology of New Hampshire: I was freezing and suf-focating. I was catching whatever it was that Daisy had. Jerry Rosen drifted over, very solicitously. "How ya doin'?"

"Fine. He did great tonight, don't you think?"

"He did okay, considering."

"Considering what?"

"Well, he still hasn't really *defined* himself," Rosen said. Just what I needed.

"Oh, come on."

"I mean, what does he really stand for, what does he believe in?"

"Oh, for Chrissake, Jerry, you've seen him work fifty times by now. You know what he *stands for*."

"Tell me."

But there wasn't time. The second wave of scorps was heading my way now. They would want a react to whatever the opposing spinners had laid down. And now they were all over me, and the questions—it was weird—were about *process*: How would we be able to soldier on with the press all over us about Cashmere? How would we be able to get our message out? Wouldn't we just be on the defensive now? The press was asking this. It was surreal. I don't know what I said to them: nothing much. I looked to see what was happening to Laurene and Richard—also working the spin room for us. (Spork was preparing for *Nightline*.) But I couldn't, and I couldn't afford to look too hard. I was talking—wallpaper talk, nothing talk. And, meanwhile, thinking it through. The opposing spinners probably hadn't said anything about Cashmere. They'd talked about the feeding frenzy. "Gotta wonder how Jack's gonna get his message out with you assholes all over him." Something like that. And so the scorps, dumb animals, came with that: How you gonna get the message out with us all over you? It made perfect sense. Wonderful sense. Everyone was clean (except us). Everyone could shave tomorrow. They weren't scumbag gossip reporters, they were media analysts. The scorps weren't reporting the trash, but how we *dealt* with the trash. The story hadn't really broken yet—and already it was one step removed: the press was reporting about how the candidate would deal with how the press would report about the story.

More of the same on *Nightline*. The show opened with shots of Gary Hart overwhelmed by reporters in 1987, and then a question, very precise, very efficiently put by Koppel, in his austere, authoritative way: Is this the sort of feeding frenzy that Jack Stanton will be facing now? Is it possible for any candidate to survive this sort of treatment? Is it fair? "We'll be joined by a top adviser to Governor Stanton, and also by a professor who has studied this phenomenon and written a book titled *Feeding Frenzy,* and the media critic for *The New Yorker.*"

Poor Arlen. He sweated, stumbled, fell. He looked like a regulation American, but he was far too nice, and not nearly quick enough, for this sort of duty. We watched him, horrified—a group of us, in Richard's room at the hotel—as he actually analyzed the difference between the Hart case and ours. "Well, Ted, Hart appeared to be caught in the act in 1987, but there's no evidence this time that . . ." Blah, blah, blah.

"WORK FOR *US,* YOU DORK," Richard screamed.

"He should be outraged," Daisy said quietly, stricken, watching her boss destroy himself. "He should be calling out Koppel for the phony he is. The guy is legitimizing this fucking thing—a bought-and-paid-for supermarket tabloid story—and Arlen is letting him get away with it."

The worst came at the end when Koppel asked the professor what the prognosis for Jack Stanton was. "Does anyone ever survive one of these feeding frenzies?"

"Well, Clarence Thomas did, but at this level . . ."

The asshole from *The New Yorker*—tweedy, supercilious—jumped in: "Ted, if Jack Stanton had been around for twenty years, was a well-known figure in American life—someone like Governor Ozio, or Donald O'Brien, the Senate majority leader—and some . . . floozy appeared with a story, well, it would be dismissed out of hand. The burden of proof would be on her. But most people don't know who Jack Stanton is. This is the first thing they'll hear about him. You've got to figure this will be a crushing blow. You've got to figure he's history."

No one said anything. Richard kicked over a chair. One of the muffins, a college kid named Alicia, was in tears. I walked down the hall to the Stanton suite. Uncle Charlie answered. "He's over at Dunkin' Donuts."

"When did he go?"

"After Arlen began to sweat."

"Say anything?"

"Broke a few things."

"Charlie, could you do me a favor? You go get him tonight. I'm just wiped. I need some sleep."

It was 2:28, digital time, glowing red in the achy exhaustion of the night, when Daisy knocked on my door. "You want to catch my cold?" she asked.

We made love, slowly, carefully, very much aware of the fragility of the moment, intent on not causing discomfort of any sort. It was not particularly passionate or transcendent, but it wasn't campaign sex, either. The kindness of it was memorable, and touching. She sniffled afterward, and coughed a bit. I felt a dampness on my chest: tears.

"Are we fucked, Henry?"

"I don't know," I said. "But we were wrong about Cashmere. The crucial variable isn't her. It's *us*. People don't know him. They look at him and see another pol—another overambitious trimmer who thinks he can get away with anything. They don't know how smart he is. They don't know he cares. We've gotta find a way to get that out, to let them know."

She was hot, feverish, on me; she shuddered—chills. I held her closer. "You got any Sudafed?" she asked.

I don't remember much of Saturday. Another bad day. The frenzy intensified. I saw it on the news that night—it had penetrated the weekend network news. (Not much else was happening in the world; the weekend anchors didn't have the stature of the regulars, so they could dive in where Dan and Tom and Peter feared to tread.) I saw it in Jack Stanton's eyes, when he came in that night: he couldn't quite believe what he was experiencing, the dream of a lifetime had dissolved into . . . this. He seemed crushed, his eyes dead. He didn't want to see anyone; he watched basketball on the tube alone. (Susan was out at a women's college—a fabulous event, I later learned; she was sharp, aggressive, funny. Her strength in the face of this embarrassment was strange. She was drawing attention to her perfection, which only served to remind people of her husband's imperfection—it was, I realized, a vengeful act.)

I walked back to my room, lay down on my bed, stared at the ceiling. Richard marched in right behind me, lay down next to me, stared at the ceiling. "So," he said, "he figured he was God. He figured that Cashmere McLeod would be so fucking honored, so fucking thrilled, so breathless at the prospect of sucking the governor's dick, that she would never betray the secret. She would carry it with her, in her heart, to the grave, hoping that he would secretly put a rose there from time to time, or at least send over Tommy in the Bronco to make sure the grass was trimmed."

"No, it's not that," I said. "He's not so good at seeing ulterior motives."

"Henry, he *is* a fucking politician."

"That's different—that's the arena," I said. "He catches everything in the arena. You see him when Harris used the word 'moral' last night? I never even talked to him about it afterwards—didn't have to. I just knew he caught the nuance."

"Yeah, ol' Natural Forces is road-testin' ambition."

"So where are we now?" I asked.

"A place I've never been before."

"I can't believe it's over," I said. "The whole thing just seems like a mirage. It's not really happening, y'know?"

"It's happening."

"But I get the feeling we're gonna pull through," I said. "I don't know how."

"What do you mean, he's not good at seeing ulterior motives?" Richard asked.

"He wants to think the best about all his friends," I said. "He's desperate to think the best. You know what Momma says, he was always like that. The Sunshine Kid."

"Except for the thunderstorms."

"They pass," I said.

"We haven't even had time to prep them for Brinkley," he said. "I just can't wait to hear George Will utter the words 'Cashmere McLeod.' That should knock us down a couple of points right there."

"He won't. Not his style. He'll do Chicago."

"So who does Cashmere?"

"Cokie—or Sam Donaldson. Susan figures Cokie. Remember she asked about her at the meeting yesterday?"

We worked through it. We did the entire interview. It was reassuring. In our version of Brinkley, we lived to fight another day. "Y'know," Richard said finally, "we just take these things. Think 'em through like we would normal stuff, like a debate or an issue or a week. We might even pretend our way into thinking we got a normal campaign here."

"It's like you're taking a shit in the woods," I said, "and this wild boar makes a rush at you . . ."

"Fuck you. Your tight little black ass never saw no woods. Face it, Henry: the toughest thing about this campaign for you is they ain't got Au Bon Pain in New Hampshire."

We lay there, not saying anything for a moment. "Cashmere McLeod," Richard said. "Cashmere Fucking McLeod. Can you imagine? One thing you can say about Jack Stanton: he ain't proud. Our governor is not afflicted by the sin of pride. Y'knowhat-tamean?"

"BUMMMMMMMMERRRRRRR! BUMMMMMERRRRR!"

"Good morning, Libby," I said. It was just after six on Sunday morning. "Is this my wakeup call?"

"What a fucking BUMMMMMMMERRRRRR!"

"What, Libby?"

"She's got tapes."

"Who's got—"

"Cashmere, the hairslut. The cunt's got tapes."

"Of?"

"Who do you think? Mario Lanza? It's our Jackie. She's got luuu-uuuuuve tapes."

"How could she?"

"Who the fuck knows. The Dustbuster SUSPECTS, but who the fuck knows?"

"Suspects?"

"Yeah. Henry, you get your ass down here fast as you can. You tell Jackie and Sue, then move your ass down here. I'm gonna show you the south side of Mammoth Falls."

"What's she going to do with the tapes?"

"Play them at her press conference tomorrow, you MORON. I do not have TIME for INEPTITUDE. I will tell you precisely what to do: One. Get out of bed. Two. Pee in the potty. Three. Wash yourself. Four. Go down the hall and wake up the Stantons. Five. Tell them the cunt's got tapes."

"You think they should know before Brinkley?" I asked, knowing the answer.

"JESUS H. PENNYPACKER, you just can't get GOOD HELP these days. Henry, you want Sam Donaldson to tell 'em? Get the fuck out of bed. Pee. Clean yourself. Tell them. Get on a plane. Come to Mama—I'm gonna show you somethin'."

I knocked on their door at seven. They already had their game faces on. Susan was wearing a tweed suit, a Chanel scarf; she hadn't put on her shoes yet. She was sitting at the table with the *Times,* the "Week in Review" section, drinking tea. The governor was standing, holding three ties, trying to decide. He was moving toward her. He was saying, "Hon, which d'ya think?" She was standing now, examining. It felt like the quiet scene just before the monster comes.

I did not try to finesse it. "Governor," I said, "I was just on the phone with Libby. She says that Cashmere McLeod has tape recordings of you and her talking on the phone, and she's going to play them at a press conference tomorrow."

Susan hauled off and slapped him right across the face. It was a perfect shot, a resonant *splat*—God, she was even good at that. His cheek flushed immediate pink, his chin dropped, his hand rose—not against her—but to massage himself. Neither of them said anything at first. She turned away, faced the plate-glass window, sun streaming in.

Then he said, "I'm sorry."

"How bad?" she asked. Him? Me? I wasn't sure.

"Don't know," he said.

"Did you tell her you . . ." She looked over at me. "Henry, could you excuse us, please?"

Oh, absolutely.

We were sucked through the gauntlet into the television station, a howling of scorps restrained by rope lines. Everything was sharpness: bright, glary sun off the snow, darkness and stiletto winds in the shadow of the building. We came through the howling like a fighter and entourage—the governor and Susan, smiling and waving, followed by various advance and press people. I felt so protective, I just kept moving with them, staying as close as possible, *adhering* to them, through the greenroom, into the studio itself, where they were fitted with earpieces and planted side by side in front of several palms and a snowy slide of Manchester—a mixed metaphor, I thought. (It was the only idle thought I can recall about that morning.) So intent was I that I didn't realize I'd come a step too far, into the studio with them, and wouldn't be able to hear the questions as they were asked from

Washington. I would just sit there, behind the cameras, watching them, and try to pick up the question and questioner from facial expressions and responses. Surreal.

So it was:

"Good to be with you, David. . . . Yeah, it's cold, but these are friendly people up here, remind me a lot of home. . . . No, not really disruptive. I think if you came up and hung out with us for a day, you'd see that what the folks are really interested in is the future, what we're proposing to do about jobs and education and—"

A smile—an awful, empty, dead smile. "No, George, they just don't seem very interested in that sort of stuff. They just don't seem to see it that way. They're worried about their country and their kids. This election is about the future.

"Well, yes, I was against the war. But I never broke the law. I wasn't even officially arrested. . . .

"No way. No way. Down my part of the country, we respect the military. . . .

"Prudently, I would hope. But I would not hesitate to use them."

Another smile—wider, far too gawky. "Now, Sam, you're not really gonna dignify that trash, are you? I mean, you look at the rest of that paper: 'Space Aliens Ate My Credit Card'?" (Where did he get that line? It sounded like Richard.)

A harder look. "No, I'm not gonna dignify that—and I'm disappointed that at a time when the American people have an awful lot they're concerned about, and want to talk about, that we'd be distracted by—Sam, do you know how many mortgages are technically in default in New Hampshire at this very moment? Twenty-five percent."

An even harder look, a slight reddening. "No. It never happened. It's not true. Yes, we did. We did have some tough times in our marriage, but we worked our way through it." I realized they didn't look like they'd worked their way through it. They weren't touching. And just then, quietly, Susan slipped her hand in his.

He nodded. He was listening. "I don't think that would be fair, Cokie."

And, suddenly, Susan jumped in: "You are making an assumption. You just don't know. I mean, Cokie—where have you *been* these past twenty-five years? People have suffered and struggled and been through all sorts of crazy things. So yes, we did have some tough times. But we're still here. And if you want to draw a political lesson from that about Jack Stanton's character, it has nothing to do with inconsistency, or what was the word you used?" She almost laughed. "Untrustworthiness. It's the exact opposite: this man does not give up. He will work through the tough times. He will wake up every morning and bust his *butt* for the American people." That was an interesting calculation: a lot of the postgame chat would now be deflected from Cashmere McLeod to whether or not a prospective first lady should be borderline profane. (Of course she should, if a Democrat.)

But, I also realized that she had made the sharpest response of the show. She had the sound bite. She came off looking fine. He, on the other hand, was a runner-up for best supporting actor. When the lights went off, she dropped his hand as if it were a dead rat.

He strolled out humming a country tune, then singing it:

> "Please, Mr. please
> Don't play B-17
> It was our song, it was her song,
> But it's o-o-ver . . ."

I rode three planes to Mammoth Falls, through the Sunday brightness. The first was a commuter to New York, filled with scorps, most of whom attempted to chat me up. Then, seeing it wouldn't get them anywhere, they snoozed or riffled through the Sunday *Times*. After that, I was free. I was anonymous, unrecognized for the first time in a month. I wandered the main terminal at La Guardia, browsed the bookstore, bought a volume of stories by Alice Munro. I flew to Cincinnati, a window seat. There weren't many passengers; it was light, and bright and airy. I felt as if I could breathe again. I read Alice Munro, sentence by sentence—reading for craft rather than plot, reading from a remove rather than diving in, wanting to keep perspective, wanting to appreciate something pristine, unhurried, carefully thought out.

At the terminal in Cincinnati, I began to feel less free and more empty. There were families, parents and children, boarding planes; I watched the children. There was a middle-aged son, a decent-looking man, pushing an older woman—his mother—in a wheelchair toward a gate. There were two priests, laughing. There was a group of large black kids—college kids, I could tell, enthusiastic, not sullen, but dressed sort of streety, cutting a wide, noisy swath through the terminal. (Even at our most hopeful best, we could still seem awkward, inappropriate, too emotive for these white folks, I feared.) But America seemed a happy place—happily oblivious of the tortured complications involved in the selection of its next president. This seemed amazing, and sane. There were basketball games on in the airport bars, people laughing and drinking beer surrounded by fluffy piles of down coats and overnight bags; soon the Super Bowl preview show would begin. It was, I suddenly realized, Super Sunday. I was invisible; no one noticed me. Well, there was one girl, Asian (Filipino?) or maybe Hispanic—we saw each other, and nodded, and went on.

I called around, waiting for the plane. I couldn't find Richard or Daisy. I called the suite and got Lucille. "Wasn't Susan just fantastic?" she asked. "*Everyone* is saying that."

It was late afternoon when I boarded the next plane, also mostly empty, for Mammoth Falls. It was dark when I landed, but there was a warm breeze blowing up from the Gulf.

Olivia Holden had settled into a small, charming white clapboard house on a quiet street north of the capitol. The living room had a couch and a large console TV, but it was filled with files as well, and an L-shaped table with a computer and printer and fax machine along the back and side wall, away from the picture window. There was a microfilm viewer, and Peter Goldsmith was hunched over it, rolling old *Mammoth Falls Gazette*s, stopping, taking notes. He looked up, said hi. Jennifer peered out from the kitchen, "Hey!" she said, "want some tea?"

"HENREEEEEE." Olivia, out from a bedroom she'd made into an office. "Gotta get movin', gotta move our *butts*—word o' the day, since Susie popularized it—gotta head south, get to Sailor's, and watch Ol' Cashmere spill her soul and shed her tears with an expert." She put on her outback hat and her vest and threw an arm around Jennifer and—I could have fallen over—gave her a long, soulful kiss on the mouth. Jennifer smiled at me, blushed a little, shrugged. "You take care of yourself now, dear," Libby said softly, tenderly, in a voice I hadn't heard before. "I'll be home for dinner."

Olivia drove—it was a red Jeep Cherokee—and didn't speak. She had the radio on, public radio, Brahms Symphony No. 4. I tried to engage her: "So you met Jack and Susan in Florida, working for McGovern?"

"Yep."

"What were they like?"

"Glorious. Golden, golden."

"They came down together?"

"Henry, don't you have any respect for the music?"

We took the interstate south of town, then a two-laner west, into the hills, piney-woods country, then a left onto a dirt road. The symphony over, Libby briefed: "Salem 'Sailorman' Shoreson. Old friend of the family. Jumped bail, went to Canada. It wasn't much—a disorderly, destruction of property, during the Days of Rage. He was really running from the draft. Came back in '77, Carterized. Still had to do a little time up north for jumping bail, but it was country-club time."

"Friend of the family?"

"Grace Junction. Knew Jackie since elementary school, would stop a bullet for him. Maybe two."

"So what does he do?"

"Electronics—obviously. Henry, do I have to walk you through every fucking thing?"

There was a cinder-block wall in the forest, whitewashed, with concertina wire on top, small cameras mounted on top of the wall, an ornate wrought-iron gate. Libby stopped the car, rolled down the window; a speaker box rose up from the ground. "Whut you *mean*, Miss Scarlett?" said the speaker box: Butterfly McQueen, *Gone With the Wind*.

"Telegram for Leon Trotsky, you DIMWIT," Libby said.

The gates swung open, and there was music, a perfect sound system, sound coming from everywhere—the Stones: "Let's Spend the Night Together." We proceeded up a circular drive to a large hunting-lodge-style cabin. Sailorman was waiting for us there—blue jeans and work shirt, round, bald, long unkempt beard, a kindly face.

"Greetings, Olivia," he said—a squeaky voice that didn't go with the rest of him.

"Sailorman, your country needs you."

"Ready to roll, honey," he said. "How was the booby hatch?"

"A better class of drugs than the old days," Olivia said. "Not ups or downs—eveners-out. I am *eeeeeeee-ven* now."

"Sure, you are," he laughed. She belly-laughed, slapped him on the back.

Sailor had quite a setup. Wall-to-wall dials and screens and gizmos. It looked sort of like a cross between a radio station and a recording studio—he produced some bluegrass bands there, just for fun, he said. There was a big screen TV amid multiple monitors, and we settled in to watch the Cashmere McLeod Show on CNN.

It was a zoo, for starters. They had set up the press conference in a New York hotel ballroom—and there must have been two hundred reporters there. Forty camera crews. I had been feeling free, if a bit weird, with Libby, but now the awful, claustrophobic New Hampshire mania was back.

Then, Cashmere: a puffy, chunky, bulldoggy woman—curly dark hair, not long; breasts, but no waist; and legs, abruptly short but shapely—she seemed intermittently alluring, sexy in sections. Sometimes you can look at a person and can see who they were when they were young—their schoolyard selves; there are others who carry with them a premonition of age. Cashmere was like that: you could see where she was headed. It was not a pleasant sight. She was wearing a black suit, white blouse, far too much makeup. She had a lawyer, bearded, double-breasted—he might have been a member of the local Playboy Club in the old days. She had a tiny little voice.

"Governor Jack Stanton see-dyou-ced me," she said, to an aurora of clicks and flashes.

Libby hooted.

"Judy Holliday," Sailorman said.

"And I can prove it," Cashmere said. "I have tapes."

There was a gasp and bedlam. The lawyer took the podium: "Miss McLeod will not be taking questions," he said. "This will not be an inquisition."

"Right," I said, "*we* get the inquisition."

It soon became clear that Cashmere's role was to stand there and daub at her mascara. The lawyer was running the show. "The tapes were recorded, on Miss Mcleod's phone machine, over an eighteen-month period," he said. "The last recording was made in November, just before Thanksgiving. I will play a portion of it now."

And you could hear a crackly, distant Jack Stanton—and a very clear Cashmere McLeod.

JACK: We're going to have to cut [crackle, mmmf] this off for now.
CASH: But you said you loved me.
JACK: I just have to be careful, honey. Anyway, I'm spending almost all my time in New Hampshire now.
CASH: But you said no one could do the things I did to you. I could come up there.

"God, what a whiny bitch," Libby said.
"Shhhh," Sailorman said.

JACK: When this is over, we'll get together.
CASH: Remember that time you had me meet you in Dallas. Ahhh, I get hot just thinkin' about it.
JACK: I've got to go.

It *was* shocking. I was shocked. It was his voice. Libby turned to Sailorman. "Well?"

"Can't say for sure. I'd have to see the tape. But it sounds real. Maybe one or two splices. But who knows? I'm hearing it thirdhand."

"I'm gonna kill him," Libby said. "How could he be so DUMB?"

The lawyer was holding up another tape. "This is one from last summer," he said.

JACK: So what you doin' tonight?
CASH: Prayin' that you'll pay me a call, darlin'.
JACK: . . . Stay at home and crack open a bottle of Chablis?
CASH: That's not all we'll crack open.
JACK: You think it's at all possible to get [*crackle, crackle*] laid tonight?
CASH: I'd say it's entirely likely.

JACK: I'm . . . too horny to think straight.

CASH: I can take care of that. What about your wife, sugar?

JACK: We're doin' okay, dontchathink?

"JESUS H . . ." Libby said. "How could he be so completely fucking fucked-up stupid?"

"He was calling from a cellular on that one," Sailor said, "which immediately makes it more suspicious. There were a couple of abrupt cutoffs. Let me replay it."

The lawyer was taking questions, but neither he nor Cashmere was answering them. Sailor had turned off the sound on screen. Then Cashmere was walking off. I was beeped. Richard. I called him.

"Whatchathink?"

Something was . . . I was thinking—something was just past the edge of my consciousness. It was torture, worse than an itch, something red and inflamed and inaccessible, like a rash in my mind. "Hey, Sailor, could you play that again?" I asked.

"Sailor?"

"Yeah—listen, Richard, gotta go."

"Whaddaya mean, gotta go. We're in deep shit, and you gotta go? What the fuck is the matter?"

"I'll tell you in a minute. I'll call back. Gotta go."

"Henri, she's a slut, dontchathink?"

"No question."

"But those tapes are gonna be trouble. We may be dead."

"Listen, Richard, something's . . . Hey, Sailor, the *second* one. Richard, where are you?"

"With him, in Mississippi. You wouldn't believe it: big crowds, like they don't get CNN down here. It's like it used to be."

"I'll call you right back. But let me go now."

Okay.

JACK: So what you doin' tonight?

CASH: Prayin' that you'll pay me a call, darlin'.

JACK: . . . Stay at home and crack open a bottle of Chablis?

CASH: That's not all we'll crack open.

JACK: You think it's at all possible to get [*crackle, crackle*] laid tonight?

CASH: I'd say it's entirely likely.

JACK: I'm . . . too horny to think straight.

CASH: I can take care of that. How about your wife, sugar?

JACK: We're doin' okay, dontchathink?

"Again," I said.

"What?" Libby asked.

"Again," I said. He played it again. It was torture. It was déjà vu.

"Let's take it line by line," I said. "Sailor, can you guess where it's been spliced?"

"Guess, yeah. Say for sure? Who knows. Okay, first line."

So what you doin' tonight?

"That's a pretty abrupt cutout."

. . . Stay at home and crack open a bottle of Chablis?

"Picked up in midsentence, I think. At least, it's possible."

You think it's at all possible to get[crackle,crackle] laid tonight?

"The breakup in the middle might be cellular static, or they might have used it to cover."

"Wait a second," I said. It was coming. "Wait a goddamn fucking second. Play that again."

*You think it's at all possible to get [*crackle, crackle*] laid tonight?*

"Again."

"What?" Libby asked.

"AGAIN, dammit."

*You think it's at all possible to get [*crackle, crackle*] laid tonight?*

"Yourself. Yourself." I said. "Un-fucking-believable. You think it's at all possible to get YOURSELF laid tonight! Me! He was talking to me! It was New Year's Eve. Again, again—from the top."

So what you doin' tonight . . .

"Abrupt cutout, right?" I asked. "It was 'What you doin' tonight, Henri.' I remember he called me Henri."

. . . Stay at home and crack open a bottle of Chablis?

"He was asking me if I was going out to party that night. Jesus Christ, we got her!"

"You got her," Libby said. "WE don't."

She was right. There was no way to prove it.

"At least not yet," Libby said. "BUT WE WILL. Henry, you call the boss and tell him never, ever, on pain of his fucking life, talk on a cellular phone again. Me and Sailor are going to cook something up."

I beeped Laurene. "This is just amazing, Henry," she said. "It's a zoo. We got a full plane with us—and you know what they're seeing? A full ballroom, one hundred dollars a head, in Baton Rouge. That was breakfast. We're in Jackson now. We've got a full ballroom for lunch. A standing O. Congressman Mobley introduces him, 'These attacks on Jack Stanton are attacks on *our* integrity, our regional integrity. We know who Jack Stanton is and what kind of governor he's been—and we don't cut and run when our boy's in trouble.' Henry, who'da thought it'd be a lucky thing for us these white boys down here still fighting the damnyankees?"

Laurene! We were all getting goofy. "Before you take off for Birmingham, you've got to get him for me," I said. "How long you think?"

"Ten minutes. So how was she?"

"Ridiculous, but devastating in a way. But I think we got her."

"How?"

"Can't say. Listen: you have to make sure that his very first call is to me. No other calls. This is absolutely urgent."

We were driving back toward Mammoth Falls when he beeped me. "Henry?" he said, his voice hoarse. He sounded awful. He coughed. "It was bad?"

"It wasn't good," I said. "When you called me from Marco Island on New Year's Eve, it was cellular?"

"Let me think. Why?"

"Because they've been listening in and taping. Remember, you told me to, uh, enjoy myself that night? Well, they took it and used it. Now you're having a conversation with Cashmere about getting laid and being horny."

"They *played* this?"

"I'm afraid so."

"That's outrageous. She can't get away with—"

"Well, sir, there's no way we can prove it didn't happen. Although Libby does have an idea. But you've got to be more careful—on the phone. You've got to assume that they're listening to every last cellular conversation you have."

"Lemme talk to him," Libby said, ripping the phone from my hand.

"You ASSHOLE," she said. "Don't pull that outraged puppy shit with me. Sailor thinks some of the other shit she played was real. God, I wish we'd castrated you when we had the chance."

"Libby!" I said, "You're *talking* on a cellular phone."

"OH SHIT," she said and calmed down. ". . . Uh-huh, uh-huh. I've done a lot of that already. Got affidavits from her first husband, her sister—but it doesn't do us *all* that much good to prove that she's a lying slut who fucked around. That is . . . like *manifest*. That is not an ELUSIVE CONCEPT, you undisciplined shit. Ooops! I'll get it done. Okay. 'Bye."

We drove along. It was clouding up. Around a bend, near the airport, I could see the modest spires of Mammoth Falls. "Of course, Henry," she said, softly, dangerously, "there is one thing we could do that would—it might—ice this case. Some risk would be involved."

She pulled off the highway at the Cranford Exit, just south of downtown. It was a formerly fancy area, large old houses—rooming houses, now—and vacant lots. We stopped in front of a *faux* plantation-style house, white paint peeling. "The law offices of Randolph Martin Culligan," she said. "I am about to do something crazy. If it backfires, I can plead *non compos* whatsis. And you can say you had no idea, since I'm not going to tell you." She turned toward me. Her blue eyes were soft—not crazy—now. She was as reasonable as I'd ever seen her. "But still, you might find yourself in an awkward position. You can leave me to go in there alone—I will understand, I won't hold it against you—or you can come with me. There will be absolutely no advantage for you in coming with me. There may be disadvantages. But you can come if you like."

"But what—"

"No QUESTIONS, Henry," she said. "Faith or nothing."

Faith. She dialed a number. The phone was answered. She hung up. "It's a go," she said. She grabbed her satchel, put on her bush hat. We went.

Up an outside staircase, around the back. The sign on the door: THE LAW OFFICES OF RANDOLPH, MARTIN AND CULLIGAN. She laughed: "Can you believe this shit? Randy's made himself into three partners." She rapped on the door. No answer. She raised a sneaker and kicked it in.

"What the—" Randy Culligan was up, behind his desk, holding the phone. He had scraggly brown hair, horn-rimmed glasses, a brown, long-sleeved knit shirt with a yellow argyle pattern across the chest, gray pants. A thoroughly undistinguished human being; an overachieving clerk.

"A triumphant day!" Libby said. "Perhaps your best ever! Is that Cashmere on the line? Oh, let me say hi."

"No, it's not. It's . . . not."

"Say good-bye to Sherman, then. We've got business." She sat down in one of the folding chairs in front of Culligan's desk; I took the other. This was a small outer room—normally, a reception area (for a doctor's office, at one time, I would have guessed). There were rooms behind. Randy probably lived there. The office was a catastrophe. The desk was a mess, there was plywood paneling, fluorescent lighting. There were diplomas on the wall, and pictures of Randy Culligan shaking hands with various local politicians, including Jack Stanton. The look on Governor Stanton's face as he gave Randy Culligan a meaningful handshake—two hands on his one—was distressfully warm and friendly. There was not a hint of reserve in it.

"It's not Sherman, either," Culligan said as he hung up. He had a deep, juicy voice. But he was a lousy liar: clearly, it had been Sherman Presley.

"Well now, Randy," Libby said expansively, "you've branched out. Electronics, now?"

"I don't know what you—"

"You've been recording your friend the governor's private conversations, haven't you?"

"Now, Olivia," he said, "why would I want to do a thing like that? I'm a big Stanton supporter. Always have been. He's putting this state right on the map."

"Well, Randy, I've only been here but a minute and you've already exhausted my patience," Libby said, reaching into her satchel and pulling out a very long, iron-black, ridiculously menacing gun. She didn't point it at him; she just sort of put it in her lap. I am not an expert about such things, but if it wasn't a .357 magnum, it was something equally dreadful. It was almost a parody of a gun—it was so foolish, so extreme. I could not take this seriously. This was not happening.

"Randy, I'm going to want a signed confession," Libby said.

"Libby, put that thing away before you do something stupid and get yourself into trouble," Randy said.

Now she pointed it at him. She stood up, put her arms straight out and together, and pointed the gun right at his face. "Randy, you wet fart of a human turd, you ambushed Jack Stanton and you're gonna admit it, or you're gonna die."

"Libby, you're crazy!"

"CERTI-FUCKIN'-FIABLY!" She said. "And I'll go right back there. Happily. And you will be in heaven."

Randy suddenly noticed me. "You'll go to jail too."

"I don't know anything about this," I said, surprising myself. I was able to say this, to move my mouth and all the rest, because I could not believe what I was seeing.

"He's shocked," Libby explained to Culligan. "He had no idea. Now, Randy, you gonna write this out in longhand?"

"I . . . I *don't know what you're talking about.*"

"OH YES YOU DO, SHITBIRD," Libby said and she moved very quickly—just astonishingly fast—around the desk, behind him, putting a choke hold on Randy Culligan with her left arm and pointing the gun straight down at his crotch. "And I've got a *better idea:* I'm gonna shoot your NUTS off."

His head, quickly red, was crushed between her two giant breasts, which were like earmuffs on him. "I'm a *gay lesbian woman,*" she said. "I do not mythologize the male sexual organ," she went on, jamming the pistol into his crotch. He started up; he yelped. "Now, now, now," she said. Her face was red, her eyes were wild, her hat rolled off her head onto the desk. "You TINY SCUMBAG, I *know* you did it. You're on retainer to the *Flash,* I KNOW that—and

you, stupid little shit, you couldn't just make do with the calls you
had. You had Jack Stanton, but you figured the world is as stupid as
you are—you had to EMBELLISH. Well, mister: YOU ARE
FUCKED."

"I . . . I . . ."

I must say that I found her very convincing. But if this had gone on
much longer, I would probably have had to make some sort of move
to stop her. I couldn't even begin to imagine what I would do if she
actually pulled the trigger.

"You have a choice to make, and very quickly," Libby said, yanking
his neck. "But you know *me,* Randy. I would have ovarian cancer for
Jack and Susan, especially Susan—and you are *embarrassing* them. You
are ruining the *party.* And I would just be SICK TO DEATH if you
fucked up the campaign. I would want to DIE. So, you're going to
have to decide: *just how desperately crazy is she?* And you're going to
have to do it now. One . . . two . . ."

"Okay. Okay, okayokay," he said.

"Very good, verrry wise," she said, loosening her grip and moving
the gun from his crotch to his head. "Now I want you to be eloquent
about this letter you're about to write, and penitent. I want you to be
guilt-ridden about your jealousy and greed. You could not live with
yourself if you deprived America of this man."

"The willingness to be violent is a force multiplier," Libby said afterward. "That's the reason why the Mafia has been so successful over
the years. Those boys are just like everyone else, except they're willing to be violent."

Libby was crazier quiet, I realized, than she was manic. And she was
very thorough. She was not going to let it go at that. The confession
was not going to be enough, she was certain. The perfidy had to be
plain. It had to be demonstrated. And so she sent Sailorman up to
Washington to trail Ted Koppel around in an unmarked van and tap
his car-phone conversations. This proved an inspired bit of whimsy.
On the way into work that Tuesday, Koppel called his producer and
said the following:

"What do you want to do tonight?"

"Do you want to do the Stanton thing?"

"I think that's sexier than Bosnia."

"What sort of guests should we have?"

These were spliced together with appropriate responses from the Cashmere tapes—and played on *Nightline* that Wednesday by Daisy, who was this week's designated hitter, after Arlen's pitiful display (and after Marty Muscavich once again demurred, thereby arousing Susan's suspicion—was he entirely loyal?—and, ultimately, ensuring himself a one-way ticket to Palookaville).

Daisy, however, was irresistible. She seemed tiny, funny, enthusiastic—she had all the qualities of a very precocious child. Only she could have gotten away with actually playing the Koppel-Cashmere tape, surprising him with it. Only she could have had him laughing after the last exchange:

TED: What sort of guests should we have?
CASHMERE: How about your *wife,* sugar?

"Now, this . . . obviously . . . has been concocted," Koppel said, chuckling a bit nervously: no man wants to raise even the appearance of lasciviousness, and Libby—bless her heart—had shown how easily such appearances could be manipulated. "You did this to make a point. Right?"

"Yeah. Isn't it a stitch?" Daisy burbled. "I mean, can you imagine anyone taking that sort of thing seriously?" Then she moved for the kill: "And yet the outcome of an American presidential campaign may be influenced by this sort of garbage. Shouldn't you guys in the press be ashamed of yourselves? Don't you owe Governor Stanton an apology?"

People were jumping up and down on the sixth floor of the Hampton Inn. Richard was beyond words: "Canyajust . . . Canyajust . . . Nevahbelieveit . . . y'knowhattamean?"

Jack and Susan came out of their suite, walked down the hall, hugging people and smiling. Down by the elevator landing, where there was a larger space and people could gather, Stanton said a few words: "I want to thank you all for sticking with us, for working so hard, through all this." His voice was hoarse, his face red, his eyes watery.

He was in a gray nylon jogging suit, with blue stripes and green pip-
ing and had no shoes on. He was, I noticed, blimping up—all those
late nights with Danny Scanlon were taking their toll. He had an arm
slung over Susan's shoulders. (She was smiling and had an arm around
his back.) "Now we have less than two weeks to go before this election, and we have to work hard—we have to get this thing back on
track. But I know that with your help and God's good grace, we'll do
what needs to be done. This hasn't been easy for us"—he looked
down at Susan. "It's been pretty awful." He stopped, he was beginning to get a little misty. "But—we're—still—*here*!"

"You want to do the Stanton thing?" Daisy asked later that night, trying to bring her voice down to Koppel level.

"It's sexier than Bosnia," I replied, gathering her in.

But not that much sexier. Daisy was effusive and animated, but distracted. She wasn't quite with me. She was out there, in the world
now. We had regressed to campaign sex.

George Will's question when the Stantons were interviewed on the
Brinkley show—which I hadn't heard, of course, and hadn't even
wondered about, and only found out about later when I read the
transcript—proved prescient: "Whatever the facts of these incidents,
your arrest in Chicago and this . . . unfortunate business involving
Miss . . . McLeod, do you think it's possible the American people
might conclude that you are more trouble than you're worth? They
usually expect a bit more stability and dignity in a president."

Yeah, well. I soon found myself wondering if old George might be
right. We had been badly damaged. We were so out of touch, so completely removed from reality that we'd expected our rousing rebuttal
to the Cashmere fiasco on *Nightline* to *take care* of it: if life were a
movie, it would have. As if Libby's remarkably flagrant and heroic ef-
forts were enough to turn the tide; as if Sailorman's electronic parlor
trick—the Koppel-Cashmere Tapes—really meant anything; as if a
"confession" from a sleazebag lawyer could erase the image and, especially, the awful woman's name—or change the impressions left by

the tapes, some of which, I had conveniently forgotten, *were* real. The affair *had* happened. (Even if it hadn't, there would have been the presumption of guilt—he was a politician.) But we'd allowed ourselves to be convinced that because some of it wasn't true, none of it was. We had allowed Susan to convince us of that. It was a lawyer's trick, and she was a fine lawyer.

But that conviction did not exist very far beyond the edges of our little campaign, our little world. I actually expected the movable zoo would dissipate after we destroyed Cashmere's credibility. I needed to believe we'd get back to the game Jack Stanton was so good at, the game we'd been winning before the craziness began. But nothing had changed; indeed, it grew worse.

Most Americans didn't watch Brinkley or *Nightline* (or the evening news, for that matter). They were just beginning to hear about us, in ways we couldn't predict or control—a joke on Leno or, more likely, their morning drive-time radio program; a rant on some call-in show; and, of course, it was now there on every supermarket checkout line in America (where the *National Flash* headline—SEDUCED AND BE-TRAYED BY STANTON—loomed in all its stupid, garish enormity). Cashmere's credibility or lack of same didn't matter; she was assumed a slut. But Jack Stanton was a presumptive president. He had to be more than credible, he had to be above suspicion. We could destroy Cashmere and still be destroyed by her.

I thought about this, but not for long. Right at that moment, we were deep into New Hampshire—and the rules were somewhat different there than in America, or so we thought. We were known in New Hampshire. We had, a few weeks earlier, been awesome there, about to run away with this election. People—political people—had made commitments to us, had put their reputations on the line, had bought in; they were continuing to work. But, even there, we were beginning to lose altitude. Leon was tracking every night and we were drifting down, having reached a peak of 37—after the second debate, to 34, on Monday night, after Cashmere's press conference, to 32, on Tuesday, 31, on Wednesday, 29, on Thursday. It was slipping away.

And Jack Stanton was sick. The weather had warmed some; it was rainy and slushy on Thursday—and we all felt like wet flannel. We rushed in and out of overheated buildings all day; from hot and sweaty to chill and damp. His eyes were glassy, his face was red; he was running a fever. We plied him with cough drops and hot water with lemon and honey; but he was dragging. He did a Kiwanis lunch in Manchester and had nothing going for him. He slumped in the van and fell quickly asleep as we headed for an after-school Drug-Free America rally in Nashua. We had trouble rousing him. He looked at me, blinked and croaked, "Can you get me one of those hot toddies, Henry? How much more of this we got today?"

At the Drug-Free America rally—which consisted of lots of kids from different schools brought together at the largest gymnasium-auditorium in the district—he began to cough and couldn't stop. "'Scuse me a second," he wheezed. "Someone get me some water?" The water didn't help. He began to shudder, the water was cold and he was chilled. He barely finished; the audience didn't ask questions—it seemed an act of sympathy. Bart Nilson, who was next on the program, caught Jack offstage. "Look, Jack, you want some advice from a guy who spent his whole life campaigning in the north country?" He put a solicitous arm around Stanton's waist. "Take it down for a couple of days. Get your strength back. You could run yourself right into the hospital."

There was a warmish, foggy mist in the night air as we came out of the auditorium; it fuzzed the absurdly tall gooseneck lights in the parking lot; it felt like airborne perspiration. Stanton leaned against the van, his head resting against his arm. Suddenly, he buckled and heaved. "Mitch—take the governor!" I said. Then I turned around to make sure none of the scorps had caught this. Rob Quiston, the AP guy, was about fifty feet away, approaching the wire van. Most of the other scorps had stuck around inside, since all the candidates were scheduled to appear at the antidrug dog and pony show. "Hey, Henry," he shouted, "what's going on? Sounds like someone blew lunch?"

"Ray Lefebre," I said, naming one of our New Hampshire people traveling with us that day. "He's got the flu."

"How's the governor?" Quiston asked.

"He's got it too," I said. "But he's okay."

He was out cold. Laurene was already on with Richard. "He wants you," she said.

"How bad?" Richard asked.

"Pretty bad," I said. "In fact, I'm kinda scared about this. We should get him to a doctor. Bart Nilson just told him to take a few days off."

"Bart'd like him to take the rest of the fucking campaign off," Richard said.

"Naww, it wasn't like that," I said, realizing how sappy it sounded (though Bart's empathy had seemed real). "But listen, Richard. We gotta talk about this. We may have to take him down for a few days."

"We got less than two weeks here," Richard said. "We have that stupid fucking fund-raiser in Los Angeles on Monday. What*ever* possessed you to schedule that fucking thing? So let me see, we take him outta here for the weekend, then he's in LA Monday, he's not back until next Tuesday. We're losing altitude, we got twelve days left and you want to take us out of here for one third of those days?"

"We may not have much choice," I said. "Can you get a doctor in there to meet us?"

"How far you out?"

"Half hour."

"Hey," he was screaming into the staff room, "we got any doctors up here we can trust?"

The doctor, whose name was Myron Milburn and who looked like a doctor, said Governor Stanton had a pretty serious case of bronchitis, that he had to rest. "And I told him—and he understands this—that he is in danger of pneumonia, if he doesn't lie down and stay down for a couple of days. He won't be of much use to you anyway." He was talking to me and Richard and Brad Lieberman and Lucille—as if we were forcing Jack Stanton to do this, as if we were *using* him somehow. "He's lost his voice. So no talking for forty-eight hours. Doctor's orders."

Susan said we would go home. And so we did, early the next morning. The team scattered—Howard and Lucille back to New York; Richard, Arlen and Daisy to Washington. Brad Lieberman stayed up in Manchester, organizing a door-to-door drop of Jack Stanton videotapes. I went back to Mammoth Falls with the Stantons and Uncle Charlie: it felt as it had in the beginning—and the memory of our early days together, the hope and warmer weather, was profoundly depressing.

We arrived in Mammoth Falls around midday on Friday. It was as if the campaign were over, as if we'd lost. It was a time of day we'd normally be in overdrive, moving from lunch to lunch—we were doing three a day by that point, doing press interviews between stops, making decisions between interviews, moving too fast to be conscious of anything except the moment, the flow, the great whoosh. But the airport was gray and empty. A car—a limo, not the governor's Bronco—was waiting for us on the tarmac.

He walked out of the plane between Susan and Uncle Charlie, wearing his nylon track suit, a blanket slung over his shoulders. He didn't have his usual "Hi, I'm *here*! just off the airplane from someplace terrific" face on. He wasn't working. His face was blank. He didn't look for me to say good-bye; it was as if I were no longer a part of his life.

"Well, I think I'll head over to the office," I said.

Susan glanced back at me, shrugged, smiled. "We'll call," she said.

An eternity passed, a whole day. The rest of us talked; we kept in touch. We talked about buying more airtime; we talked about what we had on the air. We talked about restructuring the campaign, stripping away the deadwood after New Hampshire, if there was an after–New Hampshire. We talked about replacing Arlen with Daisy; we needed a change of pace.

Late Saturday, Susan called: "Call everyone. We'll meet at five P.M. tomorrow at the Mansion."

"How's the governor?"

"Better. Not great. Henry, we've got to figure out a way to get back on top of this thing."

And so, the following evening, we moved all the fruitless, frustrating conversations we'd been having to the governor's mansion. He sat in a wing chair in the study, in striped pajamas and a light blue terrycloth robe. He was still coughing; his eyes were glassy and red-rimmed; his skin was blotchy. He had some of his voice back, though. "We just have to work," he said, pounding his fist on a wing. "We have to work, work, work."

"Thing is," Richard said. "We gotta figure out how to seem less . . . political. I'm worried that the folks parked with Harris are gonna stay there, and some others gonna join 'em. Thing is, all this shitstorm has made people even more sick of politics than they were—and that works to that asshole's benefit. Sick of politics? Ol' Natural Forces just as sick as you are."

"Turns out to be more than a fart, huh, Richard?" Lucille said. "I told you we should nuke him."

"Too late for that now," Richard said.

"Why?"

"Because the folks are beginning to associate *us* with politics as usual," Daisy said. "We go negative on their native son, and they'll run us out of town on a rail. We need to find some way to reestablish all the positives we were building."

A phone rang. Brad Lieberman said, "Richard, it's Leon. For you."

"Numbers," Richard said. "I smell numbers."

He walked out to the pantry hall, which led from the study to the kitchen. He stood there, twirling the cord, twirling it, saying, "Uh-huh, uh-huh, uh-hah. . . . And it ain't done yet? . . . Okay, champ. Seeyalater."

Richard walked back into the room. He shrugged. "We're cratering," he said. "Down fourteen, last two nights. Leon says he's not sure we're done dropping yet."

I was frozen, shocked. It was unimaginable. It was over.

"Who's ahead?" the governor asked—calmly, it seemed.

"Undecided's killin' everyone, almost as strong as we used to be, Governor—'bout thirty-three. Harris got twenty-five. You're hanging in with fifteen. The other two got 'bout ten apiece. Cats n' dogs got the rest."

"So they're not going to Harris," Stanton said. "They're hanging back. We can win them back."

"Gov'nor," Richard said, "we've all been in a lot of situations like this an', y'know, it's hard—and we haven't much more than a week, and you may not be done dropping yet."

"So you recommend we quit?" Susan asked.

"Naww, I—"

"All right, I want you all to listen carefully," she said. "Is there anyone here who doubts we have the best candidate? Is there anyone here who thinks these attacks on us haven't been *orchestrated,* part of a plan to wipe out the strongest Democrat before he took off? We are not just going to fold up our tents and go home, and give them what they want. We are going to fight these next ten days. We are going to work our tails off. We won't go negative—on the air. But we will go right into Mr. Former Senator Lawrence Harris's face in debate. We may not win, but we're gonna let them know that we've been there—and that we'll be back."

Then it was the governor's turn. "I've been thinking about Danny Scanlon," he said. Richard suppressed a groan. "You look at Harris's program and it's all about sacrifice—gas taxes, less money for this and for that. He says it's all for his grandchildren, and he has a point. We do have to provide for them. But there's nothing, not a goddamn thing in there for Danny—and all the other folks like him, and the folks that are better off than him, who may not be crippled but who work their butts off every day and just don't see anything comin' *back* from their government. Those are our folks. That's why we're doing this. Someone's gotta look out for them. . . . They're undecided right now. Can't say as I blame 'em. Can you? After all the crap they heard about us, the last few weeks? It's a rational decision, an *informed* decision on their part. They were our voters and they're gone, and we have to make them come back. Now, how do we do that? We gotta get out there and see as many of them as we possibly can, and let them know we'll be working for them night and day. If we can convince them that we're for them, that we'll fight like hell for them, then they won't care about all the garbage that's been dumped on us. They will see the light and come our way."

I wasn't so sure about that. None of us were. But *Stanton* was, and no one had the heart to tell him otherwise. We hugged him (even Richard did), clapped him on the back and walked out of there like kamikazes.

The next morning I went to the office to straighten some things out. Daisy, Richard and I had been up most of the night, thinking through ad strategies, ways to reinforce the governor's Danny Scanlon point, ways to get at Harris without going nuclear. Now I wanted to call around to some of our local people in New Hampshire, let them know we were about to raise $850,000 in one night in Los Angeles and we'd be coming back strong. We'd be leaving for Los Angeles in early afternoon.

At about eleven there was a commotion in the outer office. Terry Hickman, the guitar-playing muffin, came back and said, "Henry, there's a rather large black gentleman, a Mr. McCollister, who says he's got to speak to you."

"What's he want?"

"Won't say. Says he's been calling. Says he came by last week."

"Ask him to come back next week."

"Says he'll bust down your door if you don't see him right now."

He came in. He was wearing a dark church suit and held a dark church hat in his hand. I thought he might be a minister. "Ain't you rememberin' me, Mr. Burton?" he asked. "I figure mos' the other folks 'round here don' know me from a spent shell, but you—"

Right, a brother. He was . . .

William McCollister. Fat Willie, the Barbecue Man. And as soon as I knew who he was, I didn't want to hear what came next. After the meeting at the Mansion, I had persuaded myself to go down in flames for the Stantons with honor. William McCollister was about to remove the only tolerable part of the bargain. I could feel it.

"You don' answer yo' phone messages?" he asked.

"I try," I said. "I get a lot." He seemed reluctant to get on with it, so I nudged him: "What can I do for you, Mr. McCollister?"

"I came 'round last week," he said.

I didn't say anything, so he had to continue—and I could see it wasn't something he wanted to do. "My daughter, Loretta . . ."

I nodded.

"She . . . with child," he said. "And she say Governor Jack Stanton's the daddy."

V

We flew a Gulfstream to California and couldn't talk. The plane had been made available by a prominent music-industry homosexual several weeks earlier, when our prospects seemed more plausible. (The "rental" rate was giveaway cheap, the policy implications troubling.) It was, however, a lovely thing—all walnut and leather and crystal. It didn't rattle down the runway, as our usual crate did, but seemed to squirt, then lift effortlessly. I stared out the window; the wing tips were folded abruptly upward, like a paper airplane. Was there an aerodynamic purpose for that or just whimsy, a rich man's toy? The opulence was nervous-making, inappropriate, especially that day. We were tanking in New Hampshire; we had a potential paternity suit in Mammoth Falls.

There were six of us in the plane, matched pairs: the governor and Susan, Lucille and me, Uncle Charlie and Momma—Stanton had thought Momma would get a kick out of the Los Angeles starpower; she would go on from there to Las Vegas for a day, then meet us in New Hampshire for the grand finale. The others were playing hearts while Susan read and I moped. The governor was up and talky, slapping down cards, telling everybody what everybody else had, taking wild, meaningless risks—and singing. He sang "Red River Valley." He sang "Blue Eyes Crying in the Rain." He had a determination, a fierceness to him now. The campaign was no longer about winning but about personal survival. It was about the possibility of humiliation. He could not imagine such an outcome—it couldn't be true; his national career *couldn't* be over before it began—and this conviction gave him a giddy, febrile power.

I was annoyed, frustrated—too many crosscurrents, too many confusing personal entanglements. I had just left William McCollister, somber and embarrassed; my mother and Arnie would be waiting for us when we landed at Santa Monica. I'd been stunned by Willie's dignified befuddlement. He could not imagine his friend, the governor, betraying him in that way. He was confused; he wanted me to help him figure things out. He had not come to make a demand. His utter decency was unbearable, searing—the pain of it all, the promise of pain to come, was overpowering. It was real, unslick, unspinnable. It was not Cashmere. It couldn't be taken to Libby for Dustbusting. It had to go directly to the governor. But we hadn't had an opportunity to talk. I tried to imagine how I'd tell him about *this* one. I tried to rehearse it. I couldn't; my mind was blank.

Somewhere above the desert, Willie's sense of loss and bemusement propelled me into my own: Mother, waiting at the other end of the arc. Our relationship was affectionate, if placid—a mutual decision had been made, somewhere along the way, that we would let it go at that. She was a great believer in calm love. Even Father's departure had been oddly untempestuous. There were no scenes; he just left. He went to the American University in Beirut, as a Visiting Something-or-Other. He had never told Mother about the application; it must have been in the works for months. He never told her he was leaving, that their marriage was over; he just packed a bag and left. I was ten. They corresponded: "What does this mean?" she wrote him. "Whatever you want it to mean," he replied. Later, in a letter to me—it came out of the blue, unbidden, when I was in college—he wrote: "You may wonder what happened between your mother and me. It became untenable, through no fault of hers. I could not accept her unwillingness to see our differences. She did not care to acknowledge the issue there. In her mind, it was simply two people finding each other, and I needed to know why—or perhaps how: how she could make a leap so effortlessly, across territory normally so dangerous and melodramatic; how she could pretend that territory did not even exist. Her placidity un-nerved me. Her inability to *see* my color—a quality that at first seemed so fetching in her, so exhilarating and optimistic—ultimately became a statement I could not accept: that my color wasn't important. It seemed she did not know me. It was unbearable."

Mother's composure *was* unnerving. She mourned him. She hoped the phase would pass, that he would return. Then he went on from Beirut to Kuala Lumpur, and finally to Cairo. After three or four years—the process was seamless, unobtrusive, distressingly rational—she determined that it was not a phase, he was not coming back, and so she moved on. I was sent away to school. She made herself avail-able, but discreetly so. She did not inflict any trials or errors on me; ultimately, though, there was Arnie, who was unexceptionable. He was Armenian, which I perceived as not quite white—to have gone all the way back to Missouri or its equivalent would have been an im-plicit recognition that her marriage to Father had been a bridge too far. But Arnie was a step toward safety, at least *I* had seen it that way. No doubt, she hadn't. Her lapidary humanity was unassailable. Sud-denly, riding that Gulfstream, I experienced a wave of anger and nau-sea: my father's confused, resentful blood pumping in my heart. We swirled down, into Los Angeles, through filthy air.

The governor and Susan were immediately snatched up by the music hotshot, who was small and neat, wearing a silver silk shirt—open at the neck—and jeans and running shoes. He got to Stanton first, be-fore staff, before we even left the plane—he bounded aboard. "Greet-ings, Fritz," he said to the pilot. "You didn't shake up the governor, did you?" Then he crouched next to Stanton and whispered, "Wel-come to LA, Governor. We've put together a small group for you, back at the house," he said. "Warren is there. Barry thinks he'll be able to come. Tim and Susan. Then we'll go on to the event."

He followed the Stantons out of the plane, wrapping a consoling arm around Susan. His attentions weren't fawning or respectful, I re-alized; they were an act of charity. And so it didn't surprise me at all when John Conroy, our tall, amiable California coordinator, draped an arm over *my* shoulder as we walked to the terminal and said, "How're you?" I nodded. Then: "Henry, you are about to attend the most lav-ish Secretary's Night Out in the history of Los Angeles. Everyone as-sumes we're dead. They think it's the better part of valor not to stare at the corpse, so they're giving their tickets to the steno pool. We are feeding the mailroom tonight. Should we tell the governor?"

"No," I said. What difference would it make? He'd sense it soon enough, if he hadn't already, from his benefactor's mortician act. I could predict his reaction: anger, at first. He'd be pissed at the big shots. But then he'd look out at the audience and think, Hey, all these other people are here—I can still sell *them*. Then, a growing confi-dence and renewed sense of power when he did sell them. And, ulti-mately, a bouyant optimism: I ain't dead yet.

I didn't want to deny him that process. It would be good prepara-tion for New Hampshire. Lost in my mental staff work, I almost walked past Mother.

"Henry!" she said. She looked lovely, tanned. Arnie, who looked very LA—double-breasted blue blazer and light gray slacks, dark blue shirt with a white collar open at the neck, gold chain at the neck—stood just behind her, a hand on her shoulder, at the door of the gen-eral aviation terminal. I kissed her hair; she hugged me; Arnie patted me on the back.

"Governor!" I said, a bit too sharply. Susan turned abruptly, looking for bad news. Then smiles. The governor and Susan doubled back. I saw him check out Mother—it was reflexive when he wasn't care-ful, if the woman was particularly good-looking—then he overcom-pensated by giving Arnie a deeply meaningful handshake, a two-stager: two-handed, then an arm-drape over Arnie's shoulder. "We're in the same boat, huh, Arnie?" He said, glancing at me. "Sur-rogate fathers to someone older than we are."

Arnie laughed. "I used to feel, when we'd visit Henry in school and we'd all go out, that he was chaperoning," he said.

"He's the best," Stanton said. "Master of the universe."

"Cut the crap," I said, too jovially, distracted by all my roles and responsibilities, by the soft, west side breeze and the glare—how easy it would be to just stay in LA and be comfortable—and the jet fumes.

We began to move through the small terminal, all plate glass, potted palms and aviation sorts. The governor looked about, spotted the men's room—and I had a decision to make. I followed him in. It was a two-holer. I had to go but didn't. I stood by the sink as he went. "Governor," I said.

"They're great," he said. "Your folks. Just great—wish we could just stay out here and—"

"Governor."

Now he got it. He looked at me hard.

"What is it?" he asked.

"Fat Willie, the Barbecue Man, came by headquarters this morning," I said, reaching for calm but quavering a little. "His daughter is pregnant. She says you're the father."

He betrayed nothing. "Who else knows?"

I shrugged.

"What does he want?"

"Just to tell you. He was embarrassed, I think."

The governor wheeled and slammed the wall, open-handed on the tile. The sound was something between a slam and a splat. "I just can't catch a break, can I?" he said. He moved past me to the sink, leaned on it, stared in the mirror, ran water. "I want you to call him— No. I better do it. I need him to understand this is some kind of mistake," he said, with an earnest intensity that was pretty convincing. "I need to have some— How pregnant is she?"

"Didn't say," I said. "I don't think he knows."

"Can't be more than a few months, can it? Four, five months tops. And the girl?"

I didn't know what he was looking for.

"Yeah," he said. "How could we know? But he'll give us a week, right?"

"I suppose," I said.

He was calm now, emotionless; I had never seen him so cold. There *was* something weird here. "This stays with us, okay? Don't tell Daisy."

So he knew about Daisy. It was amazing what was known, and not known. Everyone knew everything, except for the most basic things. "Do you want Libby?"

"*No!*"

He turned away from the mirror, leaned against the sink. "They all think I'm dead," he said. "They're gonna look at me and not look me straight in the eye. It's gonna be sickening. The worst will be the ones who try to commiserate, the shitbuckets who had troubles of their own, who got caught smoking crack or feeling up a teenager. The ones who got bombed and strafed by the press. They think I'm one of them now. Soon, Henry—someday, I predict, there will be a fraternal order of those who've been raped by the media. We'll have our own old-age home, like the Will Rogers Institute, or whatever they do for bad actors out here. Ours'll be: The Mike Milken Home for the Fatally Flawed." He stopped, folded his arms over his chest, stared down. I was ready to move him along, but he wasn't ready to go. "A lot of them aren't going to show tonight. I don't care. I won't give them the satisfaction. Henry—" He stared at me very hard, his blue eyes rheumy and rimmed with pink, but riveting. "Henry. You will never be ashamed that you did this. Do you understand? You will never have to swallow it, or duck it, or apologize for it. I am not going to let that happen."

The door swung open. Conroy. "Guys?" He said.

I went with Mother and Arnie for an early dinner at an airy place on Melrose, with brick walls, a high ceiling and billowy fabrics suspended in air—sharp, breathtaking swatches of color: royal blue, wine red, chartreuse. We would have this time, then go on, have dessert and listen to the governor speak at the Beverly Hilton. It was almost a shock to be among normal people, people who didn't know everything, people who couldn't read your mind. It was annoying. That was, I realized, the other thing about Mother's composure—it was uncomprehending. She couldn't sense my confusion and utter discomfort, much less the aggravating impact the sultry ease of Los Angeles had on it. She was pleased to see me. She was proud of me. She was concerned the campaign wasn't going so well. "He seems a wonderful man," she said.

"And she's a looker," Arnie added. "I wonder what it is. . . . So what are you going to do next, Henry?"

"Go back to New Hampshire," I said, purposely avoiding Arnie's real question: what was I going to do after the campaign folded. I realized, suddenly, that Mother and Arnie were living through this embarrassment too. But they were okay; they were living through it in an LA sort of way. It didn't matter that I was associated with a campaign that had become something of a national joke. It was a credential. It made me a marketable commodity. Arnie would be able to say, "Henry used to work for Jack Stanton," and in Los Angeles, in show business, they would know what that meant. I would be considered a veteran, a gladiator, someone who understands how bright the spotlight could be, who had worked at media riot control, and that experience would make me valuable—to other candidates for The Milken Home. I realized that Arnie was about to offer me a job, and that it wouldn't be charity.

"It's all right," I said. "It's a tough time. Look: Under normal circumstances, we'd be dead. And yeah, I know it looks like we are—and we might be—but, then, you think: Who's gonna beat us? I just can't imagine any of those guys doing it. I mean, who can? Y'knowwhat-tamean?" I said, racing, sounding like Richard, sounding insane. "So we play it out. We go day to day. We got a week. A lot can happen in a week. Even if Harris beats us there, where else is he gonna win? So, I'm not— But you know, it's not an easy business."

"Henry," Arnie said. "When it's over. Your mother and I have been talking. When it's over, I can make a place for you—I mean, I could really use someone like you. It's nice out here, you know? You should enjoy life a little before you kill yourself working like this."

"Thank you, Arnie," I said. "But at this point I don't know that I'd be alive doing anything other than this. It's the strangest thing—like being a mine worker. New Hampshire is like working in a mine. You get this great, tactile pleasure from chipping away at it. At least I did, when we were working retail, coffee to coffee, winning the activists one at a time, before he became a household name. I sound nuts, right? Well, being here, in Los Angeles, is just so completely strange. It's like coming out of the mine, being blinded by the light. It's like almost *painful* being exposed to all this light."

Mother was discomforted by my discomfort. She had no idea what I was getting at and probably never would. So I did the next best thing: tried to reassure her that it was only temporary. "There are people—

Richard Jemmons, Arlen Sporken—who do this over and over, who can't live without it," I said. "I'm not like that. I'm doing this once. I made a commitment to Jack Stanton and I'll see it through. But I don't think I'd have the stomach for this business, the desperation and intensity of it, if I didn't have a real rooting interest."

"Well, if that's the case," Arnie said, laughing a little, "maybe we'll see you out here next Wednesday."

"Yeah, it may not last much longer than that," I agreed. "But if it doesn't, I'll be real upset. He's got some problems, some weaknesses—that's for sure—but I think Jack Stanton's capable of doing some really great things for this country."

His speech that night was awful, but not desperate—a plus. He stayed in control. He saw immediately what he was up against, a replacement audience and an unreachable one at that; the ballroom at the Beverly Hilton seemed distended and over-air-conditioned, the audience chilled and seated way at the other end of the hall from the podium. But that, I realized, was only my sense of room. These were people quietly, furiously engaged in one another, desperately checking out how the competition looked and dressed, performing intricate physiognomic calculations: whose cheekbones or breasts or fanny might lift them up from the mailroom or out from behind the reception desk; who had come up with the slightest hint of a new look; who had locked into the ephemeral Hollywood calculus of sensuality and sophistication. They were geniuses at such evaluations; it was their basic grammar. They did it the way Leon read a poll or Daisy cut a spot. And so they paid Jack Stanton no attention at all. And he did something I'd rarely seen him do: he mailed it in. He didn't even try to distract them. It was an unlikely act of discipline, the conservation of energy—a sign of very intense seriousness on his part.

Mother, of course, thought he was very inspiring. Arnie mumbled some encouragement but clearly figured that Stanton had given up, that he was dead. I felt a reflexive twinge of elation: he was focused. He was ready to return to New Hampshire.

I can sleep on a plane. Usually, though, the sleep is light enough that I'll sense it and wake when the engines slow and the descent begins. That night—perhaps it was the Gulfstream—I was deeply, comfortably asleep when we hit the runway in Manchester. We seemed to land hard. I was up with a start. You could feel the cold even before we got off the plane; you could feel it through the plane. It was still dark, but there was a sense of impending grayness. Several people, bundled in goosedown, determinedly waving our familiar red, white and blue STANTON FOR AMERICA signs, stood next to three vans. We had come all this way—and gone nowhere. We were still in the same place: it was like Chutes and Ladders. We climbed ladders; we slid down chutes. We always arrived at the same airport, the same time of day, the same caravan waiting to take us to the same places, all of which we'd hit several times by now.

The cold was painful after Los Angeles. We moved into it reluctantly. The governor looked at me—and this was the first time I'd ever seen him anything less than totally enthusiastic about entering the arena—and shrugged: Here we go again. Mitch was there to take suitcases, help Susan down the slippery stairway. And then, as we came off the plane, people emerged from the vans—and began to applaud, a deep, solid gloved affection. Stanton walked down the line of them, hugging them—eyes tearing from the cold, or perhaps just tearing. The last was Danny Scanlon, with a box of apple fritters. "B-brought you somethin', Governor," he said.

Stanton looked around at us, glowing, with a goofy grin. "God, it's good to see you, Danny—why aren't you at work?"

"Took the week off. I'm working for you now."

"Well now, isn't that— Listen: everyone gather around." And we did, in a tight huddle, arms entwined, warm on top, but with a bitter wind whipping our legs. "I will never, ever forget you coming out like this for us," Stanton said. "We have a tough week ahead. We may not win. But I can promise you this: no candidate will work harder these next seven days than I am going to. And you will never regret this. And I will never forget it. . . . So what do we do first? Mitch?"

"We've got the McLaughy Wire Factory plant gate, but that isn't for another hour."

"C'mon, there must be something we can do before that," the governor said. "A diner or— Danny? Where's your competition this time of morning?"

"Silver Moon'll have some folks," Danny said.

Silver Moon it was. Stanton moving down the counter, then over to the booths, shaking hands. Truckers, factory guys with dark brows, lined faces, knit caps, staring at him, shaking their heads, smiling private smiles: "What you doin' up so early, Governor?" one asked. "You startin' the day or just endin' it?"

"Last week, fellas," he said. "Workin' double shift. What can I do for you? What you want to know?"

They looked at each other, thinking: So what about Cashmere? But no one had the guts, so one of them asked, "So you gonna take our guns?"

"Only if you've got an Uzi or a bazooka."

He moved on, and kept moving. He was up now. We all were. At one point, he jumped out of the van at a red light and began knocking on windows, waving, shaking the hands of fellow motorists. As we moved from plant gates to markets, I broke off and went back to the hotel, where Arlen, Daisy, Lucille, Richard and Leon were in the Stanton suite—it was as if they'd never left, as if we'd always be there—arguing over the last week's media buy.

"Who's gonna watch the fucking thing?" Richard was asking. "They're just gonna be pissed off at us for preempting 'America's Most Fucked-Up Home Videos.' "

"You know what we get out of thirty-second spots now?" Daisy said. She was sipping a Diet Coke. "Nothing. Thirty-second spots only reinforce the bad shit—that he's just another politician. You ain't gonna thrill 'em with bands and flags now, you're not gonna move 'em on health care. We gotta let them listen to him, take him on, hit him with their best shot—y'know? We gotta let them see that there's something there." She looked at Lucille. "Flannel shirts and ax-tossing ain't gonna make it anymore."

"But if we go dark, they'll think we're folding," Arlen said. Interesting: he and Daisy were taking conflicting positions. She was stepping out, away from him; the rift we had assumed, and subtly encouraged, was now open—she might have to find new work after the campaign. I hadn't had a chance to talk to her about any of this; I couldn't remember the last time we'd had a moment, a nonstressed phone conversation. Saturday night? Aeons ago.

"There's something to that," Daisy said, pulling back—acknowledging that Arlen did have a point. "Maybe we cut the buy, or cut the TV, go more to radio? More bang, less bucks?"

"That's not nothin'—you technocrats figger that one out," Richard said. "The big question is the Jackathon. What do you think, Henri?" Richard asked. "Seems to me we hit a weird fucking place when the advertising guru's goin' *responsible* on us. Ol' Daisy Mae here wants to take us down—no more spots—and blow it all on a telethon Saturday night."

"Saturday night?" I asked. "Who's gonna be watching TV on a Saturday night?"

"All the people who might not trust a candidate who fucks around," Daisy said. "Leon, tell him about Cashmere."

"She's got higher name recognition than Bart Nilson," Leon said. "So?"

"What good does a thirty-second spot do us at this point?" she said. "We've got to figure out a way *not* to be a typical politician."

"How we doin', Leon?" I asked.

"Stable," he said. "Finally. Harris's movin' a little. Up near Undecided. We're half that. I'm a little worried about Charlie Martin. They may be ready to give him a second look. Reason they haven't so far is there's been so much bad news 'bout us. Crowded him out."

"Oh, here's another thing," Richard said. "You want to hear the best fucking thing yet? Ozio's back. At least, he's within a hundred miles. He's giving a speech at Harvard tomorrow night. Says he isn't encouraging a write-in campaign, but there's, get this, no way he can, morally—morally!—stand between a voter and his or her conscience if she or he wants to write in his name or names."

"Great," I said.

"Forget Ozio," Daisy said. "Actually, it may not be bad—say he takes two or three percent. We weren't getting that anyway—right, Leon? It just takes from Harris. Anything that takes from Harris we are just in fucking love with."

"Look," Lucille said, "we gotta decide." She was standing over the dining room table, holding a Magic Marker. Seven large pieces of poster paper in front of her. Seven days. "We've got a rally set for

Concord Saturday night. Do we kill it or what? What are the logistics? Where's Lieberman?"

Daisy called him at the Manchester headquarters. "Durham? . . . Yeah, but we want real people, not just college kids. In fact, if we do this, I want someone independent—get some fucking newspaper people, not the *Union Leader,* someone real—to pick the audience. The other thing is, if we do Durham, can we still do Concord? Push it back how much? . . . You think that's late? Okay. We'll talk about it. And we have until when for the buy? . . . Okay."

She looked around the room: "We can do it out of the public station at the university. We have until noon to decide. Someone want to call the governor?"

He came in for an hour in the afternoon and napped. I saw him just after he awakened, bleary-eyed, feverish, coughing, eating—polishing off some of the dreadful, reheated Campbell's minestrone the hotel peddled through room service. "Okay, Henry, we gotta call Willie," he said. "You make sure no one comes in here while that's happening. Where's Susan?"

"Nashua," I said. "Nursing homes."

"Good." He dialed it himself. "Willie? Hey, man—got your mojo workin'? . . . Yeah, well, it'll pick up when the weather turns. Look, I know this must be just awful for you, just the worst. And I'm gonna help you through this every way I can, just like always. But you gotta know: I didn't have anything to do with this. You understand?" He really sounded convincing. "God, Willie. You know, with all the talk around about, ah . . . me, I'm sure she was thinkin'—well, you know, how kids are, teenagers. . . . Yeah, I know. I know. You and Amalee worked real hard at raisin' her right. I can't *imagine* what this would be like. But you have to know, Willie, I'll be standin' right by you in this. I will help every way I can. . . . She's gettin' care, right? That's important now. You don't want her thinkin' 'bout doing anything crazy now. . . . Now, look, I've got to get through the next week up here. It's gonna be a rough pull, all this stuff they're throwin' at me. But I'll be back for a few hours next week and we'll sit down and work this out. . . . Be cool now. You have to give me this chance, you have to believe me. . . . It's gonna work out. I know it seems dark right now, but you still gonna' get the chance to open that branch up in the nation's capital, just like I said you would. I'd just die without your magic sauce—and without your friendship, Willie. . . . I'll stand with you now. . . . Anything you need, my man."

He hung up and stared into space.

Danny Scanlon was waiting for us in the lobby with more apple fritters. The governor didn't wait for the van; he grabbed two right there—not good. There was a lot of action in the lobby: camera crews from Japan and somewhere in the north of Europe—Sweden, maybe—were getting ready to move out; campaign workers; scorps. Cal Allerad, an enormously successful mail-order businessman who was running a vanity campaign against the president in the Republican primary and had put something like six hundred thousand dollars on the air was trying to chat up scorps, who weren't buying. Over in a corner, Geraldo, who was taping a week's worth of shows in two days—sex and politics, stress and politics, media gurus, etc., etc.—was giving instructions to his staff, which seemed to consist only of astonishingly good-looking women. He spotted Stanton and abruptly tried to plow through the crowd. "He's gonna want you as a guest," I said. "The answer is no."

"Governor, Governor," he said.

"Hey, buddy," Stanton said, looking just incredibly pleased to see him. "What brings you up to the frozen north?"

"*You!* All America wants to know how you're gettin' through this. There's a lot of sympathy out there, Governor. Folks think you're gettin' a bum deal."

"No kiddin'." Stanton wasn't buying. He was eyeing the door, beginning to move.

Geraldo moved with him. "Look, you need to get your side of the story out. I can help you. We can do it any way you want, you set the ground rules."

Stanton stopped, stared at him: "Okay. Here are the ground rules: I'm the host and I pick the audience. How 'bout that?"

"Well," Geraldo said. "What about me?"

"Take the day off." Stanton laughed. "Go skiing. Look, I'm sorry. We've got a very tight schedule, and a very tough race." And we pushed on past him, toward the doors.

Jerry Rosen was moving out the door just as we were, although I didn't recognize him at first, all bundled up with a knit cap pulled down over his eyebrows. He looked ridiculous, as if his mother had just dressed him for school. "Hey, Jer, you look like Nanook of the North," the governor said.

"Cold out there, Governor," he said. "How you doin'?"

"Pluggin' away. You comin' to Portsmouth with us?"

"Naww—goin' down to Boston to see Ozio." He seemed almost apologetic. "Gotta stick with the local story." He shrugged.

Stanton put a conciliatory arm over his shoulders. "That's okay, Jerry. You gotta do what you gotta do. So, what'ya think?"

"Not good," he said. "I hear the *Globe* tracking has you down to the high teens. They say Martin's beginning to hot up."

It was old news—but interesting. We'd known the bottom had fallen out since Sunday; the scorps were just beginning to catch on. Rosen figured we were dead. You could see it in his body language, you could hear it in his voice.

"Jerry," Stanton said, fixing him with the old, entirely compelling Stanton intensity. "Listen to me. This is not over yet. It's not—" and he began to cough. We moved toward the van. Stanton ducked in, then looked back toward Rosen and smiled. "I'm gonna surprise you, Jerry."

"I *hope so,* Governor," Rosen said, opening up a little—then shutting down again abruptly, looking quickly around to see if any of his colleagues had caught his moment of weakness.

"Asshole," Stanton said, as we rolled off. "I'm last week and he's lookin' for next week. If he thinks next week is gonna be Ozio, he's nuts. But it's interesting, none of them think next week is going to be Harris. That fucker is going to win this thing, and everyone's already discounting it. They are looking for another storyline. If we're close, if we do better than expected, we're their story."

"You think so?" I asked.

"Who knows?" he said. "Danny, where are those fritters?"

"Here, G-governor," Danny offered them up front. "Y-y'know, y-you're gettin' too f-fat to be a corpse."

"Fatten' me up for the kill," Stanton said. "Least I won't die hungry."

The funeral would be well attended. The crowd in Portsmouth that night was astonishing. They were jammed into a small, bare, cinder-block union hall—it was an obscure local of a dying craft, a nineteenth-century vestige: the steamfitters, pipe welders or iron benders—something like that: a fraternal organization for people left behind, shipyard folks. They were sallow, defiantly overweight, both men and women wearing union or tavern windbreakers, sock hats, the men with facial hair, some of the women in curlers and smoking long cigarettes. There was a table in the back with coffee, cookies, tuna sandwiches on small, soft dinner rolls; another table with Stanton literature, which seemed as stale and discolored as the tuna. We were reaching the end of this thing.

We came in through the rear, through a rush of noise—Terry O'Leary, an ancient, gray man dressed entirely in polyester (burgundy jacket, yellowish shirt, stained striped gray tie, gray slacks) was playing jigs on the accordion, smiling wide through scattered teeth. He stopped when the governor came—played the first, famous bars of "Hail to the Chief," which would have seemed a cheesy sort of mockery if the old man hadn't assembled himself upright, in some distant shadow of martial dignity, chin tilted up, shoulders square. The music silenced the hall. Jerry Delmonico, the local president—an aging Elvis, his pompadour gone gray and thinning in the back—welcomed the governor, and said, "Now, Terry, howsabout let's play the national anthem." Which Terry did, and they all sang along, and then recited the Pledge of Allegiance. I could see Jack Stanton was moved: this was the other end of the earth from the crowd in Los Angeles. It seemed, I thought, as if they hadn't been following the news the past few weeks, as if they had suddenly materialized from some pre-tabloid, pre-skeptical past—but that was wishful thinking on my part. Mickey Flanagan, the young—but ancient in the Boston way—advance guy who'd worked this stop, found me off to the side of the hall, grimaced and shrugged. " 'Smatter?" I asked. "This is good. You did great."

"I did nothin'," Mickey said. "He's a celebrity now. He's in the *Flash* and he's real—it makes all the other things in the *Flash* seem real too. Space aliens. Miracle diets. He's given credibility to all the world's garbage. He's a touchstone of the tabloid faith. You can light candles to him."

I wondered if Stanton had picked that up. But of course he had, and it didn't matter. He would use whatever tools available. He was locked in now.

"I want to thank you for coming out tonight," the governor began. "I know you work hard, and don't have much time to relax."

"Some of us have more'n we'd like," a younger, angry sort interrupted.

"Right, right. I understand that. In fact, let me see a show of hands, if you don't mind. How many of you have work now?" About half raised their hands. "How many of you are looking for work?" About a third. "Those of you who are working—let me ask you a question. As you look around the room at your brothers and neighbors and cousins who aren't as lucky as you—what do you see? Y'see people who wouldn't work if we gave 'em a chance? Y'see people who'd rather stay home and watch the soaps?"

"*I'd* rather stay home and watch the soaps," a big, blowsy woman in curlers said, and they all laughed. "I'd rather do anything than punch in at Rizzuto's Dry Clean—"

"I'll bet," Stanton said, laughing along with them. He was with them all the way now. "My momma worked jobs like that when I was comin' up. And you know what? Before I was born, my mama was a sales clerk at Harry Truman's haberdashery in Kansas City—that's how Democrat we Stantons are."

There was a pleasant buzz, an intimacy in the room. (I had never heard the Truman line before.) The governor was reaching out for them. "But after my daddy died and I was born, I remember seeing Momma come home from work, just bone-weary—y'know what I mean?" Heads were nodding. "I know she wanted to talk to me, and play with me, and ask me what I learned in school that day—but sometimes, you know how it is, you're just too tired to do anything but pop a dinner in the microwave—though we didn't have microwaves back then, of course—and blob out in front of the tube."

"You've got that one right," the blowsy woman said.

"So I know it isn't easy for the folks who *do* have work, either. The moms who have to work and have to worry 'bout what their kids are out doin' after school. And I'll bet there are more than a few dads who lost these shipyard jobs and have had to catch on doin' . . . whatever."

"Doing shit," someone shouted.

"Hey, you know what?" Jack Stanton said abruptly. "I am going to do something really outrageous here. Hell, everybody thinks I've bought the farm in this race anyway, so I got nothin' to lose. I'm going to do something really outrageous: I'm gonna tell you the truth."

Cheers and laughter. "Yeah, I know what you're thinking: He must *really* be desperate to wanta do that." More laughter. "But okay. You've had to swallow enough sh— ah, garbage."

"You can say 'shit,' Governor," said the blowsy woman. "We're X-rated."

"Me too, if you believe what you read in the paper," he said, and the place exploded. "Now look, now look. Let me get serious a little. Let me tell you something. Truth Number One. There are two kinds of politicians in this world. Those who tell you what you want to hear—and those who never come around." There were cheers and laughter. "The second kind, the ones who don't come 'round *here,* they're the ones who tell the uptown folks what *they* want to hear. Those boys don't deliver much either."

"'Cept at tax time," the blowsy woman said.

"Fair enough. They do deliver then. But what's anyone done for *you* lately? Right?" Applause. They were curious now. They wanted to know what was coming. (So did I.) "Well, I'm here now, and I'm lookin' at you, and you wouldn't believe me if I told you what you wanted to hear in any case, right?" Nods and applause. "So let me tell you this: No politician can bring these shipyard jobs back. Or make your union strong again. No politician can make it be the way it used to be. Because we're living in a new world now, a world without borders—economically, that is. Guy can push a button in New York and move a billion dollars to Tokyo before you blink an eye. We've got a world market now. And that's good for some. In the end, you've gotta believe it's good for America. We come from everywhere in the world, so we're gonna have a leg up *selling* to everywhere in the world. Makes sense, right? But muscle jobs are gonna go where muscle labor is cheap—and that's not here. So if you all want to compete and do better, you're gonna have to exercise a different set of muscles, the ones between your ears."

"Uh-oh," said the woman.

And Stanton did something really dangerous then: he didn't indulge her humor. "Uh-oh is right," he said. "And anyone who gets up here and says he can do it for you isn't leveling with you. So I'm not gonna insult you by doing that. I'm going to tell you this: This whole country is gonna have to go back to school. We're gonna have to get smarter, learn new skills. And I will work overtime figuring out ways to help you get the skills you need. I'll make you this deal: I will work for *you*. I'll wake up every morning thinking about *you*. I'll fight and worry and sweat and bleed to get the money to make education a lifetime thing in this country, to give you the support you need to move on up. But you've got to do the heavy lifting your own selves. I can't do it for you, and I know it's not gonna be easy." He stopped, paused. There were no smartass remarks now.

"Y'know, I've taken some hits in this campaign. It hasn't been easy for me, or my family. It hasn't been fair, but it hasn't been *anything* compared to the hits a lot of you take every day. Takes a lot more courage to keep your family together, to keep on moving through a tough time, where you don't know what's comin' next, whether the paycheck's gonna be there next week, who's gonna pay the doctor bill, the mortgage—all the worries you have.

"So I've taken a few shots, but I can live with it. I'll get by. Hell, I'm lucky—I got my picture on the cover of a national newspaper. Maybe not the one I would've planned on. . . ." There was some laughter, but this had become as intensely serious as I'd ever seen a political gathering. "And you know what? My picture there means that some-one—maybe some group of people—thinks I'm worth taking a shot at. And you've got to ask yourselves: Why? Why is Jack Stanton worth the ton of garbage they're dumpin' on his head? It may be because that's the way things are in this country now—if the garbage is there, or can be made to *seem* like it's there, you dump it.

"Or it may be that there are two kinds of politicians—the ones who tell you what you want to hear and the ones who don't bother tellin' you anything at all. And maybe some folks aren't very *interested* in there being a third kind. You should think about that when you cast that vote next Tuesday."

And silence. As if they were thinking too hard to applaud.

"Henry?" Daisy said. "Why do I always come to your room?"

"It's neater?"

"No, seriously."

"Seriously? Hey, it's three in the morning."

"No, turn over," she said. "Look at me."

I looked at her. Her hair was tousled, and over her eyes; the tortoiseshell barrettes she used to pin it back were on the night table. She was cute. She was not beautiful. She was, more to the point, right there—in my face. The allure of Daisy was also the difficulty: she caught everything. She let nothing pass. "I know you care," she said.

What to say.

"Henry."

I brushed her hair back with my hand; I did it twice.

"What I mean is, I would like to experience you in a noncampaign environment," she said.

"You may get that chance soon enough," I said.

"What I mean is . . . is exactly that. Next week. If we're in a non-campaign environment next week, I would like to experience you in that. Okay? Henry?" She looked at me. She went on. "I've got lots of miles. Miles and miles of miles. We could go to the Caribbean. I've got so many miles on American, we could take the space shuttle. We could lay on a beach. We could lay on a bed. We could really get laid—it'd be lahk pahradahse, we could have a wet bar in our room, room service, y'knowhattamean?" she said. "We could lick our wounds. We could lick each other. We could drink rum drinks—y'know with little turquoise parachutes."

"Parasols."

"So you're on?" She giggled. "Gotcha. *Nailed* ya."

I pulled her close, kissed her hair. "What if we're *not* in a noncampaign environment?" I said. "What if we're still alive?"

"Well," she said. "For us to actually be alive—I mean, alive alive, not just Jack and Susan being stubborn and ridiculous. For us to actually be alive would take a run—and probably a Harris fuckup—that would be so spectacular, such a rush, that it would probably be even better than noncampaign sex with you. So that would be okay too."

"How do you know how noncampaign sex with me would be?"

"Extrapolation. But, Henry, surely you—rational, sensible, dark-hearted you—surely you don't think we'll be alive a week from now. I know it was a hundred years ago—yesterday—but remember *Newsweek*?"

Newsweek had buried us with a derisive piece called "The Anatomy of a Flameout." Someone inside—Sporken was my guess—had given some classic distressed-mood-of-the-staff quotes. We were assumed toast. It was time for the consultants to start peeling off, cutting their losses, feeding the scorps obituary matter in order to fertilize the soil for their next campaigns. I was waiting, and dreading, the first sign that Richard had folded his hand. And here was Daisy, trying to act the classic professional, trying to distance herself, getting ready to go. "You see Nyhan in the *Globe* today," she went on: " 'A synthetic candidate meets his polyester epiphany?' Jeez."

"The Boston scorps all love Charlie Martin," I said. "He's hip. He's funny. He's almost Irish. Only trouble is, actual human-being folks don't get his act. They don't think running for president is performance art." I went up on one elbow. "Daisy, you should have seen Jack tonight—with the shipyard folks. Totally focused, disciplined, daring, just a great fucking candidate. He absolutely locked in. He bull's-eyed."

"It's garbage time—no one's playing defense," she said. "When you ain't got nothin' there ain't nothin' to lose."

"I don't know," I said. "A week is a long time."

"Not when you're dead." She sighed.

"Daisy, do me a favor," I said softer, but harder. "Don't do the hard-ened professional number, okay? Don't play hired gun. I still care about them—Jack and Susan. And I think you do too."

"Not as much as . . . you do," she said. "And: Shit—not as much as I do about you. Look. Henry. Okay. I'll admit it: I'm freaked. I'm pretty sure I fucked up my situation with Arlen these past couple of weeks. He seems cool enough, but he probably thinks—on some level—that I angled my way into the Stantons' hearts. No white boy from Mississippi, even a progressive one, likes to be upstaged by his junior partner. So I don't know what kind of future I have there. I also don't know what's going on with you." She didn't give me a chance to say anything—since she knew, perfectly well, that nothing I could say would meet her expectations. But she wanted the expectations out on the table, figuring that I was a decent enough guy not to slam-dunk her gratuitously, and so she hurried on. "I do suspect I got a commitment from you on the parasol drinks. I believe I tricked you into a quasi-commitment by forcing you, Mr. Pluperfection, to correct me when I said parachute instead of parasol. I believe that if I'm clever enough to do that, I deserve a whirl."

"Daise," I said, feeling—I don't know. Feeling something. "You deserve more than a whirl. But you gotta believe we may not need to count frequent-flier miles for a couple more weeks. If for no other reason than to humor me."

"Okay, I believe. Sort of."

An interesting thing happened the next day. People began to show up. Patsy McKinney, the blowsy wiseacre from the Portsmouth shipyard meeting was waiting for us in the lobby of the Hampton Inn at 6:00 A.M. "So where do I sign up—where you want me to work?" she asked. We sent her over to Brad Lieberman. By midday, three busloads had arrived after a long two-day trip, from Grace Junction—elementary school classmates of the governor's, the high school principal, half the faculty—and Beauregard Bryant Hastings, the Stanton family doctor, a fabulous-looking fellow, thin almost to the point of consumption, and *tilted* somehow, sort of like the Tower of Pisa, wearing a cape and a hat and small round glasses, like James Joyce, but with a long, wild mane of white hair: "Johnny," he said to the governor (it sounded like "*Jawhneh,*" as if a cotton boll had lodged in his throat, or perhaps it was just that his vocal chords had been sanded down by a lifetime of bourbon). "We ahre gon' to *educate* these Yawhnkehs 'bout the intrahcahcehs of inspahred governahnce, y'heah?"

College classmates drifted in; Susan's law students from the state university, and people we'd met and connected with along the way: Ms. Baum, the lady who ran the library literacy program in Harlem; Russ Delson, the state treasurer of Tennessee; Minnie Houston, a community activist from Cleveland—dozens like that, ready to do anything, lick envelopes, go door to door. The Hampton Inn was full, as was every room in Manchester, so Lieberman bought out whole motels in cities and towns around the state and dispatched groups to Nashua, Portsmouth, Lebanon, Keene. He did this so smoothly it was almost as if he had anticipated the throng. Our whole operation, so totally dispirited just days before, was running effortlessly, in high gear.

On Thursday, Bill Johnson, the deputy attorney general of Alabama, was in the lobby of the Hampton Inn, waiting for us as we came in from a lunchtime swing. "Billy, what on earth? You up here for a ski vacation? President's Day weekend or somethin'?" Stanton asked.

"I figured you needed another black face up here to sell these skinflint Yankees."

"Billy—"

"Shut up, Jack," Johnson said, hugging him. "Just put me to work."

"Billy—I'm probably gonna get my ass kicked."

"That's why I'm here," Billy said. "See: I don't believe that for a second. I figure you're gonna pull this out somehow, and I want to see it personally, for myself, and tell the grandkids. I want to see how you handle this, case I ever find myself runnin' statewide."

"You won't be in a hole this deep."

"Jack, don't go tellin' no nigger about the depth of holes in Alabama. Just put me to work."

"Henry, tell Brad to put the attorney general here in charge of something, somethin' we can monitor, see if he's gotten any better at politickin' over the years."

And so it went, each time we walked into or out of the palm and plastic lobby of the hotel. It seemed a slow-motion version of *This Is Your Life,* and it caused great huggy effusions from Jack Stanton. We were all, in fact, on the edge of tears, anger—exhaustion. But the candidate seemed to feed on it. He used the exhaustion and emotion to become a still more extravagant version of himself; he campaigned wonderfully. He was running on sheer willpower now; he was not entirely sensate, and the ceremonies of the stump—meeting, greeting, talking, walking—were performed reflexively, relentlessly, but brilliantly. He could not make strategic decisions, he could not deal with staff, but he could lock in on any crowd, answer any question. He was getting sick again; his face was flushed and he was coughing—and he had to be aware of the pounding he was getting from the scorps.

It had reached the point of disgust. They didn't understand why he wouldn't just quit. Didn't he know he was history? Everyone had written it. An entire industry existed to analyze such things, a universe of scorps, talking heads, pollsters, consultants, free-range wisemen and gurus—and they had all taken up residence in Manchester now. They filled the lobbies and saloons, rented all the cars—there were crowds everywhere, at all hours. It was instinctive, habitual; a quadrennial homing ritual. There was a liturgy; there were myths, patterns and ceremonial offerings. Jack Stanton had now been designated a ceremonial offering. It was a familiar role, reassuring to the tribe—he was George Romney, Ed Muskie, Gary Hart, the favorite who turns out to be Humpty-Dumpty. His fall would be an occasion for portentous false humility among pundits, for ruminations on the hubris of conventional wisdom prematurely arrived at; he would become a cautionary tale, remembered in years to come, and chuckled over. *What was her name again? Cashmere McLeod!* There would be ritual pleasure in watching him fall; there would be analysis of the quality of the splatter. If only he'd just get on with it.

The late-night saloon chat at the Wayfarer, Richard reported Friday morning, had drifted into the next phase: speculation about who might rejoin the campaign when Stanton dropped out. Ozio, Larkin (yes, there was talk about my old boss, I was amazed and disheartened to learn), some other hero. "It's wounded pride, y'knowhattamean?" Richard said. "They told the world he's dead, they want him to fuckin' die already."

"So what do you tell them?" I asked. We were sitting in the bedroom of Brad Lieberman's suite, waiting to do debate-strategy prep; in the outer room, muffins were hustling the phones. It sounded like a real, live campaign.

"I tell 'em we stopped sinkin'. I tell 'em we're still in second. I tell 'em Lawrence Harris is a favorite son. We'll clean his clock down south." Richard eyed me. "Don't worry, Henri. I'm still on board. I'm even about one quarter believin' the motherfucker'll figure some way out of this box. In fact, put me down as believin' that all this door-to-door retail shit he's been doin' might be clickin' on some half-conscious level. Shit, no one else's goin' anywhere. And I have never seen *anybody* work this hard. Yesterday, you shoulda seen him. He's standing in a mall in Nashua, midafternoon, just standin' there, y'knowhattamean? Standin' there, patient, answering the stupidest fucking questions from civilians that I have ever heard. Answering questions like, How can we get a stop sign over at the corner of Forest Lane? And, Can you help get my tax assessment lowered? Stone selfish, stupid people. And he's just patient as can be, explainin' this and that, the answer man. Hey, we blow this, we can open a string of Friendly Government Centers, servicing mall-rodent idiots. 'For a small fee, Governor Stanton will solve your problem.' "

"Fuck you."

"Yeah, you got that right—fuck me," Richard said. "Tell you one thing, though. He is a horse. Got two busted ankles, someone ought to put him down—but he's gallopin' down the stretch. You can only imagine what he'da been like runnin' whole. He'da been fuckin' Secretariat. We'd be plannin' the convention by now. Instead, we're— Hey, Henri, what *are* we gonna do next Tuesday night?"

"What are we doing tonight?"

"We are going to *gang-rape* Lawrence Harris." A distinctive—and surprisingly welcome—voice, boomed. "I am talking ANAL VIOLATION *in extremis*."

"Oh hi, Libby," Richard said. She stood in the doorway, darkening the sun. "You get a weekend pass? This work release or somethin'?"

"SCUMBAG," she said. "You are lucky to be fucking ALIVE, flashing your pathetic, wrinkled wiener at my darlin' Jenny. If it'd been me, you'd be a member of the Vienna Boys Choir by now. What the fuck have you brought this campaign anyway? You gonna save Jackie's ass with your brilliance this weekend? Oh," she said, spotting me, and diving an octave: "Hel-lo Hunnn-rah."

"Hello, Big Bopper." I said.

"Excuuuuse me, Henri," she crooned. "Elegance will not CUT it. We're up against it now. We are in the shit."

"Okay, Libby," I said. "What would *you* do tonight?"

"Watch my ass," she said. "Watch that mangy fucker Charlie Martin. Can't do much about Harris, but that mangy fucker wantsa move up on us."

"Not bad for a lunatic," Richard said. "Speaking of which—" Lucille came in, followed by Howard Ferguson and Leon Birnbaum.

"Pollster!" Richard saluted. "Whatcha got for us?"

"Bupkis." Leon jiggled. "No movement."

"Bowel movement," Libby said. "We gotta *make* it move."

"Can't do that by just watchin' our ass," Richard said. "Waitaminute, waitaminute, Olivia Holden—I am *discernin'* something here: could it be heinie-mania? You walk in, wanting to gang-rape Lawrence Harris. Your debate strategy is watch your ass, you talkin' bowel movements. Is there some sort of message here? You got the gripes? You stricken, or what?"

"Jemmons, stow it," Lucille said. "We've got business. Where's Daisy?"

"Cutting radio spots," I said.

"What?" Lucille asked. "Whatwhat?"

"You *know* what," Richard said. "What we said, what we agreed on—the veteran guy on Vietnam, that surgeon from Laconia on health care."

"What about the greenie?"

"We said no to the greenie," Richard said.

"We did *not,*" Lucille insisted. "This is a huge enviro state."

"The fuck it is."

"In the party it is."

"And Larry Harris got every last fucking one of them with his Natural Forces bullshit." Richard was up, shouting, taking it out on her. "Lucille, you are the stupidest—"

"ALL RIGHT. WE KNOW THAT," Libby intervened. "What we need to figure out is what we DON'T know."

"We don't know how to win this thing," Richard said. "You got any ideas, honey?"

A muffin at the door: "Henry! You better come. I got the editor of the Nashua paper. Sounds serious."

It did sound serious, in a ridiculous sort of way. The Nashua paper had an "exclusive." One of our spare drivers, a Lithuanian émigré who'd subbed for Mitch for a couple of days, was trying to make himself famous: he had heard Jack Stanton making racial and sexually charged statements, or so he said. He was intent on going public with this information now—the weekend before the primary—because the governor had promised to make the removal of Russian troops from Lithuania a major foreign policy theme, but he'd never delivered.

"Get out of here," I said. "You're kidding, right?"

"No, I've spoken to the man myself," the editor said.

"Sounds to me like a disgruntled former employee," I said, putting a finger in my out ear, trying to block the noise in the room, trying to concentrate.

"Sometimes disgruntled former employees tell good stories," the editor said.

"Oh come *on,*" I said. "You're not really gonna go with this, are you? This is horseshit. Totally unprovable. Totally undisprovable. What is it the governor supposedly said?"

"He called Luther Charles an ugly, mean-spirited nigger. And he allegedly called Harriet Everton a stupid woman with great tits. There were some other interesting tidbits, but those are the headlines."

It sounded half true, the Harriet Evergreen half. So I said, "That's completely fucking outrageous. Don't you have any standards at all? I mean, did the driver provide you with *any* supporting evidence? Did he have a tape?"

"Well, no. But he does have a track record."

"The driver?"

"No, your boss."

"Give me a break," I said. I had spent the past few weeks wondering what rock bottom would feel like. This seemed about right. "Let's say for a moment, just for the sake of argument, that everything you've heard about him is true. It isn't, but so be it. Let's say he was involved in a violent protest against the war twenty-five years ago, then used connections to skip out." I began to hesitate because the argument I was intending to make suddenly sounded weak, defensive—stupid. I was halfway along now, and trapped. Oh well. "Let's say he had an affair. What is it about that 'track record' that makes him a racist, or someone who'd make sexist remarks about your leading environmental activist? Is it just that he's fair game now—any accusation against him is presumed true?"

Silence. Maybe my argument wasn't so stupid after all—no, he was taking notes, letting me talk. "This is just bullshit, and you know it, Mr. Breen. We don't know whether this alleged disgruntled former employee even worked for us. He certainly wasn't anyone central to the campaign. You haven't even told me his name."

"Tibor Lizickis."

"Who?" But I did remember, vaguely. He drove for a few days in January, when Mitch had the flu.

"Tibor Lizickis. Lives in Derry. He's an engineering major at Merrimack."

"Look, you're going to have to give us some time to check this out. Who knows if this guy is actually telling the truth?"

"My reporter says he has confirmation that—"

"You can't give us a day to check him out?"

He gave a day, which took my day. I spent the rest of Friday on this, making calls, locating Tibor Lizickis, having him brought in. It wasn't something I had to do—I could've turned it over to Libby for dustbusting—but I guess, on some level, I couldn't bear to be part of the debate prep or any other aspect of the campaign. There was nothing to plan anymore. There would be no strategic breakthroughs. There was only the candidate, and he was moving on the moment, doing whatever felt right. He had stopped listening to us.

So I spent the day on Tibor Lizickis, and I suppose a good part of it was that someone would have to deal preemptively with the Reverend Luther Charles—and I was best equipped for that particular task. Indeed, there was a morbid fascination to it. I had spent much of my childhood listening to the grown-ups talk about what a pain it was for *them* to deal with Luther, whom they called the Fallen Angel, the member of Reverend Harvey Burton's Charmed Circle who had fallen from grace. I left a message for him at the People's

Empowerment Party (PEP) office in Washington; he called back late afternoon.

"My, my, my," he said. "Is this *the* Henry Burton? Henry the white man's Burton? 'S'appenin' my brother? Lookin' for work?"

"Not yet, Reverend," I said. "But I do need your help on something."

"You need *my* help on some *thang*," Luther Charles's first move, of course, would be to try to *race* me. He had done well for himself, playing King of the Negroes—but he knew that his reputation among those who had actually been there would never be what it was among those who'd come later. The old-timers maintained a discreet silence when asked about him, especially when asked by white journalists.

"If you need *my* help," he went on, "must be something awful big, awful big. I can't imagine that you would need my assistance with the *community* up there. Not many brothers up there in the *White* mountains. Henry—whatever could it be?"

I told him. "Ahhh," he said. "Foreign affairs. Lithuania." He massaged every word. "Henry, tell me: all them honkies gone plumb crazy? Takin' down your boy for *pussy*?" He said "pussy" with the same resonant portent as the word "community"—he didn't have a great preaching voice; it was mid-level and sort of scratchy, but he did have all the preacher's tools. "Imagine: them pale scrawny crazy fuckers rulin' the world and us doin' the laundry—it just don't figure. Why ain't they doin' *our* laundry? It's science, Henry. They do technology. That's their voodoo. And that's about *all* they got. If you need to invent something, call a European. If you need to lead or love or lift someone, phone a *brother*. Though I would guess Mr. Stanton is not deficient in the *love* department. Just like your grandpappy, Henry. In fact, just exactly like your grandpappy. I understand the governor likes his ladies. . . . melanin-enriched."

That stopped me. He couldn't know about the McCollister girl. I had to say something—and fast, before he picked up on my hesitation. "Better full-strength," I said, "than melanin-deprived. My daddy always said that you personally were the reason why blondes had more fun."

"Your daddy said that? He should talk. Your sickly paleness is testimony to his own proclivities. You hear from him, Henry?"

"Sure. He writes."

"I miss the sonofabitch—I could always identify with your pop, prodigal son and all," he said. "I have a weakness for prodigality, boy. If you want to consider a return to the fold, there might be room in my rainbow for a staffer of your shade."

Imprisonment. For an instant, I wondered if the penalty for picking a disgraced contender would be slow time in interest-group hell. I felt sick, and terrified. "Reverend, let's talk about Lithuania."

"He called me a mean-spirited nigger?"

"A disgruntled temporary driver with an ax to grind says the governor called you a mean-spirited nigger."

"You work for a guy goes 'round callin' people mean-spirited niggers? What's he call you?"

"Reverend, you think I'd work for someone like that?" A set-up line: what an idiot I was.

"Anything to pretend you ain't what you is."

"Oh Jesus, Luther. Get over it. Are you gonna make a fool of yourself yet again, blowin' up this bullshit into a racial incident? There's no leverage for you here. We're losing. You could, just for once, do the right thing. Bank it. Then you'd have this tiny decency deposit to draw on next time you feel the need to be an asshole."

"All right, Henry," he said. Just like that. "I won't bust your chops no more. But this is a debit in your own bank, a withdrawal from your Luther account. Cost you someday, plus interest."

Stanton came in about five, steaming. I told him I'd taken care of Luther. He grunted. "Where's the shitbird?" He asked.

"In your suite."

We walked down to the end of the hall. People said hello along the way, but the governor didn't respond. All the varnish was off now. "I can't fucking believe, in the midst of all this shit, I gotta massage this fucking creep. Who hired him anyway? Where'd he come from? I'm gonna kill Lieberman, fucking murder him."

We walked into the suite. Susan was there, talking quietly with Tibor Lizickis. He was pale and jittery, with light brown hair and a wispy mustache; a pathetic specimen. "Jack," Susan said, sensing his mood immediately and knowing what to do, "Tibor was just telling me about how the Russians took his father away. He was a bus driver. He had an accident, and they just—took him . . . away."

Stanton shed his overcoat. I could see that he'd sweated through his shirt. His eyes softened. "And you never saw him again?" He asked.

"No, Gowherenaw," he said. "They take him Siberia."

"And how old were you?"

"Six year."

Stanton moved toward him. There was a logistical problem. Lizickis and Susan were sitting on the couch, facing each other. The governor wanted to get in as close as possible—touching range—but he couldn't usurp Susan's position and he couldn't crouch next to Lizickis because there was a flimsy glass coffee table in the way. The coffee table would be hard to push aside; it was surrounded by comfortable chairs and a wall. He measured all this as he moved forward, making rapid geo-emotional calculations. It was Jack Stanton's vision of hell: desperately needing to make a connection but locked in a no-touch zone. He came in behind Lizickis and crouched down, propping himself on the arm of the sofa; the Lithuanian, now a Stanton sandwich, half turned toward the governor and away from Susan. "That must have been awful for you," Jack Stanton said. "Just awful. And I can understand why you'd be so intent on wanting to raise this isssue."

"Russians are pee-igs," Lizickis said, reddening. "Pee-igs."

Stanton, somehow, reached his right hand around the arm of the sofa and patted Lizickis on the shoulder. "I know, I know and I *will* do something about this. I just haven't had the chance. You know all hell has broken loose in this campaign."

"Oh, yess, Cashmere—I hear about."

Susan rolled her eyes.

"But I promise you, Tibor," Stanton continued. "And this is a solemn promise—that your father will not be forgotten. If the voters of New Hampshire allow me to continue in this race, and if, in their wisdom, the American people elect me president—I will *liberate* Lithuania."

"But you no mention now?"

"I will mention now. Tonight. I promise. But if I do, you will tell the newspaper editor that you were mistaken, that you were angry and were acting out of pique?"

"Out of what? Pee-ig?"

"You were very angry."

"Oh yes, wery angry."

He had Tibor up now, and was shepherding him toward the door, hand on his arm, soothing him. "I know what it's like to lose a father, Tibor, but not the way you did. I can't imagine your loss, your sense of rage. You must understand it's difficult for Americans—we've been so lucky. We have so much to learn from you. I really appreciate your coming. I really appreciate your bringing this to my atten— Henry, see that Mr. Lizickis gets home okay. 'Bye. . . ."

He slammed the door.

The last debate of the New Hampshire primary was held at a Catholic girls school. It would be an auditorium debate, with a live audience—good for us. Stanton always worked better to people than to cameras. There were greenrooms for this one, but no one used them. The candidates gravitated toward the brightly lit cinder-block hallway. This would be their last group appearance. They knew one another now, were fascinated and disgusted by each other; they would look back on this as a period of intensity and absurdity, sort of like a brief, disastrous marriage. There would be a bond. They would always have New Hampshire.

"Well, Jack," Bart Nilson said. "Guess this is it."

Stanton nodded. Charlie Martin came over, wearing a tie with little hot-air balloons on it. "Kinda gettin' used to the folks up here."

"They're just great," Stanton agreed. "Even after all the shit, they've been just great. They really listened. They really cared about the issues. I was just out in LA, and it was like a different country. They aren't havin' this election out there."

And now—a first!—Lawrence Harris approached, looking prohibitively academic. He was wearing a brown herringbone jacket, a tattersall shirt and forest-green knit tie; his reading glasses dangled from a lanyard around his neck. "Well, mates," he said. "Our last tango."

I could see Stanton's jaw tighten. Harris actually reached up and patted him on the back. "I just wanted to tell you fellows what a memorable experience it's been for me."

"Yeah," Charlie Martin said. "It's like we were lost in the Andes or something—the plane went down in this strange tribal culture where the only thing they care about is politics."

"Then again," Stanton said, checking out Martin carefully, "maybe we're the Donner party."

"Well," Harris said, breaking off, his work here done. "I just hope we'll all be able to unite when this is over. I think it will be very important to have a united party if we're going to win in the fall and set about the difficult work of getting the fiscal situation under control."

"Larry, I'm sure whichever of us wins the nomination will be honored to have your support," said Bart Nilson, with a deftness I'd not anticipated. Harris sniffed, grinned uneasily, retreated.

Stanton and Nilson walked together down the cinder-block hall. "Bart," Stanton said, his arm resting gently on the older man's shoulders. "Whichever way this comes out, when it's over—I'm with you. We work as a team, far as I'm concerned."

Nilson stopped, looked at Stanton. "Jack," he said. "I've been a loyal Democrat all my life, always voted the party line—but if that bloodless prick wins the nomination, I'll stay home in November."

"This is a great country, Bart," Jack Stanton said with a smile, "and 'less I miss my guess, if *that* boy's gonna' win the nomination of *this* party, he's gonna have to learn a few things about the folks."

"Pay good money to see him get that education," Nilson said.

"May be able to see it for free," Stanton said.

The candidates stood at walnut podiums in front of a deep, rich burgundy velvet curtain. It was nicer than the usual banal TV-station blue. That—plus the audience, plus the climactic nature of the event—added a depth and resonance to the proceedings; all four of the candidates seemed larger than usual, almost presidential. Especially Jack Stanton, who was on a mission that night. He took care of Tibor Lizickis in the first ten minutes. The opening question was What are the three main challenges facing the next president? The economy, of course; crime, certainly. But instead of health care, which normally would have come next, he drifted into America's place in the world. "We must provide leadership. The Cold War may be over, but challenges remain. We must encourage Russia to continue its path to partnership in the Western alliance—and we must make sure that the Russians know that partnership will not be complete until they take the final steps to disengage from their former republics, especially the Baltic republics. We must be sure that Russian troops are no longer stationed in Latvia, in Estonia, in Lithuania. And of course, there's other pressing business to take care of back home—health care—"

"Hey, Jack," Charlie Martin interrupted. "You gonna hog the whole show?" Titters from the audience.

"Jack, Jack—*focus,*" Susan whispered. We were sitting in a green-room, just offstage; the two of us and Danny Scanlon. "Take it bit by bit," Susan said. "You can't do it all in one bite."

He seemed to hear her; he pulled back. He let Charlie Martin get lost in health care, and Bart Nilson do his New Deal Redux number for a sad last time. Bart was aiming it at Larry Harris, digging it at him, talking about the need for compassionate government, a government that would meet the needs of the people. Harris was shifting impatiently, one podium to his left; he was pursing his lips. The smart move was to let the old guy have his valedictory.

"Senator, if I may," Harris interrupted.

Susan grabbed my hand. "*Good!*" she said.

"Senator," Lawrence Harris intoned, head tilted back, eyes almost closed. "We would all like to do many things. I, for example, would have loved to play shortstop for the Red Sox. But that was not a realistic wish on my part—I'm left-handed. You can't have a left-handed shortstop." The joke fell flat. Harris didn't seem to notice. He would teach us now, tell us about reality. "The reality is, we can't afford to be as compassionate as we'd like.

"The reality is, we've been spending far too much for far too long.

"The reality is, if we're going to leave a better world for our grandchildren, the American people are going to have to live with some pain. Sacrifices will have to be made."

"Larry, you gotta be *kidding,*" said a familiar voice.

"Excuse me, Governor Stanton?"

"I mean, I know you're from up here and you're more popular than a Christmas turkey and all, but I've got to wonder just what state you've been livin' in. I mean, the state I've been travelin' in—

we've all been practically livin' here these past few months—you go anywhere in this state, and you see folks who've had a great deal of personal experience, *recent* personal experience, with pain. I don't know if the word's reached you up there at Dartmouth yet, but we've got a recession goin' on here in New Hampshire. Folks are hurtin'. They're losin' their jobs, losin' their homes. Senator, are *those* the folks you're sayin' gotta learn to sacrifice? Just what else you want them to give up?"

"Governor—"

"Now, Larry, you just let me finish. Then you can go on with Economics 101." Laughter. The crowd—Harris's crowd—was with us now. "I don't mean to make light of what you're saying. We all know you've got a point. Republicans been runnin' deficits like a bunch of drunken sailors for a decade. We've gotta do something about that for sure. But we've got to fix this economy first. You keep on talkin' about our grandchildren—and we're all concerned about them. But what about the *parents* of our grandchildren? We just gonna cut them loose, let 'em drift? Larry, tell us about your plans for *them*."

No applause, but a buzzing. "I think they're looking for a leader," Harris said, looking directly at Stanton. "I think they're looking for someone who is decent, honorable, someone they can *trust*." A scattering of applause, but also a few hisses.

"Cheap," Susan said. But not ineffective. I gave our boy the decision on points, but who could say? Susan was making the same calculations. "We won the hall and the TV audience," she whispered, "but Harris probably took the bite."

Right. Stanton's case against Harris, succinct and deadly as it seemed in real life, was too long, too complicated to communicate in a two-minute spot on the evening news, especially in the standard "sparks flew among the candidates" debate wrap that broadcast scorps inevitably favored. In fact, Stanton might even come off looking petulant, petty: they'd go with the governor's "Economics 101" bite—and with Harris's "decent, honorable" riff. Harris would come off stable, straight, while reinforcing our decency problem.

"Shitty prep," Susan said.

"You think he would've *let* us prep him?" I said, defensively.

"A-any p-punch—" Danny stammered.

"Shoosh!" Susan said, flashing a stern look at him. Danny recoiled, as if he'd been shot, and Susan quickly relented, ashamed. "Danny, I'm sorry . . . go ahead."

"A-any p-punch he th-threw woulda been c-countered," Danny said, seeming to assume Susan Stanton would have the same weakness for late-night sportsblab as the governor. "He w-wins it on my scorec-c-card 'c-cause he th-threw a punch for the p-people. C-can't play rope-a-dope n-now."

Susan inhaled sharply and hugged Danny, burying her head in his neck. "No. You're right, Danny," she said, pulling back, putting her hand, full, flat on his cheek. "You're right, honey. We can't play rope-a-dope now."

Meanwhile, onstage, the storm subsided. Everyone said what he always said. The closing statements went about as expected—until Charlie Martin, who was last. "Our party has a grand tradition," he said, with a stentorian seriousness that did not quite make it. "A tradition of energy, compassion and honor. We need a candidate, a standard-bearer, who is energetic, compassionate and honorable. I ask you, my fellow Americans, to make the following judgment: Which among us has the energy, the compassion and the honor to serve and to lead?"

I could see where this was headed. So could Susan. "Uh-oh," she said.

"Senator Nilson is a distinguished Democrat. I am proud to call him my friend." Martin paused and for an instant I hoped he wouldn't pull the trigger. No such luck. "He's had a long and distinguished career—but does he have the *energy* to take this battle to the Republicans? As for Senator Harris, I know he's a neighbor of yours. He and I served together in the Senate. I know the quality of his mind. And, as president, I would want him very close by; I would depend on his advice. But his is an academic intelligence. It needs to be leavened by practicality. And Jack Stanton." He paused again—and again, I had a twinge of hope: he'd only *implied* Harris's lack of compassion. There was a chance he'd be equally cautious with us. He wouldn't want to get too graphic—and he didn't, which made it all the more brutal. "Now, Governor Stanton, we all know, is energetic and compassionate and intelligent—and he has been the victim of some questionable charges in this campaign, *very* questionable charges. But even if you believe that he has been unjustly slandered, even if you believe he is an honorable man, we must, as Democrats, make a practical judgment. Is he damaged goods?" I think I gasped: it was so stark. "Would he be able to make the best possible case against the Republicans, or would he be too busy defending himself against an incumbent—and a party—that hasn't been shy about using any and all available weapons in the past."

"Sucker p-punch," Danny said.

Susan shook her head, shrugged, and began to wander out into the hallway to greet Jack when he came off. As it happened, Charlie Martin was off first—Jack Stanton was lingering, as always, reaching down into the audience to shake hands—and Susan grabbed the senator by the arm, smiling sweetly. "Hey, Charrr-lie," she said. He stopped, gave her a peck on the cheek. "So *that's* how you got all those medals in Vietnam," she said. "What do you get for bayoneting someone in the back? The Double-Cross with oakleaf cluster?"

"Susan, it's part of the game."

"Charlie, it's not a fucking game."

Stanton came last. He pushed Susan back into our greenroom and closed the door. He slammed his fist on the top of a chair. "I just can't get a clean shot," he said.

"You did g-good, G-governor," Danny said. "You t-told 'im."

"Yeah, but I took some, too." He turned to Susan. "Was it worth the risk?"

"What've you got to lose?" She replied, coolly. But then, sensing his distress, she added, "You couldn't have said it any better than you did. Someone had to. I'm glad it was you."

My turn. "Martin was coming at you, no matter what. It's probably a good thing you took a poke at Harris—shows you can still do some damage. The scorps may have some second thoughts about your viability."

If only I believed that. I was exhausted, totally wiped that Saturday. It was a beautiful day, a sudden thaw. There was a Carolina breeze; everything was dripping, melting. But Charlie Martin had taken it out of me. His argument sounded too plausible for comfort. "Oh for Chrissakes, Henri—you are too fuckin' literal," Richard said as we speed-walked—there was no other way with Richard—from the hotel down to our campaign headquarters on Main Street. It was a good mile or so, but there was the sense now that our work was pretty much done; there was nothing more to do. We were killing time. We walked past a scruffy row of fender and lube shops. "No one gives a shit about closing statements, Henri," Richard said. "By the time that stupid fuckin' hippie kamikaze unloaded, only *God* was watchin' the show. Folks at home were channel-surfin'. Half the folks in the hall were roustin' around, lookin' for their scarfs and galoshes— y'knowhattamean? Anyways, you telling me you never *heard* that argument before? 'Damaged goods' is so old even the small-city scorps ain't writin' it anymore."

"It's one thing for the scorps to write it and another for Charlie Martin to present the world with the biggest, fattest sound bite imaginable," I said. "Y'know, Richard? *Y'knowhattamean?*"

"What is this?" Richard asked. We were near downtown now, moving through clusters of volunteers. Some were standing with signs on street corners; others were working sidewalk tables. "You think only *ugly* girls interested in politics nowadays?" Richard said. "This is like the inverse Miss America contest. You gotta figure the Republicans do better than this, right? They get cheerleaders and prom queens. We get tree huggers and NOW ninnies. We get whole armies of women who look like Lucille." Richard did have fairly mainstream taste, and a fairly constant frustration level.

"Richard, shut the fuck up and look at this," I said. It was, in fact, a remarkable scene. Downtown Manchester was a political street fair. There were clowns and mimes. The Rotary Club was giving away hot dogs. The millionaire vanity candidate was handing out purple balloons with his name on them; there was a Lyndon Larouche sound truck circling, playing Beethoven's Ninth; there were Operation Rescue fanatics waving dead-fetus posters. Harris volunteers were handing out green-and-white pom-poms. A Nilson Dixieland band played in the park facing the Holiday Inn.

"Brigadoon," I said. "By midweek, it'll all be over. Just some techies packing up. By next weekend, half these storefronts'll be empty again."

"I mean," Richard said, oblivious. "Henri—you *assessing* this talent? Pathetic. 'Lo, Tom."

Tom Brokaw was coming the other way—with Richard Cohen, *The Washington Post* columnist, and several other scorps. "Hey, Jemmons, you got numbers?" Brokaw asked.

"Steady as she goes," Richard said. "You?"

"Hear the *Globe* track has you up nudging twenty again. . . ."

"And Harris?"

"Thirty-five or so . . ."

"That boy's only gettin' one outta three in his home state with half a ton a trash on our head. Wait till we get him down home."

"You gonna make it down home?" Cohen asked.

"Well, who the fuck else gonna make it?" Richard snapped.

"Ozio?"

"In the South, in the *South*?" Richard shrieked. "You talk about *Orlando* down home, they think you talkin' 'bout Disney World. You got any other hot ideas?"

Cohen shrugged and smiled, palms up. We moved on. "Jeez," Richard said. "Heavy fucking lifting. It's like goin' through life carryin' Libby Holden on your back. And they think we don't *earn* our money."

"The *Globe* number—Leon's showing more than that," I said. Leon was, in fact, showing us moving again after the debate.

"A bump, a bumplet, a sta-tis-tical hiccup: we're still fucked, Henri."

"What do we need?" I asked as we passed Martin headquarters, which was overflowing with student volunteers. Several dozen college kids were milling on the sidewalk around a very attractive blonde who had a street map and a megaphone. She was giving out assignments. Richard gawked at the blonde. She smiled back at him. "Listen, honey, you wanta learn about the intricacies a' politics?" he asked. She shook her head slowly, sexily, and blew Richard a kiss.

"What do we need?" I asked again.

"I'm smitten," he said. "Fuckin' hippie has the best-lookin' talent—wouldn't ya know it? I'd take that girl door-to-door in a hot-flash, we'd push every doorbell in town."

"Richard, for Chrissake." We were stopped at a red light; a Harris station wagon sped past, slushing us pretty bad.

"Fuck you, asshole!" Richard shouted, then, to me he said, "We need one outta four, long as Natural Forces stays under forty and no one comes up behind us. We can limp our sorry asses outta here with twenty-five—and we're nowhere near that."

"Leon has us twenty-one on a three-day track," I said, assaying an argument I didn't quite believe, "which means last night and this morning had to be near twenty-five."

"And sample size?" Richard said. "You call four people. One of them giggles like a heathen and says, 'Well, that redneck sonofabitch sure tucked it to ol' Professor Perfect las' night. Mebbe I'm for *him*.' You think that means something? Call my broker. He'll sell you all sorts of shit."

Our headquarters, halfway down the next block, wasn't nearly as bad as I'd feared. It was alive, every bit as alive as Martin's had been. And a better sort of crowd: student vols in plaid flannel and jeans mixed with older folks in union and tavern windbreakers. "Cross between a Nirvana concert and Tuesday-night bowling league," Richard said. "Not bad. Not fucking bad at all, for a cripple."

Brad Lieberman sat at a desk in the front, working a phone, handing out piles of literature and xeroxed neighborhood maps to a line of coordinators. He waved to us, gave a thumbs-up. We squeezed past the pegboard partitions behind Brad to the larger back room, which had three long rows of tables with telephones and thirty people working them. Off to the side was another table with two large coffee urns and dozens of boxes of doughnuts, cascading, half open, half eaten. Interesting people were working the phones. Bill Johnson was back there, as well as several of the Gang of Five. And Momma, puffing Slims and radiating cheap perfume from the middle of a row, her raven beehive sticking up like a textile-factory bobbin—all of them working down lists of people who'd been called at least once in the past month. I went over to Johnson when he put down the receiver. "How's it goin'?"

"Twos and threes," he shrugged. "We ain't lightin' it up."

"No fours?"

"Shitload of fours. But you gotta expect that. Count every hangup a four. Where's the candidate?"

"At the mall," I said. "He's just gonna stand there and work the mall all day, if you can believe it."

"No touring?"

"He said every minute in the van is a minute wasted. He figures he'll get a steady flow all day this way—"

"He's a fucking horse," Johnson said. "Always was."

Richard came over. "Henri, you ain't lived till you heard Momma work a phone. 'This is Mary-Pat Stanton, the candidate's momma. *Now you gonna vote for mah boy or not?*' Hot shit!"

"Richard," I said, getting sort of excited now, "let's get Ken Spiegelman off the phone and see if he can give us something for the candidate to say on the telethon tonight about health care." Spiegelman was a Gang of Five member from the University of Chicago. He was young, slick, accessible—too young for treasury secretary but building his portfolio.

"Why, that's just *brilliant,* Henri," Richard said, diving into the middle of Momma's row and retrieving her. "We say the exact right twenty-five words 'bout health care tonight, and we'll just . . . walk *away* with this thing. Right? I got a better idea."

He wrapped an arm around Momma, cupped his hands: "HEY EV-ER'body, listen UP! Best-lookin' woman in the room got somethin' to say. Go 'head now, Momma. Gwon stand up on this here chair."

Momma didn't need much prodding. She was wearing a flagrant orange-and-white State U. tracksuit. "Y'all havin' *fun*?" she croaked, and she smiled, her big, broad lipstick-and-mascara face bursting into utter glee. "Wal, listen. Ah *know* you workin' hard foh mah Jackie, an' he's the best a momma could have, and y'alls the best friends our family could have, an' ah ain't got no highfalutin' talk like Mr. Senator Lawrence Harris." There were hoots and whistles. "But in mah book, y'alls are just EX-CEPTIONAL. With a gang lahk this, we could do serious *damage* in a roadhouse—y'get me, Jemmons? We could jus' rip *up* a joint."

"Momma, I was thirty years older, I'd be lickin' your ear!" Richard said, playing to the crowd—which roared.

"And ah'd be squealin' like a pig," Momma said, doubling over, hands on her knees. I had to admit: I'd never fully appreciated Momma until that moment. I'd considered her something of an em-barrassment, a joke. But she had everyone in that room up now, and feeling good. Every face was beaming. She was her son's mother.

"Now listen up y'all. Ah'm a-gonna set down now, 'fore ah fall down. But ah love ya, and ah'll never forget ya. Win or lose, come rain or come shine, ain't this just GRAND!" She started down, to whoops and applause, then went up again: "Now, jus' a second, jus' a second. Ah'm a-listenin' to what ah just said—and ah would like to *amend* it a little—okay, Jemmons?"

"Have at it, Momma," he said.

"The lose part," she said. "Ah didn't mean to say that—win or lose. Mah boy ain't gonna *lose*. You folks ain't gonna *lose*. Ah don't see a loser in this here room. And ah've seen more than a few losers in mah sorry ol' life." The place was rocking, hoots and whistles. "But mah Jackie ain't no loser, and y'alls his friends and you ain't losers neither. So listen up: We are going to *win* this thing. We are gonna steal this thing right out from under Mr. Senator Lawrence Harris's nose. Then we gonna go on down home and *whip* his sorry butt. And that's all ah'm a-gonna say."

VI

We lost New Hampshire, but not badly. It rained Election Day, and that was good for us. Stanton voters proved to be as devoted to the candidate as he had been to them—in fact, according to the exit polls, an implausible number said the deciding factor was that they'd actually *met* the governor. And so we did somewhat better than Richard's one in four; our 29 percent was more than Nilson and Martin combined. Harris won, of course; but he could manage no more than 38 percent in his home state, which gave us hope.

Election Day itself was strange, empty. We slept in. We packed our bags. We went to the movies. We saw *Wayne's World*. Daisy and I held hands; Richard jiggled; Lucille—an unexpected delight—had a rowdy and infectious laugh. Halfway through the movie, I went out into the lobby and called Brad Lieberman. The first wave of exit polling was coming in. "We're alive," he said.

I went back in, whispered the results to Daisy on my left and Richard on my right. Daisy squeezed my hand and stuck her nose in my ear. "No Caribbean this week," she whispered.

"Disappointed?"

"Yes—and no."

We shared an umbrella walking back across the asphalt expanse to the Hampton Inn. We walked with our arms around each other, very close and comfortable. Richard and Lucille went ahead, separately, their black umbrellas bobbing in the wind. Mountains of snow were stacked around the light poles; everything was gray and white. "I'm beginning to feel nostalgic," I said. "We've lived our lives around this parking lot. I can't count the number of times I looked out over at the multiplex and wished I was at the movies."

"And I can't remember them ever having a Werner Herzog," Daisy teased.

"And all the nights I had to slog across over there and retrieve the candidate from Danny's Dunkin' Donuts. You wonder what Danny's going to do with himself now."

"I wonder what the candidate's going to do with himself now," she said, "without Danny's Dunkin' Donuts."

We stopped just outside the lobby door, under the marquee, but still under the umbrella and turned to each other, and kissed. It was a serious kiss, our first public display of affection.

"Henry?" she said, meaning: Did that mean what I think it meant?

"Yes," I said. It did.

She looked at me, her eyes widened; she put her hand on my cheek. "What are we going to have him say tonight?" she asked.

"That it was a moral victory."

"Henry?"

I looked at her.

"Do you think the telethon helped us any?"

"No," I said. "He did it by sheer force of will. He did it on Saturday, standing at the mall all day. He did it on Sunday and Monday. I mean, have you ever seen anybody do one-on-one like that? But the telethon wasn't a bad idea," I added quickly, remembering that it had been hers.

"Henry?" she said. "Is this . . ."

"I think so."

". . . or are we just relieved that we won?"

"We didn't win."

"We didn't die," she said. "So we won."

"We better go inside."

She kissed me again, quickly, open-mouthed, on the lips.

.   .   .

Jack and Susan were both up in the suite working the phones, thanking local supporters. "I will never forget this," Jack said, over and over. "I will always remember what you did for us here."

Susan hugged me. It was a big day for hugs.

Jack was off the phone now. He came over and shook my hand. He was wearing a white shirt, suit pants, no shoes. "Henry, I'll admit it: last night, I thought we were dead."

"Well, Leon's last track didn't help much," I said.

"He couldn't measure intensity," he said. "Our folks just felt more strongly about this election."

"That's because of you, sir."

The governor ambled over to the table. There was a fruit platter and some sandwiches. "*Don't!*" Susan said. "You fell off the wall, you didn't crack—but you're still looking like Humpty-Dumpty."

She said this lightly, but with an edge. He narrowed his eyes, and took some grapes. "Henry, how early can we get on and off, and go home?" he asked.

"Polls close at eight," I said. "You've got to stay and do the nets. You want to do *Nightline*?"

"No!" Susan said. "And no press conference. Those jerks had us buried, all of them. Let 'em stew in it."

"Well, we aren't gonna be able to make 'em disappear," Stanton said.

"They weren't able to make *you* disappear either," she said. "And so they'll have to come to terms with that. We're going to tighten this up now, Henry. We've got a new set of priorities. We'll do local TVs first, networks second, local pencils third, national pencils last."

"And pundits never?" Stanton laughed. "C'mon, they're there. We can pick and choose. Henry, get Richard and Daisy and all—get 'em here 'bout six. We'll thrash this out. Also, have Laurene schedule the nets. We'll do 'em all tonight. We'll do the morning shows from Mammoth Falls tomorrow, from the Mansion—okay?" He looked over at Susan; she nodded. "And okay, Mrs. Stanton—no press conference. Henry, y'all come on the plane with us. Tell Richard and Arlen and Leon, and whoever else we got here to stick around and work spin. Then get their selves down to Mammoth Falls by tomorrow night. Y'know, I'm gonna miss this place."

"So many wonderful things happened to your reputation here," she said.

"No, really," he said. "It was okay. It was a rite of passage. You realize how *amazing* these folks are, voting for me after all this shit? There was a time, last night, it was getting on toward ten o'clock, and I was working—what?—my eighth restaurant, table to table? And I knew most of these damn people wouldn't be voting for me—hell, half of them wouldn't be voting, period. And I come to this table, two couples 'bout our age—teachers, lawyers, something like that—havin' dessert, getting ready to split the bill. Back home, the kind of folks that would've been friends of ours. Up here, they're gonna be voting Harris without even thinkin' about it. One of the women teaches preschool. She asks about Head Start. And y'know, we just start *talkin'* about it. I forgot we were in a campaign, damn near sat down and had a cup of coffee with 'em. She was smart. You could tell she was good at what she did. And I told her about some of the things we'd been messin' with down home."

"Tish Miller's thing," Susan said.

"Yeah," Stanton said, moving over to the wing chair where Susan was sitting, leaning down, putting his hands on her shoulders, staring her in the eye. "Tish Miller's one of *mine*—inspirational model, right, sweetheart?"

"Okay, okay."

"Anyhow, this woman says to me, 'Governor, from all I've heard and read during this campaign, I'da never guessed you knew or cared about this stuff.' "

"I wonder why," Susan said.

"No, it's not just them—not just the scorps," he said. "It's us. It's me. We gotta figure out how to communicate what we *love* about what we do. We've gotta show them we're doin' this not for ambition or glory."

"Not *just*," Susan said, but softer. She was with him now.

"Not just, not only—but because we love *doin'* for the folks, finding things that work. We gotta think about how we can do that—right, Henry? Because, you know what? I would be willing to bet you anything, I *got* that woman's vote today."

"Now all you have to do," Susan said, "is personally meet and greet the other two hundred fifty million Americans."

"Fine with me," Jack Stanton said. "But first, I want to go home."

Home. We landed in deep night. There was no moon. There was, however, a soft breeze coming up from the Gulf, carrying with it a moist hint of spring. I stood by the river for a moment before going up to my apartment. The river seemed familiar, an old acquaintance; it flowed quickly, silently, as if it were a well-oiled piece of machinery, doing its job. My apartment was less familiar. I hadn't slept there in a week, but it seemed much longer. The place felt dusty, moldy. Several of the plants along the river window had died. I turned on the television. CNN was telling it our way. We were alive, and Lawrence Harris was breathing more life in us yet: his sound bite was pompous, trite. "The people of New Hampshire have sent the message that they are ready for fiscally responsible governance," he said, without a hint of a smile. "I expect the rest of the American people will respond favorably to this message as we move along." Then the clincher: "I think we are growing up as a nation."

Lovely. I opened the refrigerator and winced; something had gone bad. This presented me with several decisions. Clean the fridge or let it fester? A Perrier or that lone bottle of Heineken? Fester. Heineken. My own personal victory party. I lay down on the bed, watched CNN some more. It was pundit time. Several Washington scorps were talking about the "weak" Democratic field and who would save it. Ozio's non-write-in campaign had fizzled in New Hampshire. They showed a clip of the governor of New York rushing into or out of a building. He seemed perturbed. "I never asked for it, I never encouraged it," he said, "so why should I comment on it?" And so, the anchor wondered, If not Ozio, who? Larkin? Someone was saying *very* definitively that Larkin would soon jump in. "You don't know anything," I told the television and shut it off.

I noticed the collection of Alice Munro stories I'd bought a month earlier splayed open on the coffee table across the room. Had I left it like that? Cruel and unusual punishment for a book (I hated broken spines; I was willing to endure personal discomfort to maintain the integrity of a spine). It seemed a long way to go, but I got up and walked across the room. The book had been left open to a story called "Bardon Bus." I began to read the first paragraph in the half-light; it was bold and yet wistful—perfect. I snapped on the reading light, lay down lengthwise on the couch facing the river and read myself to sleep there.

Jack Stanton woke me in the morning, banging on the door. "Henry! Henry! Rise and shine!" He was wearing a yellow knit shirt, leather jacket, jeans and cowboy boots. It was eight o'clock. "Jeez, you look a sight," he said. "Fell asleep in your clothes, huh? Didn't watch me, all fresh and confident, on the morning shows? Well, get on up. We're going for a drive, goin' down to Grace Junction. Hey, look—I even brought you breakfast: a banana, an apple, black coffee—all your favorites."

"Why Grace Junction?"

"Dunno. Take a drive. See some country. See Momma. C'mon, Henry. Get yourself showered and shaved. I'll just sit here, read the paper, make some calls."

The Bronco was downstairs, Uncle Charlie lounging in the back. I rode shotgun; the governor drove—and sang. He had the radio turned way up. He sang tentatively on the new songs, more confidently on the oldies. He turned the radio down when "Achy Breaky Heart" (which was just gathering steam about then) came on. "I hate that goddamn song," he said. "I have always hated gimmick songs, even when I was a kid—'Purple People Eater,' 'How Much Is That Doggie in the Window,' the Singing Nun. People should have more respect for music than that. You know, it's like politics. You should always have respect for what you're doing, respect the ceremonies and rituals, respect the audience."

He was certainly feeling chipper. He drove south on the interstate about thirty miles, sticking right on the speed limit, then turned west on a two-lane state road toward Grace Junction. It was an uncomfortable sort of day. The sun was warm, but the air was cold—the wind had shifted around north and carried with it memories of New Hampshire. The governor couldn't find the right mix. He lowered the windows, and it got cold. He raised the windows and it got stuffy. When he lowered the window just a little, the whistling made it hard to hear the music. "Henry," he said, snapping off the radio and lowering the windows about ten miles out from Grace Junction. "I'm gonna go over Doc Hastings', get some blood pulled. I think it's about time we dealt with the McCollister situation."

I'd been dreading this moment. Fat Willie had been there in New Hampshire, in the back of my mind. He would blindside me whenever I began to feel optimistic (when there was no cause for optimism, the McCollister situation seemed moot—a pragmatic callousness I did not admire in myself). But I never really thought it through. It was too awful. I never seemed able to fix on it, to analyze it, to make a judgment. Sitting there, beginning to freeze a little in the Bronco, I suddenly realized why: I could not allow myself to believe that Jack Stanton would take advantage of Fat Willie's teenage daughter; and yet I couldn't believe he hadn't.

"Deal with it?" I asked.

"Tomorrow, I want you and Howard to go over there, to Fat Willie's, and lean on him a little," the governor said. "Not really *lean* on him—but tell him we have to resolve this thing, establish paternity. Tell him we want the girl to have an amniocentesis. Explain what that means, in detail. Tell him it's a long needle through the belly button. Tell him to explain that to Loretta. Henry, these aren't sophisticated people. They're good people, but not sophisticated. I think you present this to them, tell them that I am insisting on it, that I had my blood pulled already. Chances are, the girl will back off her claim."

"Why me?" I said, shivering. "Is it because I'm—"

"It's because Willie chose you," he said. "*I* didn't. I can't help it if he can't see past skin color."

"Maybe he just thought I'd be sympathetic," I said, knowing that was only part of the truth.

"Look, you don't have to say anything. Howard knows what to say. But you should be there, since he came to you."

I turned toward the open window. The air was sharp but fresh; it smelled of newly turned soil. We were riding through raw red-clay farmland. It was exotic country; the roadsides were the color of a squeezed fingertip. I remember thinking it must be tough to farm such land. "Governor," I said. "If I'm going to do this, there's something I need to know."

"*I am not the father of that child,*" he said.

Grace Junction was Onawachee County's seat. It had the requisite domed, two-story county-court building on the town square and a gray granite Confederate War Memorial that was particularly grisly: "These, Our Sons, Gave All in Glorious Struggle." There was a tablet for Civil War dead, two more for World War I and II, and a fourth for Vietnam, which was practically empty—leaving plenty of space for the next war. The governor's father, William H. Stanton, was listed among the World War II dead, though he had never lived in Grace Junction.

The square around the court building was half populated now—law offices and the Willows Funeral Home on the north side; Presley Drugs and the Florida (the most popular, and political, café in town) on the west. The south had several thrift shops and a gaping hole where Zucker's furniture had once been; the east side had Meyer's Stride-Rite Shoes, the Modest Values dress shop and more vacant storefronts. Despite the strong sense that time had passed it by, this was a fairly pleasant square, as such places go: the sidewalks were red brick, set in a herringbone pattern; the courthouse was framed by live oaks. Daffodils were blooming now; spring was coming. The town seemed green, lived-in—not stark or defeated, as so many rural towns were.

We entered town from the east, through Black Town, which was mostly shotgun shacks and cinder-block convenience stores, set in a web of train tracks, dilapidated garages and auto repair shops. The sawmills—mostly closed now—were on the south side of town. White folks lived on the north and west; rich folks north, rednecks west. Momma lived on the west side, in a tan clapboard house on a double lot. The governor had offered her a new house in Mammoth Falls, a brick house on the north side of Grace Junction—anything she wanted—but she was a creature of her place and wanted to stay put. "The gals wouldn't know where to come for our Wednesday poker party if I picked up and moved," she said.

Momma was sitting out on the front porch, bundled up in a heavy sweater over her usual State U. tracksuit, when we pulled up. "Hooray, hoo-rah, yeeee-hah!" she said, tugging him down by the neck and planting about an ounce of lipstick on his cheek. "You did it, honey."

"Well, I survived," the governor said. "By the way, what on earth happened to you? You just took off, never said 'bye. When'd you get home, Momma?"

"I left there on Monday. I shoulda stayed, I know. But I was just too nervous, bitin' my fingernails, pacin' the floor, practically drippin' in my britches. I was *intendin'* to stick around, but then I heard a whole bunch of Grace Junction folks was takin' out on Monday, so I went with 'em—Doc Hastings and all."

"Goin' over see Doc now," the governor said. "Henry, Charlie— you guys keep Momma company. We can all meet up at the Florida for lunch."

"I'll come with you," Charlie said. "Got some business with Jerry Conway over at the County Barn. Owes me some money off New Hampshire."

"You take odds?" Momma asked.

"Naw, just straight—fifty bucks on twenty-five percent."

"I did better'n *that,*" Momma said. "Jackie, you makin' your Momma a rich ol' lady."

"I get a cut?" the governor asked.

"I'll give you ten percent on my take in November," she said. "Now, get outtahere. Henry, what's your pleasure? Cup a coffee?"

It was an old-fashioned house, a sane person's house. It probably hadn't changed much since the governor was a boy. The living room was on the left, dining room on the right, with the kitchen behind. The dining room had a solid old mahogany table and chairs, with matching sideboard—good stuff: Momma had come from gentry. There was a dark green horsehair Chesterfield sofa with antimacassars along the wall in the living room, flanked by a La-Z-Boy and a maple rocker with a crocheted seat cushion—all facing an enormous console television, which seemed the only new piece in the house. There were several oak lamp tables with doilies, a magazine rack next to the La-Z-Boy (Momma subscribed to *Time, Good Housekeeping, Sports Illustrated* and the *Smithsonian),* shaggy chocolate wall-to-wall carpeting. There was a mirror on the wall behind the sofa, portraits of her parents on the back wall and a large campaign poster of her son, looking very seventies and glamorous running for attorney general, over the television. We moved on back to the kitchen, which was light and large, and had more photos—Jack as a boy, Jack as a teenager, Uncle Charlie, other folks I didn't recognize.

"You have any pictures of Jack's father?" I asked.

"Over here," she said. "Here's the two of us in Kansas City."

It was a studio shot. They were holding hands, their heads together—lovebirds. She wore a lot of makep back then, too; he had a sort of Ronald Colman look—dark slicked-back hair, pencil mustache. He was in uniform, a private first-class. The governor, it was clear, looked a lot like his mother; he had her nose and mouth.

"So: you did say coffee?" she asked, already pouring some from a Mister Coffee. "'Bout losin' my mind. Take anything?"

"No thanks, just black," I said. "What was he like?"

"Oh, he was just glorious," she said, sitting down at the gray Formica table with chrome legs. "You know the story, right?"

I'd heard the story, but I wanted to hear it from her. "You met at the USO?" I asked.

"Yes sirree," she said. "He was a friend of Charlie's. I was up, visiting Charlie—he was about to ship out. Kansas City was *the* place back then, don't ask me why. But it was just swarmin' with fellas. And so there I was, and Charlie introduced me to Will Stanton—and he asked me to dance. It was a Glen Miller, "Gettin' Sentimental Over You"—or was that Dorsey? Anyway, it just clicked, and I mean clicked, like a lock tumblin'. You only get a few moments of magic in a life, I suspect, and that was mine. He knew it. I knew it. We didn't wait for the formalities, if you know what I mean. But we did get ourselves hitched before he went. Charlie was best man. We had a couple of weeks, long enough for Jackie to get planted."

She paused. "Was that when you worked at Harry Truman's haberdashery?" I asked.

"Oh shit, who told you that? Jackie? Gawd, Henry—let me tell you somethin': kids'll believe anything. Truman's was well bankrupt by the time *this* girl hit town. I mean, he was vice president of the United States by then, fixin' to move on up. People'd point out where his store had been, but it was long gone. I guess I told that to Jackie just to tell him something. He always wanted to know everything there was to know 'bout his daddy, but there wasn't all that much *to* know. I had him for two weeks, and I can't remember two better weeks in my entire life—and then he left, and he died at Iwo. And he's buried somewhere out there. And his son is going to be president of the United States someday."

"And Uncle Charlie, did he win the Congressional Medal of Honor?"

"He won some sort of thing, came home a mess. He lay on that damn couch in the living room, shakin' like a leaf and screamin' in the night. But I think it was Jackie pulled him out—he was devoted to Jackie, like he was his own." She paused. "Y'know, Uncle Charlie isn't really *Uncle* Charlie. He's not my brother—not by blood, least-ways. Momma and Pops inherited him from Daddy's best friend, Junior Treadwell—tree fell on Junior, he was a lumberjack, back when they were lumberin' these woods; then Junior's wife, Johnetta, got womb cancer and died. My folks took him in—I was a little girl. So Charlie's real name is Treadwell, not Malone. But we was raised brother and sister, and my folks did adopt him."

"Tough life," I said.

"Yeah, it was real," Momma said. "Not like now. Up in New Hampshire, I saw all those folks goin' around in goose-down jack-ets—and I was thinkin' to myself, we didn't have nothin' like that at all. We didn't have any *insulation,* y'know? It was just us and life. 'Ac-centuate the positive, e-liminate the negative, and don't mess with Mr. In-between.' People seem to do more things but take less chances nowadays. You mind if I light up?"

"Not at all. You were fabulous up there, in New Hampshire," I said. "You really lifted everyone's spirits—and, believe me, that was some heavy lifting."

"Awww, I was just runnin' my mouth. You know, Henry," she said, lowering her voice, "we used to have separate drinking fountains here in Grace Junction. A lot of us weren't too proud of that, but we didn't say nothin'—till Jackie started eatin' over at the Florida."

"The Florida?"

"Yeah, no kidding. That was Mabel Brockett's place, over in Black Town, before she got big and moved it downtown. That was Jackie's doing, if you want to know the truth. He started eatin' there when he was in high school. Y'know, they were havin' the sit-ins 'bout that time over in Nashville, and Jackie wanted to do *something*, so he sat in at Mabel's, though no one noticed it or gave two shits, a white boy sitting-in in Black Town. Can you imagine? But he knew what he was doing. Mabel was the best damn cook in the piney woods, and Jackie began talkin' her up—in school, you know. He started doin' takeout, takin' orders from his classmates, 'cause none of them had the guts to go on over to Black Town. Anyways, Jackie got this notion: he wants Mabel to cater the Senior Prom. And it became this big deal. They had an election over it—and that election came to be how Grace Junction argued it out over integration."

The phone rang. "Yeah, yeah, we're comin," Momma said. "Henry's been talkin' my ear off." She hung up the phone. "C'mon, son, you ever ride shotgun with a blind ol' lady behind the wheel?"

We took the scenic route into town. She showed me all her friends' houses, the Baptist church where they used to go, the Methodist church where she had her AA meetings, the Assembly of God she went to now. "I'm a Christian, sort of," she said. "I don't drink no more, smoke only a little—when I'm nervous, or I feel like I'm gonna be nervous. But I asked the Lord to forgive my gambling, and my Lord is a forgivin' fellah. He'll let me cheat on everythin' but the drinkin'." We parked in front of Presley's Drugs, down the block from the Florida. "You hear of Sherman Presley?" Momma said. "That was his daddy's pharmacy. Al Presley was the leading seg in town."

"He still run it?" I asked.

"No, he took a heart attack and died," Momma said. "Sherm was long gone, too damn smart to get stuck down here—like Jackie, only mean. So Ruth Ann, Al's daughter, inherited the store. Her husband, Ralph Winter, runs it."

"And how did the Florida move downtown?"

"Well, this wasn't exactly *prime* real estate after Wal-Mart's come in, and Mabel had this built-in clientele, all the kids who'd started in on her chicken and ribs in high school—so she took the leap. If you can believe it, it was the one time Jackie and Sherman Presley ever worked together on somethin'. They both backed her—Sherm, I think, 'cause he wanted to step away from his daddy's seg ways in people's minds. Jackie, 'cause he's Jackie."

It wasn't quite noon, but the Florida was nearly full—and the governor was holding court at a round table in the front corner, next to the window. There was a sign on the wall above the table: JACK STANTON'S TABLE. There was a big, strange hand-painted photo of the governor on the wall, which made him look like a corpse, and smaller photos—of Jack and Susan eating there, of Jack and Momma and Uncle Charlie, of Jack and a wraithlike black woman who had to be Mabel Brockett.

"Is Mabel still around?" I asked Momma as we walked in.

"Naw, her daughter Peetsy-Mae, runnin' it now. HEY, honey, howya doin' sweetie-pie, what'sup, killer?" Momma was working her way down toward Jack's table, shaking hands and blowing kisses to all comers. The crowd was a mix of courthouse and feed-store types. She knew everyone, of course. "Lunch's ON THE HOUSE!" she shouted. "*Jack's* buyin'. Only kiddin'! Only kiddin'! Y'alls oughta buy Jack his meal, given the tourist business gonna be comin' through here when he's president of the United States."

"Sit down, Momma," Jack said, standing up. "Half these folks ain't even gonna vote for me."

"I'll swallow my pride and vote for ya," said a middle-aged man who had the looks of an insurance or farm-equipment salesman—he wore a short-sleeved white shirt with a pocket protector—"if it means more business."

"C'mon, Joe Bob," Jack said. "You ain't voted Democrat since Roosevelt. And it's *always* meant more business, 'spite what the Republicans say."

There was laughter and applause, and we sat down. Doc Hastings was there, but not Charlie. "Where's your uncle?" Momma asked.

"Losin' his fifty dollars back to Jerry and the boys," the governor said. "We'll pick him up on the way out. Doc and me just talkin' 'bout what comes next. Doc thinks we breeze. I'm not so sure."

"You're the class of the field, son," Doc Hastings said. "Name the man that can beat you."

"I dunno," the governor said. "They don't know me. They don't know who I am, and I don't know how to get it across."

Doc Hastings shook his white mane, put his hand on the governor's forearm. "You always figger out a way to get it across, son." Suddenly, he had tears in his eyes. He stuck a long, slim finger behind his small, round glasses, digging out the moisture. The governor wrapped an arm around the old man's shoulders. " 'Scuse me," Doc Hastings said, to me. "I've known this boy too long."

Momma was looking away. "Hey, *Peetsy*," she shouted. "Cain't we get any *service* over here, or we second-class customers?"

The Mansion was smelling of popcorn that night when I arrived for the meeting. I went to the kitchen, where Susan and young Jackie were emptying one bag and sticking another in the microwave. Susan was wearing a Yale sweatshirt and jeans; she had her Coke-bottle glasses on. She looked sort of rabbity and tired but not bad, considering all she'd been through. "No more doughnuts," she said, carrying a bowl of bleached white popcorn over to the counter. "This is now the official snack food of this campaign. Henry, you eat this stuff—you lose weight. It has negative calories." She put her hand on my forearm, kissed my cheek. "Have a taste."

It smelled like popcorn but tasted like chewed-over paper. "You think he'll go for this?" I asked.

"He'll go for anything," she said, "if you provide it in sufficient quantity."

We met in the study. The last time I'd been in that room—and it seemed several years earlier—had been the Sunday night before we went to Los Angeles, the night we found out we were cratering in New Hampshire. The mood was different this time, and so was the room— the furniture had been arranged in a circle, with the governor's armchair in front of the fireplace. This room, like the rest of the Mansion, had an unlived-in, Ethan Allen showroom feel to it—quiet but undistinguished furniture and colors, very pale yellow walls and baby blue carpeting, dark wood breakfront and end tables, a square, lime-green sofa, leather chairs, brass lamps with dark green shades. Richard was already there, Lucille and Howard Ferguson came in together, Dwayne Forrest—the governor's agribusiness pal—was there, Brad Lieberman, Arlen Sporken, Leon Birnbaum, Laurene Robinson, Ken Spiegelman.

"Okay," said the governor, still wearing the yellow shirt and jeans he'd worn to Grace Junction. "Let's do it. I have a few announcements, and then I'll turn this thing over to Howard. Actually, that's the first announcement—Howard's now, officially, our campaign manager; Henry Burton will be his deputy." That was news to me. "We're in a new phase of this thing now. We need to rethink and retool and reorganize a little bit. Dwayne Forrest will be our campaign chairman, which means he'll watch out for the money. And Ken Spiegelman—you all know Ken, right?—has somehow convinced the neocons up at University of Chicago to give him a leave of absence to run issues for us. Okay, Howard."

"All right," Howard said. "First things first. How we hangin', Dwayne?"

Dwayne Forrest was a tall, thin man except for an explosively large stomach. He had a graying crew cut, sharp blue eyes and a beard. He was wearing a tweed jacket, aquamarine chamois shirt (no tie), khakis and Timberland boots. He had the look of a man who dressed, and did, as he pleased. "Well, we're bone-dry now—but we got some stuff cookin'. Now that the campaign's come down home, we'll be doin' a series of twenty-five-dollar cocktail parties and fifty-dollar-a-platers: you'll be eatin' chicken and peas most nights the next month, Governor. We got somethin' set for every state capital in the region. A five-hundred-dollar-a-plater in Atlanta, another in Houston, another here in Mammoth Falls. We're workin' on several big hits in New York, for when that comes around. Meantime, we got some interim cash-flow problems—but nothin' we can't handle. Our friends at Briggs County Bank'll smooth out the bumps."

"Okay," Howard said. "Brad?"

"Dorsey Maxwell's got us a deal on a plane, a seven-twenty-seven—old Southern Airways thing, configured for first class, front and rear," Brad Lieberman said. "Big logistical question now is, you want the Service?"

My mind wandered as they discussed pros and cons of adding Secret Service protection. That stuff, the schedule and the money—I couldn't care less about. In fact, that night it was an effort for me to concentrate on the things I *liked* thinking about—what came next tactically and strategically, the road out from New Hampshire. I was wiped; played out. As I looked around the circle, the people who'd been most involved in New Hampshire all seemed in similar shape—lying back, staring at the ceiling, doodling, yawning. Except for Howard Ferguson, who seemed cool, untired, unreadable, immutable. I wondered if he dreaded the next day's business—the visit to Fat Willie's—as much as I did. I wondered how he'd handle it. I'd known him for six months and didn't know him at all. I found myself wishing I could talk to Daisy about it, ask her advice. I knew she'd be appalled. *I* was appalled. I found myself wishing—for the first time since I'd signed on with Jack Stanton—that I could be someplace else: off in the Caribbean somewhere, with Daisy.

Then, finally, the governor cut off the techie talk. "Richard, we learn anything useful today?"

"Hotline says ol' Natural Forces is shoppin' for a guru. May go with Strunk and Wilson, may go with David Adler. In any case, I guess this ain't no 'classroom exercise' anymore."

"David Adler, huh?" the governor said. "He still in the business?"

"He'll work one or two a cycle—no straight party stuff, just guys he likes, moderates. This might be his sort of gig, high-profile and quirky. But look, either way, this ain't New Hampshire. We are now free to batter the shit out of Harris, hang him with his own words— Arlen and Daisy're already workin' on some spots."

"Governor, this is not rocket science," Arlen Sporken said. "The man has proposed some crazy stuff."

"Basic rule of politics," Richard said. "There are some issues that are so complicated, you never talk about 'em—'cause your opponents can distort your position too easy. I suspect Lawrence Harris has raised nearly every last one of those issues. His head is on a platter."

"Say Adler took Harris on, how would he play it?" the governor asked. He was intrigued by this turn.

"High road—inspirational shit," Richard said. "A nation in crisis, looking for a different kind of politician. David's made his money. He wants to go out a saint. Anyways, he doesn't need to go low road— not so long as he's runnin' against, ah, *you*. Right, Leon?"

Leon shrugged, embarrassed. "Leon?" Susan asked.

"You don't want to know," Leon said. "Okay—two numbers, nationally. Among Democrats. Is Jack Stanton trustworthy enough to be president: thirty-eight percent say no."

"Well, that's not so bad," Lucille said.

"Thirteen percent say yes," Leon continued. "The rest don't know."

The governor, color rising, tried to snag a bowl of popcorn on the floor with his cowboy boot but knocked it over. He looked down, debating whether to squat down and get it. "Amazing those damn things don't just float up in the air, so little to 'em." He looked up, "Okay, Leon, don't keep us in suspense—what's the other number?"

"It's on a series of personal qualities, head-to-head against Harris. 'More thoughtful on the issues,' two thirds haven't got a clue, but the other third, he clobbers you—twenty-four to eight."

"Only eight percent of the American public think I'm thoughtful on the issues?" Stanton asked, a deep red now.

"Only eight percent of Democrats," Leon said. "But your come-back in New Hampshire hasn't really registered yet, and Harris has got problems, too: he's *nowhere* down here. He's at three percent in Georgia, six in North Carolina, thirteen in Florida—approval, that is. Name rec, he's not much more than a third."

"So, Richard, you're him—what do you do?" Susan asked.

"Play regional. He's probably got Maine this weekend. Win Massachusetts, try and establish myself out west—Colorado may not be a bad state for him. Hope to survive Super Tuesday by pulling a Dukakis—picking off enough in south Florida to seem plausible, then pray for a split in Illinois and Michigan. And nail us in the big states back east—New York and Pennsylvania."

"He's not gonna play in Illinois or Michigan," Brad Lieberman said. "You imagine him sellin' auto workers on a gas tax? You think he's ever *met* a black person?"

"We've got to stop him before that, down here," Richard said.

"It's not a question of stopping him," the governor said. "It's a question of starting *us.* I mean, if this is a fair fight, a normal campaign, we can take him out easy. Arlen and Daisy probably got the silver bullet in the can already—am I right?" Arlen nodded, started to speak, but Stanton put up a hand. "But that's not our problem. Our problem is, the American people think I'm an airhead. Now, Arlen, you tell me how we correct that in thirty seconds?"

"Issues spots?"

"Spots are *spots,*" the governor said. "They're like this shitty cardboard popcorn. They don't fill you up. We need to figure out some more basic way to connect."

"You could try some speeches," said Ken Spiegelman, his first foray on our turf. "You could give a series of speeches, real thoughtful speeches, lay out the differences with Harris on taxes, foreign policy. . . ."

"No one would cover them," I said, maybe a little too abruptly. "Actually, it'd be worse than that. The scorps would ignore the substance and use the *fact* of the speeches against us, as a failed ploy, part of the horse race—Stanton trying to compete with the intellectual Professor Harris."

"Anyway, you're not gonna win that cohort, the MacNeil-Lehrer tribe," Leon said, so matter-of-factly that it almost seemed cruel. Jack and Susan glanced at each other quickly, then both, simultaneously, stared down at their hands. "You've got some promising grazing land farther down the ed and income scales—and those folks aren't going to respond to elegant policy formulations."

"So tell me," the governor asked. "How do we move this thing from retail to wholesale? How do we do the stuff we did in the malls and the union halls the last few weeks, how do we do that if we're hopping from tarmac to tarmac in a big plane, shut off from the folks by Secret Service? Except, of course, for the folks we touch up at fund-raisers? How do we reach the folks 'down the ed and income scales,' half of whom think I'm just that bozo in the *National Flash*? . . . How *do* you do politics in a country that hates politicians? How do we show 'em who I really am?"

No one had a clue.

"So, am I a pumpkin?" Daisy asked. It was one in the morning. I was asleep. "Are you asleep?"

"Unh."

"Sorry."

" 'Sokay . . ."

"I can't believe you're back down there—and I'm up here," she said. "It's like what happened to Lloyd Bridges when he surfaced too fast on *Sea Hunt*. My stomach hurts, like someone's wringing it out. My arms and legs hurt—and you're asleep, and pissed at me now, because, I mean, after all: don't you have a *right* to get some sleep?"

"Don't worry about it. How're you? What's new?"

"You tell me. Am I a pumpkin?"

"Huh?"

"Well, they have the first big post–New Hampshire meeting down at the Mansion. Half the known world is there. Arlen is there. Lucille is there. I'm not invited. What gives, Henry?"

"Nothing. It probably doesn't mean anything." But I *had* wondered about that. "Everyone's still a little foggy. Nothing happened at the meeting, except Howard's campaign manager now—"

"Howard the Furtive Cipher? *That* should straighten things right out. What else happened?"

"Richard said Harris's probably gonna hire David Adler."

"That's old news—Hotline this morning. I heard it was gonna be Paul Shaplen."

"Who?"

"Old labor guy—used to work for the Mine Workers, ran a couple of the reform campaigns. I think maybe the one where the guy got killed. Works out of Louisville. Guess Harris figured this guy could help with two colors—blue-collars and rednecks. Not a bad move, if he's any good. But this isn't an easy game."

"Tell me about it," I yawned.

"I'm sorry, Henry," she said. "For waking you, and for being paranoid after hours."

"No, it's okay. Wish you were here."

"I'm thinking about it, thinking what it's like there right about now—the silence of that place, the river, your orderly refrigerator, your warm little body."

"Could be warmer," I said.

"This is even more pathetic than campaign sex," she said. "Phone sex."

"Are you doing something I should know about?"

"No, but I may after I hang up," she said. "Night, sweetie."

I met Howard the Furtive Cipher at campaign headquarters in midmorning. He was in his usual costume—rumpled gray pin-striped suit, flower tie. He offered a thin, ironic half-smile. "You're not really my deputy," he said immediately. "And I'm not really the campaign manager. We do what we always did."

"React calmly in the face of utter turmoil?"

Another thin smile. "Whatever they want us to do," he said. "Let's go. You know the way. You drive."

We took his rented white Taurus. I thought about engaging him along the way, but I was too nervous. Howard was as ever—calm, pale, ultra-energy-absorbent. He stowed a battered brown-leather briefcase in the backseat. He sat next to me, staring straight ahead. He was a man who never seemed curious, who never fidgeted.

It was a fine, sunny day, and Fat Willie was outside, taking down the heavy plastic windbreak, preparing his place for spring. He was wearing a fresh white shirt and pants, and a red "M.F. Boosters" baseball cap. He started a smile when he saw me, but stopped when he saw that the white man getting out of the car was not Governor Stanton. "'Mornin'," he said, tentatively.

Howard did not introduce himself. He just stood there. "Willie," I said, "this is Howard Ferguson. He works with the governor too."

Willie eyed Howard. Howard nodded, offered a hand, said hello.

"Well," Willie said finally. "What can I do for you?"

Howard said nothing. This was going to be awful. "Willie, could we sit down and talk a minute?" I asked.

"Sure 'nuf," he said. "Can I get y'anything? Coffee?"

"No thanks," I said. Howard said nothing, but shook his head—no.

Willie led us to the picnic tables just to the side of his kitchen trailer shack, an area still protected by the plastic windbreak. He sat down facing us. Howard put his attaché case flat on the table in front of him, clicked it open, took out a yellow legal pad and what looked like court papers, then clicked the case shut and stowed it. Willie watched all this very carefully—which, of course, had been Howard's intention: intimidation. Willie glanced at me; I gave him nothing back.

"Mr. McCollister, the governor is very concerned about this situation with your daughter and the possible damage it might cause to his reputation," Howard Ferguson began, his voice as small and hard as a bullet. Willie glanced at me; I gave him nothing back, God forgive me.

"He wants to see it resolved. He wants paternity to be established, definitively, as soon as possible."

Willie was confused. Was this man saying the governor wanted to *admit* paternity? "The governor's a—"

"He wants your daughter to have an amniocentesis performed so that paternity can be established," Howard continued, barging through whatever it was Willie was going to say. There were no wasted words, no wasted movements. This was the way black folks *figured* white folks did business—no grease, no grace, no emotions. Howard, who came from midwestern hard-sod stock, was the quintessential, lipless white man.

"A what?" Willie said. He wiped his brow. He looked at me. I stared at the table.

"It is a procedure, performed at the hospital. Amniotic fluid is drawn from your daughter's womb. Genetic material is analyzed. It can be compared with the governor's blood to determine whether or not he is the father."

"I don't—" Willie said.

"It's a common enough procedure," Howard said, more casually. He was talking down to Willie now. "It is used to determine the health of the fetus—and that is why you will say you want it performed, to make sure the baby is healthy."

"How do you . . . get the fluid?"

"A needle is inserted through the abdomen," Howard said. Willie didn't quite wince; he wiped his eye. "Don't worry, Mr. McCollister—this is a common procedure, and the governor insists that it will be performed by the very best people available. Your daughter will be treated at Mercy Hospital, which will also ensure confidentiality."

"Mercy, huh?" Willie said. Mercy was considered the white folks' hospital. "And the governor wants—"

"The governor *insists*," Howard said. "There are people, Mr. McCollister, who would like to destroy Governor Stanton. He doesn't believe you are one of them. He believes you are his friend. But he can't allow this. *You* can't allow this. I am sure your daughter is a fine young person, but she is a child, and children are impressionable—and there has been a lot of news about the governor in recent weeks. She hasn't said a word about this to anyone?"

Willie shook his head. "I tol' her," he said. "She's a good girl."

"Well, I certainly hope so," Howard said. "You wouldn't want to jeopardize your relationship with the governor and Mrs. Stanton. The governor wants to do everything possible to help you through this time. The Stantons are prepared to be very generous. This procedure will cost you nothing. The governor is prepared to cover all pre- and postnatal expenses. He will do this because he believes you are his friend. But you must cooperate. We must determine—to everyone's satisfaction—that he is not the father of that child. I'm sure you understand his position."

Without waiting for a response, Howard pulled up his attaché case, put his phony papers back in it. He stood up, offered William McCollister his card. "Please call me at this number, and we will make all the necessary arrangements."

Willie nodded. He shook Howard's hand. He didn't shake mine; this time, he didn't even look at me. .

We pulled away and I felt dizzy. Howard sighed. "What do you think?" he asked.

"I don't know."

"I can't believe she won't tell someone, tell a friend, and then we're fucked," Howard said. "Well, maybe not. Say she tells some friends, say it begins to get around—we can just say it's a copycat, a copycat Cashmere." He laughed—a thin, throaty heh-heh, the bloodless fuck. "There might even be a blowback from it, a sympathy reaction, work in our favor."

"They're good people," I said. "And if she *doesn't* tell anyone, doesn't that indicate she's probably making this thing up?"

"That she's pregnant?"

"No, about the governor."

"You believe that?" Howard asked.

I missed a red light and was nearly hit by a truck coming the other way. I pulled over to the side of the road, sick to my stomach. I leaned out the door and vomited.

Howard just shook his head.

The next few weeks were strange, amorphous. The metabolism of the campaign changed. There wasn't the intensity of New Hampshire.

Our political family was splintered. Richard, Arlen and Daisy were back in Washington. Brad, Howard, Lucille and I were in Mammoth Falls. Susan worked her own schedule. And the candidate flew about, doing foolish, mechanical things. He did a lot of satellite interviews. These would happen around midday, in a television studio—inevitably a flat, nondescript building with satellite dishes, located in an industrial park. He would sit in a room alone, backlit in mentholated blue. He would have an earpiece and a glass of water. He would have a list of stations and anchor names:

> WHRC—Charlotte, NC—Richard and Cheryl.
> WGUL—Charleston, SC—Brody and Kelly.
> WANB—Anniston, AL—Kelly and Chuck.

And so on.

He would do ten, twelve, seventeen at a shot. Five minutes each. Always the same. Always the same first question—and the same evasion: "Awww, Kelly—I don't think folks really care about that. They're concerned about the economy. About what's gonna happen down there in Charleston when the base closes." They were also concerned about what the government was going to do about crime, about education, about . . . It was awful. He would rip out the earpiece when it was over and stomp around. "Tell me, Laurene," he said one day, "what was it about America twenty years ago that caused every third woman, white and black, to name her daughter Kelly?"

"I dunno," Laurene said. *"Charlie's Angels?"*

The governor was suffering from severe human-contact withdrawal. He would devour every employee in every television station, lingering over their personal stories and their problems, hungry for the sort of campaigning he'd done in New Hampshire. But there was very little of that now. He did three states a day, unless it was Florida or Texas, where he did three markets a day. The weather was better—it was spring—but he didn't experience it much. He experienced airports and hotel ballrooms and hotel rooms, and the plane.

The plane was as hermetic an experience as the rest of the campaign, only more intense. He could feel the presence of the traveling scorps in the rear; there was the *appearance* of interaction—he'd go back once a day, just before takeoff, chat in the aisle, say nothing. Laurene and her people tried to keep the scorps occupied—a losing battle, since *nothing* was happening most days, at least nothing they could see or report. It was all fund-raising and local organizing, and five-minute noninterviews with local anchors. I was happy, for once, not to be too much a part of this. I traveled with the candidate several days a week, mostly weekends, when the bigger public events—debates, rallies—happened; the rest of the time I spent back in Mammoth Falls, working the phones, doing stuff.

I didn't hear anything more from Howard, or anyone else, about the McCollister situation, and I never asked. I let it slip into the black hole that was Howard Ferguson's portfolio: it was the campaign manager's job to worry about the unspeakable. But I was obsessed by it, pained by it. I'm pretty sure I dreamed about it—horrible dreams that lingered just beyond the edge of my consciousness. I was disgusted by what I had done. I was ashamed. I didn't want to think about what came next. I started running again. Daisy and I agreed to go see *Terminator 2* simultaneously, in our respective cities—she, for the third time—and then talk about it. I was beginning to like action movies.

The campaign unfolded much as we expected. We lost Maine. We lost South Dakota—Bart Nilson won that, even though he'd already dropped out. The next day he endorsed us, and we put him on the plane with Stanton, hoping his prairie integrity would give us a boost in Colorado. We certainly needed one. Harris was all over the air, running a spot we called "Rocky Mountain Hiya," in which he stood in a mountain meadow wearing a plaid shirt and said, "Hello to you, Colorado. My name is Lawrence Harris and I'm running for president. I'm a college teacher, a former United States senator from New Hampshire, which is a state very much like yours—a beautiful state, a place where people really care about the environment, but a place that's suffering some tough economic times, just like Colorado. I think our government should *do* something about that. We can invest in the future, invest in environmental technology, create new jobs while building a cleaner future for our children." And again, as in New Hampshire, there was a rush of children into his arms. "And our . . ."—he was laughing now—"grandchildren."

"Shit, he's a pol," Richard said on the phone, after seeing a dub of the "Hiya" spot. "All of a sudden he wants to start spending fuckin' *money* on the fuckin' *environment*! Is *pork* a natural force?"

"Well, he never said he didn't want to spend money," I said. "He just said he wanted to raise taxes."

"Henri, coupla things about that spot got me worried," Richard said. "Notice how they have him saying college *teacher* instead of professor? And the way spending money on the environment flows naturally from his 'Natural Forces' bullshit. This guy Shaplen ain't bad."

"But he's still stuck peddling Lawrence Harris."

"No one knows who or what Lawrence Harris is," Richard said. "And no one's gonna know. He's gonna be in and out of this state by next Tuesday. All they gonna know is what they see on the tube. He could get up there and say, 'I'm Lawrence Harris and I used to play professional football,' and no one'd know any different, specially since we ain't *telling* them any different. You can't convince Jack to fire off one of our silver bullets?"

"No. He's positive negative'll boomerang," I said.

"How about comparative?" Richard said. "Hi, I'm Jack Stanton and I'm a human being. My opponent is Lawrence Harris, and he has a cork up his ass."

"Forget about it."

"So we're just sittin' out there doin' Fast Times at Bronx Science?"

Which was what Richard called our main Colorado spot, which featured Jack Stanton speaking to high school kids—and giving a much less convincing version of the speech I'd seen him deliver at the union hall in Portsmouth: "No politician can promise you a secure future," he said, sitting on a school desk in a dark suit, a demographically correct display of acne-free teenagers in front of him. "We're going to have to compete hard against the rest of the world for the best jobs—I want you to have a leg up in that competition, and so I'll work overtime to make sure our schools and colleges are second to none. But we're all going to have to work harder."

"It's a fucking reversal of fortune is what it is," Richard said. "Harris is promising pork. We're promising hard times. And you know what? People *still* think we're the airhead. This ain't makin' it, Henri."

I knew that. I knew it even better after Harris clobbered us in the Colorado debate, the Saturday night before the primary in Denver. It was a strange evening. Susan wasn't there. I flew in last minute. There had been no real debate prep, just Stanton and Bart Nilson putting their heads together with the plane people—Ken Spiegelman, who was flying around with the candidate, keeping the governor's mind occupied, talking issues, and Laurene. None of the political folks were around. I caught up with the candidate just as the debate prep was breaking up, just as he was about to walk through the labyrinthine postmodern series of overhead walkways from the hotel, through some other building, into a generic concrete and cinder-block convention center. The debate would be held in a stark, overlit corner of a large, echoey warehouse of a room, empty except for two thin rows of spectators.

It didn't feel good. And it was strange to see Charlie Martin still there, waiting, when we arrived. I'd almost forgotten about him. He was out of money and out of the news but still hanging around in the race and onstage. It must have been painful for him: he was extraneous, the story had passed him by. He tried to attack both Harris and us, but no one paid him any attention, especially not after Harris lowered the boom on us.

Actually, Stanton walked right into it. He went after Harris playfully, as if he didn't quite take him seriously. "You say you want to improve the economy and the environment, *and* invest in the future—and yet you are proposing the stiffest gasoline tax increase in history," the governor said, with a not-very-convincing chuckle. "How you gonna improve the economy by taking money out of people's pockets?"

"Well, that's a difference between you and me, Governor Stanton," Harris said—insufferable, obnoxious. And lethal. "I *tell* the people how I'm going to pay for the things I want to do. You don't."

"That's not true, Larry, and you know it," Stanton shouted—suddenly, stupidly, out of control. "I've proposed a tax increase for the wealthiest Americans."

"Which won't raise a quarter of what you'll need to keep all the extravagant promises you've made, Jack," Harris said. "You see, folks: this is politics as usual."

"Larry, for God's sake."

"This is what the American people are sick and tired of. This man will say just about *anything* to get elected."

The governor maintained his discipline admirably after it was over. He even chatted with scorps. He did not trash his room. He trashed mine. "Fuck all, Henry!" he said, barging in about midnight, as I was commiserating with Daisy on the phone. (The debate had looked as awful in Washington as in Colorado.) "Fuck all. We can't get it together to do even a half-assed prep?" He pounded his fist on my desk. "I—can't—fucking—believe it!" He swept the lamp off the desk, knocking it into the television cabinet, smashing the bulb. "So what the fuck was I supposed to say, 'No, Larry, I won't say just about anything to get elected—just a couple of things I don't quite believe'? What was I supposed to fucking say?"

"I don't know," I said.

He picked up the desk chair and smashed it down, cracking a leg. "Henry, this *sucks.*" He sat down on my bed. "What do we do now?"

"Stick with the plan," I said. "We'll win down home."

"The scorps have already discounted that," he said. "It won't *mean* anything, except in delegate count, especially not after tonight. You *know* half of Washington was watching this damn thing. That's all they do up there, watch C-SPAN. They break up dinner parties, they hold the dessert. The hostess says, 'We'll have baked Alaska in an hour, but first let's watch Stanton and Harris mess each other up.' And then they congratulate themselves on how much better they would've done. What did Daisy say?"

"A bunch of nasty things about Lawrence Harris."

"Great. Just fucking fabulous." He was calmer now. "Henry, I think this is the worst it's been. New Hampshire was bad there, for a few weeks, but I always felt I could *do* something about it. I could work, go to a mall, stand out on a street corner, whatever. But, you know what? This is one big empty country. You stand on a street corner and the cars whizz by. I don't know how you do politics if you can't *see* the folks. Dunno if I *want* to do politics if you can't see the folks. I was born too late. I would've loved torchlight parades, whistle-stop tours. You know?"

He stood up. Thought a moment. Sat down again. "You think we're gonna get a Washington candidate? Larkin?"

"I don't think so," I said.

"He'd be good," Stanton said. "He'd come out, work hard, stay on message. He's clean."

"He's sterile."

"Henry, my man," he said, standing again. "Sterile is what's happening. Larry's the next thing to sterile—he's smart, he smells of chalk and erasers. You can trust a fella like that. Not so sure you want to vote for him: he might assign homework. But you can trust him. Good thing he doesn't understand Stanton's Third Rule: You don't want to go around campaigning for office and acting too smart. Certainly not book-smart. The only kind of smart that folks in this country'll tolerate is *country*-smart. See, if it's just me and Lawrence, I may have a shot—if I can make him look prideful and preachy and cold and pointy-headed. But I can't attack him frontally. I know Richard and all of them are itchy to drop the big one. But it's too damn dangerous, given how people think of me."

"But can you just let him keep on hammering you, the way he did tonight?"

He shook his head, as if to say no. "Damnedest thing," he said. "I watch elections all the time, study 'em, *love* 'em. Usually I can figure out what each guy should do, doesn't make a difference if they're Democrat or Republican—there's always something. But I can't crack this one. I can't figure it out. Probably just too close to it—that's why you hire hired guns, I guess." He moved toward the door, opened it, then turned: "It's also why, I gotta tell you, Henry, if I'm a God-fearing Democrat sitting in Washington tonight, or maybe even someplace else, and I've ever had an itch to be president of the United States, I may be scratching just a little."

Two things happened the next Monday that changed Jack Stanton's mind about going negative, and set us on the strange path that led to the third candidate he was dreading. The first was a scary Leon poll from Florida. We were ahead, but not convincingly—35 to 21, with a lot undecided and Stanton's negatives at 45, and 62 percent saying they'd like to see another candidate in the race. "You know what it looks like?" the governor said. "It looks like New Hampshire in reverse. If we can't do better in Florida than he did in New Hampshire, we may be mortally fucked."

The other thing was that Lawrence Harris—or, more likely, Paul Shaplen—made a mistake. They went negative on us in Colorado. It was a strange ad. It started with drums and deep horns and pictures of the war in Vietnam, the flag waving, and then scruffy protesters marching in the streets. "When our country was at war, Jack Stanton didn't just opt out—he used *pull* to get himself out." A jail door slid open with a rusty squeak. "Now our country is facing another crisis." And there was Lawrence Harris, back in the damn meadow: "It's a silent crisis. A fiscal crisis. An economic crisis. I'll *face* that crisis. *I* won't run away."

"Have you seen it?" I asked Richard by phone. Stanton had asked me to stay with him after the debate. We were trying to make sure we held our base in Georgia, which would be voting the same day as Colorado. We were in Macon, at one of those rare events the governor actually enjoyed—a town meeting at a local high school. It was probably a waste of time, but I'd argued for it with Lucille, who was now doing scheduling: "It's like vitamins," I said. "It keeps him pumped the rest of the day."

But he wouldn't need the stimulation this day. He knew about the poll and the ad before he started the town meeting—and he seemed to race through the questions from the audience, impatient, on autopilot, giving stock answers instead of locking in on the folks: this was, I realized, how politicians who were not Jack Stanton routinely worked these sorts of events. Having caught the drift, I went outside—it was a fabulously warm and bright day; birds were singing—and called Richard.

"Yeah, I saw the ad," he said. "It's completely fucking bizarre, like they started to do one spot, a slice-and-dice on us, then suddenly changed their minds. I mean, what are they *after* here? Enviro veterans? It's fucking idiotic. If they wanted to go negative, whyn't they just use that clip from the debate where he lit us up?"

"Because Jack mentioned that Harris wanted to raise taxes right in the middle of it?"

"Mebbe," Richard said. "But the 'politics as usual' line was dynamite. And then the 'He'll say anything to get elected' without a comeback from Jack: slam-fucking-dunk. I'd wear that out, I was them. It wouldn't even be perceived as going negative: It's like a fact, y'know? It's reality. He's just sayin': Lookit what happened last Saturday night—y'knowhattamean? It's a no-brainer. But you know what's even more fucked up? Why on earth did they go negative on us—in *Colorado*—in the first place? They shoulda waited, sprung it on us in Florida. Weren't you the one saying Shaplen was so good?"

"No, you were. You liked 'Rocky Mountain Hiya.' "

"He's a union Jew?"

I didn't know. Richard believed there were three basic categories of Democratic Party pols: Bostons, Southerns and Jews. Shaplen, coming from the Mine Workers and Louisville, had been intriguing. "I think he's Jewish," Richard said. "Shaplen could be anything right? Shortened Shapiro maybe."

"What difference does it make?" I asked.

"Know thine enemy," he said.

"The Jewish move would be to go negative in Colorado?" I said, teasing him.

"No, that's just it. The Jewish move would be to be freaked by cowboys. Be cautious. Drop the big one in Colorado to make sure Stanton doesn't come back and win it—and use a patriotic spot, a flag-waver. You gotta love it. Y'know, it probably has something to do with the mine workers never having much luck organizing out west—least, not as much as back east. Western labor guys tend to be scary, anarchists—Wobblies, gun nuts. The guys from Brooklyn go out there to organize, they figure they've gotta be Wyatt Earp."

"Richard, that is ninety-eight percent bullshit," I said. "You don't even know if Shaplen's Jewish."

"Oh, he's Jewish. And he's fucked up bigtime. He knows we're fighting with one arm, he knows we ain't gonna go negative first. So, I would've held off till Florida, then clocked us there."

"He might do that anyway," I said.

"He might," Richard said. "But it won't be as elegant. He's lost my fucking respect—and he's given us the opportunity to fight back. I was figuring on having a knock-down, drag-out with ol' Jackie, get him to whomp this shitbird before he whomped us. I was expectin' to have to threaten to quit or start exposing myself to muffins again. Y'know? But that may not be necessary now. Shaplen did our work for us."

"Not Shaplen—it's more Leon," I said. "Stanton'll care more about the poll than that stupid ad."

"Probably so," Richard said. "Whichever: my guess is our Jackie'll be ready to play."

It certainly seemed so. Stanton raced out of the town meeting in Macon, back to the plane for a short hop to Atlanta, with his game face on. "Call everyone," he said in the car. "Get Richard, Leon and Libby. I want them at the hotel tonight. Tell Libby I want to see every fucking vote Harris cast when he was in the Senate, especially on foreign policy—tell her to check *committee* votes on that, if she can. I think he was on Foreign Relations, right?" I nodded. "And tell Lucille I want to cancel everything but money events in every state but Florida, and start working up some new stuff there. Radio shows. The old folks listen to a lot of radio. And let's see what Daisy has. Call Daisy, have her come down too, bring her silver bullets—that should make you happy, Henri. Tell her to pack a bag. We'll set her up with an edit studio in Miami—or maybe Orlando, they've got facilities there now, and it's more in the center of the state. Have Brad figure it out."

He sat back, stared out the window. "If we can't build me up," he said quietly, "we are going to tear that mother-fucker down. I am going to break his fucking back."

The Florida campaign opened symmetrically. On Tuesday night, Harris celebrated his Colorado victory in Miami, where he was trying to build a base along condo row—and we celebrated our Georgia victory up in Tampa, trying to protect our strength among "yellow dog" Democrats in the northern half of the state. On Wednesday, both campaigns moved into enemy turf and unveiled their secret weapons.

Harris's was Freddy Picker, which didn't seem such a big deal at first. I remembered him vaguely, but fondly. He was one of the New Southerners who'd suddenly materialized in the 1970s, the first politicians elected with both black and white votes south of the

Mason-Dixon line. I was a teenager then. My grandfather was a decade dead, my father was several years disappeared, but those pale, bland Southern Democrats seemed a down payment on the family dream. It was a whisper of a revolution; there wasn't much blood or lust to it, just the promise of Northern money—new factories, new branch offices—in return for the appearance of racial harmony. Amazingly, the Crackers went for it. It happened so smoothly nobody noticed. But I noticed. I saw Jimmy Carter coming, even before the series of speculative articles in *The New York Times* at the beginning of the 1976 campaign: could a little-known Southern governor make a name for himself in national politics? That seemed dense. Of course he could. If he'd managed to get himself elected governor of Georgia with both black and white votes, what *couldn't* he do?

Fred Picker had gotten himself elected governor of Florida around that same time and was speculated upon as well. There had been a Picker-for-president moment—but it had come and gone, just as he had. I didn't remember his being disgraced or defeated, but . . . Had he served one term or two? His name never surfaced anymore. I hadn't heard or thought of him in years—until the Thursday before the Florida primary, when he suddenly appeared, with Lawrence Harris, at a Tallahassee press conference.

"I am very proud to announce," Harris said, wearing a seersucker suit that vibrated crazily on television, "that former governor Fred Picker has not only agreed to endorse my candidacy, but he will chair my effort here in Florida—and he will remain with me, after the primary, in a significant advisory capacity. I think most Floridians know that Governor Picker is a man with little tolerance for politics as usual. They understand what it means when a man of his integrity steps forward."

At which point, Freddy Picker stepped forward. He was still trim—in fact, he seemed tauter, more serious, than my fuzzy recollection of him as governor. He had a great hawklike nose and arched eyebrows that seemed playful, ironic. He was wearing a blue blazer and a muted plaid shirt; no tie. He had the look of a man who, after no small struggle, had come to terms with himself—though perhaps just barely. His eyes were sharp, dark; he didn't scan an audience, the way most pols do, but darted from face to face, like a bird. You could sense an edge of wildness in those eyes. He looked out at the assembled scorps, blinked once, and said, "You guys are *still* ugly."

"Governor," asked a television blonde, who was not ugly, "what brought you back into politics after all these years?"

"Well, electing a president is serious business—but this hasn't been a very serious campaign, except for Senator Harris here. And we need to *get* serious. I think this country needs to get its act together. I was thinkin' about bringin' out my old broom," he said, suppressing a laugh. "You children probably don't remember, but that was how I ran in '74—time for a clean sweep. But that just doesn't seem *technological* enough now. Need to keep up with the times. Need a more modern contraption—maybe a Dustbuster."

Libby Holden's screech could be heard all the way from Mammoth Falls. It was as if someone had broken our code.

"Governor, what's your opinion of Jack Stanton? You say this hasn't been a serious campaign—is that his fault?" Tom Rickman of *The Miami Herald* asked.

"Well, he does have serious hair."

When the laughter died down, Fred Picker continued, "Look, I'm sure Governor Stanton is a fine man—but we have an extraordinary man right here, a man who's willing to tell it straight to the American people." He put an arm around Larry Harris, who had faded into the background a bit—indeed, Harris came across in black-and-white, compared with Picker, who was, ineffably, Technicolor.

"Senator Harris, would you consider Governor Picker as a running mate?"

"Well, it's a bit premature to be speculating about that," Harris woofed, chest puffed out. "But Governor Picker certainly is the sort of person you'd see in a Harris administration."

"Not so fast there, Senator—I've only signed on for a week," Picker chided, playfully squeezing the candidate's neck. Then, turning serious, "But I will be out there, between now and next Tuesday, helping this man every way I can."

Laurene Robinson and I had our heads together, watching this on her transistor television in the lobby outside the cafeteria-auditorium at the Mogen David Senior Center in Pompano Beach. My beeper vibrated—it was Daisy.

"You *see* that?" she asked.

"He's good," I said. "Picker."

"The governor see it?"

"No, he's eating lunch with the Old Testament."

"He's gonna be thrilled with that hair line," Daisy said. "You think this guy's gonna make any difference down here?"

"Do endorsements ever make a difference?" I asked.

"It half looked like Harris was endorsing Picker," Daisy said. "Someone should tell the professor that seersucker plus TV equals death. He looked like a carnival ride. Probably caused mass vertigo outbreaks in half the nursing homes in Broward County. And if Picker is gonna have a 'significant advisory role in the campaign' after Florida, how come he said he'd only signed on for a week?"

"Who knows," I said. "You *care* about that?"

"Whenever any candidate who isn't mine comes up with anything that isn't bad, it gets my attention," Daisy said.

"You having fun at Disney World?" I asked.

"Just hangin' out, ready to roll," she said. "But I don't know what it is with these guys. You get the feeling they haven't thought it through. They're still running that stupid Vietnam spot from Colorado. Here, in Orlando. Saw it last night, just before Letterman. You gotta figure they'll come in with a Picker endorse spot now. But what else? Why aren't they up with more? Where's the strategy here?"

"Well, they don't know what we're doing yet either."

"Yeah, and neither do we. You think *our* guy is ready to go for it?"

"Who knows?" I said, remembering that he had whiffed on attacking Ozio. "We'll know in a minute. Seeya."

The cafeteria-auditorium of the Mogen David Senior Center was a profoundly depressing room, a file cabinet for human beings: cinder-block walls painted beige, a high narrow line of crank-open windows throwing sharp slants of sunlight across a pea-soup linoleum-tile floor. There were metal and Formica picnic tables in orderly rows; each had a centerpiece—Israeli and American flags. At the front of the room, hanging on a red brick wall, was a dreadful representation of a turquoise-and-brass menorah topped by an oversize Star of David. Scattered about on the walls were faded Israel travel posters and sad, shaky amateur artwork. Near the door was a bulletin board

with photos of a recent field trip to the dog track and announcements of canasta tournaments, lectures and "Singles Mix Nights" to
come. It all seemed antiseptic, perfunctory, a depository. But, then, we
weren't there to spread joy, either. This was not going to be a moment
I would cherish.

Stanton was sitting at one of the picnic tables, surrounded by extremely old people, eating soggy tuna on white. I found myself wondering if he had extinguished his sandwich in something more than
the usual two bites, and hoping that he wasn't poaching off his neighbors' plates. (I also found myself giggling at the thought that maybe
his lunch companions were so fogbound they wouldn't notice if he
made everyone's lunch disappear.) I watched him sitting there, with a
blue velvet yarmulke precarious atop his head—nodding respectfully,
listening, the good son—and, suddenly, the whole thing seemed absurd. The idea that we were about to nuke Lawrence Harris here, in
front of these demi-oblivious people.

He was introduced by a spry fellow named Mort Silberberg, who
said that Jack Stanton reminded him of Jack Kennedy. "This boy," he
said, "has got the charisma. Believe me, he's got real pizzazz. He's the
next president of the United States, Governor Jack Stanton."

The governor stood, bobbing his head and spreading his arms—
more good-son choreography, as if to say: Well, here I am . . . and
does anybody need anything from the store? It seemed condescending, transparent; unworthy. I realized that I was in a foul mood—hoping he would actually do what he was supposed to do, but not really
wanting to see him do it. *This* would be politics as usual, Stanton as
accused.

He seemed tentative. He meandered through his usual stump
speech, as if distracted. But he was preparing himself for the kill—
which came brilliantly, quietly, sadly. "I want to speak for a moment
about my opponent, Senator Harris," he said. "An excellent man. A
learned man." Then he paused, shook his head. "But there are some
differences between us. I think you should know about them—and,
quite frankly, I was surprised and disappointed to discover some of his
positions on issues of interest to you and me. For example, I agree
with him about the importance of reducing the deficit. I think that's
very important. But in his eagerness to cut spending, Senator Harris

has made some questionable proposals. Look in his booklet, *Saving the Future*. Look on page eighteen, third paragraph down: he wants to 'study' a reduction—perhaps even a freeze—in cost of living adjustments for Social Security."

There was a rustling in the room, like a breeze passing through a tree, and you could hear the old people whispering to one another, or maybe just to themselves, "Social Security, Security, curity, curity—ity-ity . . ."

Stanton measured the breeze, let it pass. "Yeah," he nodded sadly. "I know, and *you* know, how important it is for your Social Security to keep up with the prices at the grocery store. And you know how prices keep going up! I have this chart—some of my young people will distribute it to you—showing how prices in south Florida have gone up during the last ten years—and how your Social Security has *just barely* kept up with them.

"I also disagree with Senator Harris about Medicare," Stanton said, which caused another breeze—stiffer this time. He waited for them. "He wants you to pay more—page twenty-three in his book. Let me read: 'Part B co-payments should be adjusted for income to reflect the program's original intention of a fifty-fifty split between government and recipient.' He also adds, I want to be fair here, 'The poor should not be affected by these changes. In fact, we should try to alleviate their co-pays wherever possible.' Now, let me try to explain what this means—"

"It means we pay more and *schvartze*s pay less," said an explosively bitter little man in a short-sleeved white shirt, madras Bermuda shorts and sandals.

"No, that's not true," Stanton replied, though not quite vehemently enough to suit my taste. "And I believe it's very important that every senior gets all the medical care he or she needs, regardless of race or creed. But what Senator Harris is doing here is *opening the door* to changes that may have an adverse impact. I don't think we can take that chance.

"There are other things in the senator's book. I would recommend that each one of you read it carefully before making this very important decision about the future of our country—and read my literature, my issue papers too, of course," he said, pausing again, walking a few steps, turning slightly. "But there is one other area where Senator Harris and I disagree—and that is foreign policy, specifically the Middle East."

There were whispers and shushes throughout the room. Stanton held out his hands, quieted them down. "When he was a member of the Senate Foreign Relations Committee, my opponent had to cast a great many votes regarding the security and the future of the state of Israel."

"No!" shouted a woman wearing sunglasses and shellacked hair of a color that did not occur in nature.

"Now wait—I agree with many of his votes," Stanton said. "But there were some . . . Well, I think it's important to stand with our friends—and our country has no better friend than the state of Israel. And when we do have a difference of opinion, it should be settled privately. Many of us had mixed feelings about the incursion into Lebanon ten years ago, but I don't think I would have called Israel the 'aggressor' state as Senator Harris did. I think we all know who the aggressor *really* is in that neighborhood. Nor would I have voted for a resolution opposing the construction of new settlements on the West Bank. Like many of you, I may question the wisdom of such settlements, but I am opposed to interfering in the internal affairs of an ally—unlike my opponent, apparently."

And with that, muffins distributed a list of selected statements and votes Lawrence Harris had made about Israel to the handful of scorps loitering by the door. The scorps didn't even wait for Stanton to finish speaking but immediately came at me, flushed and righteous with the prospect of having some *news* to report for a change: "Henry, are you guys actually saying Harris is anti-Israel?" Bob O'Connell from *The Washington Post* asked with utter disgust.

"Absolutely not," I said. "Harris has supported Israel—but there are times when his support wavered."

"And Stanton's support would *never* waver?" asked Tommy Preston, a black reporter from *The Dallas Morning News.*

"Come on—that's not the point," I said. "Don't you think it's time we all took a good look at Senator Harris's record?"

"Henry, this is pretty thin stuff," O'Connell said, looking up from the handout. "Did he ever vote against giving aid to Israel? Did he ever vote to reduce aid in any way?"

I let that pass and responded instead to the vile Felicia Aulder of the New York *Daily News,* who sneered: "You guys must be scared that Harris is beating you here, pulling this kind of crap."

"These are facts," I said. "They are documented. We have differences with Senator Harris on a number of issues. Are you saying we shouldn't point out those differences?"

"But, Henry, this is—"

"And what about those ads Harris put up in Colorado—the antiwar protesters, the jail door. That was high-minded?"

The scorps—satisfied they had picked me clean—rushed off to the lobby, eager to call their bosses. I turned back to the candidate, who had finished speaking and was now in furiously filial mode, awkwardly embracing an elderly woman in a wheelchair while simultaneously looking up and shaking a frail gentleman's hand. Others crowded around and he worked them perfectly, lingering with them, listening, touching, connecting. Twisting around to hug a woman in a walker, he lost his yarmulke. He was about to reach down for it, but a woman with orange hair and absurd breasts that spilled from a peasant blouse got there first. She smiled at him naughtily, then hooked her arm through his and pulled him toward her, nuzzling her chest provocatively against his ribs. He succumbed to this, smiling goofily and bending down in a half-squat so she could place the yarmulke back on his head, then remaining there as she took his face in her hands, stared at him dreamily and kissed him full on the lips, leaving a hideous tangerine smear. He smiled at her, lost in all the touching and hugging, then looked over at me—and seemed to startle. I realized that I must have been frowning.

The next few days were brutal, but very effective. It was almost too easy. Richard had been right: Lawrence Harris had offered us his head on a platter. We went up in every Florida market that night with "factual" ads about Harris's intention to raise the gasoline tax, cut Social Security and Medicare, lay waste to the American dream. It was a saturation bombing campaign—you couldn't watch the evening news or any of the top-five daytime shows favored by senior citizens without catching a Stanton ad. (We did the Middle East number more selectively, with flyers in condo-land and shills calling in to radio shows.)

I am tempted to say that Daisy's ads were classy. Certainly, they were elegant—several cuts above the usual Texas Chainsaw negative spots politicians tend to favor. An announcer said: "Here are some things Lawrence Harris says he would like to do as president." And, in a light, ironic tone, he read passages from *Saving the Future,* always citing page and paragraph numbers. As he read, words appeared on the screen: "Will raise gas tax 50 cents—*Saving the Future,* page 7" and "Will cut Social Security—*Saving the Future,* page 18." These were the only visual images. At the end, there was a picture of Lawrence Harris—not a mean, ugly or befuddled one, as is the usual practice, but a nice, tweedy one—and the announcer said: "The Harris Platform. A fifty-cent gasoline tax. An attack on Social Security. Less money for Medicare. Can we really afford that?" And a "Stanton For America" slide.

Harris responded quickly, though not very effectively, with one of the moldy-oldies of political advertising. He stood next to a television set and rolled one of our ads, then froze it with his remote control clicker: "Just *look* at this," he said, much too hot for television. (In fact, there wasn't very much to look at—just the "Will raise gas tax" slide.) "Haven't we had enough of this kind of garbage?" Harris huffed and puffed. "Jack Stanton doesn't want to talk about these issues. He just wants to scare you. Well, I don't think Floridians scare easy—and I'm convinced that you are sick of politics as usual." He said "you are" instead of "you're." It seemed stiff, cranky. It worked for us.

That was on the air by Friday night. We heard about it in Houston, where Stanton was working a $500-a-plate picnic for one thousand Texas Democrats. We scooted out of there, flying back to Orlando at about 10:30 central time, a planeful of sleepy, barbecue-stained scorps in tow. We landed in Florida just past one in the morning and walked into chaos at the Magic Kingdom West Motel, where a complex of suites and connecting rooms on the second floor served as our makeshift headquarters. Phones were ringing, muffins hustling, the Xerox machines and faxes churning. Leon, Brad and Richard were in the outer room of the Stanton suite working the phones, eating pizza and listening to a fierce argument in the bedroom. Women arguing. Lucille and . . . Daisy? I looked at Leon, who shrugged eloquently—

he didn't know *what* was going on back there—but he gave me a vigorous thumbs-up and said, "Numbers are good. We're holding, he's folding." Brad, talking to Howard Ferguson back in Mammoth Falls, handed me a condo-land flyer: "Lawrence Harris and Israel: The Facts." Richard was shouting at someone in Miami: "Of course we want the support of the Latino community. Wait a minute." He covered the phone: "Hey, Henri, you better go give your girlfriend some aid and comfort back there, man."

Stanton snagged a cold, congealed slice of pepperoni, peppers and onions on his way to the bedroom—where Susan was working the phone with a finger stuck in her ear, and Lucille was screaming at Daisy: "We gotta come back at him! We can't let him get away with this."

"What we've got is working just fine," Daisy said. "I told you. I told her," she went on, turning to the candidate and me. "We've been moving ever since we went up with it."

"Jack, you want to respond to this asshole," Lucille said, speaking of Harris (but glancing at Daisy). "Show him."

Daisy showed him a tape of the ad. The candidate grunted. Richard came in. "Ol' Natural Forces learnin' 'bout life in the kitchen? Looks pretty sweaty to me."

"What do you think?" Stanton asked him.

"I think," Richard glanced carefully at Daisy, "a campaign this short and intense, an ad don't have much shelf life. We gotta come back with somethin' new by Sunday."

"We've *got* inspirational positives in the can," Daisy said. "We should close this out on the high road."

"I don't know about going positive at this point," Susan said, off the phone.

"The theory is," Daisy said, "we've nuked Harris. We want to give them some reason to come out for us."

"What are we planning on using?" Stanton asked.

"You, on the desk again," Lucille sneered. "Always on the damn desk. Health care. You think that's gonna fly after this piece of shit?"

"It's not just the desk," Daisy said, rising to it, truly pissed: "It's crowd shots, excitement, music, you with kids and seniors, people listening, responding."

"Henry?" Susan asked, and I wondered why she was choosing me to scorch Daisy.

"Tough call," I said. "Anyone have any ideas about what *sort* of negative we might come back with against Harris?"

Actually, Daisy did—but she didn't know it. "Why don't we just click off *his* spot?" she scoffed.

"Not fucking bad!" Richard said. "See, the governor could do it casual, funny—make fun of this shitbird's negative. Do it just the way Harris did: Start off with our spot—reinforce our message in a backhand way. But then you pull back and it's actually *his* spot: You show Harris clicking off our spot. Then, surprise! You pull back again and now it's Stanton, clicking off Harris and kinda laughing about how silly this politics business is, y'knowhattamean? Sayin', 'Yeah, I saw this piece of shit too, and did you notice how this stuckup–dipshit–asshole still ain't admitting that he wants to raise the gas tax and cut Social Security. Dontcha think it's time to just Vote Smart? Vote for a human being.' Y'knowhattamean?"

"What? What?" Lucille asked, or perhaps said.

"Vote Smart," Daisy said. "Not *entirely* implausible."

"Smart doesn't work," Leon Birnbaum now said, joining the deliberations. "I tested it. I tried it a bunch of ways. Nope. Can't do it. People think we're being defensive because the perception of Stanton isn't—uhh, smart."

Everyone looked at the candidate. He was all business. "Susan?" He asked.

"Too complicated?" Susan asked Daisy. "A click too far?"

"Maybe," Daisy said, but then: "Leon, this a big checkers-playing state? You test for that?"

"Seriously?" Leon asked. "I haven't. I could check if—"

"Not seriously." Daisy laughed. "But I was just thinking. You know how people always say the loser was playing checkers while the winner was playing chess? Well, maybe we should reverse that: Harris the intellectual plays chess. We're down with the folks—we play checkers. And my man, Mr. Jemmons, may have come up with a double jump here: We jump over our negative *and* his counterattack and land on the other side of the board. Which means we've been *kinged,* we can go backwards and forwards. We sort of make fun of him, saying Ain't *he* a stuck-up sonofabitch."

"Right—exactly—exactly right," Richard said, bursting. "Why the fuck not?"

"What's going on?" asked Brad Lieberman, just off the phone. Daisy explained it. "Well, I've got some bad news," Brad said. "If you're gonna do it, you gotta shoot now. I don't suppose any of you've seen Lucille's four-market plus a dinner in Nashville schedule for tomorrow?"

He passed it around. Several people whistled.

"Wait a minute," Daisy said. "Lucille—you were arguing for cutting another spot, when the fuck did you think we'd be able to shoot it—?"

"You don't have twenty-four-hour production capability?" Lucille asked.

"As a matter of fact, we do," Daisy snapped back.

"Then what's the problem?"

"Sanity," Susan said. "Even Jack needs a couple of hours' sleep every few days. So, Jack—over to you."

"Let's do it," he said. "I like it. What the hell."

"Okay," Daisy said. "Shoot, then sleep. Or sleep, then shoot?"

"Shoot first," he said. "I ain't gonna be able to sleep in this madhouse. I'll sleep on the plane."

"It'll take an hour or two to script it, set it, rouse the crew," Daisy said.

"Okay. Three-forty-five at Universal," Brad said.

"Deal," Stanton said. "Anyone want to play some hearts?"

We called the spot "Click-Click." I don't know if it influenced many voters, but it certainly drove Lawrence Harris around the bend. We had it up by Sunday morning. Everyone in Florida who watched David Brinkley, *Meet the Press* or CBS *Sunday Morning* saw it. Everyone watching the NCAA basketball tournament that afternoon saw it. It was all over the news that night and the morning shows on Monday. Harris, a jump too slow, was stuck with his first "click" ad—which seemed prehistoric and self-righteous to anyone who'd seen ours. Leon's postgame analysis showed that the numbers, which started breaking our way on Thursday, kept moving in the right direction through the weekend—"Click-Click" didn't start or stop anything. But then, it was hard to say what, if anything, worked in a campaign that came and went so quickly—it may have been nothing more complicated than the fact that we appeared to be confident, playing offense, and Harris was wobbly, on the defensive. It may have been that a stiff, chilly New Hampshire college professor just wasn't going to sell down South, period.

No debate was scheduled for Florida, but Harris was desperate to have at us. He made his move Monday afternoon—and a weird move it was. We were driving from Palm Beach to Miami in the Stanton Van South, trailed by two buses full of scorps, stopping to shake hands at malls along the way and doing radio call-in shows in between. It was a good day, an *up* day: we were winning. The sun was shining. Stanton was in a good mood. The scorps were lax and happy, taking it easy. After New Hampshire and the weeks of tarmac-hopping, the past few days in Florida had been an unexpected blessing for them, a vacation almost—and a nice story besides, with Stanton taking off the gloves and Harris slugging back. There wasn't much news left to report in Florida now and everyone knew this would be the last day of good weather for a while: we'd be heading back to Mammoth Falls, then up to Chicago to start Illinois-Michigan week, after an evening rally in Miami Beach.

So it was a lazy afternoon. We shook hands at a Winn-Dixie strip mall in Palm Beach, then started south. The first of the radio shows scheduled for the afternoon was the most obscure, but also the most fun—Izzy Rosenblatt's, which was broadcast out of a closet in West Palm. Stanton sat up in the front of the van with the phone, shoes off, sipping a Diet Coke; I listened in on my Walkman. We had arranged for the press buses to broadcast all three shows on their speaker systems, which probably doubled Rosenblatt's usual audience.

Izzy, who was eighty, had a sense of humor but not much of a following. His show was called the *Israel Rosenblatt Hour,* but he liked to call it "Shmooze for Jews"—and he kept it light, gossipy; no serious policy stuff for Izzy, mostly nostalgia and spritz. In fact, what he *really* wanted to know from Stanton was about Momma and where she liked to go in Vegas, who her favorite acts were and whether she took another card or stood pat when she was holding 16. Stanton was talking about how her favorite song was Kenny Rogers's "The Gambler" when Izzy interrupted him and said, "Funny thing, Governor, we've got Senator Harris on the phone . . . Well, this *is* an honor."

Stanton turned around and looked at me.

"Senator," Izzy said, "we were just talking about Governor Stanton's mother and how she just loves Vegas—does your mother have a favorite vacation spot?"

"My mother is dead."

"Oh, I'm sorry."

"And Jack Stanton should be ashamed of the way he's scaring a lot of other elderly people down here."

"Scaring?" Izzy said.

"He's telling them that I'm going to cut their Social Security and—"

"Aw, c'mon, Larry," Stanton interrupted—but calmly, casually. "It's in your book. It's part of that 'classroom exercise' you were so all-fired huffy about up in New Hampshire."

"Jack, you let me—"

"GENTLEMEN!" Izzy said. Then laughed: "Hey, folks, it worked."

"Jack," Harris resumed, "everyone knows what you're doing down here, the sleazy politics you're playing."

"Izzy," Stanton said. "Okay if I get a word in here? I'd like to ask Senator Harris a question."

"Go ahead, Governor."

"Now, Larry, I'm looking at your campaign book, page eighteen—paragraph three." He wasn't looking at the book. He had memorized the passage. But it sounded good. "What exactly does it mean when you say you want to 'study' a freeze in cost-of-living adjustments?"

"That's only one possibility," Harris said. "We might want to rework how COLAs are calculated."

"He isn't talking about soft drinks, Izzy," Stanton said. "A COLA is a cost-of-living adjustment. It means that we raise your Social Security to keep up with inflation. Senator Harris doesn't think that's such a good idea."

"Now *wait* a minute, I didn't say that," Harris said.

"Well, what do you mean, Larry? It's right here in your book."

"I'm saying it has to be studied," Harris said. "Who knows? We might even want to raise COLAs."

"*Raise* them?" Stanton asked, feigning surprise. "But it says right here you want to study *freezing* them. Folks, I've told you what I'd do: I won't mess with your Social Security. Senator Harris can't seem to make up his mind."

"Jack, that's outrageous."

"Larry, you want to go on to Medicare, the Middle East—I'm happy to talk about all your problems."

Izzy wasn't. He wanted his show back. "Senator Harris, do you have a favorite comedian?"

"This whole campaign is a joke," Harris fumed. "It's a clear demonstration of why people are disgusted with politics and politicians, why it's so hard to have an honest discussion of the issues."

"Larry, I'm telling them what my positions are," Stanton said, "You're the one who—"

"You're *distorting* my positions!"

"No," Stanton said. "You just can't defend your—"

"Not when you play these games— Folks, we just can't afford to keep spending money like this."

"But you just said you might want to spend *more* on COLAs," Stanton said. "Larry, I think you're confused."

"But I . . . I . . ." Harris seemed to cough twice. "Excuse me," he said. "Unh," he said. "Listen," he said. "Excuse me." And the line went dead.

When the Izzy show was over, Stanton asked: "What happened? Did he hang up or what?"

I didn't know.

"You think he's okay?"

He was on the evening news. We watched it from the hotel suite we'd taken for a couple of hours, getting cleaned up for our last rally in Miami Beach. Richard and Susan had joined us. The four of us would fly to Mammoth Falls in a Beechcraft after the rally; the scorps would get a last night in Miami and meet us in Chicago on Tuesday.

"Well, he looks all right," I said.

"That was a noon rally," Stanton said. "Look, there's Picker."

Freddy Picker, in a plaid shirt once again, had an arm around Harris, who looked decidedly uncomfortable. Picker seemed tanned, healthy, confident—especially in contrast to poor Harris, who was clearly furious about everything that was happening to him.

"When this is over, we should talk to Picker," Stanton said. "I always liked Freddy. Smart guy."

"I saw him Saturday night," Richard said. "He did warm-up for Harris—big rally at the fairgrounds, and he wasn't half bad. He woke 'em up. Then Harris put 'em back to sleep again. You can't do a 'classroom exercise' at a county fair."

"He rough on me? Picker?" Stanton asked.

"Rougher'n a bull on a sheep. He's got a responsive chorus goin': 'What does Stanton *stand* for?' He says, 'Y'know, Stanton says he wants to do this and this and this, but you can't do it, cause there's no money—and so, you gotta ask yourself, "What does Stanton *stand* for?" ' And so on. It was pretty good the-yater, gotta say."

"What's his story?" I asked. "Where's he been?"

"He got elected Watergate year," Stanton said, with some disdain, "and quit after one term. He just up and quit."

"Why?" I asked. "Did he screw up?"

"Not so far as anyone could tell," Richard said. "Had a weird scene at a press conference. What was it—you remember, Governor?"

"He was going to announce for a second term," Stanton said. "And he surprised everyone. 'I changed my mind,' he said. 'I'm goin' home.' It was real strange. I don't remember hearing much more about it. I was gearing up for my own run. But y'know, everyone thought Freddy was the real deal. It could've just as easily been him as Carter. More easily: He was the governor of Florida. Still looks pretty good, doesn't he?"

"Looks *better,* lost his baby fat," Richard said.

"I'll give him a call tomorrow," Stanton said. "Congratulate him on the campaign and see what gives."

We did our Miami rally, which went nicely. Stanton spent the ride to the plane on the phone with Leon, who had wall-to-wall good news. We were holding strong throughout the South.

I called Daisy with the news. "So what's with Harris?" she asked immediately.

"He can't be too happy," I said.

"No—you didn't hear?"

"What?"

"He didn't show for his evening rally in Lauderdale."

"No shit," I said. "Hold on a second. Hey, Governor, Harris blew off his Lauderdale rally. Daise, they say what it was?"

"Well, Picker was kind of mysterious. He told the crowd Harris was feeling under the weather—but when the scorps nailed him afterwards, he said he wasn't sure. He hadn't seen Harris. But Mrs. Harris said it was a serious case of the flu, or maybe food poisoning."

It was a massive heart attack, but we didn't find that out until about nine the next morning. CNN had the ambulance shot and Harris being rushed into a hospital, an oxygen mask over his face. I was back at our headquarters in Mammoth Falls, calling around, when the news came on. I called Marty Rosales, our Miami guy.

"*Two* heart attacks," he said. "A little one after the dustup with Jack on Izzy's show. He went back to the hotel, had a heart guy come in to see him—and then, kaboom: the big one last night."

"How big? Anyone know?"

"Well, you know Shirley Herrera—she did some advance for us? Her sister is a nurse over at Lauderdale, and she heard he's in a coma."

"Shit. CNN just said 'serious' condition."

"Well, a coma's serious," Marty said.

"Sit tight, Marty. You hear anything firm, call us at this number." I gave him the number at the Mansion, where Richard and I were scheduled to meet with Stanton to work up something for that night in Chicago. "And tonight we'll be at the Palmer House, okay?"

Richard was jiggling; I was freaked. It seemed cataclysmic, incalcula-ble. "You ever had anything like this?" I asked.

"Nope," he said. "Dark side of the moon."

We were on our way over to the Mansion. It was chilly, a mid-March day, sun ducking in and out of fast-moving clouds. Richard was riding shotgun, jiggling his legs with his hands pressed between his thighs, a mildly obscene form of meditation. Usually, he thought out loud. But he wasn't saying anything now. He stared out the win-dow. It was, without doubt, the strangest moment yet: Richard, speechless.

And then it got worse. I was so wrapped up in my own thoughts, trying to play it out, that I didn't quite grasp the significance of what I was seeing in the crescent driveway as we pulled up to the Mansion. There was Susan. She was walking with someone. She had her arm around a woman, a large woman. Their heads were down, close to-gether. We pulled up and Susan looked up, her eyes red. The other woman kept moving forward, looking down. She was large and dark, wearing a church hat and a navy blue sailor dress. She looked up at me as I got out of the car, rivulets down her cheeks—Amalee McCollis-ter. I just went numb, staring at her. They moved on past us, and Susan glanced back at me—furious.

"What the fuck was that?" Richard said.

"Nothing," I said.

"Henri, I *know* nothing. That wasn't nothing. Who was that lady—I've seen her. Henri"—he grabbed me by the shoulders—"what the *fuck* is going on here?"

"Nothing, Richard. Nothing. You've gotta trust me on this. Please."

Richard eyed me. His natural opacity had evaporated. He was right on me. "Fuck this shit," he said, and walked on inside. "This cam-paign is just one long fucking blind date."

Stanton was in the study, his head in his hands. He looked up when we walked in. His eyes were red too. But about what?

"I didn't want it to happen this way," he said.

What? Richard and I just looked at him. He was in his wing chair. He had a blue suit and white shirt on, no tie; he was holding a red-and-blue striped *politician's* tie in his left hand. He had selected it thinking, no doubt, that the American public would see him for this first time that night as the probable Democratic nominee. From the way he was holding it, I could tell that he'd selected it *before* he'd learned about Lawrence Harris. He had already made the semiconscious calculation that he would have to go to a less aggressive tie. I knew him so well—parts of him.

"It's my fault," he said.

What? Richard and I sat down on the lime-green couch. I thought of all the meetings we'd had in this curious, impersonal room, most of them horrible, but none quite so numb and weird as this. It was possible, I realized, that he wasn't yet aware that Amalee had come to visit Susan. In fact, it wouldn't be at all surprising. It would be very much in keeping with the mysterious emotional concavity of their bond: the most blatant transgressions often had to be ignored.

"Dammit," he said, slamming a fist down. "I was so prideful. Henry, you heard me yesterday. I was so smug with him—I could have treated him with more respect. But I was going for the kill. I wanted to *humiliate* him. You heard that in my voice, didn't you? I didn't need to take it that far. We were going to whip his butt anyway—I could've been gracious, y'know? It would have been smarter. We were going to need him down the road. He's a smart guy—and he was *right* on the damn issues—you know that, right?"

"But he was a pompous sonofabitch," Richard said, "and he rubbed your nose in it."

I was relieved that we were on *this* crisis and not the other. Stanton stood, still holding the tie in his left hand. "Yeah, and I rubbed his nose in it right back—but that's not how you win the big ones. You have to *be* big to win the big ones, and I played it like a fucking county commissioner. *Dammit,* I wish for once I could just get a clear shot—y'know? This was gonna be it. Tonight. So what do we—no, I *know* what we do. We take it down until we know more about him."

"Take it down?" I asked.

"I tried to reach her at the hospital," he said, moving on, "but she hasn't returned my . . . Can't blame her, canya?"

"What about Paul Shaplen, or Picker?" I asked.

"You want to try?" he asked.

. . .

So I tried. I reached Shaplen about four in the afternoon, just before we got on the plane to Chicago. "The governor's really ripped up over this," I said. "He wants to convey his sympathy to Mrs. Harris."

"Fuck him."

"C'mon now, Paul."

"C'mon now yourself, asshole. You think she's got any fucking thing to say to the prick who put her husband on life support?"

"On life support?"

"Fuck you, Burton. Some people'll rent out their pigment to any old piece of shit that comes along."

He was magnificent that night. He had me go out, kill the music, calm the crowd. I don't remember what I said, but they were stone quiet when he came out with Susan. Both of them looked awful. All the networks, I later learned, broke into their schedule to broadcast this moment.

"This is a night for prayer, not politics," Jack Stanton said. "We stand here humbled by fate, mindful of God's power, but we must also keep in mind His grace. Tonight our thoughts and prayers are with Lawrence Harris, and Martha, and their children. We have been competitors this season and sometimes spoke in anger, but always from a base of genuine respect. I think the people of Florida, and throughout the South, will understand if I forgo thanking them for their support this night, forgo any talk of victory or defeat, and ask them to join us in a moment of silent prayer."

He kept his head down for considerably more than a moment. When he lifted it, a tear had slid halfway down his left cheek. He wiped it and said, "I am canceling all campaign events until further notice. I hope you understand. And I hope God, in His infinite wisdom, will soothe and heal and bring comfort to Lawrence Harris and his family."

There was a scattering of applause, but Jack Stanton stopped it by putting his hands out, palms down, then raising his right index finger to his lips, "Shhh," he said. "Not now."

. . .

I was on the phone with Daisy about midnight.

"I wish I was there with you," she said.

"I wish you were, too. I feel just, I don't know. It's like this whole thing just went off a cliff. We're still in midair, falling."

"Imagine what it would've been like if we lost," she said. "What do you think happens now?"

"I have no idea," I said. "I'm stumped."

There was a knock at the door. "Someone's at the door," I said. "It's probably him. I better go. I'll call you later."

"If it's him, it may be a lot later," she said.

But it wasn't him. It was her. She stood there in the doorway, in bare feet, seeming smaller than usual. She was still wearing the plain navy blue dress and Chanel scarf she'd worn on the podium. "Well, aren't you going to invite me in?" she asked, curtly.

"Of course."

She walked in. I closed the door.

"You *sonofabitch*," she said, and slapped me across the face. "You cruel, heartless sonofabitch. Amniocentesis?" She slapped me again. "You motherfucker." She shuddered and suddenly wailed, "Ohhhh-hhhhh," and began to sob. She was shuddering and sobbing and she leaned into me, her hands tucked onto my chest, separating us slightly, her head on my left shoulder. I put an arm tentatively around her, patting her back. She lifted her face, mascara-streaked and uncertain, needy for once. She moved her hands out, away, and put her lips on mine. Then she opened her mouth, and I had a decision to make.

Oh, shit.

VII

"S o, Governor Stanton," Don O'Brien asked in his thick, caramel voice. "Can I offer you a Harp?"

"A Diet Coke," Stanton said, "if you've got any."

I was back at the beginning of time. Senator O'Brien raised himself—massive, ursine—from behind his walnut-and-brass desk and went to the doorless closet where he kept the small refrigerator. The little office was dark and denlike. There were soft lights, heavy gold curtains, no views. O'Brien, uncomfortable in large and light spaces, had given his formal office over to staff and hidden himself in a support room beyond. There was the desk, which took up about a third of the room; Stanton and I sat in two chairs facing the desk; Dov Mandelbaum, the senator's young strategist—my former counterpart—sat behind us on the small sofa along the back wall. On the walls were photos of Don O'Brien with every president since Eisenhower, and three others: a laminated cover of *Time* magazine from sometime in the early seventies, featuring a Don O'Brien who looked very much as he did today—white hair, huge red face, bulbous nose and thick lips, but with longer sideburns, his one concession to that inelegant moment in time. There was also a photo of Senator O'Brien—the son of a Southie garbage hauler—receiving his honorary degree from "the Hahvihds." And dominating the room, above the sofa where Dov sat, was a portrait of the senator's deceased wife, Fiona, smiling, head tilted slightly, an overpowering kindness emanating from her eyes. Don O'Brien spent every day staring directly at that portrait.

"So what can I do for you, Governor Stanton?" Donny asked, returning to his seat with a Diet Coke for Stanton and a cup of tea for himself.

"I want to ask you for your support."

Don O'Brien threw back his head and roared appreciatively. It was a reference to the senator's favorite political story—how he'd come home from his first, losing congressional campaign and thanked his neighbor Mrs. Aggie Murphy for her support and she'd said, "But, Donny, I didn't vote for you." O'Brien, crushed, reminded her that he'd gone to the store for her and shoveled her walk free of charge for twenty years, so why on earth *wouldn't* she vote for him? "Because you didn't ask," she said (or so he claimed).

Stanton, of course, realized that O'Brien's support would not be forthcoming that day. Dov and I had negotiated the logistics of this meeting carefully. There would be no statement of support, no photo op. But Donny *had* agreed to meet with us, which seemed a victory. It meant that Larkin would have to meet with us as well—which was, I was certain, Donny's primary motive: he lived for Lark's discomfort.

"Jack, I've been watching you," O'Brien now said, warmly, "and you puzzle me. I watch you on Sunday nights, on C-SPAN—*Road to the White House*—it's taken the place of Ed Sullivan in my life. It's quite amazing: they'll show you, or Larry or Bart or that pipsqueak Charlie Martin, just shaking hands for a half hour. Can you imagine? Who'd ever want to watch such a thing? Except for the likes of us, of course. So we have our own private network now." He smiled, shaking his head, looking up at Fiona. "Only not so private. Not much we can get away with in private anymore, huh, Jack?"

O'Brien sipped his tea, leaned forward, elbows on the desk. "Anyway, here's what puzzles me about you: You are very good at this. That is abundantly clear. The thing that makes you so good is, you really do like *them*—the folks—don't you? You seem to enjoy yourself with them. That's important—they'll cut you some slack if they think you like them. You give a nice speech, too. But I have never seen a politician carry so much trouble around with him. You're like that cartoon character—what's his name, Dov?"

"Pigpen."

O'Brien chuckled. "Pigpen. A permanent cloud of dirt follows him around. It worries me, Jack. A cloud like that doesn't happen by accident. I know, this latest thing—Larry's coronary—isn't really your fault, though the way they keep playing that Izzy Whatchamacallit tape on the news, over and over, doesn't help any. And I know that it's not the way it used to be—everyone gets taken apart these days. We all suffer. They have an eighteen-minute report on *Eye-to-Eye,* or whatever they call that show, about *me,* playing golf in the Bahamas with the insurance industry—it doesn't look good. So there's no such thing as security anymore. No more safe seats. It's hard for us to legislate confidently if we're all walking on tiptoe, if you know what I mean. Everyone feels the heat. But what I wonder about you is, do you *need* the heat? Are you one of those boyos who like danger—a skydiver?—or . . ."

Stanton started to respond, but stopped—intelligently—realizing there was nothing to be said here. "The other Jack—Kennedy—he was like that," O'Brien continued. "A perfect skydiver. He was like one of those Greek heroes who forgets he isn't a god. He was a Mick who forgot he wasn't a WASP. It's okay for the gods to live dangerously. They can come down, rape and pillage, run off with our daughters, turn our sons into sparrows. But if a man mistakes himself for a god, they will find a way to humiliate you. They will have their revenge. Discipline is how we show them reverence. But you, Jack, seem to enjoy tempting them."

"I've made mistakes," Stanton said.

"Perhaps one too many," O'Brien said.

"Perhaps," the governor said. "But I've learned from them. And I've survived. You may not be thrilled by it—but I'm still here, and I'm not going away. If someone wants this nomination, they will have to come in and take it from me."

"A big if," O'Brien said. "You've driven the stock down, unfortunately. There may be no takers. Not from here, anyway. Larkin—I can tell you what he's thinking. He has made his calculations. It's too late for him to get into many of the primaries—a couple, maybe."

"California," Dov said.

"He won't come in just for California," O'Brien said. "He is a cautious man—right, Henry? He'd want to test his act on a smaller stage first. He likes sure things. Henry used to be his balls." He looked over at me, curious. "This fellow doesn't need *those,*" he said, nodding at Stanton. "So what are you giving him? You loaning him your conscience, Henry?"

Stanton shifted in his seat but stayed calm. "You know, Jack, I don't know if William Larkin would take the nomination if we handed it to him at this point," O'Brien said. "The president is likely to be re-elected, whoever runs against him. That would leave Bill looking to be a university president next December. Lousy work. More fund-raising than here, and you don't get to cut deals." O'Brien looked for a laugh; Stanton obliged with a chuckle. Donny wrinkled his brow, tossed a dismissive hand. "No, the Lark won't take that chance. He's been here—how long, Henry? Twenty years. Made an elegant move to the leadership—took *you* by surprise, didn't it?" he said, to me again. "Anyway, we've all been living with Republican presidents for a long time—some real stinkers, too. Another four years of it won't kill us. But we don't want to be *embarrassed,* either, if you know what I mean, Jack. You make a fool of this party, we could lose some seats in November—might even lose the Senate again. I wouldn't be pleased by that. Have to move all my stuff across the hall."

O'Brien leaned back in his chair, stared up at Fiona. He had said his piece.

"I can win the nomination and beat the president," Stanton said forcefully. I'd been hoping for something more puckish, more clever—Donny was testing him now—but the governor had decided not to take any chances. His toughness was the issue, and he would play this as tough as he could.

O'Brien laughed. "Dov, incumbent presidents beaten this century?"

"Taft, Hoover, Carter."

"Beaten by Wilson, Roosevelt and Reagan," O'Brien said. "So you are telling me, Jack, that the incumbent is in a class with the former and you are in a class with the latter?" He laughed again and shook his head. "Tell me another one."

"If not Larkin, who'll take it from me?" Stanton said.

"I don't know," O'Brien said. "But we can always work out something . . . respectable. And we will, if you don't pull this together. I can promise you that. If you come out of California with one delegate less than a majority, you will find yourself back in Mammoth Falls, cutting ribbons and distributing highway contracts, by the end of July."

"And if I do pull it together?"

"I will admire your perseverance," O'Brien said. "In fact, I already admire your perseverance. There are worse qualities a politician can have."

"If I pull it together," Stanton asked, "will you place my name in nomination?"

"Not very smart politics, Governor—an old fart like me, doing that. I play golf with the insurance industry, a sin apparently even more troublesome to Americans than diddling a hairdresser, if that's what you did. No, I won't place your name in nomination, Jack," O'Brien said, rising; ending it. "But I will do what I won't do today. I will stand on the steps outside with you, and have my picture taken."

Which was about as good as it got that week. Not bad, in fact: O'Brien's was an entirely reasonable position. Few others were ready to give us *that* much. The meeting with Larkin, which followed immediately—a cloud of scorps trailing us from one end of the capitol to the other—was surreal by comparison. The Lark would not deign to discuss politics with Stanton. He reminisced about the last time he and Marianne had had dinner with Jack and Susan. He asked about young Jackie; he talked about his own kids. He became passionate, and very detailed, about the intransigence of the Japanese in trade negotiations. Stanton showed he could be equally passionate, and even more detailed, on the same subject—and, in the process, sent the message that if Larkin wanted to challenge him, he would give no quarter. I thought it was an impressive performance. Larkin looked over at me from time to time, coolly, not unpleasantly, bland lashless eyes unblinking; I unblinked back at him. Stanton walked out of there furious, disdainful. "Please, God, I want that gelding," he whispered.

We gave the press some time then, in the statuary hall outside the House chamber. We couldn't not. "Governor Stanton, what if anything do you think you accomplished here today?" A mousy woman from AP asked.

"Had a chance to sit down with our congressional leaders, get to know each other better," he said casually.

"Did either of them ask you to withdraw?"

"Absolutely not."

"Have you read A. P. Caulley's piece in the *Times*? Do you have a reaction?" Caulley, who always tapped the purest—if not quite the freshest—vein of conventional wisdom in Washington, had called three former Democratic Party chairs who expressed alarm, though not directly for attribution, that a man of Jack Stanton's character seemed destined to win the nomination.

"No," Stanton lied. "What's he say?"

"Well, that a lot of leading Democrats think you don't have the character to be president."

"Well, look," he said. "I'm mostly interested in what the *people* think. If they think I should go home, my guess is they'll figure out a way to get the message across."

"Will Bill Larkin challenge you?"

"You'll have to ask him that. Fine with me if he does. Our party should have its strongest possible candidate next fall. Any of these folks can prove they're stronger than me, I'll support 'em."

"Have you talked yet with Mrs. Harris?" A young woman from *The Boston Globe* asked. "Have you apologized?"

"For *what*?" Stanton glared at her. It was a smart, controlled flash of anger. None of the reporters would have the guts to say, "For baiting him into a massive heart attack."

"Look, we have a serious situation here," Stanton said, turning instantaneously sober. "I have suspended campaigning. I know it's hard, but maybe we should all show a little restraint for the next few days—till we know more about Senator Harris's condition. Thanks."

That day in Washington, the Friday after the Florida primary, was strange and remarkable in many ways but truly memorable only in one: it was the first time I ever saw Daisy in a skirt. It was a kilt, to be precise, of a heathery plaid—and much shorter than the kilts I remembered from school; she was also wearing a black blazer, a sky-blue turtleneck, dangly enamel earrings, black stockings—and heels. She looked spectacular. We met at a restaurant near the White House that was deep in mortal trendiness at that moment, offering Washington its first haute, high-concept, hyperdesigned, if not quite distinguished, Tex-Mex cuisine.

"My God, look at you," I said. I was standing at the bar, watching the door. I hadn't *recognized* her at first. "Do you do this often?"

"Get dressed?" she asked. "Only when I'm depressed. It's okay?"

"It's fabulous," I said. "You're depressed?"

"Aren't you?" She snaked an arm around my waist and whispered in my ear. "Let's drink margaritas, go home and get laid."

"Sounds good to me," I said. But something was up. She was pressing. "Here comes Richard."

It took him a while to reach us. This was Washington. Everyone knew Richard—knew all of us, more or less—and he took his time, working his way along the bar, shaking hands, slapping backs and chatting, his honks and bleats overwhelming even this incredibly noisy restaurant. Unlike Daisy, Richard looked the same here as in America: blue blazer, white shirt, no tie; and his signature, pressed, too-tight, too-short jeans—and white socks and running shoes. "Assholes in megavulture mode tonight, y'knowhattamean?" He greeted us. "Let's get a table."

"Smoking, okay?" Daisy said.

"'Sweird, Daisy Mae. I always forget you smoke. I used to smoke—you know that?"

"I'll bet you did," she said, as we were led to a corner table in a nearly depopulated room. "Never underestimate the pariah factor: smoking'll get you a quiet table, and fast too."

"You know how I stopped?" Richard said. "I smoked two hundred cigarettes—ten packs—in a single day. I decided to gorge myself on 'em, y'knowhattamean? My throat was killing me, thought I was gonna die by lunchtime. So you know what I did? I switched to *Luckies,* then to *Pall*-fucking-*Mall,* the strongest, harshest worst damn things I could find. It was the most disgusting thing I ever did that didn't involve sex or politics. By nightfall, I needed an iron lung, I needed to be fumigated, or sterilized or some fucking thing. I surrounded myself with ashtrays, full of those stale, disgusting pieces of shit—put 'em all around my bed that night. Next morning, I woke up, blew lunch, could barely talk—my throat was killing me so much—and I never touched another damn one of those things again. You should try it, Daize."

"Don't think so," she said. "Only smoke four or five a day, no big deal. Reminds my friends I'm not an absolutely perfect person—right, Henry?"

"That, and your taste in movies," I said.

"So?" she said. "Tell us."

"Boy, it is *weird* being back here, doing the same old shit," I said, "being a supplicant in Donny O'Brien's office, feeling the Lark's cool breeze, seeing all these tactical people—reminds me why I left town."

"But you love it, too," Daisy said, always the unambiguous junkie (but a little worried now that I might not be). "It's what you do."

"It's what I did," I said. "Y'know, I can't remember the last time I was here. But it didn't take a nanosecond to remember the feel of the place: everybody's so *on top of* everything. The guy at the dry cleaner's has an opinion about the emissions-trading provisions of the Clean Air Act, the Ethiopian cabbie wants to know if Donny's gonna block cloture on capital gains. It's like being trapped inside talk radio: a city full of crank callers with nothing else in their lives, nothing better to do. It's why the rest of the country thinks we're nuts."

"Blah, blah, blah," Richard said, appropriately. Trashing Washington is one of the world's most gratuitous pastimes. "What happened up on the hill today? And where's a waitress? Or is this place too trendy to have *help*? Hey, YOU."

A very hip young woman wearing black lipstick and black combat boots ambled over. We ordered drinks. Daisy had a frozen margarita with a double shot; I tried one too. Richard had a Diet Coke.

"It wasn't a disaster," I said, when the waitress wandered off. "The candidate was fine. I think he scared the shit out of the Lark, outtalked him on Japanese trade policy. But it was just . . . weird. I kept thinking: Is *this* the prize? Is this what we've been running to win?"

"We win, it changes," Daisy said.

"Guys, I wouldn't go 'round worrying too damn much about winning this week," Richard said. "You hear what Marshall Gordon's gonna say on Sunday? We should 'step aside' because of all the shit that's gone down."

Marshall Gordon, who'd been writing a column in the *Post* since before forever, was the unimpeachable voice of moderate sanity in Washington.

"Step aside for what?" Daisy asked.

"For the Wi-i-i-se Men to uncork the magic bottle at the convention," Richard said, shimmering his hands like a hoodoo man. "All them geniuses who've been doin' so well by the party—doin' well by doin' good, y'knowhattamean?—they gonna haul their two-thousand-dollar suits into a room and restore sanity to the process." He flipped a bird then. "Fuck *them*. And then when it happens, when they've picked the pope and vice pope, they'll leak it to ol' Marshall Gordon. It sure beats havin' an election. It's this week's parlor game: What's the *real* ticket, who's in the room when it gets decided?"

"My guess," Daisy said, "is *their* guess is something like Ozio-Larkin, right?"

"The real question is, which of us winds up on the *Today* show Monday morning to respond to Gordon's column," I said, not wanting to play the What If game. "Who goes on *Nightline* Monday night? Why is it that every other week we've got a new miniwave of crap to wade through?"

"Send Libby," Daisy said. "Fuck 'em all."

"Fuck 'em all is right," I said. "This is bullshit. No one's gonna *do* anything, no one's gonna come out and stop us. You could see Jack sensed that today—he paid his respects and was tough as nails. You sit in the same room as him and the Lark, and you realize what a flimsy contraption the Lark is: he'd get blown away if he ever actually walked out into the street and came after us. These guys are moles. They live in that building, they go rummaging around after each other through piles of mole shit. They don't do sunlight."

"Don't *have* much sunlight right now, Henri," Richard said, as the drinks came. He took one long, nearly obscene gulp and said to the waitress, "Honey, you think you could bestir yourself to bring me another." He smiled at her sneer, then turned back to us: "Check it out:

We're stacked up in the clouds, circling the runway. We're all sitting around, scratching our balls—"

"Mixed-metaphor alert," Daisy said.

"Well, shit, Daisy Mae," Richard said. "They are having fucking *elections* in Michigan and Illinois—got more delegates coming out of Chicago than we spent a year driving ourselves crazy over in New Hampshire. And we're not out there, working it. No one is. Y'ask me, we should just fuck all this humble respectful shit and send him out, do some town meetings, win those suckers, shut these assholes up."

"He won't do it," I said. "Not yet."

"He better soon," Richard said. "This is America. It may not be the brandy-and-bullshit crowd, but someone's gonna come after us. It's drivin' me nuts, trying to figure out who. I checked down the road, see whether Charlie Martin could get back in, or even Nilson."

"He won't," I said. "He's with us."

"When's the last time *you* saw him around?" Richard said, stopping me. Richard, as usual, was thinking through worst-case scenarios—all of which had come true so far, though that hadn't done us much good in preparing for them. "Henri, use your fucking head: someone is gonna come after us. We're heading to New York. Ozio? Could Ozio use Harris's line? Y'know, drop a hint—if you vote for the vegetable, you can still stop Stanton? Ozio can still get on in California, though he's gonna have to move his butt."

"He won't," Daisy said. "He'll do some body language. He'll do what he can to fuck us in New York, but he's not going to make an overt move. Overt isn't in his racial memory."

"*Someone* is coming after us," Richard said, then began to peruse the menu. "What is this, one of those places where you can build your own pineapple-guacamole chimichanga?"

Everything about sex is banal except the anticipation. The act itself, though undeniably satisfying, is memorable no more than a handful of times in the course of a life—and imperfect more often than not. I can remember every twitch, glance, touch, hint—the way my *hair* felt—the afternoon Daisy and I first made love in Mammoth Falls. With Susan Stanton, though, there had been no anticipation, no expectation. (Okay: a stray thought, occasionally—but she was *Susan Stanton*, the world's most fortified bunker; it wasn't anything you could think about in broad daylight.) But it happened. It happened in a semi-numb realm of physical experience, a reflexive part of the brain and body—it happened too quickly to engage the imagination. She even *smelled* distant and formal, all soap and hair spray. I'd never, I realized, made love before to a woman who used hair spray. It made her hair feel stiff, and it preoccupied me. I found myself thinking about the stiffness of her hair rather than what our bodies were doing. When her body finished what it was doing, she made a barely audible grunt, a door closing. She gathered her clothes in the dark. She didn't say anything, or do anything, or touch me or kiss me good-bye. I saw her silhouette as she moved, brusquely, through the amber crime-light crack between the curtains of my hotel room; that was all I saw. She didn't call the next day, or the days after, which was a relief, but a tiny, guilty disappointment, too.

Sometimes, even the anticipation is banal. My reaction to Daisy that night was entirely predictable, straight out of the "Wear Something Different" chapter of *How to Please a Man*. I was crazed horny. My hand was up under that little kilt as soon as we jumped in a cab; I was moving on her as soon as she opened the door to her house. She had a bandbox row house on Capitol Hill, a tiny Washington place. She turned on the lights; I turned them off.

"Henry, a *skirt* will do this to you?" She turned on the lights again, a row of track lights along the right wall. "Don't you even want to look around, see who I am?"

"I know who you are. You're smart and honest and orderly. You have a bookcase filled with politics and thrillers. You have—what's this?" I started to laugh. She had a vertical display rack, the sort of thing you'd see in a poster store, with an array of old movie posters, hanging on the wall to the left of the bookcase.

"I couldn't make up my mind," she said. "I couldn't settle on just one movie. You walk in and see, *The Sands of Iwo Jima* or *Casablanca* and say, 'Oh, she's one of those.' Of course, if you pinned me up against the wall and said, 'Choose one,' I'd have to go with *Sullivan's Travels* and

I've got it right . . . here." She flipped to Veronica Lake and Joel McRae, eternally romantic and cool, preternaturally American.

"Great movie, good choice," I said. "Why not go with it?"

"'Cause *all* of these are great. I bought 'em. I paid good money for them. They *are* originals. I wanted to be able to see them all. So what would your choice be, Henry—*Rashomon*?" She said this with a tinge of . . . something in her voice. I ignored it. She let me ignore it—until after we made love, upstairs, in her bedroom with the four televisions. I didn't notice the televisions until afterward, which said something about my state of mind and the intensity of my anticipation that night. I liked the bedroom, despite the televisions. She had it painted a dark Chinese red. There were four gold-framed Thomas Nast drawings on the wall. The bed was queen-size, with crisp, cheery blue-and-white checked sheets and pillowcases beneath a navy comforter. The lighting was soft, although there was a goose-necked brass reading lamp that arced in from the right side of the bed. I hadn't asked her about it, but I realized that she'd never lived with a man in that house.

"See, this is different from campaign sex," she said when I'd subsided. "There is a campaign going on out there—somewhere—but we're not part of it right now."

"And—?"

"Not fucking bad at all," she said, nuzzling her nose in my ear. But that wasn't quite true. I had sensed her holding back; bemused by my enthusiasm perhaps, or maybe something else.

"You want anything from downstairs, a Diet Coke?"

She returned, wearing a mohair shawl and nothing else. She tossed me the soda. It was strange, her casual nakedness: a new level of intimacy for us—we were always working our way through new levels, slowly and carefully, one at a time; we hadn't reached one yet we couldn't handle.

"So, why didn't you tell me about the McCollister girl?" she asked, trying to sound offhand.

"He told me not to tell anyone. He specifically mentioned you. I guess he figured that if you knew, Susan would."

She nodded. She didn't say anything.

"Look," I said. But couldn't figure out what to say next.

"So you went and scared Fat Willie into having his daughter get an amniocentesis. I don't get it."

"He figured Howard would scare her *out* of getting an amniocentesis—and that would make it go away."

"Brilliant," Daisy said. "He didn't understand that Fat Willie would do whatever his friend the governor asked?"

"So she went?" I asked.

"You haven't been following this, step by step?" she asked. "It's your baby—as it were."

"Willie came to *me*," I said.

"So that makes it—"

"Horrendous. You think I enjoyed it? I didn't want any part of it. I didn't want to think about it. I *didn't* think about it—I didn't even know she'd gone for the amnio."

"It was a *late* amnio, real late," she said. "It was too late to do a chorionic villus sampling—CVS. It's the latest thing, through the vagina, not the abdomen. They take pre-placental material. Might've been a little easier on the kid. But she's got herself a placenta now, feeding little Jackie McCollister or whoever it is. Anyway, we'll have a result in a couple of weeks."

"How do you know all this?"

"Susan put Libby on the case. She's practically moved in with the McCollisters."

"Of course," I said. "Look. That day with Howard—it was the worst thing I've ever done."

"But you did it."

"He insisted it wasn't his baby."

"And you believed him?"

An important moment for us, Daisy and me: "Not entirely," I said. "If I'd believed him entirely, it would've merely been awful—not the complete fucking horror that it has been. He did volunteer to have his blood taken, so I had to figure he was in the clear, and you know how dangerous it is to have something like this floating out there. The girl could tell a friend, the friend could tell another . . . and he could be absolutely innocent, and the whole campaign could come down. You think we could handle another scandal? Fuck. Not even a scandal. You think we could handle another *denial*? But still, there was—is—

something bugging me about this. Something in my gut: I don't believe he's absolutely innocent, y'know? And even if he is, in this case, I realized that I wouldn't put it past him—taking advantage of that girl. And you cannot imagine how ashamed I was. Howard did the heavy lifting—and a cold sonofabitch he was. But I was complicit. Willie came to me. He trusted me. And I guess, what it was, was—I had to give the governor the benefit of the doubt. I mean, if it's true that it's not his baby, then this had to be done, right?"

"And what will you think of him if it does turn out to be his baby?"

"I don't know. A lot less, I imagine. Daisy—" I sat up. "I don't understand *how* I think about this. I don't have a fucking clue. It's like—compartmentalized. There's the politician, the guy we've all invested in, and then there's this. How do *you* think about it?"

"I haven't, until recently—obviously," she said. "And then I was pissed."

"At him?"

"At you."

"I'm sorry," I said. But I found myself wondering: Was she pissed because I hadn't told her or because she hadn't been able to sense there was something important I wasn't telling her? The latter, I realized, was potentially more threatening. It meant there were things she might never know about me, ways she couldn't trust me, ways I could hurt her.

She was crying, quietly. I put my arm around her and pulled her toward me. She resisted, but she came.

We won Illinois and Michigan, but no one noticed. *We* hardly noticed. Other things happened that day. In Fort Lauderdale, Martha Harris—a sturdy cranberry-oat-bran muffin of a woman—held a press conference at the hospital where her husband remained in a coma. I was back in Mammoth Falls, at our headquarters. All activity stopped when Mrs. Harris came on the screen; she had the Stanton campaign's undivided attention.

"First of all, I want to thank the American public, all of you, for your remarkable outpouring of affection," she said. "I would especially like to thank the children of America—my husband, Senator Harris, was doing this for you, and, clearly, you understood that. The letters and drawings and everything we've gotten during the past week—I've read some of them to my husband. I think he can hear you . . ." Her voice broke now. "And I'm sure he is, as I am, more hopeful than ever about the future of our country. But hope is not enough. We need to do more."

And I thought about Richard: Right again. Here they come. "A great many of you have written asking us how we might keep the Harris movement alive," she said. "I think it's obvious, at this point, that my husband will not be able to continue his campaign for the presidency. But *someone should*. And so I have asked former governor Fred Picker of Florida, and he has agreed, to carry on for us—to continue to raise the issues." And now Freddy Picker moved somberly into the frame, head slightly bowed, hands clasped together in front of him. He was, finally, wearing a tie—blue-and-gold striped, it appeared. "And carry our message," Martha Harris continued, "all the way to the convention—and *beyond,* if possible. Both Lawrence and I learned to love Freddy Picker over the years, and especially over the past few weeks. He has been a devoted friend. He knows the meaning of honor. He understands what this country needs, and he will continue what we have begun, in an *honorable* way. And now," she said, tears suddenly spurting from both her eyes, "let me turn this campaign over to Governor Picker."

He was crying too. He brushed a tear from his right eye with the back of his hand, kissed Martha Harris lightly on the cheek, took a deep breath, stared down, as if in prayer, and then looked up, his fierce eyes quiet—different. There was a scattering of applause in the room. CNN had only one camera on scene, so it was hard to tell how many people—and reporters—were there, but it seemed pretty cramped. "I hope you'll excuse me," he said. "This is a very emotional time. I have a brief statement, and then I'll take a few questions—a very few, because, quite honestly, I haven't thought this through yet. Mrs. Harris approached me with this idea only yesterday. I was honored. I felt I couldn't possibly say no." He was staring directly into the CNN camera. I thought about the logistics of this: there were probably ten cameras facing him—and he had made sure to find the one that was broadcasting this live, nationally. "And I will try my darndest to express the themes that Lawrence Harris has begun to lay out for the American people in a manner consistent with the spirit of his campaign. Today I've spoken with several of our party leaders, and told them what Mrs. Harris has asked me to do—"

"Have you spoken with Governor Stanton?" a reporter interrupted.

"No," he said. "But let me make this clear: I am not running against Jack Stanton. I am running for Lawrence Harris."

"Does that mean you agree with every position he has taken in this campaign?"

"Most everything," he said. "There may be some differences in personal style, differences in emphasis—but I think Senator Harris was doing something important, and challenging, in this campaign, and I intend to carry that forward."

"Do you think you can win the nomination?"

"I'm not *trying* to win the nomination. I am just trying to continue what Senator Harris began, trying to give the American people an honest choice."

"But if you won the nomination—"

"It would be premature for me to discuss that, since I haven't given it a moment's thought. And that's why I think it'd be best to cut this session off right here. I've spent the night thinking about how I wanted to start this thing," he said, talking to CNN again, "about what gesture might convey the immense respect I have for Senator Harris, and the humility I feel at this moment, and the need for all of us to pull together as a country and give of ourselves. So I decided, since we're here in the hospital, that I'd just go down and donate a pint of blood."

There was a groan in Stanton headquarters, which had been stone silent to that point. And I must admit, I was shaking my head, too—and sort of half wondering who'd buzz me first: Richard, Daisy or the governor.

It was the governor.

"Jesus Christ, Henry. *We* should've thought of that," he said. "The blood thing."

.   .   .

We had a conference call that afternoon. It was a cumbersome thing—the governor and Susan at the Mansion; Howard, Lucille and me at headquarters; Richard, Leon and Daisy in Washington.

"All right," Stanton said. "What now?"

Silence.

"Good thing I've got all you geniuses on board," he said. "Okay, I'll go first: We start campaigning again immediately, Connecticut and New York. Howard, I want to see a New York schedule—and strategy—this time tomorrow. Beyond that, I'm stumped. How do we treat this guy? Do we ignore him? Debate him? Treat him like a candidate? I assume Harris has a ballot line in every state. Does he have full slates?"

"He's had some trouble slating. As for ballot lines, we *could* have knocked him off in New York," Howard said. "But you didn't want that."

"Right," Stanton said. "And one thing is absolutely certain at this point: we are not going to do *anything* that smacks of politics. We're gonna get the League of Women Voters' Seal of Approval for every last fucking thing we do. We're gonna be more high-minded than public television. But, within those parameters, we gotta be smart. Richard, how do we run against this guy without running against him?"

"Well, first thing," Richard said. "You gotta expect he's gonna be the flavor of the week. And it's all gonna be golden. The TV stuff, the profiles. He'll be interviewed everywhere the next few days. We're gonna have to be patient and see what he does."

"Any guesses?"

Silence, then Daisy: "Well, obviously we have no idea how he's gonna campaign, how it's gonna look, but my gut says he's going to jettison a lot of Harris's excess baggage. He can't junk the Virgin Uses tax, but he can slim it down, de-emphasize it some. Same with the Social Security COLA. He seems smart. He may be tougher for us than Harris."

"What do we know about him?" Susan asked. "Where's his family? Why'd he quit being governor? Where's he been all our lives?"

"He's divorced, isn't he?" Richard said.

"The point is, we don't know," Susan said. "We're going to need Libby to do a Nexus."

"Meanwhile," Stanton asked, "what do I say tonight—after I thank the people of Illinois and Michigan for this victory no one is gonna care about? No—wait a minute. I've got a better question: Howard, *can* he stop us? Let's assume the party takes the Donny O'Brien position: I get no help from them. We've got to make fifty percent plus one on our own. Can he stop us?"

"Yes," Howard said.

"Easily?"

"Yes."

"Don't we have a thousand some-odd delegates already?"

"We're running at about fifty-five percent, depending on how we do tonight," Howard said. "And if we keep running at that rate, we're okay, by a little—even assuming most of the superdelegates hang back and take their sweet time making up their minds. We've got commitments from about two hundred fifty of the seven hundred sixty-eight super-D's now, mostly the ones from down here—though who knows how solid those are."

"Howard, we damn well better find out," Stanton said. "I want a list of names—no, I want to know every damn thing about every last one of them, what they want, what they need. I want you to set up a super-D squad, keep track of them—figure out ways to put me in touch with 'em. And I want to talk to each one of them in the next month. And I also want the word to go out, these seven hundred sixty-eight superdelegates are *family* now, you treat 'em like Momma. They say Fetch, you go fetch. Y'hear? Now, Howard, why is it you think we're in such deep shit?"

"Wellll . . ." Howard said.

"Well *what*?"

"It's just, I know New York," Howard said. "Everything is driven by the tabloids there—the TVs make their news decisions off the tabs—so Cashmere was a bigger story than in most places, and Izzy Rosenblatt got played like a Mafia hit. I would guess we'd have a struggle on our hands there against anyone. And if we start losing primaries, all bets are obviously off."

"Leon, do we have New York numbers?" Susan asked.

"I don't," he said. "But the Marist poll has you at twenty-two with fifty percent or so undecided."

"And the rest?"

"Harris was running at eighteen percent comatose, pre-Picker."

"Sweet Jesus," Stanton said. "So what do I say tonight?"

Again, silence. Then, Daisy: "One thing is, you've got to be prepared for questions about Picker giving blood today."

"Why?" Stanton exploded. "What on earth do I say about that?"

"Well, it was his big moment today. It's a great gimmick. You gotta figure it's gonna be an issue. You're gonna be asked about it. You're gonna be asked when the last time you . . . gave blood was." She hadn't realized what she was saying until halfway through the sentence.

There was a stony silence in the ether. Stanton, Susan, Howard, Daisy and I all knew when, and why, Jack Stanton had last given blood.

"Maybe you should go down to Mercy and give a pint tomorrow," Susan said, saving us all from the silence.

"It'll seem copycat—cheap," Lucille said.

"Better cheap than having a bunch of scorps all over us, asking whether or not you're gonna match Picker's pint, and if not, why not," Richard said.

"What makes you think they'll be all over us?" Lucille asked. "Reporters are cynics. They'll see the blood-giving for the cheap stunt it was. You don't want to look like you're panicking over this guy."

"Well, aren't we?" Stanton asked.

I called Daisy after *Nightline;* various Washington talking heads had predicted that Fred Picker was just a stalking horse for Larkin or Ozio. Jeff Greenfield did the lead piece, which was filled with wonderful file footage—Picker, with long sideburns, wearing what looked like a tangerine leisure suit, brandishing a broom over his head as he ran for governor in 1974; there was also footage of the strange press conference when he dropped out four years later. "I thought I was gonna announce that I was running for a reelection, but I changed my mind," he said, eyes shifting about, bleary, nervous. Greenfield said that Picker's action had never really been explained, that he had lived quietly on a plantation just north of Tallahassee ever since, sharing custody of his two sons with his former wife, Antonia Reyes Cardinale—the daughter of a prominent Cuban émigré businessman. They had divorced soon after he left office. "There are always suspicions raised when a politician leaves office abruptly," Greenfield concluded. "No doubt, former governor Picker will have to deal with them in the days to come. For tonight, though, Fred Picker must be considered a significant, and formidable, new force in what has become an entirely bizarre presidential campaign. And I've got to say, Ted, that pint of blood was the first tangible thing we've gotten *from* any of these candidates this year."

Daisy was a mess. "I am a complete fucking nincompoop," she said. "Henry, I swear to God I didn't realize what I was saying until I was halfway through the sentence. You think I'm dead?"

I thought she had hurt herself. But I didn't know what to say. I didn't know what she'd want: to be soothed, or to be told the truth. "You're as alive as anyone I know," I said, not very convincingly—and pissed at myself for being so awkward, so reticent, so sappy. "More alive than most."

"Henry."

"Yeah, okay. The truth is: I don't know. You can't tell with them. It *sounded* the way you said it happened—that you didn't realize it until halfway through. It was the hesitation that hurt."

"And then the silence," she said. "Conference calls are so fucking weird. It's like you're having a meeting in a cave."

"Look, Daisy," I said. "I can't tell you don't kill yourself over this, because I know you're killing yourself over this. But you've done great stuff for this campaign. The Stantons know that. And they're gonna need all the help they can get now."

"I'm a fucking idiot," she said. "I feel all—" She was about to say "alone."

"Don't," I said. "I'm here."

"You're *there,*" she said, "down in the darkness, surrounded by The Great Books, with the river flowing outside your window." Her voice broke. "I need you here."

"We'll be together in New York by the end of the week," I said. "Looks like we'll be there for a while, too."

"Ugh, that means the ultimate horror: proximity to Mom," she said. "Henry, I'm gonna ask you a favor. An enormous, humongous, completely out-of-bounds favor. Will you let me take you home, have dinner with my mom?"

"Sure," I said. "Why not?"

"You'll see," she said. "And you've also got to promise that nothing said or done or implied by my mother will affect your feelings toward me, okay?"

I laughed. "Daisy," I said. "Don't worry about tonight, okay?"

"Oh sure," she said. "You *know* I won't. Henry, look. I promised myself I wouldn't start saying anything, or even thinking it, until the campaign was over and we were, like, sane again, y'know? But there *is* something happening here with us, isn't there? I need to know."

"Yes," I said, without hesitation.

"And we don't have to talk about it anymore now, Henry. Or say any of the words. We can wait till this is over and we can think clearly, but I'm really feeling kind of quivery and gelatinous over you. Oh, and one other thing," she quickly added, pulling back from the brink. "Freddy's not a stalking horse for anyone. He's *better* than Ozio or Larkin. And the blood thing was brilliant. You saw how Greenfield handled it. I knew Lucille had to be fucked up about the press reaction, as always. I mean, the way the guy said it, the ease, the humility—fucking fabulous. I wonder why he quit."

"So, Governor," Bryant Gumbel asked at 7:11 the next morning. "Why did you quit politics in 1978, and why are you back now?"

The camera was too close in on Freddy Picker. He seemed squished into a corner, a leaf of the inevitable potted palm flopping over his shoulder. But he was cool. His black eyes were alive—they were naturally intense, but he could soften them to great effect and he did so now. "Well, Bryant, I thought it was important to carry through on what Senator Harris was tryin' to get across," he said.

"And should we consider you an actual candidate for president or just a stand-in?"

"Well, we'll have to see about that," Picker said. "For now, I just want to give the folks a choice. It's been a while since I've done this, not sure I'll be any good at it."

"Governor, why *did* you quit in 1978?"

"It was a lot of things," Picker said carefully. "I was a lot younger man then, a lot less patient. Got frustrated with how long and hard you had to work to get anything done." He paused, for a carefully measured moment of time, and then said, "And there were some personal problems."

"Well, I suppose someone's going to have to ask this question, Governor," Gumbel said, trying—unsuccessfully—to sound remorseful about it. "What sort of personal problems?"

"Family problems." Picker said, then stopped. He was very disciplined. You had the sense that he was in complete control of the situation.

"I know this can't be easy for you to talk about."

"No, it isn't, Bryant. But I guess it's part of the game now, and so I'll be candid, in the hopes that people will respect the privacy of my former wife, who is not a public figure." He was looking straight at the camera, calm, clear-eyed. "What happened was I got too wrapped up in the business of being governor and began to neglect my family—and my wife fell in love with another man."

I think I heard Gumbel gasp. Or maybe it was just me. The simplicity and calm of the statement were breathtaking.

"I quit, in part to see if I could salvage my marriage," he continued. "But I couldn't. And so I did the next best thing, I resolved to be as good a father as I could—I tried to make sure the boys knew that they had two parents who loved them. And I think if you ask them, they'll tell you that we made it through okay. They're off in college now—and they were both big Lawrence Harris supporters, and when Mrs. Harris asked me to do this, they were *very* enthusiastic. I guess you could say I'm doing it for them."

"Awesome," Richard said. "As good as I've ever seen."

"What do we do?" I asked.

"Just stand around slack-jawed, playin' with ourselves and hope to fuck our eyes are deceivin' us," Richard said. "We're facin' a tidal wave with a sump pump."

The sump pump's name was Richmond Rucker, and he was the mayor of the City of New York. He had come out of the Harlem clubhouse, a formal, distinguished-looking man with a reputation for both kindliness and modest intelligence, neither of which was deserved: he was devious smart and vicious mean. He would endorse us because he and Howard Ferguson had been close for years—and because Orlando Ozio wouldn't. (Democratic governors and mayors of New York were famous for detesting each other and playing out their enmities obliquely, but obviously.) Ozio would, of course, endorse no one. He was above that.

He would hint, though.

We assumed the hints would be devastating. And indeed, Ozio quickly—and very publicly—went to New York Hospital and gave blood the day after Picker announced.

The schedule that Howard and Lucille concocted, with the help of the Rucker organization, reminded me of the agenda Larkin and I had suffered through when he'd visited the Soviet Union in 1987, only in reverse: instead of happy peasants and Potemkin villages, this was—relentlessly—unhappy interest groups and urban devastation. There was no spontaneity, no contact with citizens who happened not to be members of some organized group with a specific grievance. Every last stop seemed synthetic and massaged; these were New York liberalism's stations of the cross.

"Is this going to get us there?" Stanton asked that afternoon, when Howard presented his plan at the kitchen table in the Mansion.

"You go with what you got," Howard said. "This is what we have. Did you talk to Rucker?"

"He said he was happy that I was going to endorse UCSER," Stanton said. "What the fuck is that?"

"Urban Coalition Supporting Economic Recovery," Howard said. "It's this group of mayors Rucker pulls together every year or so. They want to goose urban spending."

"How?" Stanton asks.

"Who the fuck knows," Howard said. "They have a phantom piece of legislation—direct grants to cities."

"For how much?"

"Forty billion."

"A year?" Stanton asked. Howard nodded. The governor whistled. "You're kidding."

"He demanded it," Howard said.

"Howard," the governor started softly. "You and I have been bud-dies since forever. I love you like a brother. I don't trust anyone on this earth more. But you *never, ever, ever* commit to a *money* figure on my behalf," he said, banging the table so hard the coffee mugs were jumping. "*Never!* Do you fucking understand?"

"We need him," Howard said calmly.

"We can find a way to goddamn have him without his fucking blood money!" Stanton screamed. "This kind of shit is death in Amer-ica. You won't get eighteen votes for it in the rest of the country—and now I'm gonna have to slip-slide my way out of it tomorrow."

"There's one other thing," Howard said.

"Whut?"

"Luther Charles wants to be part of the event at City Hall."

Stanton looked at me. "Why?" I asked Howard.

"He said he wanted to begin 'the process of engagement.' "

"Now, what the fuck is that?" Stanton asked.

"The mating ritual," Howard said.

"Henry?" Stanton said. He knew how I felt about Luther, but this whole conversation was distasteful.

"Where is Rucker on this?" I asked, knowing the answer.

"Deferential to Luther."

"Okay, I guess it's on me, then," I said. "I'll call Luther and—Gov-ernor?—set up a separate meeting? At the hotel?"

"After the news cycle," Stanton said.

I placed a call to Luther Charles when I returned to headquarters, and then sat idly, swiveling in my chair, waiting for him to respond. It was a darkish day; the giant plate-glass windows in our old auto dealer-ship, so often blinding bright—and seducing a stubborn sunniness from the staff, even at the diciest times—now seemed wet and woolen, tamping down spirits. (The fact that the phones were just not ringing, that all politics seemed fixed on Picker, didn't help.) I found myself thinking about Daisy, thinking about how she looked in that kilt. The past few days, I realized, I'd been thinking as much about Daisy as about the campaign.

In fact, the campaign was feeling a bit foreign to me now—a first. The whole New York scenario was wrong, I knew that. It was the politics of reflex and obligation. You saw the obligatory groups, you made the obligatory promises—more money for the cities, an embassy in Jerusalem for the Jews, the release of a gun-running IRA terrorist for the Irish. But what worked for Jack Stanton had been less predictable, more spontaneous. Or maybe it was just that this was Howard's moment and I hated the son of a bitch. In any case, I took it out on Luther. I took some chances I probably shouldn't have.

"Lit-tle bro-ther," Luther purred. "Why is it that I only hear from you in times of trouble? Sometimes I suspect the white politicians of this world look on old Luther as the Salvation Army, ready to help with the *community* in times of disaster. But I don't play that game. I am the Salvation *Liberation* Army. I will save their asses if they will liberate my people."

"Luther, this thing tomorrow isn't a good idea," I said, suddenly realizing that I'd made a careless mistake. I should have called Bobby Tomkins, Rucker's guy, and gotten him on board. Indolence is one of the perils of low morale, which is why it's so hard to turn around a campaign heading south—which was why Jack Stanton's New Hampshire performance had been so remarkable.

"Isn't a good idea?" Luther repeated. "*What* isn't a good idea?"

"You showing up at the Rucker endorsement."

"The mayor say that?"

"No, I haven't talked to Bobby yet, but think about it," I said. "You think the mayor is gonna want to be upstaged by the Luther Charles Salvation Liberation Army Review? I know you worked this through Bobby, I know he's your guy—and *you* know Richie Rucker will kick the shit out of him, make his ass suffer, when the deal comes down, you hog the spotlight and the mayor turns out to be a bit player in his own endorsement of Jack Stanton. Now, why, Luther, would you want to cause Bobby such pain?"

He didn't answer. "Henry, your boy needs me," he said instead. "I am very big in the Apple—but I'm not gonna come cheap. He will have to negotiate for my services. The Salvation Liberation Army has staffing needs. And I'm gonna need a plane and a budget."

"Luther, get real," I said. "The governor will meet with you to-morrow night at his hotel. He's willing to talk. But don't make stupid demands."

"Do I use the servants' entrance?" He said. "Carter gave me a plane and a budget. Mondale gave me a plane and a budget. You sayin' Jack Stanton isn't interested in support from the *community*?"

"I'm sayin', Luther, that you are talking to me," I said. "And I know you can rouse the community to come out and vote—for you. I don't know how much good you can do us, or how much harm. The governor likes you, Luther—he enjoys your brand of bullshit. But the days when you could walk in and just demand a 737 and ten thousand dollars a week are over—and if you start in, showing up where you shouldn't, distracting folks at the Rucker endorsement tomorrow, Stanton isn't gonna have anything to say to you at all."

" 'Showing up where I shouldn't' "—Luther mimicked me. "If you're black, get back."

"Luther, give it up."

"I may have to have a discussion with Richmond Rucker about the viability of his endorsement," he said.

"Be my guest," I said.

"It would be embarrassing if he pulled back now."

"Yeah, it'd do wonders for his reputation for decisive thinking."

"Henry Burton, my, my," he said. "Ain't you the stony-assed pol. You need to locate your *soul* vein. Mebbe you should give some blood, like ol' Freddy Picker—now, *there's* a white boy with soul. Though I 'spect he's got himself a microscopic Johnson, his wife runnin' off like that. You imagine, the dude just coming out and *sayin'* it to Bryant like that?" And Luther switched to a white man's voice: " 'My wife fell in love with another man.' " Then back again, "Jee-hoshaphat. The Caucasian Trustometer shot up into the *iono*-fucking-sphere. White folk love that shit. Black folk, they wonder about his willie."

"So, Luther, are we set for tomorrow night?"

"Fuck, no. I don't need to see your master right now, he gonna be like that. But I will do you a favor, Henry. I want to further your ed-ucation. You gonna be stayin' your place?"

I hadn't thought about that. I did have a home in New York. I hadn't been there in months. "I'm not sure," I said.

"Yeah, the hotel life is contagious. Am I right, my brother? And a body man got to stay close to the body. But howsabout we meet up in your old nabe, the West End Bar?"

At which point, I sensed a great rush of air.

"HEY, AMNIO MAN! HEY, AMNIO MAN!" It was Libby, just barging in, doing a riff on the old "Hey, Culligan Man" commercial, waving a roll of brown wrapping paper in her hand. I began gesturing wildly, waving my arms, trying to shut her down. "HEY *AMNIO MAN* . . ."

"You there, little brother?" Luther asked. "Something happening?"

"No. Yeah, the West End Bar. What's this about?"

"You'll see. Say, eleven?"

"Right." I hung up.

"Hey, AMNIO MAN," Libby said. "AMNIO MAN, AMNIO MAN."

There were times when Libby just seemed crazy, ready for re-admission. This was one of them. "For God's sake, Libby," I said. "You want the world to know?"

"Henry, my little bitty shitheel traitor motherfucker asshole," she said softly, sweetly. "They are going to know. I think, I suppose. They may."

I slumped in my chair. It felt like the eighth time someone had run over me that day. "Okay, Libby, what's up?"

"I'LL GET TO THAT," she said. "But first a word from our sponsor. 'Hey, AMNIO MAN! Hey, AMNIO MAN!' Henry, Henry, Henry—the girls' team thought you were *simpatico,* a fella we could do bidness with. And you *go along with this SHIT*?"

"Libby, what'd you want me to do?"

"NOT." She said, "NOT GO ALONG."

"I was under a direct order from the governor."

"*Sieg* FUCKING *heil,*" she said. "Nuremberg for you, babycakes. Now, look at this." She unrolled the brown wrapping paper on my desk. It was a series of double boxes—seating charts, I realized. "These are all of Loretta McCollister's classes," Libby said. "She's the star pupil," pointing to gold stars marking her place in each class. "She *wishes.* But let me direct your attention to the *green* stars." Second and fourth periods, there were green stars next to Loretta's gold. "They represent the lithe young body of Kendra Mason."

Libby looked at me, to be sure I knew what was coming. I did, unfortunately. "Roger Melville-Jones paid her family a visit two days ago. That dimwit limey *prick.* She lives with her mother—and three half-whatevers by different daddies. And you know what? They are very interested in MOVING UP IN THE WORLD."

"Libby, be quiet, for Chrissake," I said. "So what did you do, take out your gun, go over there and shoot them?"

"HA FUCKING HA," she said, but then she did quiet down. "He offered them one hundred thousand dollars right there to be on *Sex Lives of the Rich and Famous* or whatever he calls that syndicated piece of cat-hocker."

"And the McCollisters?" I asked.

"Completely *mortified,*" she said. "Fat Willie shut down the shack, took a 'vacation' for a couple weeks, slapped Loretta around for opening her mouth too. You know, Henry, those are fine people. Melville-Jones comes to the door and asks Willie, 'Is your daughter pregnant?' And he says, 'None of your fucking business—you don't get off my property, I'm gonna call the cops.' And shitheel says, 'Is the governor the father?' And Willie says, 'The governor is a friend of mine' and slams the door. I mean, Henry, how could you let Howard Pencil-Penis DO that to Willie, without stepping in that day?"

I let that pass. "So all Melville-Jones has is a girl who says another girl says the governor made her pregnant?"

"Henry, he doesn't represent *The New York* FUCKING *Times.*" Libby said. "He also has a nondenial denial from the father of the bride."

"On camera?"

"He don't leave home without it," She said. "My guess, we hit *Sex Lives of the Rich and Famous* early next week."

"This is—"

"Uglier than a hairy ass," she said.

"Can we get firmer denial from Willie?"

"Henry, you really do take the fucking cake," she said. "He could make a fucking fortune off us, he's been stand-up throughout—and you're asking him to LIE for us?"

"Not lie," I said. "I don't know. I'm sorry. You're right. Anyway, anything he says'll be used against us. Where are they?"

"I don't know if I want to tell you, *amnio man.*"

"Libby—"

"They're up in a fishing shack in Montgomery County I advanced for them. Nice trout stream. Willie can stand out there and cast all day, thinkin' 'bout the business he's losing," she said. "Oh, he'll have plenty of business when he gets back. This'll be *good* for business. Folks'll want to come around. Folks'll *always* remember who he is and what his daughter said the governor did. They'll come by, just to see if the kid has Jack's wavy hair and shit-eatin' grin. He will never just be Fat Willie again. I could fucking KILL Jack for this."

"He says he's not the father," I said.

"He's not," she said, crossing her arms and giving me a wicked look.

"How do you *know* that?" I felt an adrenaline rush, a sudden exhilaration. "You got the results?"

"Not for a couple of weeks, says Dr. Sharon Wilkinson, O.b.g.y.n. R.S.V.P.A.S.A.P," she was spinning out again, "P.D. FUCKING Q."

"Then how do you know?"

"TRUST THE DUSTBUSTER," she said. " 'It was just my woman's intuition, but I was into wishin' you were here.' Remember that song? Oh, *you* wouldn't. Too trashy. Oh Henry, Henry, Henry, Henry—poor *child:* it doesn't *matter* whether he did or didn't, if she ever FUCKING ONCE said he did. And we know she said it at least twice: to her daddy and to Kendra 'I'm-Going-to-Disney-World' MASON. Henry, grow *up* already: shit begets shit. Cashmere made ANYthing possible . . . And, whether he did it or not, you think Jack Stanton wouldn't be capable of fucking the McCollister girl? You think he *didn't?*"

"Libby, I don't get it. Why would—?"

She cut me off. "Oh shut UP, Henry," she said. "Why ask why?"

"Because it's just too fucking weird," I said.

"Weird isn't the word for it," she said. "Try *disgusting.*"

"Then what are you doing here?"

"Ohhhhhhh Henry," and she looked at me, suddenly sane. "We are here because they need us here."

Luther Charles, like Jack Stanton, was the sort of man who created vibrations whenever he was in a room; the molecules moved differently, there was a sense of anticipation. And so it may well have been animal magnetism—rather than just a glint of light off his gold cuff links—that led my eye directly to the reverend when I walked in the West End Bar, just after eleven, the next night.

I was somewhat jazzed, in any case. New York did that. It was like reverse jet lag; everything was faster, noisier, more vivid than Mammoth Falls. I had walked the streets of my old neighborhood, agog with the life of the place, the sheer number of people: bums and full professors wandering about mutually befogged, pasty-faced Upper West Side types shopping the Korean fruit stands, Puerto Ricans with boom boxes and gold jewelry hanging on the corners. If you could handle this, everywhere else in America seemed half-speed and half-filled. I not only could handle it; it was, arguably, home. I debated whether to stop in and check out my old apartment. I got into the building itself, then chickened out, daunted by the expectation of roaches scattering in the light, daunted by the reminders of what my life had been after William Larkin and before Jack Stanton, the caesura it had been. I did, however, stop in on Mrs. Flores, the super, who had been forwarding my nonjunk mail to Mammoth Falls. She was small and round, and given to unflattering tank tops. "Henry, you *back*?" She said. "You governor man he mess up all over de place . . ."

"No, just checking in," I said. "I was just in the nabe, figured I'd pick up the mail."

"You go up?"

"No."

"I keep fix. Have been two months, I bomb the fuck out of *las cucarachas.* 'S okay now, but they back soon. When you come back, Enrico?"

"Who knows?" I said. "Maybe soon. Any mail?"

"I just send last week, but this come few weeks before that. Gets lost *abajo* my dream book."

It was from Father. It seemed not only from a different place but from a different time: my old pen-pal days, when the letters from Mohammed Siddiqi in Lahore came in delicate, sky-blue envelopes. This letter was painfully thin. It consisted of a single sheet of tissue paper and a single, manually typed sentence:

Are you actually working for this man?

There was no Dear Henry or Love, Father. There was nothing on the page but the sentence. It seemed a physical assault, but different from Susan's slapping me across the face—more like a full-fisted punch, dead center on my stomach; I could hardly breathe. And then I was furious: the son of a bitch had no right. He didn't have enough of an investment in my life to intrude like that, to hurt me like that. In retrospect, though, it was perfect—perfect timing, given what transpired that night at the West End Bar. It was as if Luther and Father had coordinated this attack, their last desperate effort to salvage Henry before he slipped irredeemably into the vale of the pale.

So, jazzed and smarting—reeling, actually—I spotted Luther immediately, sitting in a booth at the West End, looking conspicuously substantial in blue pinstripes and a white shirt with French cuffs and a gold collar pin (his tie, red and black divided vertically, seemed defiantly downscale, a foot firmly planted in the Sunday service). He had put on weight over the years and lost some hair; Luther had peaked in full Afro and dashiki—rage defined him, and became him. He looked plucked now; Luther in a suit was like Dukakis in a tank.

He was with a woman, her back to me. He acknowledged my approach with nothing so welcoming as a smile; it was more a nod, then a handshake—a greeting for a white person. "Henry," he said, "this is Gail Powell, a law school classmate of your current employer—and a member of the band."

"Of the band?" I asked, sitting down next to her. She was a striking woman, long and beautiful, her classic African profile accentuated by closely cropped hair, the first scattered ringlets of gray contributing to the air of dignity and integrity. She was wearing a pearl-gray silk blouse and dark slacks, a small gold cross necklace, simple pearl earrings.

"Partners Three." She smiled, nodding over to the bandstand. "Some pals from the firm—Jennings, Jenkins and Abercrombie. We noodle here, now and again."

"This sister—" Luther began, but was interrupted by the waitress. I assessed the table: Luther was drinking coffee, Gail Powell something brown—bourbon, it seemed. I had gotten into the habit of drinking margaritas with a double shot—Daisy's drink—but clearly that would not do in this company. I ordered a beer.

"This sister can tell you some things about Jack Stanton," Luther said.

"Some *things*?" I asked.

"Well, we had a thing," she said, beyond cool.

"More than a *thing*," Luther said. "Tell him."

"Yeah, more than a thing. We were pretty tight. There were times when—well, you know Jack."

"I know him now," I said. "What was he like back then?"

"Same as now, maybe a little shinier," she said. "He glowed."

"You knew Bill Johnson?" I asked.

"Of course," she said. "There weren't enough of *us* not to know each other, not to be in each other's face on a daily basis—you know, we were pulling for each other, pullin' hard, didn't want to be embarrassed. And I've got to say, Jack was right there with us—fair number of the white boys didn't even see us, too grogged out with the ambition-sickness; others made a pass at it; but Jack was right there. He was *easy* with the blood, you know what I mean? He didn't have to work at it. And he could sing the birds from the trees. There were times when I thought—I actually did think—he and I would open up that little mom-and-pop legal services clinic he always talked about."

"He *used* the sister," Luther said.

She laughed lightly. "Now, there's a news flash: Black Woman Used by White Dude. Luther, lemme lawyer you a little: use ain't abuse. I can tell you all about abuse."

"You knew Susan too, I guess?" I asked.

"Oh yeah," she said. "But not so well. You're too young to remember the old toothpaste commercials—Colgate with Gardol, the invisible protective shield. With Susan, it didn't just stop at the mouth."

"He didn't love her?" I asked.

She laughed again. "I thought you *worked* for the man! Jack loved her. Of course he did. He loved her. He loved me. He loved every stray cat in the quad. That boy is not deficient in the love zone—he's got more than enough to go around, and it's all legit. He's never fakin' it. I'm sure *he* thought he and I were gonna settle down, open a legal services clinic and have mocha chip babies—whenever he was thinkin' it. Trouble was, he was thinkin' too many other things too."

"He led the sister on," Luther said, halfheartedly now. This wasn't turning out the way he'd expected. "He went with the white girl because an interracial marriage wouldn't be politically *viable*."

"There is that," Gail said, sipping her whiskey, rolling the glass between her palms, studying it. "But you always had two things goin' on with Jack—your mind and your heart. In my *mind,* I knew I'd never really have him. He was too needy, and it wasn't the usual male kind of needy—it wasn't just come and blow. He was needy the way a woman is, he needed the physical proximity more than the other. You wouldn't know about this, Reverend," she said wickedly, looking across at Luther. "He was . . . darling." She seemed almost surprised by her choice of words. "He was a lovely boy. Your heart went out to him: he found a way to make you do that. And no, Luther"—she wagged a finger at the reverend—"it wasn't exploitation. I don't think it was ever about domination, having his way. It was about needing, and just getting off on being close. He got as much pure pleasure out of just being there, touching, bein' touched, watchin', hangin' out, as any man *I* ever knew."

She turned and looked at me. Her eyes were, simultaneously, onyx-sharp and heavy-lidded. "Of course, in my *mind,* I knew Jack Stanton was scheduled for something other than legal services—and in that way, Susan was the obvious choice. But it wasn't the cold thing, the *partnership,* people say. I'd be willing to bet you anything that he *got* to her, same way he got to me, same way he got to all of us. I'd bet you anything he *penetrated* that white girl's invisible protective shield. If he hadn't, *he* couldn't have married her. You've gotta know that Jack can't stand not being loved. Other thing is: if he didn't, *she* wouldn't have put up with his shit all these years. Too proud. Listen, fellas, I've got to . . ."

I stood up, allowed her to slip past. She was much taller than me. "Reverend," she bowed. "Mr. Burton." She kissed my hand. She took a step away and said, "You know, Henry, I was going to say, it's too bad: he woulda been a great guy if he hadn't wanted to be a great man. But that'd be cheap, wouldn't it? Anyway, I bet—somewhere beneath all the bullshit—he's probably still a great guy."

She moved off, done with us, moving toward the music. "So, Luther, that was my education?" I said when she'd gone.

"Look at her," Luther said. "That is one sad sister. She still not over that sucker. And that's your fate too, Henry. He's makin' good use of your pigment. But what do *you* get out of it? What power do you have? You gave up your heritage and your leverage to carry a white man's coat."

I couldn't take my eyes off Gail Powell. There was a weary erudition to her, a bluesy wisdom—I wondered if she was a different, crisper Gail Powell at Jennings, Jenkins and Abercrombie. She went over to the bandstand, joined a white piano player and a black drummer; she played bass.

"She plays bass?"

"Yeah, you don't often see it," Luther said. "Sister playin' bass. It's *puzzling,* given how much the sisters get off on that instrument—plucks their magic twanger, least that's what they say," he said, checking me out. "My, my, Henry Burton—you think I'm *crude*. Well, ain't you ever your grandpappy's grandkid! Hey, how much you remember the great man?"

"Not much," I said. I remembered his fingers, my little ones threading through his big, thick ones; I remembered the smell of cigars coming off him. "He read me James Weldon Johnson—"

Luther immediately launched a recitation:

"When I've drunk my last cup of sorrow—
When I've been called everything but a child of God—
When I'm done travelling up the rough side of the mountain—. . . ."

Luther boomed it out, eyes toward heaven. Heads turned in that dark, boozy room. He was, certifiably, one of God's Trombones.

"That *was* his favorite, wasn't it?" I said.

Luther nodded and skipped to the end: *"Lower me to my dusty grave in peace."* He was standing now, waving his teaspoon, playing to the crowd. *"To wait for that great gittin' up morning—Amen."* He luxuriated in the "gittin-up" just—just exactly—as Grandfather had. Luther sat down. He looked at me. We looked at each other hard—for the first time, really; we had made a connection. We could talk now. He searched my face, as if he were looking for traces of my grandfather in me, or maybe my dad.

"Did he teach it to you?" I asked. Then, before he could answer, I moved closer to the point: "What was he like?"

"God," Luther laughed. "He was like God, 'cept he had faults, and we knew all about them—but he was *still* like God, still the voice from the mountaintop, looking down at us, looking down at *me*. I was always the token, the ignorant street nigger in his Charmed fucking Circle. Too bad he didn't get to know you, he woulda just *loved* your scrawny ass. You're just his type. Classy. Pale. Dignified. Rev was black as night, but he loved the yaller boys, 'specially the ones come up from the un-i-*verse*-sah-tah," he said venomously.

"He went to Hampton," I said.

"The un-i-*verse*-sah-tah!" Luther insisted. "Where'd your daddy go? University of Chicago? You look at the roster, the so-called Charmed Circle. Where'd Rev. Artemis Jackson go? Yaller Arty went to Yale. Like that. The Rev loved brothers who ate chicken with a knife and fork, 'stead of their hands. Wore shirts with collars. I'd never seen such a thing. I come up out of the South Side. My daddy could have been anyone on the block. That discomfited him, the Reverend Mr. Burton. He was also discommoded by my lack of patience and manners and couth. And he was *also* discommoded by your father's lack of . . . interest."

"It wasn't a lack of interest," I said. "He was just interested in other things."

"He was *interested* in being interested in other things than the Rev was—that's for damn sure," Luther laughed. "He wanted no part of the crusade. And he was, most assuredly, *not* into reconciliation. That made us a pair, your daddy and me. We were among the first who weren't colored, the first who were black, years before Stokely and them found the proper word for it. Colored was nice—colored meant you could be mocha or magenta, or chartreuse; you could be pleasing to the eye, like a Monet water lily. Refined brothers we called *water-*

colored, your daddy and me. See, the lovely thing about black was: it was not nice. It was opposition, darkness. It was a great big FUCK NO. It was too harsh for Rev: he was colored."

"But that doesn't sound like my father—angry," I said. "I don't remember him ever raising his voice. He just kind of kept his distance . . . from everything."

"Ironically," Luther said. "He kept his distance ironically. See, he *knew*. He knew the Rev's get-together-with-whitey shit wasn't gonna make it. He also knew my fuck-the-motherfuckers gambit didn't have much of a future. He was—well, you know this—he was into antiquity, looking to where our sorry asses came from. He knew the get-together-with-whitey shit wouldn't make it, and not just because those sick motherfuckers *still* can't even look us in the eye—but because *we* were too damn uncomfortable in our own skins to negotiate credibly, no matter how fuckin' *proud* we play-acted back then. We weren't ready to be equal. Can't blame us, I guess. We had just cause. We were movin' with all deliberate speed. But that's why I could never understand—"

"What?" I asked, but I knew what.

"Your mother," he said. "I never could understand what he saw in her, aside from the obvious. But then, look at the sister"—he nodded over to the bandstand, where Partners Three had drifted into a slow, dreamy version of "Time After Time," Gail Powell caressing the bass, eyes closed tight. "She coulda had any man. She didn't want none of us. You can't say shit about other folks' lovin' or not lovin'. I can't tell you what kind of voodoo your mother laid on him, or what was in your daddy's heart." Luther smiled. "The heart is a lonely hustler."

We were quiet for a moment, listening to the music.

"Henry," Luther finally said. "Your daddy ain't around, so I'm the only member of the Rev's rump caucus available to do the honors. So listen: I know you can't do my thing. I know you're *embarrassed* by my thing. It ain't worth doin' much longer anyways, most likely. But we were kind of countin' on you to figure out the *next* thing. Y'know? Booker T. Washington was full of shit, right? We can't live with them like the fingers on a hand. We always gettin' thumb-fucked. We can't live with 'em, can't live without 'em, can't ever fuckin' trust 'em— and who wants to, anyway? Truth is, they are just plain disgusted by us, most of 'em. So the Rev's thing won't work. My thing won't work. It's on *you* and yours to figure out the next move."

"Me?" I said. "Jesus, Luther. You think I got some mission just because of my last name? I'm not a preacher. I'm a pol. I do what I do. I'm good at it. I like it, most of the time."

"Exactly so, little brother," he said. "You could've been a dentist or a golf pro or go off to Cairo like your daddy, but you chose to be in the arena—and so it falls on you. I know you went with Stanton 'cause you figured you might be the second most powerful man in the world if he won."

"I did not," I lied.

"Right, there's always the toothpaste woman, right?" Luther said. "She's number two. But you figured it was your ticket to the West Wing. And who knows, you might've got there. But even if you had, even if you do—you got more important business than that, takin' the Rev's business the next stop down the line. I hoped it would be me, you know. I wanted it to be *me,* not those sophisticated academia niggers. I was the rightful heir—and, man, I couldn't fuckin' handle it when he died. I cried and cried, and yeah I made my move too. And the Circle been talkin' trash 'bout me ever since. Luther, the Fallen Angel. Well, get thee behind *me,* suckahs! Who made the brothers feel better about their selves, me or the yallerboys? I ran for the president, debated those white boys, damn near took 'em out. And down on the street, they were listenin' to those debates like they listened to Joe Louis in the thirties."

He stopped. He seemed to realize he'd gotten into self-justificatory bullshit, and that wasn't where he wanted to be. He smiled a little and said, "Henry, I *hated* the Rev's fuckin' ass. But I hated him like a son hates a father, knowing that he'd never see me the way I wanted him to. And you're his blood, and I don't care what your rationale is, but the Reverend Harvey Burton would not have been *proud* to see his grandson a servant to some Southern governor."

"Oh come on, Luther," I said. "You know he's not just some Southern governor."

"That's not the point, son," he said, his eyes softening, reaching a big hand over onto my arm. "It ain't the quality of the governor. It's the quality of your service."

. . .

That Saturday was awful. We were supposed to launch our New York campaign with a rally at Restoration Plaza in Bed-Stuy, then Stanton would helicopter up to Connecticut for a quick round of events. Rucker had Bed-Stuy wired, we were told. Great pictures for the Sunday papers, we were told.

The place was desolate. No one was there. It was as if someone had done *reverse* advance work, as if the heart of Bedford-Stuyvesant had been evacuated. There was a band playing in the empty plaza, a soul band with a woman screaming off-key Chaka Khan. (This woman, we would later learn, was the sister of the press secretary of the deputy mayor for economic development, and would cost the Stanton campaign two thousand dollars.) There were five or six heavily bundled and not very enthusiastic volunteers (billed at one hundred dollars per head, for the afternoon) ready to distribute Stanton literature and bumper stickers and stick-on buttons to anyone who happened by. But no one was happening by.

It was, to be fair, an unappetizing March day—cloudy, near freezing and blustery. But it was a Saturday, the NCAA basketball semifinals wouldn't start till later that afternoon, and Rucker had promised a crowd. We arrived in a van, trailed by a press bus filled with our national regulars. (The utterly unregenerate and incorruptible New York scorps would never hit us up for transit—they arrived separately, in their own cars, with special press plates that enabled them to park illegally just about anywhere.)

"Henry, I am not stepping out of this van until we find the mayor and figure out what the fuck is going on here," Stanton said.

I called Bobby Tomkins. "Where are you?" I asked.

"Here," he said. "We're in a holding room across the plaza. I can see you just pulled up. Let's get it on."

"Where are the people?" I asked. "Where's the crowd?"

"A fuckup," Bobby said. "We got fucked. We were depending on the Brooklyn organization to advance it—but you know how things sometimes are between the Brooklyn and Harlem organizations. There's, you know, a rivalry. Sometimes they don't want us looking too good. And I'm sure, in this case, they probably got a message from Albany saying this might not be a time for Harlem to shine. 'Course, if you ask them, they'll tell you some incredible story about signals missed and wasn't it supposed to be *tomorrow*? But I won't bullshit you: they fucked us."

"Whut's goin' *on*?" Stanton growled, turning back toward me from his usual spot in the front seat.

"The mayor—" Bobby said.

"Hold it," I said to Bobby.

"What do you mean, *hold it*?" Stanton screamed.

"The mayor—" Bobby said.

I cupped the phone. "They screwed up, something about Ozio and the Brooklyn organization—but this is all they've got for us."

"So what do they propose we do?" Stanton asked.

"So what do you want to do?" I asked Tomkins.

"The mayor wants to go ahead with it," Bobby said.

"The mayor wants to go ahead with it," I told Stanton, who ripped the phone out of my hand. I gave him a look. He gave an immediate, contrite flicker of response. But still.

"Bobby, you tell the mayor I ain't going ahead with no goddamn thing that involves me speaking to three stray dogs and a wino," Stanton said. "He whut? You're kidding? Bobby, put him on the goddamn phone. He won't? Shee-it! I guess we have a standoff."

He hung up. I asked what the story was. "The mayor, if you can fucking believe this, wants to deliver his speech. He wants to speak to this empty plaza. He says it isn't empty: there are scorps. He says he's already issued a press release and a text, so he has to deliver it." Stanton was nonplussed—half laughing and half about to punch out a window. "If it's anything like that snoozer he gave the other day at City Hall, endorsin' me, he probably ought to think twice. But I don't think *that's* within the realm of his capabilities. Oh, the other really terrific thing is: he won't talk to me on the phone. He thinks it's *improper* for principals to talk on the phone."

"Well, we've got to work out something," I said. "I'll go over and talk to them."

"I've got half a mind to just pull out of here. But yeah, I guess you're right," he said.

"So what should I settle for?" I asked.

"*Settle* for?" Stanton asked, petulant.

"What do you want?"

"A crowd."

"Short of that," I said.

"To fucking kill that asshole," Stanton screamed, then calmed. "I don't know—maybe we should just work the streets."

"All right," I said. I walked across the plaza, past scraggly, newly planted linden striplings, toward a vacant storefront where two mayoral security guards framed the door. The area was empty in the distinctive, depressing manner of overly optimistic urban renewal cityscapes; it had recently been spiffed up—brick walkways, an Africa Pride mural—and teetered at a sterile apogee of nondecline. Wind whipped fat bunches of undistributed "Stand for Stanton" handbills against brick planters and into the whitewashed corners of the plaza. Several New York scorps moped about the storefront entrance, but— happily—they didn't recognize me.

The mayor did. "Mr. Burton," he said, not rising from a desk planted below a bare lightbulb in the middle of the empty storefront; indeed, he hardly looked up from a Greek salad in a tin take-out tray. "This is unfortunate."

"Hey, man," Bobby Tomkins said, coming over, shaking my hand. He was a large man, with a dark battered face. It hadn't surprised me to learn that he had played nose tackle for Kutztown State and came from a freeholding Pennsylvania farm family—he had a sane, steady decency to him. He was truly embarrassed by this.

The mayor wasn't. "Mr. Burton," he said, "when do you think the governor will see fit to emerge from his vehicle and allow us to begin this event?"

I couldn't tell if he was mocking me with this bitter formality or whether he always spoke like that. He sat regally in the midst of the re-developed but never reoccupied storefront; there were stray ladders, bare Sheetrock walls, blueprints and a thin layer of construction dust. He was wearing a black satin Spike Lee "40 Acres and a Mule" baseball jacket over a white shirt with a perfectly starched collar and an elegant silver tie. An aide stood to the side, carrying a severely unwrinkled blue double-breasted blazer in clear plastic wrap on a hanger. There was a boom box on the desk. The mayor was listening to latish, lugubrious Billie Holiday: "I Don't Know Why I Love You Like I Do."

"The governor," I said, "isn't going to give a speech to an empty plaza."

"The governor abuses my hospitality," the mayor said, again barely looking at me. I didn't exist; I was dirt.

"I think, sir, the governor's trying to do you a favor," I said. "The way things stand now, the national press will report tomorrow that Richmond Rucker can't raise a crowd in Brooklyn. We have to find a way around that."

"The way things stand now, young man," he said, finally looking at me with rhiney blue-green eyes and unconcealed disdain, "the New York press will report continuing friction between the Harlem and Brooklyn organizations—several paragraphs down. Their lead will be that Governor Stanton's campaign has had a rocky start in the city, that it is having difficulty engendering much enthusiasm, and then there will be a graph or two reporting on my speech denouncing federal indifference to our situation in the cities and reminding people about the UCSER initiative."

I was tempted to say: Right, we need UCSER to build more urban wastelands like this one—and I wonder how many of your pals got construction contracts? But I am a professional, as was Bobby Tomkins, who gave me a you-see-what-I-have-to-deal-with-I'll-bet-you-got-troubles-too look. "Mr. Mayor, I mean this with the greatest respect," I said. "But there is no way on earth Jack Stanton is going to join you at that lonely podium in that empty plaza unless you find some people to fill it. The governor would like to discuss this with you directly. All you have to do is pick up the phone."

"That would be unseemly," Rucker said. And that was all he said.

I looked at my watch. "Mr. Mayor, it's now one-fifty. I'm going to walk across that plaza and tell the governor about this and then, at two o'clock, Governor Stanton is going to begin a walking tour down Fulton Street, accompanied by the national press."

"Don't *threaten* me, boy," he said, rising, leaning forward on the desk. "And who ever taught you manners? Don't look at your watch in the presence of a superior, unless he asks you the time. And tell the governor that at two o'clock, I'm going to deliver my address here, in the plaza, with him or without."

. . .

"So I walked back across and told Jack," I said to Daisy as we rode the E train that night out to Forest Hills. "And we went our way—and Rucker gave his speech, and the press was all over both of us, and the story tomorrow will be about the public rift between the governor and the mayor, and the disastrous start for the Stanton campaign in New York."

"Shit," she said. "And the Furtive Cipher, was he all apologies?"

"No," I said. "Howard said, 'You have to handle the mayor very carefully.' And Jack said, 'Like toxic waste?' Actually, the weird thing—and, of course, you could have predicted this—was that Jack was feeling pretty up after all that street work. He had a *wonderful* time on Fulton Street. And I think we got some great pictures out of it. He must have hugged every overweight black woman in Brooklyn."

"So he lives to fight another day?" Daisy asked.

"I don't know," I said. "He always does. Daisy . . ."

"What?" she asked, and took my hand. We pulled into Queens Plaza; people got on and off.

"I keep thinking about the conversation I had with Luther Charles the other night. It started out about the usual bullshit, him endorsing us or not, the terms of his blackmail—but it somehow moved on to my grandfather. He talked a lot about the Rev and about my father. You know, I'd never talked to *him* about it. I just remember the others riffing on him, dismissing him. All my 'uncles' in the Charmed Circle had their take on Luther, they laid it on him all the time—and no doubt they were right. But he has his side, too. That's what I learned the other night. He loved the Rev as much as any of them, and he really knew my father—better than I do, most likely. Anyway, Luther finally said: the Reverend Harvey Burton would've never wanted his grandson to be a servant to some Southern governor. I told him Jack wasn't just some Southern governor. And he said, maybe not, but you're just a servant."

"Luther was *gaming* you, Henry," Daisy said, outraged. "You aren't a servant. You know that. You *run* this thing. More than anyone else. Don't you see how people—Jack, Susan—look to you in any given meeting? Someone comes up with a goofy idea, you lift an eyebrow and it's done. You are Mr. Sanity. They'd be lost without you."

"Isn't that what people always say about the good butler?"

"Henry, you are deputy campaign manager of a presidential campaign—and the campaign manager is an asshole, and everyone looks to you: you call that being a *servant*? By that standard, the only people who aren't servants are CEOs."

Well, yeah. Okay. I looked around the subway car. It was an old habit of mine: scoping the car, thinking about what sort of society the passengers would form if we were stranded in a tunnel; what would happen if we learned that nuclear missiles were heading toward New York and we only had ten minutes to live, which woman I'd want to pair up with before the *great gittin' up morning*. This car was pretty empty. There were sales clerks coming home after a long day at Macy's or Bloomie's; they were immigrants—Indians, Pakistanis, Latinos—exhausted, but relieved, *thrilled* to be where they were, on a New York subway, heading home. There were older, Jewish men and women, coming home after a Saturday afternoon of culture in Manhattan. There were several thermonuclear love-in candidates among the salesclerks: good-looking brown-skinned girls, carefully put together, the sort of girls you see behind the makeup counter. They could have been Latinos, South Asians, almost anything; ethnic distinctions were being pureed in Queens. Under normal circumstances—all my life, in fact—I'd flirted with these girls in subway cars, made eye contact, smiled, fantasized. But here was Daisy, fiercely holding my hand, and I looked at her as I might have at a stranger: I would never pick her out of a crowded car. She wasn't unattractive; she was cute, close up. But she was not the stuff of fantasy. Her hair, which flopped down over her eyes when we made love, was pinned back precisely on both sides, barretted. She had dressed a bit for the visit to Mom. She was wearing a black, simple, elegant overcoat, a wine-red scarf, a white silk dress shirt and black slacks.

And the very act of looking at her that way, as a stranger, became a self-fulfilling prophecy: I felt disconnected, I didn't know her. This was, I realized, about the most banal thought in the male-female courtship playbook. But there it was, and she sensed it.

"Henry, it's been a really shitty day," she said. "And just wait till you meet my mother."

Her mother was dressed like a Gypsy, or perhaps the "sale" rack at a secondhand folk costume store. She wore a high-necked, embroidered—red and black on white cotton—Russian-style *narodniki* blouse; a floor-length black Indian skirt with elaborate creweled flowers in horizontal bands, and a multicolored Andean (or perhaps African) bandanna, which covered her head. I thought for a moment that she might be a recent chemotherapy patient, but stray wisps of gray snuck out at her ears—this head covering was a fashion statement. She was wearing dangly Mexican silver and turquoise earrings. The immediate effect was . . . too much.

She seemed to gasp as she opened the door to her apartment, as if to say: You actually brought him. "Ruth Green," she announced, sticking out a hand. "I am so *pleased* to meet you."

Her apartment was the museum of the Popular Front—bare, undistinguished Danish modern furniture overwhelmed by an international brigade of *people's* art: the Ben Shahn Sacco and Vanzetti poster, in which the Italian anarchists are made to seem simple, bemused immigrant workingmen; the famous Martha Graham photo, head down, fist at forehead, everything akimbo in glorious consternation; a Fasanella poster; Guatemalan wall hangings; Dagon sculpture. And enough plants to create a weather system. On her coffee table, placed with an almost grotesque lack of subtlety, was *Plowing Our Field, Planting A Dream: Sermons by the Reverend Harvey Burton.*

"I've been so *nervous* about this," Ruth Green said. I could see Daisy in her, Daisy older, lonelier, slouched a bit; it was not an attractive thought. "I keep thinking about the Langston Hughes poem. *You* must know it." Incredibly, she began to recite:

> *"I know I am*
> *The Negro Problem*
> *Being wined and dined*
> *Answering the usual questions*

That come to white mind
Which seeks demurely
To probe in polite ways
The why and wherewithal
Of Darkness U.S.A . . .

and then it goes on," she sputtered. "There are more lines, I don't remember all of it, but eventually the white host says, *'I'm so ashamed of
being white.'* And . . . I know I shouldn't, but I can't help feeling that
way. I do, I do. This is such a racist country. We've been so ugly toward,
ahh . . . each other. It's so difficult to break through the barriers and,
you know, talk. I mean, I was such a devoted *follower* of your grandfather's. I can hardly believe you're, Daisy's . . . Which is why I've been
so nervous." She stopped. Looked at me. Blinked. "I just wanted that
out on the table. It's so awkward between the races most of the time,
but I guess you two have dealt with that in your own way."

Yikes. Daisy rolled her eyes, then said with them: See, I told you so.
I thought: I have stumbled into Negro Poetry Month. First Luther,
now this; they were symmetrical. With Luther, the poetry had been a
lovely, nostalgic breakthrough; this was quite the opposite.

"Can I get you something?" Ruth Green asked, calming a bit. She
had worked hard on her opening statement, and was relieved that it
was now over—and was quite oblivious to its impact on the company
assembled. "Seltzer? A beer?"

"A beer," I said.

"I'll have one too," Daisy said, not having been asked—not having
been looked at, so far as I could tell, by her mother.

"You know where they are," Ruth now said to her. "Why don't
you get three."

As soon as Daisy walked out into the kitchen, Ruth turned to me:
"Don't you think Daisy's underemployed? She's got a PhD in public
policy. She did her thesis on structural flaws in the Canadian single-
payer system. She should be doing serious *policy* work, don't you
think? She should be at the Urban Institute or something. I don't like
this political commercial business—negative advertising, always negative. How can you raise up the people, always being so negative?"

"She's very good at it, Mrs. Green," I said.

"Did she ever tell you I used to do population control work for the United Nations before I started teaching?"

Daisy was back with the beers, mortified. "Mom, policy-shmolicy," she said, too cheery, handing me a can of Bud Light. "You design these things, the politicians screw them up. Nothing ever really works."

"Daisy! Really. You sound like a neocon. Henry, policy does *matter*, doesn't it? Tell her. Daisy, you couldn't bring glasses?"

I looked at Daisy. I started to say something, but she jumped in: "Of course policy matters, Mom. It's just not what I like to do. And I'll get the glasses."

"So you sell soap."

"Let it go, Mom."

"Did Daisy ever tell you about her father, may he rest in peace?" Ruth asked, turning to me again, as Daisy returned to the kitchen. She had her daughter's eyes. Or rather, her eyes were shaped like Daisy's. She didn't have Daisy's eyes. Daisy saw everything, and always understood what she was seeing. It was disconcerting—looking into Daisy's eyes and seeing them blind.

"He was a union official," I said.

"An *organizer*," Ruth said reverently, glaring reproachfully toward the kitchen, as if Daisy hadn't explained her father well enough. She stood up, went over to the plain maple sideboard, opened the top drawer and came out with a picture of Daisy's father. He had a mustache, wire-rimmed glasses and a sly, knowing smile: he had seen everything, too. "This was Max," Ruth said. "Max did the toughest work, organizing textile factories down South. He was beaten, badly beaten, once in Greenville. He had his heart attack in High Point, North Carolina." I nodded, trying to communicate that Daisy had told me all this, though Ruth didn't appear to notice. "Anyway, he always said the reason organizing had gotten so hard toward the end was *television*. Marx, he said, didn't *know* from opiates. And here's Max Green's daughter, doing television."

"And not even public television," Daisy said, returning. She had been here before, obviously.

"Go ahead, make jokes," Ruth Green said, suddenly morose. "But you could be doing something for the people."

"Mom, what's for dinner?" Daisy asked, clearly hoping to move things along.

"Boneless chicken breasts," Ruth said. "It's in the refrigerator. There's also some fresh broccoli. Daisy, could you be a darling girl and fix it up for us? You're so much better than I am at that sort of thing. Henry and I will set the table. And could you cook up some rice?"

More symmetry: Daisy came after me that night in the hotel the same way I'd come after her on kilt-night. There was an edge of desperation to it, an edge of—please, *please* disregard what just happened, I can make you *very* happy. But she was trying too hard; we were all arms and elbows; at one point, she bit my earlobe and I said "*Ouch!*"

"So," I asked afterward, "what *are* the structural flaws in the Canadian single-payer system?"

"Oh God," she said. "I know you know I'm not her. I know that. But you see pieces of her in me—like, maybe, the fact that I'm saying this right now. *She* would be doing this. *She* would have bit your ear too hard. Shit, shit, shit, Henry." She pounded the pillow, sat bolt upright, zipped her mouth shut and threw away the key. "Mmmpf, mmmpf, mmmmpf," she said.

I reached down, over the side of the bed, and came back with the key. I turned it in her left dimple and unzipped her mouth. "I'm sorry," she said. "Really, really sorry."

"Don't worry about it." I said, but she could tell: I had been freaked by her mother.

"Henry, I'll make you a deal: If we turn out to be, like, together— I mean, for a while—" she said. "If it'll make you feel any more comfortable, I will *kill* my mother. Literally. I'll do it with my own hands."

"If you really want to hurt her," I said, "maybe you should hire a couple of *proletarians* to do the job."

"They could tie her to a chair first, and make her watch hours upon hours of negative spots," Daisy said. "And then force her to actually *cook fucking dinner* for them. And then they could strangle her while reciting Langston Hughes."

She was up on one elbow, playing with my hair. I was staring at the ceiling. "Henry, why are we here?" she asked. "Why aren't we at your apartment?"

"I don't know," I said. "I have the feeling it's not my apartment anymore. I'm not the guy who used to live there. Or maybe it's what Luther said: body man's got to stay close to the body. Or maybe, it's just that Mrs. Flores doesn't do room service."

"Henry, do not buy that servant shit," she said. "It's race stuff. It's Luther fucking with you."

"I don't know," I said. "Jack grabbed the cell phone out of my hand today during the Rucker business—and *Rucker*, he acted like I was lower than dirt. Luther's got me noticing that stuff now."

"That makes them assholes," she said. "It doesn't make you a servant. Henry, you can't let this stuff get to you."

But she knew it was getting to me. All of it.

There still was a presidential campaign going on, though it had surprisingly little to do with Jack Stanton. Our Rucker Ruckus/Stanton Standoff (as the Sunday *News* inevitably put it) was news in New York, but made barely a ripple in the rest of the country.

The rest of the country was madly in love with Freddy Picker. It was a sudden, hectic infatuation. He would appear on the covers of *Time* ("Picker Fever"), *Newsweek* ("Make Room for Freddy") and *People* ("Pickermania!") that week. He would be interviewed, by Lesley Stahl, on *60 Minutes* that Sunday night; it had already been taped, Picker and Lesley walking the grounds of his environmentally correct Florida plantation. He was wearing a denim work shirt, overalls, high riding boots and a camouflage cap. "You're a hunter, Governor Picker?" she had asked.

"Not for sport." He smiled. "For food. I can rustle you up some Picker-shot quail for dinner, if you want to stick around."

He was, as Daisy had sensed, *very* good. He moved, ever so easily, away from Lawrence Harris's more extreme positions—no more talk of a Virgin Uses fee or a fifty-cent tax on anything. "Everybody knows we got to do *something*," he said on his first Larry King show. "But it'd be sort of foolish for me to stand up here now, in the middle of a campaign, and say just exactly what it is we're gonna do, Larry. To close the deficit we need to raise some money." He casually turned away from King and addressed the camera. "Senator Harris figured there were ways we could do it that would also protect the environment. I think that's a pretty damn good idea. But we've got to wait until this country elects a president and he sits down with the folks in Congress and works out the precise details."

"You're saying Harris was wrong to be specific?"

Picker laughed. "Awww, c'mon now, Larry. That's not worthy of ya'. You're tryin' to play gotcha. The folks know what I'm sayin'. Next topic."

We still didn't know all that much about him. The first profiles were flattering, of course. He had been a businessman before becoming governor, had moved his family's Pensacola-based oil equipment supply company into oil lease speculation, and traded brilliantly—catching the wave just before the first Arab oil embargo, then leaving the business to his younger brother, Arnie, in order to dabble in politics. He appeared to have a great sense of timing. He launched himself into the 1974 gubernatorial campaign as a Democrat against the exhausted, befuddled incumbent. He campaigned in a leisure suit, with a broom—the broom, the leisure suit, the sideburns, the hawklike nose and eyes, the big smile made him immediately popular with political cartoonists, and soon the public. His marriage, in midcampaign, to Antonia Reyes Cardinale, the daughter of a wealthy Cuban furniture dealer (and a Nicaraguan heiress), helped with the normally Republican Latino vote. He won election easily. A big future was predicted. It was one of those victories that the Washington political columnists, always in the hunt for new talent, picked up on immediately. A charismatic big-state governor is always worth checking out.

Libby's research turned up a ripple of speculative columns about Picker soon after he took office. He did not discourage the speculation. He said, "Being president might be a fun thing to do—they need some sweeping out up in Washington, too." But he never really acted on it. He never really acted on much of anything as governor—there were no great Picker initiatives, no great Picker scandals, no great Picker tax increases or tax cuts. Things seemed to run pretty smoothly. He was well liked. Two sons were born. There was another ripple, smaller, speculating that he might make a good vice presidential candidate in 1976—but Jimmy Carter's surge pretty much put an end to that; a Georgia-Florida ticket would never fly. He endorsed Carter. "Hell, we practically grew up in the same neighborhood," he said. And then: Nothing. Until the strange press conference in March of 1978, an event that had clearly been planned as the announcement of his reelection campaign. There were photos of Picker, black hair parted in the middle and curling down over his collar, looking anguished; his wife, an exquisite woman, dark hair pulled back in a bun, standing just behind him to the right, holding one of their sons in her arms—and tears in her eyes. After the famous line "I was gonna announce for reelection, but I changed my mind," he had added: "I guess I'm just not cut out for this work. You want a more patient man than me. I hope you'll indulge me a little by not asking too many more questions about it."

There was a headline over an analysis piece in *The Miami Herald* several days later that pretty much summed up the local press reaction to Picker's retirement: HE JUST GOT BORED. There was no speculation about personal problems or marital difficulties. And by the time the divorce was announced, six months after he left office, Freddy Picker was no longer news.

"It's just a giant fucking LOOK fucking HERE sign, a solid-gold invitation to scrutinize, dontchathink?" Richard said that Sunday morning, sitting in the coffee shop of our nondescript Lexington Avenue hotel, near Grand Central. "But everyone's too damn lovesick to do much looking now. They'll get around to it, a few weeks. 'Course we may be deader than Eleanor Roosevelt by then. Shit, Henry, how much would you trust any of these guys who said he *just got bored*? How many of 'em get bored with power, with all these nubile teeny-bop muffins and munchkins paddin' around sayin', 'Ooh, Governor, can I get you this? Or maybe *that*? Can I clip your toenails?' "

"Maybe he's different," I said. "Maybe he's the real thing."

"The real thing? What on earth is that, Henri? There's no such thing. Not in this business. Not in this century."

"FDR?"

"Okay, but only because he was a cripple and had to live with pain every day," he said. "FDR minus polio is George Bush."

"Oh, come on."

"Callow, cheery rich boy, summers up in Maine, sends a lot of thank-you notes. Henri, never underestimate the educational power of sheer fucking pain."

"Maybe, then, Picker's been educated," I said.

"Mebbe," he said, taking a sip of Diet Coke, which—along with a barely pecked-at stack of pancakes—was his breakfast. "But it's a *curious* thing, dontchathink? It's got ol' Libby curious. Bumped into Lucille 'smorning and she told me Libby was kind of obsessing on Picker—turned out she *worked* for him in '74. Well, not really worked. She volunteered. She wore a button, said: 'I'm a Picker Person.' 'Member all these folks—Jack and Susan, Lucille, the Libster— all of them were working for McGovern down there in '72. Libby stayed on, hung out in Margaritaville. Gotta figure, if there's anything there, she'll wrastle it to the ground."

"If there's anything there," I said.

"When has there *not* been anything there lately?" Richard said. "There's always something there. He's a pol. Lookit the moves he's makin'. You don't come down off Harris's high horse smooth as he has and *not* be a pol."

But that wasn't quite true. Picker wasn't acting like the sort of politician *we* were used to. He hadn't brought on any consultants; in fact, he'd let Paul Shaplen go. He had announced, on Larry King, that he wouldn't do any thirty-second spots. Or polling. Or focus groups. "I'm not going to hire a bunch of folks to tell me what you're thinking and how to get at you," he'd said.

"Maybe you're right, Henri," Richard scoffed. "Maybe he ain't a pol. Maybe he's fucking Jesus Christ. Ain't hard to be the Jesus of the week in this business—for a week. *Two* weeks, though, kinda stretches the envelope."

"The blood thing is saintly," I said.

"The blood thing is politics, a fucking stroke of genius," Richard said. "Do you realize that every last one of my clients, every last one of the mangy suckers, called this week to ask if they should go down and donate a fucking pint of blood? It's like it was after that Supreme Court nominee, what was his name—Ginsburg? Yeah. After he said he'd smoked a couple joints, every last one of my clients called within twenty-four hours to find out what *they* should say about marijuana. And they were *right* to ask. Scorps asked every fucking alderman in the country that week if they'd gotten high. So now it's blood."

That Sunday there were stories in the papers about blood donations increasing nationally by 10 percent. But we didn't realize just how huge the thing had become until Picker held his first and only Connecticut rally, in the Yale bowl, that night. More than twenty thousand people turned out—and some enterprising soul, unaffiliated with the Picker campaign (according to the next day's stories) set up booths outside all the entrances to the stadium, selling a variety of blood artifacts—drop-of-blood lapel pins, bumper stickers, posters with a picture of a smiling Freddy Picker, lying down on a cot, sleeve rolled up, giving blood. A logo had suddenly materialized: PICKER, with the "I" in the shape of a drop of blood.

Picker spoke from a bare stage that night. None of the usual political trappings, just an American flag. He had most of the leadership of the Connecticut Democratic Party up there with him. He was introduced by Paul Newman and Joanne Woodward. And he just stood there, frozen—frightened, it seemed—as the crowd went berserk. Richard, Daisy, Lucille and I watched it on C-SPAN. Stanton was off in Brooklyn, meeting with the Lubavitcher Rebbe.

"Who the fuck did this schedule?" Richard moaned. "We 'bout to get our butts kicked all over Connecticut and Jack's off in a *different* state sucking up to some medieval Jew?"

"You have to meet the Lubavitcher Rebbe when you do New York," Lucille said.

"You have to meet him the Sunday night before the Connecticut primary?"

"It's when he said to come," Lucille sniffed.

"So we run on *his* schedule? We run on that fuckball Richie Rucker's schedule?" Richard was screaming, red in the face. "Who the fuck is running for president here? This is the stupidest goddamn thing."

"Jemmons, I've just about had it with you," Lucille said.

"Shut UP, everybody—please," Daisy said. The candidate was about to speak.

"Okay, okay—I'm sorry," Picker said, recoiling a bit from the echo, adjusting the microphone. He was wearing a dark suit, white shirt and a striped tie. He looked like a politician, but his body language was strange, different: diffident. "This is kind of overwhelming."

"WE LOVE YOU, FREDDY," a girl shouted.

"You hardly know me," he said. "I don't know . . . I don't want you to, ah, lose perspective. I, ah . . . I'm kind of nervous up here." The crowd exploded. People were waving handmade placards with large painted drops of blood. Picker pulled a handkerchief from his pocket and wiped his brow. He really did seem nervous.

"It's weird, Henri," Richard said. "He seemed much more comfortable in front of a crowd when I saw him in Florida. But I guess it's different when you're the man."

"Now there's a candidate for your mother," I whispered to Daisy. "Humble. Apolitical. Paul Newman likes him. And no thirty-second spots."

But Daisy was transfixed. Picker seemed to be struggling. He didn't know what to say next.

"I . . . I didn't expect this," he said. "And, ah, all you folks giving blood in the tents out back, I want to thank you." The crowd erupted again. It was deafening. "Look," Picker said uneasily, "could you do me a favor and not cheer so loud?" There was laughter. "No," he said. "I really mean it. I really want everyone to calm down. And I guess I mean everyone. I guess I mean the press, and the TV folks, and my colleagues, and the folks who make a living advising my colleagues— I think we all need to calm down."

And the crowd calmed down. "This is really a terrific country, but we get a little crazy sometimes," he continued. "I guess the craziness is part of what makes us great, it's part of our freedom. But we have to watch out. We have to be careful about it. There's no guarantee we'll be able to continue this—this highwire act, this democracy. If we don't calm down, it all may just spin out of control. I mean, the world keeps getting more complicated and we keep having to explain it to you in simpler terms, so we can get our little oversimplified explanations on the evening news. Eventually, instead of even trying to explain it, we just give up and sling mud at each other—and it's a show, it keeps you watching, like you watch a car wreck or maybe wrestling." He stopped; he liked what he'd just said. "That's right. The kind of posturing and hair-pulling you see us do in thirty-second advertisements and on podiums like this one is *exactly* like professional wrestling: it's fake, it's staged, it doesn't mean anything. Most of us don't hate our opponents; hell, we don't even know 'em. We don't have the fierce kind of ideological differences we used to have, back when the war in Vietnam was on. We just put on the show because we don't know what else to do. We don't know any other way to get you all riled up, to get you out to vote. But there are some serious things we have to talk about now. There are some decisions we have to make, as a people, together. And it's gonna be hard to make them if we don't slow this thing down a little, calm it down, have a conversation amongst ourselves."

He paused. "I guess . . . I guess—you know it's funny, I never even thought of it at the time," he said. "But I guess that's why I decided to start this thing by giving blood." There were cheers from the crowd; he tamped them down. "You can't *do* much else but be calm when you give blood. You just lie there and you can think, or listen to music, or to a book on tape—you don't *feel* like spouting off all that much. And all the while, you're giving something. Not a lot. Just a pint. But if each of us turned around and thought in those terms, thought about giving a little—instead of worrying about what we want to get, or what the government is taking from us . . . If we thought about it in those terms, we'd all just naturally sort of—calm down. Don't you think? And I guess that's what I want to do with this campaign: sort of calm things down a little, and see if we can start having a conversation about the sort of place we want America to be in the next century. I want Governor Stanton to know I welcome him into the conversation—and the president too, matter of fact, if he has the time. But that's what I . . ." He stopped, distracted for a moment. He looked down at the podium, looked up again: "Yeah, that's all I want to do. And, ah, okay. That's about all I have to say now."

There was applause then, sustained and rolling applause, but no wild cheering, no craziness. He had tamed them. He had tamed us. We just stood around the television set, watching.

Finally, Richard said the obvious: "We are in seriously deep shit now."

Deeper than we could begin to imagine. If Freddy Picker seemed to be campaigning from Mount Olympus, all cool and breezy and high-minded, we were neck-deep in the Augean Stables. Nothing went right that week. Tuesday was especially juicy: We were clobbered in the Connecticut primary and the *New York Post* headline was STAN-TON'S BLACK LOVE CHILD. I had spent the past month dreading that headline, but now that it was here, it seemed almost superfluous. It seemed the nail *after* the final nail in our coffin; we were already feeling dead and buried by Freddy Picker. It wasn't much of a story, in any case. There wasn't much in the way of *facts* beyond the stuff Melville-Jones had put on his trashy TV show, and the governor denied paternity vehemently—but his denials didn't count for anything anymore. And the fact that Fat Willie had vanished was not useful. We spent that morning debating whether to admit that a blood test was in the works, that the governor had volunteered to have his blood taken—and decided, finally, that it was best to keep quiet. Any admission of involvement would imply complicity—and the blood contrast with Picker would be devastating. And the fact that we were even debating such a thing implied our utter hopelessness: in the New York press, his paternity was a fact.

Stanton was stunned. He was barely communicating. He sleepwalked through Howard's stupid schedule. The most rudimentary acts of politics—walking into an event, through the inevitable mob of cameras and screechers—became a near-unendurable agony, each movement demanding total discipline and tremendous exertion. The traditional New York politics of reflex and obligation had become twisted, distended, a forum for lunacy; our obligatory, scripted concessions weren't greeted with the usual mopey, self-righteous acquiescence, but with a fury—the blacks, the Jews, the Irish: no one was happy. All New York seemed off the edge, in the throes of some primordial catharsis. On Tuesday, after the McCollister story broke, the first feminists dressed as pigs began to appear. They waved OINK, OINK placards. They made pig noises. On Tuesday night, after Stanton graciously conceded Connecticut to Harris-Picker, he went to a downtown disco for a Women's Political Caucus benefit and could not speak because a group of gay radicals stood in the middle of the dance floor chanting, "BUGGER, BUG-GER, BUGGER, BUGGER, BUGGER."

It was an odd protest. It seemed to have nothing to do with Jack Stanton; it was just a howling. A woman, a Broadway star I didn't recognize, wearing a slinky, sequined dress, tried to calm the crowd and eventually succeeded—by reminding them of Freddy Picker's plea for civility. Then Jack Stanton took the microphone and stared at the floor for a moment. "If all *I* knew about me was what you've been reading," he said, addressing the demonstrators, "I'd be out there booing, too. And if I were living, as many of you are, under a death sentence—and if I felt that no one cared, that no one was trying to help me—"

"STANTON, YOU'RE A PHONY," shouted a young, very proper-looking woman with long, jet-black hair. She was wearing a satin emerald ball gown and the anger distorted her face, reddened it beneath her makeup; she seemed to double over, trying to push every last bit of air out of her lungs. "YOU'RE A PEDERAST. YOU'RE A SICK HETERO FUCK."

Stanton took an involuntary half-step backward, raised both his arms in what seemed to be shock, as if he had been slashed across the chest. He appeared to crumple. "I can't even begin to deal with that," he said softly.

Afterward, the governor sat in the back of the van next to me. The seat next to the driver had been abdicated. We drove uptown along desolate avenues. "Henry," he finally whispered, putting his big hand on my shoulder. "I don't know how much more of this I can take."

But he kept on taking it. He took it on morning drive-time radio shows. He took it in the tabloids. He took it on the streets, where it seemed every third New Yorker had something awful to screech at him. We finally tossed Howard's schedule and went back to what felt comfortable, stopping in senior centers and schools and supermarkets, just chatting with the folks. Even that proved controversial. At a senior center in Brighton Beach, an old woman suddenly burst into tears— she had just found out her daughter was dying of cancer—and Stanton hugged her, and began to sing "You'll Never Walk Alone." It was a strange, corny, but absolutely legitimate moment, the first time—so far as I knew—he had sung publicly during the presidential campaign. There wasn't a dry eye in the room. But the *Daily News* headline next day was: THE SINGING SINNER. And that night, Jay Leno came out and said, "You see that Jack Stanton *sang* in Brooklyn yesterday. Noooo, it was *not* Rock-a-Bye, Baby."

We endured what seemed a month of abuse, although it must have been only a few days. Toward the end of that week, I walked into the Stanton suite and found the governor and Susan, huddled together on the couch holding hands, deep in conversation with a balding, middle-aged man who looked like an Israeli army officer, perhaps because he was wearing a khaki shirt with epaulets. He was eating half a cantaloupe, filled with a great ball of cottage cheese, flecks of which dotted his chin.

"Henry," the governor said. "This is David Adler. David, this is Henry Burton."

We nodded at each other, warily. "Henry, we're tryin' to figure out some way to turn this thing around," Stanton said. "David's got some good ideas, I think."

"I wouldn't go overboard," Adler said. "You're running against a tidal wave. Chances are, you're fucked."

"I was just saying to David, maybe we could do some ads—positive ads, folks from down home, folks who know me tellin' what Jack Stanton is really like."

"Henry, you're a New Yorker?" Adler said, finally wiping his chin. "Henry, you think New Yorkers are gonna give a rat's ass what some yokel says about *anything*? Governor, I've got to tell you: Hee-Haw *never made it* here. You gotta use your kanoodle, Governor. You gotta think: what've I got that'll work in the Apple? One thing you got, you're good with the folks. I don't give a shit what Leno said, I *liked* you crooning to the old lady. It was shmaltzy, but it was real. So I figure, the only thing you can do is get down where the folks live."

"We've been trying that," Susan said.

"No, I mean on TV," Adler said. "They watch these trashy shows. They watch Oprah and Crapola. You do your thing on that, they'll be watching. It'll get through."

"It'll just be trash," Susan said. "They'll just go after him on the trash."

"Yeah, sure," Adler said, getting up from the table now, beginning to pace. He was a fireplug, with thick, muscular shoulders and fore-arms. "It'll be all about trash at first, but if he can't handle that, he ain't goin' anywhere in this thing anyway—right, Governor? You don't have much of a shot talking to them about the national debt if they think you're a—whatever."

"Jack, don't," Susan pleaded, "A president doesn't do that sort of thing. We've got to think about keeping whatever dignity we have left."

"Excuse me, ma'am," Adler said. "But who knows what the fuck a president does these days?"

He was very crude; Susan, for once, was taken aback. Our eyes met. I communicated: Do we really need this asshole? She commu-nicated: Who knows? We're desperate, Jack's casting about—let's see. "Couldn't we start with something a little bit softer?" she asked.

"Well, I know Regis Philbin from the old country," Adler was say-ing. "He probably owes me a favor."

And then I had an idea. "We've been treating Freddy Picker as if he were involved in some different campaign than this one—but, Gover-nor, he said the other night he wanted to start a conversation. Why don't you invite him to come on a show with you?"

"Why would Picker do it?" Adler said. "He could only lose. He's smart, he'll say Yeah sure, I want a 'conversation' and then work us on the details until Tishah-b'Ab."

"You may be right, but I've got a feeling he'll do it," Stanton said. "Did you see him the other night? He's not into playing games. And even if he does fuck around with us on this, at least we'll have him on the defensive. Henry, what is it, Thursday, Friday? Why'd it take us all week to think of this?"

"Because," I said, "it's difficult to think straight when you're get-ting the shit kicked out of you."

I was watching the six o'clock news in my room when Daisy came. She banged hard on the door. When I answered it, she took two steps into the room and just stood there—furious. "You couldn't tell me I was fired?" she said. "You couldn't fucking pick up the phone?"

"Wait a minute," I said. "*Fired?* I didn't know that."

"You knew about David Adler. You had to."

"Yeah, but what's that . . ." I hadn't even thought about the impact Adler might have on Daisy.

"They sent Ferguson, the assassin. He said they were going to make some *adjustments*. They were going to split the media job. Adler was going to do the positive spin, I was going to do the—the *comparative*, I think he called it."

"Well, that's not getting fired," I said. We were still standing in the short hall just outside the door to my bathroom, facing each other. "But it's not too terrific, either."

"Not too terrific?" she said. "Henry, what do you think the chances are that we'll run another fucking negative ad in this campaign? And don't you think it's kind of *insulting* that they think I can only do negative? And what am I gonna do now? Go back to Washington, work *congressional* races for Arlen or maybe get fired by him, too?"

"He won't fire you," I said.

"Right, he's too much of a fucking liberal to fire a woman. But he won't make my life particularly pleasant, or profitable, either. I'll get all the hard cases. I'll have a great fucking batting average. The word will go forth: Hire Daisy and Die."

"Look, this isn't exactly a hot campaign right now," I said. "How much of a future you think *any* of us have here? How did you leave it with Howard?"

"I told him to get fucked and walked out."

"You did?"

"What would you have done?"

"I don't know," I said. "I guess I would've just taken what they offered—and figured that after the Adler phase passed, I'd be back or the whole thing would be in the toilet."

"The Adler phase *is* the toilet," she spat. "I can't fucking believe you. Why didn't you fight for me? He's gonna do positive spin? What can he do that I couldn't do?"

"I didn't know he was going to do positive."

"And if you *had* known?"

"Well, positive isn't easy," I said.

"Henry, what the fuck does that mean? Did you *see* my positives, the ones down in Florida, the ones we didn't use?"

"Yes."

"And?"

"They were okay."

"Henry!" She swung at me then, but she wasn't as good at slapping as Susan, and the blow landed harmlessly, half on my arm and half on my chest. She came at me—to be hugged, I realized one second too late. Reflexively, I put out my hands and caught her by the biceps and held her at arm's length.

She looked at me, stunned. She looked in my eyes and saw—what? Not enough. "Oh shit, Henry," she said, shaking herself free of my grasp, wiping her eyes. "God damn you."

"Daisy—" I tried to hug her now, but she pushed me away.

"Henry, you are one cold sonofabitch," she said, and was gone.

I stood there for a moment, then turned and looked at my hotel room. I went to the window, pulled the drapes for the first time in a week and looked out—a modern office building directly across from me, men in shirtsleeves sitting in offices, well-dressed women moving between offices. Potted plants.

I went to look for Daisy. I knocked on her door. No answer. I went to the headquarters suite; no one had seen her. I went down to the lobby and found Richard—checking out.

"I'm not quitting," he said. "I'm just taking a little leave of absence."

"Richard," I said. I felt woozy. "Wait—c'mere." I pulled him from the checkout line, over to a quiet corner of the lobby. "You can't bail now."

"I'm not bailing completely," he said. "I'm just gonna work out of Washington for a time. Scorps call me, I'll talk strategy and bullshit, just like always, tell 'em how Picker's the flavor of the week and Jack'll be back, like he always is. Jack or Susan call, I'll talk strategy and bullshit with them, too. But I ain't sticking around here right now. I ain't taking no marching orders from that fucking *mesomorph.*

Y'knowhattamean? Fucking guy says to me, 'I do two hundred sit-ups a day, how many you do?' So I look at him and say, 'Two hundred 'n' one.' Y'knowhattamean? Me and David Adler come from different parts of the jungle—so, Henri, let him have his fucking day. This thing's 'bout gone anyway."

There wasn't much I could say to that.

"Henri—look, man, I been through this shit a hundred times," Richard said. "That's what these guys do. They love you, they stop lovin' you. They say, 'I'm payin' this guy ten thousand dollars a month and he ain't made me God just yet, so fuck 'im.' "

"But this was different, wasn't it?" I asked.

Richard laughed. "Different doesn't even begin to describe it," he said. Then he softened. "Yeah, Henri—it was different. He was worth it. But, you know, I'm always relieved to be gettin' home. Much as I like room service, I'm scared shitless on the road, 'specially when a campaign starts goin' sour and you have time to think. Y'knowhattamean? I'm always afraid I'm gonna keel over and die in some hotel room, alone in my underpants, working for some stranger who can't give a speech to save his fucking life. This shit we do is a lot of fun, but ultimately—it sucks. Au revoir, Henri. 'C'est la vie . . . say the old folks.' "

" 'It goes to show you never can tell,' " I replied, completing the Chuck Berry lyric.

"You're okay, my man," Richard said. "Take *care* of your ass."

I lay flat on my back, fully clothed, paralyzed, staring at the ceiling. I couldn't believe it. The assholes had staged a coup; no, they hadn't even *staged* it, they had fallen into it. Richard and Daisy were gone; Howard and Lucille were still around but they always would be—and now David Adler would be calling the strategic shots. I could not imagine being a part of *that* campaign. I could not imagine getting up off the bed. I would die alone, in a hotel room sixty blocks from my actual home, which I didn't have the courage to live in. But at least I would not die in my underwear; I lacked the energy to take off my clothes.

. . .

Susan came late that night. She knocked on the door. I let her in. She walked past me into the room, turned the desk chair toward the bed and sat down on it. "You okay?" she asked.

"No," I said.

"I know," she said. She didn't say anything for a long while. She was wearing a charcoal-gray suit. She had just come in from some event, I realized. "Things are happening—and I just can't believe they're happening to us, that they're real," she said. "You read the paper. You see Jack's name. I see *my* name. And you can't believe the people they are talking about, saying these things about, are anyone you know, much less us. Henry, *you* know us. This is not what we're about."

"History," I said, "is what we're about."

Her eyes filled with tears, but she held them in place. "I know you must be hurting," she said. "I know it's a difficult moment—with Daisy, and Richard, going. I didn't want them to go, you've got to believe that."

"And the governor?"

"He thinks Adler may help . . . in New York. I'm like you: not so sure about that. But Lord knows we need help." She said this almost airily, sarcastically. But she caught herself, and began again more quietly and seriously. "Henry, we need help. And I have to ask you a personal favor. Please, do not leave us now. I don't know if we could survive it. Daisy, Richard—that's bad enough. But if you were to go, the impact on everyone—the staff, the muffins—would be devastating. The impact on Jack would be . . . unimaginable. And you know how *I* feel about you," she said, staring at me evenly.

"How's that?" I asked, taking a leap into uncharted territory. "You know, I've kinda been curious about it since that night in Chicago. I mean, what was *that* all about? It didn't seem to have all that much to do with *me*. Was it that you were feeling lonely? Needy? Or were you just trying to play catch up with the governor, after Amalee McCollister told you about Loretta."

"Henry!" she said. "That is just too cruel." Then she softened a bit. "But I guess I deserve it. It was wrong. I *was* needy. I wasn't thinking."

Me neither: I was just reacting. I remembered the way she'd left that night, gathering her clothes, slipping through the slant of anticrime light, the rift in my curtain. I realized that I hadn't felt any residual titillation since. That was odd. Susan Stanton was not unattractive; the forbidden nature of the event had been extremely provocative. But I hadn't allowed myself to be aroused by it. It had been service, not sex—a strangely humiliating service, part of my disgraceful role in the McCollister business. Now, however, watching her perform in my room as Susan Stanton, watching her struggle for something more intimate and emotionally compelling than Susan Stantonhood, I suddenly remembered her tongue, her hands moving on me—and I found myself growing excited.

"Henry," she began again, oblivious to my arousal. "Jack loves you. He needs you now—not as his deputy campaign manager but as a friend, a member of the family. There aren't many people he can trust. He trusts you. Please don't leave him—not now, not like this. Stay with us for a little while, until we have a better sense of how this is going to resolve itself. It may not," she said, her voice catching now, "be very long. But please, don't cut us loose."

"All right," I said, without nearly enough hesitation, reacting to her emotion, surprising myself.

She rose, gave me a peck on the forehead, and left.

I thought about this afterward. I thought about loyalty. It was the ultimate attribute of the perfect servant, and I was nothing if not loyal—to my employers. I was more loyal to the Stantons than I'd been to Daisy. I had sat there, considering all the angles while David Adler made his pitch, all the consequences for Jack Stanton and the campaign. But I hadn't given a moment's thought to the impact it might have on Daisy. It hadn't even crossed my mind—and she knew that. Of course, I could never have stopped Stanton from hiring the asshole. But I could have said, "What does Daisy think about all this?" I could have at least said that; I could have thought of her. If she and I were involved in something deeper than a campaign romance, *shouldn't* I have thought of her? And if we weren't involved in something deeper than a campaign romance, what sort of game had I been playing, what sort of stunted creature was I?

I looked in the mirror and saw—the butler. I was, Susan had said, practically a member of the family, which was the most banal compliment one can pay a menial. (Then again, she hadn't said *practically*. She hadn't qualified it at all.) And then, as I built up a doleful, self-pitying head of steam, I realized there was another, rather delicious, complicating factor here: *Luther wasn't right, either.* He had assumed my servility was a slavery atavism, a consequence of self-hatred, the absence of pride—a black thing. He had half convinced me of that. But all the qualities that made me good at what I did had come from the *other* side, from Mother: the calm and patience and acceptance, and the loyalty. Those were her things. The Burton blood—the Rev's and Father's—was too proud and angry to put up with walking half a step behind *any* candidate, perfect staff position, ready to serve: my most comfortable place in life. I laughed out loud. It was just too hilarious. I was a genius at servitude because I was half white.

Actually, David Adler did do a very good thing. He got us Geraldo—without Geraldo. (Actually, Geraldo did a very good thing by agreeing to the format.) Freddy Picker immediately accepted without conditions. It would be the one debate of the New York primary. And, of course, it became an impossibly silly media circus. There were more than 250 requests for credentials; CNN had more people there than either campaign did. "Who's doing spin for us?" Laurene asked.

"No one, so far as I know," I said.

"Well, CNN wants someone for after the show."

"You do it," I said. "But I'll tell you what: no bullshit. When they ask how we think we did, either speak for yourself and tell the truth or tell them we'll let the debate speak for itself. In fact, I'd kind of prefer the latter."

"Are you speaking for David Adler?"

"Probably not," I said. "But I have a revised contract with the campaign: I only do what I can live with."

"So maybe I should ask him," she said.

"Suit yourself."

"C'mon, Henry, get the fuck off it," Laurene said. "I'm just a working girl. This ain't an adventure, it's a job."

"I'm telling you, as deputy campaign manager, I think we should let the debate speak for itself. I'll take the fall for this, if there's a fall to be taken."

As it happened, the Pickerites came with even fewer staff people than we did. A crisp-looking young blonde named Maura Donahue approached me in the hallway outside the studio and introduced herself. "How you guys handling CNN?" she asked.

"We're not," I said. "I instructed our press secretary to say the debate spoke for itself. 'Course David Adler works his own side of the street. He could declare war on Syria."

She laughed. "But you're not going on? None of the regulars?" I nodded. "Good," she said. "That's what we've been doing."

"I've noticed," I said. "We're learning from you. Who's *we*, by the way? Show me your army."

"There's me and that's Terry Fisk over there," she said, pointing to a stocky black guy carrying a sheaf of papers. "He does schedule. I do all else. We also got the two Picker boys along—serious studs, and I mean serious."

"And you get away with that?"

"No, we're a mess," she said. "But the candidate won't let it be a zoo. He's zoo-ophobic, or something. He's big into the calm thing. No entourage, no traveling press."

"No press?"

"We just tell them where we're gonna be—y'know, put the schedule out on AP—and let them find their own way."

"Where did you come from? Harris?"

"Yeah—Terry, too. But not very prominently. The governor told all the consultant types to go home. He kept the issues shop, interviewed some of the smurfs . . . and here we are."

And there we were. Freddy Picker came out of a doorway, nodded at me—I was, probably, someone vaguely recognizable to him—and headed down toward the studio. He was not a small man, but he seemed less substantial, stooped—and sort of dour—compared with Stanton. He seemed a little lost, too—out of place in the forced cheeriness of the Geraldo set. He was quiet; he wasn't a blabber. He and Stanton sat, just the two of them, at a small round table in front of a live audience. They each had coffee mugs—Stanton drank Diet Coke; Picker, iced tea. Geraldo was supposed to open the show, ask the first question, and then it would be all theirs. No ground rules. I sat in the control room with Susan and the two Picker boys. They were tall, handsome, Hispanic and polite; they shook hands and didn't attempt any small talk; they sat down at the other end of the row of seats behind the director and his staff.

"Well, O-Kay," Geraldo said, when the bright lights came on. "You gentlemen know the rules. No chair-tossing, no claw holds, three falls and I come in to stop the bout." Stanton smiled and nodded; Picker simply nodded. Stanton seemed more comfortable, more presidential, sitting there. "And I will now ask the first question—to you, Governor Stanton. We have heard reports this week that you may be the father of a child by a teenage girl in your hometown of Mammoth Falls. You have denied this, but the girl and her family have disappeared. What on earth is going on?"

"Well, Geraldo, first let me thank you for making this forum possible—and I do hope we eventually get around to discussing matters of substance. But I will answer your question. The family involved are good people, friends of mine. I spoke with the father just before he took them to their undisclosed location, to see if there was anything I could do to help. He *apologized* to me for causing so much trouble. He said he was taking his family away because of all the craziness. His daughter couldn't get any peace, he couldn't even operate his business. He said he wanted to wait till it all simmered down. And I'd make this plea: when these good people do return home, and start their lives again, I'd hope the media would give them some peace. Governor Picker has spoken eloquently to this point. We do need to all calm down. We've got important public business to deal with and unless, Fred, you've got something to add," he said, nodding toward Picker, who nodded back, no, "I'd like to move on and ask you a question. I know you supported Senator Harris and that you've come up with a modified version of his Virgin Uses fee—"

"Not Virgin Uses, but some sort of—" Picker said.

"Whatever," Stanton replied. "Have you given much thought to how that's going to affect the working people of America, even if you do a *small* energy tax of some sort—how do we work it so they don't get whomped?"

"I haven't worked out the details," Picker said. "You know, you negotiate most of this stuff out with the Congress."

"Right, and it's absolutely appropriate that you remind the folks that the sort of things we propose in these campaigns are best-case scenarios, and always subject to negotiation," Stanton said. "In fact, there are times when our *own* ideas are subject to change during a campaign." There was laughter. The director cut away to Geraldo, standing off to the side, chuckling. But this was now Jack Stanton's show: "Let me give you an example. Early on, I proposed a middle-class tax cut. Senator Harris disagreed with that. And, looking back, I think he was probably right. I've been thinking about this—and Governor Picker, I'd like to get your feeling about it—but maybe we should do something more targeted. Say we do a *combination* of your idea and mine. We do an energy tax of some sort *and* give a rebate to average folks, say incomes of fifty thousand dollars or less, maybe an increased tax deduction for each member of their family."

Picker thought for a moment. The politic thing would have been to ignore the proposal or brush it aside, find some way to take control of the show. But Picker said, "I would think you'd *have* to consider something like that, although—as I said—I'm not too sure about the details. Wouldn't you be favoring the folks who had more children?"

"Yeah, I guess," Stanton said, amazed that Picker had just, in effect, bought his proposal. "We could have a deductions-per-family cutoff if you like."

"But can you bottom-line that?" Picker asked. "What would the net revenue gain be? We do need to reduce the deficit."

This was truly bizarre. Picker was ignoring the audience, and having a policy discussion with Jack Stanton. He didn't seem to care about the politics or television of it at all. Stanton was thrilled to go along; he was, in fact, ecstatic. "You're right—we do need to reduce the deficit—but when we bring it down, we can't take it out of average folks' hides," he said. "There are ways we can spend money more efficiently, ways we can spend less. But I think, ultimately, if you want to reduce the deficit, we're gonna have to raise taxes on the rich—are you with me on that one?"

"Depends on how you define rich," Picker said. "But yeah."

"Larry—ahh, Senator Harris—wanted to cut capital gains," Stanton said. "You for that too?"

And so it went. Eventually, Geraldo—amazed that his hot ticket had turned into a meeting of the Senate Finance Committee—jumped in and said, "Hey, guys, you mind if we get some questions from the audience?"

A middle-aged woman stood and said, "I'm a teacher. We're on the front lines every day. Governor Picker, what would you do to help us do our job?"

"Well, education is very important," Picker said. "It's the most important thing. The federal government helps with student loans, and with extra money for poorer districts—and we should continue that but, I guess—Jack, education's mostly a state and local thing, isn't it?"

"Yeah, it is. But the president has the bully pulpit," Stanton said. He seemed much more sure of himself than Picker. "He can go around the country and show what works. We can also—Fred, you forgot to mention—boost funds for Head Start." Picker nodded. "But ultimately, ma'am," Stanton continued, "I've got to say that you're right—you are on the front lines every day. I think an inspired teacher is more important than anything any ol' politician or bureaucrat can do." And Jack Stanton looked into the camera, raised an eyebrow and—quickly—winked at Susan. She inhaled sharply and grabbed hold of my wrist. "And so I think we should keep experimenting with programs that liberate teachers to be as creative as they want to be."

"Jack's absolutely right about that," Picker now jumped in, enthused. "I sent my boys to a magnet school—I was willing to put them on a bus, send them into Tallahassee. We live on a farm, just outside of town. I did that because they had a special math program for my older boy and a string program for my younger son, who's a pretty damn fine fiddler. Oh . . . uh, Felipe doesn't like it when I say that: he plays the viola. But you're right, Jack, about education. You walk into a school that works, and you can feel it immediately. If we could only get the people—the teachers and the parents, especially—more excited and involved in the schools . . ."

"Trouble is, it's tough for the families where both mom and dad work," Stanton said. They were just chatting now. "They don't have time for PTA and all the rest, like some of us do." Stanton stopped, and in a tone of voice that mocked himself, mocked all politicians, "That's why *I* favor the family tax credit."

"Okay, okay," Picker said, laughing.

"More questions?" Geraldo asked.

There were questions about Social Security, foreign aid, taxes again; and no great disagreements. Finally, an elderly black gentleman slowly pulled himself to his feet. "I think a lot of us are sick of all the bullshit in politics," he said. There were ooohs and cheers. "And while I can't follow all of what you fellahs are talkin' 'bout, I been sitting here listenin' to you, and it sure sounds a lot different from the usual. Even I can see you ain't trying to rip each other apart. Maybe you're even tryin' to work things out a little." He paused.

"Excuse me, sir, but do you have a question?" Geraldo asked.

"Yeah, I guess it's this," the old man said. "Any way we can get you *both*?"

Susan, tears streaming, was out of the control room like a shot when it was over. I was right behind her. The audience had come down to the table; Stanton, Picker and Geraldo were shaking hands with the folks. Susan and I stood off to the side, in the doorway. David Adler suddenly appeared, looking for congratulations. "Thanks, David," Susan said. "Really."

"He *dominated*," Adler said.

Finally, Jack and Picker began moving toward the hallway, Geraldo tagging along. Stanton thanked the host and said, "Geraldo, you think Freddy and I could have a moment?"

"Sure," he said. "You want a room?"

"No, here's fine." He leaned down into Picker, draped an arm over his shoulder. "Freddy, I just want you to know how much I admire the way you're running this campaign. It's good for the party, it's good for the country. And I 'spect it'll pay off for you. And thanks for giving me a chance to regain a little of what I lost."

"No problem. And thank you, too, Jack." Picker put an arm around Stanton's back. "You sure do know every little nook and cranny of this policy stuff. I'm gonna have to study up. Uhh, Jack?"

"What?"

"Nothing," Picker said. "Thanks."

"I remember days like this one—vaguely, but I remember," Stanton said in the van heading downtown. "When was it? When did this used to be fun, Henry?"

"New Hampshire," I said. "Last year. But this was good. You think it'll have any impact?"

"Nawww," Stanton said. "No one was watching. And no one cares. I mean, who gives a rat's ass that I knew more about the fucking *budget* than he does? Hell, 'f I didn't know me, I'd probably vote for him. But it's weird. It's like he's been transformed—different guy from when he was governor. I never saw anything like it. It's like he's not, like he never *was,* a politician. He doesn't have the instincts anymore, the little things we do to cut in on each other. You saw that, right? He isn't playing the game at all, not in any way. It's absolutely strange." Stanton laughed, and then seemed to have a thought: "Henry, you know what? He's not going to be able to sustain it. It's a great concept, but it's too radical. The stuff we do, the craft of it, has developed very slowly and logically over time. You ever think about the fact that the riffs we do started with George *Washington*? Andrew Jackson massaged it some, and Lincoln—and then Boss Murphy here in New York, and FDR, Bilbo and George Wallace in the South. All of them, the giants and the shitheels, have massaged it, moved it, pushed it ahead." He stared out the window at the vibrant chaos of New York. "And Freddy's doing that, too. He's moving it in a way that's probably appropriate for these fucked-up times. The game got too ornate and bullshitty. That's for sure. And he's a corrective. But you don't wrench the *art* of politics away from its roots so drastically without paying some sort of price. All the bullshit we do is there for a reason. Fuck with it too much and it'll come back and bite your ass."

Stanton turned around and pounded his fist on my knee. "Henry," he said, "there may be some life in this thing yet."

VIII

Not all that much life, it appeared. We were trounced in New York, two to one. It was definitive, crushing, a paralytic wipeout. Picker thanked New York on behalf of Martha Harris, and announced he was going home for a few days, to rest and "think about what's important, what's best for our country." We went home, too. Our campaign seemed over. Stanton didn't withdraw from the race immediately, but he returned to Mammoth Falls and the prosaic rituals of home-state governance. There was no travel schedule. There were no staff meetings. People began to leave.

I stayed. I called Daisy several times and left messages, but there was no answer. I ran along my old three-mile route, down the river and back again. I read *Middlemarch*. I went each day to the headquarters and cleared files; a few stray muffins remained, a few older women—local volunteers—continued to answer the phones when they rang, which wasn't often. I didn't dare ask the governor or Susan about what came next; for two days after New York, I didn't speak to them at all. We just needed a break from each other, I guess. There was no real rush. The primary schedule thinned out at that point; it would be three weeks before the next big one—Pennsylvania—if we remained in business that long. I tried to think about what I was going to do with my life, but couldn't.

I was staring off into space, not even pretending to be busy, when Libby walked into the office that Thursday. And that was the first thing I noticed: she walked, she didn't barge or boom. "Hey, kid," she said, scarily subdued, holding her outback hat against her chest with both hands. "I got the tests. You're a part of this. You want to come up with me and tell the gov?"

It was a perfect spring day. We walked up the hill to the capitol, which was girded by a lush apron of coral, fuchsia and white azaleas. (Jack and Susan Stanton would preside over the Mammoth Azalea Festival that weekend; I remembered Donny O'Brien's line about going back to ribbon cuttings and highway contracts—I'm sure Stanton did, too.) There was a quietly efficient, back-to-normal air in the governor's office; phones were ringing, which distinguished it from the mausoleum our campaign headquarters had become.

Annie Marie ushered us in. Stanton sat behind his desk. I realized I had never seen him there before. In fact, it had been months since I'd been *in* that office—New Year's Eve, the day I met Daisy. She was the last person I'd seen sitting there. She'd been smoking a cigarette, flipping through Leon's New Hampshire cross-tabs. She pushed her glasses up on her forehead. She looked at me—

"Well, Jack, you're in the clear," Libby said dully. This was all dreamlike and *very* strange. "You're not the father." He stared at his hands and exhaled. "Hell," Libby said, reviving a bit. "Uncle Charlie's not even the father."

Stanton glanced at her sharply. "Does Willie know?" he asked.

"Doc Wilkinson will call them," Libby said.

"We should call them, too," Stanton said. "He's gonna be feeling awful, thinking he brought this thing down. Hell, we should all go over there for dinner tonight."

He swiveled, stared out the window, down the hill toward the few scraggly, undistinguished modern skyscrapers downtown. "Henry," he said, turning back, "any press calls on this, there's no comment. And Sunday evening, we'll pull everyone together at the Mansion, figure out where we take this thing from here—okay?"

The meeting was over. Sort of. Libby wasn't getting up from her chair. Actually, she seemed to be trying to get up but was unable to put the full force of her will behind it. I had never seen her indecisive before.

"Libby?" Stanton asked. "What on earth is the matter with you?"

"Well . . ."

"Libby?"

"Oh shit," she sighed. "You know, I've been kind of . . . interested in the Picker thing," she said softly, almost mumbling. "So I made some calls—one of them to Judy Lipinsky, an old *friend* of mine, used to be a scorp—police reporter and a good one, a very tough chick. She's got an advertising sheet in Fort Lauderdale now. And she made some calls. And she, ah, found this state senator who claims that Picker . . . well, that Picker gave him some money to vote for this project—a development, south of Naples."

"When he was governor?" Stanton asked.

"Uh-huh," Libby said. "The vote was state matching money for the county to build a connecting road, and also the approval of a federal water and sewer grant. And the thing is, the project—Tidewater Estates—was being developed by Sunshine Brothers, which is a subsidiary of Sunshine Savings and Loan, which is owned by Edgardo Reyes Cardinale. And Edgardo Reyes Cardinale is the brother of Antonia Reyes Cardinale, who is—"

"Picker's former wife," Stanton said and whistled. "Jeez. Who else knows about this? What else do we know? Who's the senator? Will he talk?"

Libby just sat there. She didn't say anything.

"Libby, what the fuck is the matter with you?"

"I've been trying to decide . . ." she said, her voice trailing off.

"Decide what?"

"Whether I want to DO THIS for you, you *stupid SHIT*," she said, Libby once more. "I bust dust. I protect you. I don't do oppo . . ."

"Libby, what the fuck is the difference?"

"All the difference in the world," she said. "All the *moral* difference in the world. I'm not too interested in tearing Freddy Picker down."

"And if he's bent?" Stanton said. "If he's a crook?"

"It'll out," she said.

"Yeah, but when?" Stanton said. "Say he wins the nomination—and *then* it comes out. If it's there, the Republicans'll find it, that's for sure. They may already have it. Libby, we should at least know what they know. We should at least know what's there. Think of it as dust-busting for the Democratic Party, for all of us."

"Don't *patronize* me, Jack. We've known each other too fucking long. . . . He *cleaned your clock*."

"But you'll do it," Stanton said.

"Oh, fuck you."

"I knew you would. Henry, how would *you* like a nice Florida vacation?" he asked. "Nothin's happening around here till Sunday. And"—he was smiling now, playing with us—"you guys worked *so well* together on the phony tapes."

If the handshake is the threshold act of politics, what can one say of oppo? It is the primal impulse, the headwaters of all tactics and strategy, the oldest and most dishonorable exercise linked to the Will to Power. The Greeks did oppo; they learned it from the gods. Cassius did oppo. Even our sainted FDR used the Internal Revenue Service to scope out his opponents. It is a foundation of the trade, the darkest tool, the inevitable destination; it is where the story always ends. It can be done elegantly or not—mostly not, in the late twentieth century. It can be done reluctantly or with relish, but it will always be done.

And we would do it for Jack Stanton, Libby and I. We would do it as a ceremonial act, a genuflection to the origins of our craft, and as a release—our final service to the Stantons. We would do it almost ironically, standing at a distance from ourselves, curious about where we were going, how far we'd be willing to go. Without Libby, I wouldn't have gone—it was clear that her impulse was the same as mine, that she was propelled by the desire for symmetry, the need to tie up all the loose ends, to see it through.

"We are in *limbo* now, Henri—in every sense of the word," she said as Jennifer Rogers drove us to the airport in Libby's red Jeep Cherokee. She was sitting up front, her left hand massaging Jenny's neck. I sat in the back. "We are . . . *outside the mainstream*. We are . . . *in purgatory*. We are . . . *lost*. We are . . . *testing our limits*. You remember the stupid song, 'Limbo Rock'? You remember the words? 'How *loooooowwwwwww* can you *gooooooooo*? That's us, Henri. We are moral submariners. We dive down into the shit, hoping for a shit-balm, hoping for a cure."

"Libby, let me ask you," I said. "How did you know Jack wasn't the father of that child?"

"He was the father of the mother's ignorance," Libby said, deep into cryptic limbo mode.

"In English, Libby?"

"He gave in to the fundies on sex education," Libby said. "He wouldn't fight that fight. So the girl didn't know her vagina from the mailbox. Her folks sure as hell didn't tell her much. I had to run a goddamn sex seminar for the poor kid. She actually thought the first guy who got to you after menstruation planted the seed. In this case, the happy farmer turned out to be the *second* guy who got to her that particular month—Jarone Dixon, who sat next to her in sixth period, social studies. HOO-HAH! Seventh period was a study hall. Jarone Dixon and Loretta McCollister studied biology in a broom closet two days after she ovulated. Jarone, I can assure you, will make an entirely incompetent father."

"And the first guy who got to her that month was Jack Stanton?" I asked.

"We'll never know for sure, will we?" Libby said. "But your suspicion is as good as mine."

The Gold Coast *Time-and-Tides* was a narrow storefront in a seedy strip mall on one of Fort Lauderdale's long, flat east–west boulevards. We arrived after hours, but it didn't appear to be the sort of place where much business was transacted at any time. There was a classified-ad counter up front, then a single row of three desks; there were maps of Fort Lauderdale and vicinity on the walls above the inevitable, battered buff-colored file cabinets. Judy Lipinsky sat at the rear desk, smoking a very long cigarette. She was wearing what appeared to be a Little Orphan Annie fright wig. (It was, however, her own, actual, hyperpermed hair.)

"Hey, Lips," Libby called out.

"Hey, *tongue*," Judy replied, in what appeared to be a ritual greeting. "Who's the mascot?"

"Henry Burton, deputy manager of the very nearly defunct Jack Stanton for President campaign."

"Meetya," said Judy Lipinsky, standing now to shake hands. She was short, stacked, butchy—a feminine version of David Adler, it seemed—all shoulders and breasts and bravado. She was wearing a black-and-white polka-dot sheath, white Minnie Mouse shoes and lots of very red lipstick.

"How's Ralphie?" Libby asked.

"Gettin' on," Judy replied.

"Ralph is Judy's husband, a former statie," Libby explained. "She left me for him. She never told me if it was his gun or his badge."

"Or the fact that he ran the North Miami barracks and gave good copy," Judy said, to me. "Libby never did dig my ecumenicism. She didn't believe me when I told her my motto was 'Different strokes for the same folks.' "

"She didn't believe me when I told her that penetration is violation," Libby replied. "So, Lips, what've we got here?"

"State Senator Orestes 'Rusty' Figueroa," Judy said. "He used to work out of Miami, but he retired and settled in up here."

"Dem or GOP?"

"Cuban," Judy said. "GOP, of course."

"That means old Jackie's right," Libby explained to me. "Whatever this is, the Republicans probably already have it. That's also why it probably hasn't hit the papers yet."

"Well, there may be another reason," Judy said. "Rusty isn't what might be called an unimpeachable witness. He had a 'For Sale' sign on his door and got caught eventually—his retirement included a suspended sentence."

"So why should we believe him?" I asked.

"Because he was a crook, not necessarily a liar," Judy said. "Anyway, Lib, your instructions were *anything* on Picker, right?"

Rusty Figueroa lived in a fine, sprawling ranch on one of the man-made islands in the Inland Waterway. He had silver hair and mustache but was still slim—no paunch distended his pale yellow guayabera. He welcomed us into his living room, which was elegant, subdued—a first-class hotel lobby: pleasant but undistinguished watercolors of tropical scenes sparsely rationed on stark white walls, Persian rugs and a beige sectional couch, curving around a low, oval teak coffee table, facing a large flagstone fireplace.

"You ever *use* that thing?" Judy asked.

"Occasionally—when I have to burn documents," Rusty said. He enjoyed being a rogue. A young woman servant brought a tray with iced tea, lemonade, Coke, Perrier and a lone bottle of Bacardi. "I assumed you wouldn't be interested in alcohol," he said. "The world has become a much less interesting place over time. Even journalists and politicians eat well and exercise—a pity. But if any of you would like to join me in something stronger? Rum and Coca? No? Oh well."

We sat down on the couch, Libby and Figueroa facing each other catercornered, Judy and I farther down. Libby was controlled, businesslike—very Sam Spade. She conducted the interrogation. "So, Freddy Picker offered you a bribe to vote for this project?" she asked.

"Not a bribe," Figueroa said. "I never said bribe. I said contribution."

"How much?" Libby asked.

"A thousand," he said. "That was the going rate in those days."

"The going rate?"

"Well, there were a lot of projects going up, a lot of roads and sewers being built. Progress, you might say, was my most important profit." He was enjoying this.

"Do you have any record of it, any way to prove it?" Libby asked.

"Well"—he laughed—"I didn't keep a little black book, but if you go back into my campaign committee records, you'll see contributions there from the Sunshine folks."

"That's his brother-in-law's company," Libby said.

"His brother-in-law's company." Figueroa laughed. "And his wife's a director. And his brother, Andy, is the executive vice president. So whose company is this really, right?"

"But who approached you? Was it Picker himself?"

"Oh come on now! And you claim to be active in *national* politics?" Figueroa said. "The game has fallen on hard times."

"Did you deal with Picker at all on this?" Libby asked.

"No," he said. "Not on this. You'd see him around, though. Down in Miami. He made the scene."

"He made the scene?"

"Well, Toni's family was into everything good, if you know what I'm saying—and Freddy and Toni, you'd see them around in the mid-seventies, together and apart, sometimes very much apart." He chuckled appreciatively.

"Who was the other man?" I asked.

He looked at Judy, then Libby, then me. "Oh, you mean the guy Toni left him for?" He said. "Some Anglo attorney up there, in Tallahassee."

"And the governor, what was he like? How well did you know him?" Libby asked.

"He was okay. He was smart, he could do the job. 'Course, he wasn't the saint you're seeing now—that's like, hilarious. But then, none of us were saints back then. And everybody's a saint now. At least, that's the way it looks. That's the style. I love how everyone's working so hard to be clean these days, and they're still getting scorched—and for what? For nothing, compared to what used to go on. This is a crazy business. Hard times for party animals. You should talk to Eddie Reyes, the brother-in-law. He knew Freddy real good."

"Was he the guy you did business with?" Libby asked.

"*Everybody* did business with Eddie," Figueroa said. "He was just a real public-spirited individual."

"I need a SHOWER," Libby said as we headed south in the red Chrysler LeBaron convertible she had rented. ("Might as well live it up," she'd said. "This'll be paid off ten cents on the dollar by the defunct Stanton for President campaign.")

"Not much of a scandal," I said.

"Fucking sleazeball," she said. Her wild gray hair was blowing out behind her in the evening breeze. "I touched his *hand. YUCK: COOTIES!*"

"So, we go to see Eddie Reyes, if he'll see us," I said. "Then what?"

"Pottsie," she said. "Lipinsky's husband. Pottsie was a statie. Staties know everything. We'll have a nice quiet dinner with the Potter-Lipinskys tomorrow night."

Libby had made room reservations at a place called L'Afrique, an Art Deco hotel on the ocean in South Beach—which, it was immediately clear, had gotten high marks from Libby's favorite gay travel guide. It was a fabulous place, a carnal theme park: the bellboys were choice beefcake—dressed as native bearers, bare-chested, in loincloths and sandals (this being a politically correct theme park, they came in all colors). The lobby was fantastic, way over the top Neo-Bwana style, all palms and rattan furniture with mud cloth cushions sitting on a giant leopard-print rug. There were trickling fountains and rain-forest vegetation and zebra skins, masks, spears and thatch on the walls. The lobby bar had waiters wearing pith helmets and sarongs; other servants wafted about offering party favors and waving palm-frond fans. The piped music—very low and seductive—was Olatunji and his Drums of Passion; everyone seemed to be moving to the beat.

"BUMMMERRR," Libby stage-whispered.

"Too sedate, Lib?" I asked.

"I was expecting something more . . . bicoastal," she said as we followed a snaking slate path toward the registration desk. "At least, that's what the guide said."

"How disappointing," I said. "So, do we have to stay here?"

"It's late, I'm wiped," Libby said. "And this is going to cost the Stanton campaign a shitload of money. They charge *whorehouse* rates in this joint."

The rooms were something of a comedown after the scene in the lobby. Mine was pink and bare, with fifties motel furniture—another conceit, obviously—and jalousie windows facing the ocean. I flipped on the television, lay down on the bed and felt antsy. I called Daisy, got her phone machine and didn't leave a message.

I went for a walk. On a side street off the ocean I saw a crowd of young people—men and women, young and pretty, carrying pastel drinks in plastic glasses—spilling out from a club called the Awful Surge. I went inside and stood at the bar, which was bathed in cherry light and decorated with driftwood and seashells. I ordered a mar-garita with a double shot. A bar band wearing Hawaiian shirts was playing Beach Boys loud enough so that when you talked, you had to yell directly into the other person's ear.

The ear I chose belonged to a woman who would have been one of my classic thermonuclear-holocaust fantasies on the E train. Her name was either Claudia or Gloria. She was Latino, copper-skinned, wearing an aquamarine halter top and black bicycle shorts. She smiled at me; I smiled at her. I bought her a drink. We chatted, rudimentarily. She worked in a hotel. She asked me what I did. "ESTATE SALES," I yelled. *"WHAT?"* she asked. "I SELL DEAD PEOPLE'S PROPERTY," I said. *"YOU FROM HERE?"* she asked. "New York," I said, less confidently. "You want to dance?"

We danced: "Little Deuce Coupe" and "Surfer Girl." I am not a big Beach Boys fan—they'd always seemed an apotheosis of Caucasian dorkiness—and "Surfer Girl" may well be the stupidest song ever written, but it is very, very slow. And Claudia-Gloria snuggled close, her hands up my neck; and I put my hands down by the small of her back, just where her hips flared, touching the soft skin between her halter top and bicycle shorts. "Where you staying?" she whispered, her lips and a tiny hint of tongue on my ear.

"Uhhh . . . L'Afrique," I said.

"That's the *faggot* hotel," she said, pulling back, looking at me. "Are you?"

"No," I said, "And I can prove it."

I proved it, then promptly fell asleep. And awakened in the darkness, Claudia-Gloria sleeping softly, facing me, her mouth slightly open, a complete stranger. I shoved back, toward the edge of the bed, and stared at her, searching for signs of familiarity. There were none. I was wide awake now, feeling slightly freaked—not quite *guilty,* but alone, and the aloneness was a physical state, a dull ache—and claustrophobic, too, in that bed.

I got up and went to the windows. They were locked shut. I fumbled about, trying to crank them open; no luck. I could see occasional ruffles of white along the inky beachfront: waves breaking. I couldn't hear the ocean; I was cut off from it. Each of Claudia-Gloria's breaths seemed to fill the room, pressing against me, pushing me out. I threw on my clothes and whipped through the lobby—mostly empty now, though several bearers and bwanas were engaged in heavy petting on the rattan couches in dark corners—and I went out to the ocean, tremendously relieved by the warmth of the air and the fact that I could now hear the waves. I took several steps out into the sand, but it was squishy and uncomfortable—too much of an effort—and so I retreated to a bench on the grass strip near the sidewalk, beneath the palms, and I sat there, watching the ocean, watching the dawn come, my mind frozen, except for thoughts of Daisy and the sudden, intolerable emptiness of being alone.

Eddie Reyes was a very busy man, but he agreed to see us late that afternoon. Libby also arranged for us to have dinner with Judy Lipinsky and her husband, Ralph Potter, that evening, at Joe's Stone Crab.

"So who was the girl?" Libby asked, as we drove across the causeway to Miami that afternoon.

"What girl?"

"Henry, you've known me for how long? We're fucking partners in crime. And you're still trying to GAME ME? For God's sake, little man—you *smell* like sex. I got a *nose* for *nookie*."

I looked at her.

"Okay," she said. "I called your room this morning. She answered. She said, 'Tell your friend he's a nice guy, but it's only polite to say thank you and good-bye.' You *booked* on her, Henri? You fled?"

"Do we have to talk about this?" I asked.

"What else IS there?" Libby screeched. "You don't have much of a conversational *repertoire,* Henry. There isn't too much we can talk about—you don't know shit about music, I've never heard you discuss science or philosophy, or the *wonders of East Asia*. You're a *stunted* fucking little guy—politics, politics, politics. And there ain't much politics left for us now, is there? We are at the *END* of politics. So what you got without politics, Henri?" she said, suddenly quieting down—for effect. "You don't even have the courage to tell Daisy you love her."

"Jesus, Libby," I said.

"Pathetic, Henry."

I would like to be able to report that Eddie Reyes's office *didn't* look like something lifted directly out of *Miami Vice;* I would like to report that it wasn't all angles and starkness. But I can't. It was, and so was he. His bare rectangular desk, green marble on thin legs, stood in front of a dramatic isosceles triangle window; the room was irregularly shaped, acute and unpredictable—the art, clashing with itself elegantly on soft, charcoal-gray walls, was solid geometry: a tangerine circle, a cerulean rhombus, a royal purple square. The floor was highly polished onyx plastic. Libby, in a fuchsia-and-chartreuse tie-dyed muumuu, fit this place perfectly. I felt lost and a little giddy. Had serious, sentient humans ever conducted business here? Then again, I imagined how *we*—Libby and I—probably looked to Eddie Reyes: several exits past *serious*, that was for damn sure.

Eddie was wearing a white linen suit and a creamy white silk shirt, opened several buttons down, a gold cross nestled in his hairy chest; he had a slight paunch. His hair was dark and straight but not oiled; his sideburns were bushy and turning gray. He wore a Rolex with a heavy gold band, a wedding ring, a diamond stud earring.

His secretary, a tall woman impeccably dressed in a white blouse, tight gray skirt (the color of the walls) and black heels, served us Perrier in triangular glasses. We sat in two very austere chrome-and-black leather chairs facing the desk; Eddie stood. There was no chair behind the desk. This was a room for audiences, not paperwork.

"So," Eddie said, with the confidence of a man used to being the smartest person in a room. "Rusty Figueroa has spilled the beans. He once took a campaign contribution from Sunshine Associates. Shocking, don't you think? I hope you won't be too disappointed if I confess everything immediately. A terrible crime, giving campaign contributions."

"It's not the money," Libby said. "It's who gave it. And why."

"I gave it," Eddie said, "because I found Rusty Figueroa's philosophy of governance *enlightened*. Oh, there were some specific policy differences, but . . ."

"You were in business with the governor's wife and the governor's brother," Libby said. "You were trying to get action on a specific project from the state."

"Yes, I was in business with my sister and the governor's idiot brother," Eddie replied sharply. "As for the 'action,' *prove* it."

"I don't have to," Libby said. "It's gonna look like shit."

"I am absolutely heartbroken about that, Ms. Holden," he said derisively. "I had so wished that Freddy would get to be president." Then, diving into a cruder, faster tone: "But, I must say, if the motherfucker has to go down, it would be just *too fucking perfect* that he go down over a nothing piece of shit like this. It would be more *appropriate* than you can imagine. I'll even tell you why: Yes, Toni and I had this business. Yes, we hired that idiot Andy Picker after he drove his family business into the ground. And yes, I hoped that having the governor as a brother-in-law wouldn't be a . . . liability. But it was."

Eddie Reyes sat down on the edge of his desk, leaned toward us. "See, the Pickers were broke. Andy was as bad at trading leases as Freddy was good. Poppy didn't want Toni to be broke too, so he told me to take care of her, and yeah, I thought I'd be able to make a little dough for myself in the process. Money was falling from the clouds in those days. But Señor *Recto*—Mr. Righteous, Governor Picker—he wouldn't cut me any slack. There was a shitload of Section Eight money just lying around. I had a fucking consortium ready to roll— and Freddy said, 'No way.' " Reyes got up off the desk, began prowling the room. "So, yeah, we did do Tidewater. We did it straight up. We did it like every other fucking condo—and that motherfucker still wanted to line item *veto* it. I'll bet Rusty didn't tell you *that*. It was just fucking *spectacular* that Freddy could be so straight and so bent at the same time. It was practically acrobatic, a wonder of modern science. And so, yes—yeah, absolutely—Toni did eventually *convince* him to treat Tidewater just like every other fucking project. But I gotta tell you, the story here isn't what we did—but what we didn't do, what he stopped us from doing."

There wasn't much we could say to that. Eddie seemed almost disappointed that we didn't have more questions. He stopped pacing, shook his head. "Señor Recto. Mr. Rectum. Mr. Asshole." He laughed. "Mr. *President*? This is one fabulous fucking country, you know that?"

"But he didn't *stop* you from going into business like that," Libby tried, flustered for once, groping. "You hired his wife, his brother— and he didn't stop you. He must have known . . ."

"Known?" Eddie scoffed. "What the fuck did *he* know? He was half stoned most of the time."

"Stoned?" Libby blurted.

"Oh, dear," Edgardo Reyes said, putting his hands beside his cheeks and rolling his eyes, viciously mocking Munch. "I really have gone and said something I oughtn't. Haven't I?"

"Stoned how?"

"Toot toot tootsie goodbye," Eddie sang. "Toot toot tootsie don't cry. . . . You look disappointed," he said, reading our faces too well. "Fucking *maricón* cokehead."

"Wait a minute," Libby said. "Co—"

"Cocaine," Eddie said. "He loved the shit. Hell, we *all* loved the shit—but he's the only one of us who's a candidate for sainthood."

"It doesn't fit," I said, shocked—and sickened—by this, and *angry* with Eddie Reyes for pushing this in our faces.

"With the current Señor Recto—no way it fits, *chiquito*," Eddie purred. "You see him on the tube and he's practically a virgin. But how old are you? Where you were twenty years ago? In diapers. *You* ought to understand," he said, turning to Libby. "Are you the same now you were twenty years ago?"

"Abso-FUCKING-lutely," Libby said.

Eddie looked at her and laughed. "I'll bet you are," he said.

"I just look a little different," she added.

"But you *do* remember when everyone was doing everything, right?" Eddie continued. "You remember when people were saying cocaine was about as dangerous as marijuana. Word was, down here, they were even tooting up in the White House." And then he softened a bit: "Look, I ain't gonna testify against Freddy. I ain't gonna say a word. You were reporters, I'da given you my Tidewater rap and then sent you home. But I'm not the only guy in town. There are folks might want to make a fortune selling this to the *National Flash*. If your guy Stanton's a real shit, he'll reach out and touch someone—put in a call, start the ball rolling. I guess you guys know all about how that works. And I will fucking weep when Freddy goes down, because it will reflect back on my sister, who has put her life together okay now, and on my nephews. But he shoulda never gotten back into the game. He made the right choice when he quit in '78, came damn close to having his cover blown from what I hear. He should've left well enough alone. But down he *will* go. This is America. You can bank on it."

. . .

"I don't believe it," I said in the car heading back across the causeway. "He's just trying to lead us off the scent."

"Oh shit, Henry—why would he even bother?" Libby said dismissively. "He's not at risk in any way. Even if Freddy *did* all the things Reyes said he *didn't* do—even if he quietly helped make his wife and brother a fortune—*Eddie's* still clean. He was just a businessman, just doin' business. But Picker is fucked either way. If he didn't do anything bent, it still *looks* like shit. It still looks like four thousand man-hours of investigative reporting and Lord knows how many column inches of bullshit when the scorps get wind. And even if they don't come up with a scintilla of a fart in the end, Henry baby, the mere fact that they were looking—the mere fact that Sunshine *existed,* with Picker's wife and his brother and his brother-in-law turning any sort of profit at all—is gonna come off just marginally more benign than if Freddy had personally knocked off half the banks in Tampa. Henry, this is the world we inhabit. This is our lives. This is what *we've* been living the past few months. Why should Picker be immune? 'AL-LEGED' is an indictment in a political campaign. So, yeah, I don't think the cocaine stuff was Eddie working any detour."

"Then what?" I asked. "It was weird. It was just so . . . gratuitous."

"Payback can be therapeutic," Libby said. "You gotta figure Eddie's been storing up a shitload of pissed-*off*edness ever since Freddy went *recto* on him. And you gotta say, he's got a point—if Freddy was snowed in. I mean: Drugs but no deals? A very bent sort of integrity. I suppose you gotta admire it."

"You think it's true?"

"Well, you look at Freddy Picker back then, you look at the video-tape—and he sure was a *bouncy* little fucker," Libby said. Then: "Henry, you are an open fucking *book*. Always were. You're *rooting* for Picker."

"And what are you doing?"

"I'm conducting a scientific experiment," she said. "I am the Marie Curie of the shit world."

"Libby, we've busted enough dust," I said. "Why can't we go home now?"

"We've got to see it through," she said. "I will not consider this a satisfying personal experience unless we know exactly what Freddy Picker did and who he did it to. Even if," she added, "I'll be disappointed to learn it."

"But it'd take weeks—if ever," I said.

"How quickly, Henri, did we nail that shitbird Cashmere?"

"About as fast as the governor did, most likely." I said, surprising myself. I'd never made a joke at Jack Stanton's expense before.

"Henry Burton! Irreverence! Your conversational repertoire is like—EXPLODING—before my very eyes. If you could start discoursing— No, not even that. Just, like, personal opinions on Brahms' *German Requiem,* or maybe why you think Beethoven couldn't do opera. Does grunge have legs. Anything. You do that, we could go into business, be partners—like Starsky and Hutch—and I wouldn't be bored. It would be a life."

"You ever read *Middlemarch*?" I asked.

"George Eliot?" she said. "How could such a smart woman have such a fucking pathetic, self-destructive sex life?"

"It was the nineteenth century," I said.

"She was a rebel, she broke rules," Libby said, "and she weenied out on her own life. But then, who am *I* to talk?"

"Shit, Libby," I said. "Let's go home. What else can we do here?"

"Ralphie will know."

"Well, yeah," Ralph Potter said, hammering a crab claw and looking slightly ridiculous in his plastic bib. He was a classic state trooper, big and buzz cut, but with some irony in the crow's feet. "There were rumors."

"There were rumors he was a junkie; there were rumors he was fucking around on her, and vice versa; there were rumors he was gay; there were rumors she was gay," Judy Lipinsky said. "That was one crazy time. Coke had just come in, and it was a monster—and yeah, I guess the governor was down here a lot. He made the scene. It didn't seem like such a big deal: in the old days, it was okay for politicians to make the scene. She, the wife, was from here. And who wants to stay in Tallahassee if you're not under duress?"

I was drifting, fighting off sleep, picking at a seafood salad; I hadn't gotten much rest the night before. This was a very noisy restaurant—no problem for Judy and Libby, who could be heard in an avalanche, but Ralph spoke softly, slowly, and you had to strain to hear him.

"Ralphie," Libby asked. "What sort of rumors?"

"What you said," he said. "Drugs."

"What flavor?" Libby asked.

"Just what you said," he said, irritated. He knew something. And since he was willing—however reluctantly—to show that he knew something, Libby was sure to find out what it was. This was a negotiation. They were negotiating over discretion. Ralph was saying, Okay, I'll tell you, but I don't like this, I'm only doing this because you're an old friend. And you better be goddamn careful. And Libby was saying: I'll protect you and your source, but we both know you're going to tell me. She was saying this by not saying anything, by just staring at him, twirling great forkloads of linguini with seafood and allowing the quiet to settle in.

"Oh, for Chrissake, Ralphie," Judy finally said.

"There's a guy," Ralph said after another chastening moment of silence, directed mostly at his wife.

Libby stared at him.

"A former statie."

Libby twirled and stared.

"Name Reggie Duboise," Ralph said.

"And?" Judy asked. This was *her* interrogation now.

"He was detailed to the governor whenever the governor came to Miami," Ralph said. "He was Picker's driver. He had a problem. He owes me a little."

"What kind of problem?" Judy asked.

"A running nose," Ralph said, eyes narrowing, angry with his wife. "I was his superior. He came to me, all fucked up. He needed help—and I got him a quiet little leave, with the understanding that he'd resign as soon as he got his problem taken care of."

"Why the break?" Libby asked.

"He was a good man," Ralph said. "And a lot of fucked-up things were going down in those days, as you said. I made a judgment he'd made a mistake and could get himself clean. I didn't think humiliation would help him any."

Judy came halfway out of her chair, threw her arms around Ralph's neck and gave him a long, passionate kiss on the mouth. She turned to Libby. "See," she said. "It wasn't his badge *or* his gun."

Libby nodded: *touché*. "So where is he now?" she asked.

"Doing community work," Ralph said. "They call him the Mayor of Liberty City."

We found the Mayor of Liberty City in a garbage-strewn vacant lot on Saturday morning with about twenty twelve-year-olds wearing bright yellow baseball hats and holding large green litter bags. He was an imposing black man, a huge upper torso precarious on long, thin legs, with a gray beard and furious eyes; he was wearing a Nelson Mandela T-shirt and khaki bush shorts. "Welcome to the Little Negro Leagues," he said, when Libby and I pulled up. "This is spring training. We clear the field, we cut a diamond. If we build it, they *may* come."

"We'll help," Libby volunteered. And we did, for several hours, and it felt very good—something actually got done. It was a hot clear morning that drifted from tolerable to bleach-white as the sun dragged itself to the top of the sky; we stopped every half hour or so and gave the kids fruit juice in small paper cups. Libby quickly flushed salmon-pink; huge, dark crescents of sweat radiated out from her armpits, turning her enormous olive shift black. I was drenched and dusty as well, but not quite so spectacularly. I lost myself in the work, the first sustained physical labor I'd done in I couldn't remember how long. I didn't pay much attention to the kids, certainly not as much as Libby (who tried, without much luck, to lead them in a Smokey Robinson's *Greatest Hits* sing-along—most were too young to know the songs). By noon the lot was cleared, a pyramid of green litter bags triumphant on the sidewalk.

"You want to come back next week and rake?" Reggie Duboise asked, after sending the kids home. "Or you gonna be too busy destroying a friend of mine?"

"Where do you want to talk about it?" Libby asked.

"NO *fucking* where," Reggie said. "But there's a McDonald's a few blocks down, and it's air-conditioned."

Duboise ordered himself several Big Macs, Libby ordered herself several quarter-pounders with cheese; I had a medium Diet Coke, which tasted like liquid cardboard. "You know," Libby said, "I've never understood why they wouldn't do a Mac with quarter-pound patties."

"Fuck you," Duboise said. McDonald's wasn't built for people his size; he and Libby sitting in the same booth represented a serious population problem, but he was working the discomfort angle. He didn't want us to feel too easy about our work.

"And you know what else?" he said, taking a fierce, noisy climactic sip from his Coke. "Fuck *you*. I just want to make my utter *disgust* perfectly clear. I also want it clear that I will never say a public word against Freddy Picker; in fact, I will fucking *deny* everything I tell you now. I'm only doing this shit because I owe Ralph Potter my life and he asked me to cooperate, and he ain't asked a thing from me from the *day* he saved my life until now. But I want you to know," and he looked at me very evenly, "I think you're scum."

"You drove for the governor?" Libby asked.

"Yeah," he said, "and it was a fucking *privilege*."

"Why?"

"Because he was a decent human being who got caught up in something he didn't expect."

"Which was cocaine?"

"*None* of us had any idea what it was, except it made you feel like God. And the governor would—score. And, y'know, I don't know how it started—how it became clear to us that we were both into the shit. Maybe it was just that everyone was into it then, maybe you just saw it in each other's eyes. But, at some point, it was clear. It wasn't grotesque. He wasn't . . . like me. I was a fucking animal. But I never thought he was as fucked up as me. You know how it is, you're always doin' junkie trigonometry: I am more fucked up than A, but less fucked up than B. I thought he controlled it pretty well, but then, what did I know? I always imagined him living a *Father Knows Best* life up in Tallahassee, then coming down here to take vacations from having to be perfect. I never asked myself, Why is this guy messing with his life this way? When you're a cop, you don't look for explanations of people fucking up—you just assume it: people fuck up. But there *are* amateurs and professionals. The governor fucked up like an amateur."

"Where would he score?" Libby asked gently.

"There was a guy . . ."

"The same guy, always?"

"Yeah. Lorenzo Delgado, upper-class Cuban—a lawyer, I think. Lived in a classy old building in Coral Gables. Another amateur, at first. I think he and the governor knew each other socially, met through the wife's crowd. But Renzo got snow-blind real bad. He began to deal, and deal heavily enough to draw attention."

Libby didn't say anything.

"Yeah, yeah," Reggie Duboise said. "I saved the governor's ass. I was down in the car. He was up with Renzo. Sometimes you just get lucky. A narc you once knew will stroll up to the car, the governor's car, and say, 'I'm not so sure you want to be in this neighborhood. It's not very safe.' So I run upstairs and I found them. And I say to the governor, 'Stevie is calling you, something urgent up north.' Stevie was his chief of staff. And he—we—got out of there, just in time. And it kind of focused the mind. He sat in the backseat of the car and he began to cry, his hand up over his eyes, and I sat in the front seat, crying too. And you know, I didn't know what to do, what to say. Because we'd never really said anything in the first place, we had no vocabulary for this shit. I just got him the fuck out of there as fast I could, to the airport—out. I opened the door for him, and we just looked at each other, our eyes met, and we didn't say anything, but I knew we were both thinking the same thing: 'Is *this* who we are?' "

Duboise gathered all the sandwich wrappings and placed them neatly on the tray; he policed the area. "And then," he continued, "I went and found Potter, and I told him everything—except for the part about the governor—and he said, 'Reggie, you're a good cop. Take yourself a leave of absence, get cleaned up, and then I don't ever want to see you around a state barracks again.' I was lucky that way—luckier than the governor. There was no Ralph Potter for him to go to, and I think he needed someone. He quit the job a few weeks after that, the press conference you keep seeing on the news. I never saw him again."

"And the dealer?" Libby asked.

"Busted. Guilty. Gone. Never heard nothin' about him again either."

We sat there quietly for a few minutes, no one knowing what to do or say next.

"I don't know what you people do with this sort of thing," Reggie Duboise finally said, "and, as I said, *I'm* not gonna be any part of it. But if you use this to take Freddy Picker down, you should die slowly from cancer—unless you can look yourself in the mirror and say there wasn't a moment in your life when you didn't do the wrong thing, when you didn't get a little mixed up, head off on the wrong path. The good Lord gives us a precious ration of those. We're each allowed a few. My grandmother, who came down here from cane-cuttin' country, had this thing she'd say: *Every saint has a past, every sinner has a future.* I try to remember that when folks in this neighborhood start treating me like a *role model,* start hedging their language and acting like I'm better than they are, like they can't behave normal around me. And I try to look at the fucked-up kids 'round here same way Ralph Potter looked at me, least when they're still fresh at being evil. I don't assume they're lost, I'll give 'em a tough chance back. But nobody gets that sort of slack in your line of work, do they? One strike and you're out." He shook his head and laughed. "I guess your drug is a lot more dangerous than mine was."

There was one last favor to ask of Ralph Potter. Libby called him from the lobby of the Intercontinental Hotel in Miami, still sweaty and dusty from Liberty City, and drawing stares. We used the bathrooms to wash and change, then sat out on the patio for an hour, drinking iced tea. Finally, Libby called Ralph again. "Lorenzo Delgado was released from prison nine months ago," she said when she returned. "He's living at this address, a halfway house in Hialeah."

We arrived there in late afternoon. It was different from the other houses in the neighborhood, which were small, low, painted in Caribbean pastels, teeming with children and music and immigrant optimism. The halfway house was older, and more austere; all the windows were closed and the shades drawn. It was a large house, two stories, white shingles and a tin roof—a remnant from an earlier time.

The dirt yard had been carefully raked; there were no footprints. There was a sign above the door, EL CAMINO AL PARAISO. We rang the bell and were buzzed in. It was cool inside, over-air-conditioned, with a heavy institutional disinfectant smell. The entrance hall ceiling was painted—remarkably—in dark blue, with small stars and subtle, discretely placed angels. There were two posters on the walls: a flowery "One Day at a Time" and a more militant photo of a gay pride march, with the words "We're Here . . . Get Used to It."

A chunky Hispanic woman sat in the office, reading a *novela*. She directed us upstairs, to the sun porch, "That's where Renzo usually hangs."

We walked through a common room filled with secondhand furniture, dominated by a big-screen color television. Three men sat watching a Spanish soap opera. One had the distinctive purplish festers of Kaposi's sarcoma, another was bundled in a sweater, glassy-eyed and coughing; the third was tethered to an intravenous pole. Upstairs was a narrow, depressing hallway, studded with doorways on both sides. The porch was at the end of the hall, through an aluminum storm door. It was enclosed by screens, pleasant—warmer than inside and feathered by a slight breeze. Lorenzo Delgado was alone there. He was a small, thin man, sitting on a chaise, smoking a Marlboro.

"You're Renzo?" Libby asked. He nodded. "We'd like to talk to you about Freddy Picker."

"Oh, I've been *expecting* you. You're from the campaign, right?" he asked, but rattled on before we had a chance—God forgive us—to say *which* campaign. "Well, you can tell Freddy he has nothing to fear from me," he said in a hoarse, gravelly voice. "*Nothing.* You understand? This happened . . . after. I fucked my brains out in jail, not much else to do there—and there were so many boys who spent all day in the gym, working on their bodies."

Libby and I didn't dare *look* at each other, much less say anything. We flanked him in aluminum lawn chairs. "I like this porch," he said, "but I can't do it all the time. Depends on the weather. It's strange—my body temperature is *always* off, one way or another. Too hot or too cold. It never feels just right. Sometimes the tiniest breeze can set me off, shivering—and I can't do anything about it, can't turn it off, just have to ride with it."

I still hadn't said anything, hadn't introduced myself—and Renzo suddenly fixed on me. He appeared to check me out, a salacious glance, then he smiled and asked, "So, are you Freddy's friend now?"

"OOOOOOOOO-EEEEEEE," Libby said, as we headed for the airport. "You just knew it was gonna be *GOOD*! You just knew it was gonna be IRRESISTIBLE. And this has EVERYfucking-THING: SEX! DRUGS! CORRUPTION! And NONE of it—*none of it,* Henry, my man—NONE OF IT is clear-cut venality. It's all kind of . . . *human* and lovely and luscious. It's weakness, not evil. I LOVE THIS GAME."

"What are you *talking* about?" I asked.

"When doing a social experiment," Libby said, going into a high-pitched Julia Child impersonation, "you do not want to stir *gently*. You WANT TO ROIL THE FUCKER. You want conditions right, you want it to be really tempting, y'know? You want it luscious. THIS is *dripping* with lusciosity."

"But I don't—"

"Understand? Ohhhhh, Henry! Of course you understand. We've been on the same fucking page from the start—if you hadn't been, I'da told you to stuff it, stay home, be a lackey. So don't play dumb with me. THIS IS A TEST. Of us and them. Actually, of us and them and us again. We just passed the entrance exam. We got the dirt. We're fuck-ing unbelievable—you know that? We're so good we're . . . *lucky.*"

"Libby, what are you *talking* about?" I asked, but I kind of knew. "What are we gonna do with this shit?"

"It ain't US! It ain't what *we're* gonna do. It ain't about US!" She slammed the horn on "US." "It is now about THEM! We are going to do what we do: we bust dust and tell all. The question is, what are Jack and Susan going to DO with it? Inquiring MINDS want to know! I mean, little buddy, isn't that *really* what we're both *after* here? I mean, after twenty fucking years, I get to see what THEY're about—not just hypothesize, not just HOPE. This is it. Graduation day. They graduate or I do. Tell the truth, Henry," she said, and dived to an intense whisper, staring at me with wild blue eyes, instead of at the road, "isn't this what you're really after, too?"

"Drive, Libby, goddammit!" I said.

"Well, isn't it?"

"I guess," I said, but I knew. "What if they react the wrong way? What if they flunk the test?"

"Then it's OUR turn at bat again," she said. "Hoo-HAH! Then we get to see what *we're* made of, and we gotta hope it ain't green cheese."

"Libby," I said. "I know this is hard, but I've seen you do it before. Could you please possibly get fucking *sane* for a minute and tell me what you're getting me into?"

"NO!" She said and swerved the car onto the shoulder, slamming the breaks, stopping with a lurch.

"Jesus!" I said.

"Henry," she said, staring at me—perfectly calm, perfectly sane. (I had done it.) "Do you remember the rules we set the day we vamped on that scumfucker Randy Culligan? Do you remember how we're sitting outside his law office and I told you I was about to do something crazy? And you could be in or out, but ask no questions?"

I nodded.

"Well, sweetie," she said, taking my chin in her hand, "we're back there now. Faith or nothing. You on?"

"You're not gonna shoot the Stantons, are you?"

"Not quite," she said.

"No violence of any kind."

"Don't *chivvy* me, Henry," she said. "You on or no?"

I nodded yes, my chin still in her hand. And she kissed me on the cheek.

The Sunday morning papers had Freddie Picker being endorsed by the governor of Pennsylvania and most of the state's congressional delegation. I read it as a civilian might, without a twinge. There had been days, *months,* when I could soar or dive on the hint of a nuance in a one-paragraph item buried in *The Washington Post;* that had been my life. But the campaign was over for me now. I called Daisy that morning and got her machine again. "Daisy, *please,*" I said. "I fucked up. But does one fuckup mean that I'm cast into the outer darkness for all eternity? I miss you."

Libby called later that morning. "We meet at five at the Mansion, just before the other meeting, which is—you're never fucking going to BELIEVE this—a dinner meeting. And Fat Willie is CATERING! I guess Jack figures, if he's goin' out, might as well go out with a full belly."

"Did he ask you anything?"

"Does a woodpecker have a long, sharp nose?"

"And?"

"Oh ye of little faith."

"Well, what did you say?"

"He said, 'Any luck?' I said, 'Depends on what you mean by luck.' He said, 'Did you find anything?' I said, 'Depends on what you mean by anything.' He said, 'C'mon Libby, don't fuck with me.' I said, 'I don't fuck, I make love. You aren't gonna risk another moment of passion now, Jack, after all the shit your wiener's gotten you into, are you?' . . . So, the question is: He call *you* yet?"

"No," I said.

"He will."

He did, about ten minutes after I got off with Libby.

"So how was Florida?" He asked.

"Humid," I said.

"Oh come *on*, Henry. Not you too?"

I didn't say anything.

"I need to know if there's any hope," he said.

I carefully considered what I said next. "It depends," I said, "what you mean by hope."

"Henry, goddammit, who are you working for?"

"Governor, I'm working *with* Libby," I said. "We figured it would be best if we made our report together. See you at five."

I spent the next few hours taking inventory of my apartment, trying to figure how much there would be to pack, how long it would take to leave. Then I went for a run and, afterward, sat on a bench next to the river, which had swollen with the spring, leaving the grassy banks soggy. Of all the things I had seen and done and experienced in Mammoth Falls, I would remember the river most vividly. It was the closest I'd ever come to a natural thing. I lived next to it, ran alongside it, sat by it, slowly learned its moods—and there were times that

I could put myself in a half-trance, and imagine its swift current emptying my mind, carrying my worries off downstream. I never really stopped to consider the transcendental power of the river—I'm not very mystical, I guess—but I do find myself sitting in that spot, in my mind, from time to time, especially when I'm looking to get calm.

Howard and Lucille were with the Stantons in the study when I arrived—which was a matter of some concern. Howard telegraphed one of his furtive little ironic smiles; Lucille glared. Susan stood, gave me a kiss on the cheek and said, "What, you didn't us bring back any jelly?" She turned to Jack and asked, "Hey, did I ever tell you about this? Whenever my folks came back from Florida, they brought a package—three glass globes, globules—of jelly. One was orange, another orange-pineapple, another cher—"

"OUT!" It was Libby, pointing a finger—casually and from above, like God in the Sistine Chapel—at Lucille. "YOU ARE OUTTA-HERE, you slimetudinous sack of snail wuzzle. AND YOU TOO— YOU *ESPECIALLY* TOO," she said, whirling on Howard. "Life is too *fucking* SHORT to even have to *think* about your sorry ass. OUT!"

Neither moved. Howard looked to Jack; Lucille, Susan. "Ohhh-KAYYYYY," Libby said and turned toward the door.

"No, wait," Susan said, nodding toward Lucille, who began moving toward the door—then stopped, put her hands on her hips and said to Libby, "You are one *sick* puppy."

"HAWHAWHAWHAWHAWHAWHAWHAW," Libby said, throwing her head back and not laughing. "Out . . . OUT, out . . . OUT," she said, barking like a dog. Then, to Howard, "You too, teenie-weenie. Time to BOOK. You're leavin' on that midnight train to JAWWW-JAH! Out . . . OUT, out . . . OUT! I've had twenty fucking years too much of *you*."

"Can *I* stay?" Susan asked, as Howard left, closing the study door behind him.

"Always." Libby smiled. "Sweetheart."

"Is all this really necessary?" Jack asked.

"NO!" Libby said, then added with a sudden Scottish burr. "But it's what happens when you send a LUNATIC to do a *mannnn's* work. So *here,* Governor—feast your eyes," she said, tossing Stanton, who was sitting in his usual wing chair, a manila legal file with a metal clasp at the top. "You too, m'lady." She handed a file to Susan, who was curled, barefoot, down the other end of the green couch from me.

Then Libby handed me a copy, accompanied by a small sigh and a clear-eyed, here-goes-nothing glance. As we read, she paced the edge of the room, next to the windows, hands clasped behind her back, head down, riffling the gauzy linen curtains as she passed.

The file was untitled. The first page said "Executive Summary." It had a row of bullets, setting off capitalized names: ORESTES FIGUEROA, EDGARDO REYES, REGINALD DUBOISE, LORENZO DELGADO—and a precise one-sentence summary of their "testimony." This was followed by more elaborate accounts of our interviews with the four, accounts that seemed entirely accurate—unhedged, unbiased—to me.

Jack Stanton whistled and looked up. Libby said, "Henry, does this square with your memory of our investigation?"

"Yes, absolutely."

"Remarkable," Stanton said, shaking his head. "How on earth did he ever think he could get *away* with this?"

"Well, he *was* running against YOU," Libby said.

Stanton ignored that. "What do we do with this?" he asked.

"The *Times*?" Susan said. "Or maybe *The Wall Street Journal*—more authoritative, in a way."

Libby glanced at me. They hadn't even hesitated. Not an instant of doubt.

"Through an intermediary," Susan said. "Someone not associated with the campaign."

"I don't *think* so," Libby said.

"What do you mean?" Stanton said, twisting around back toward a corner of the room behind the wing chair, where Libby leaned against a grandfather clock, positioning herself for his discomfort.

"I don't think there's anything of *use* here," she said.

"C'mon, Libby, you gotta be kidding," Stanton said. "At the very least, the Republicans already know about the Sunshine business, and the rest is eminently gettable, soon as people start looking for it."

"Mebbe," said Libby, sliding down to the floor, knees up, palms on her knees, next to the grandfather clock. Stanton couldn't see her at all now. He had to get up and turn around, a knee on the wing chair. "But it doesn't meet *my* standards," she said.

"What on earth do you mean, Olivia?" Susan asked sardonically.

"I mean, *madame,* two things," Libby said, popping up, pacing again. "First of all, this is mostly bullshit. It's horseflop and innuendo. The Sunshine business *looks* bad, but I don't think Freddy had all that much to do with it. As for the rest, well, Reggie Duboise ain't gonna talk, God bless him. And Renzo," she said, stopping, staring directly at Susan, "you wouldn't . . . *dare.*"

She moved around the couch, directly behind me, put her hands on my shoulders. "Besides, legal eagles—point two is dispositive: Henry and I don't think the use of this material is proper. We have a moral objection. And *I* have a historical beef."

Stanton glanced at me; I gave him nothing back, the same cold void I'd once given Fat Willie on his behalf. "Awww c'mon, Libby," he said. "If you weren't gonna use it, why'd you go look for it?"

"He could've been a real shit," she said, resuming her pacing. "I didn't think he would be, and he isn't, but he *could* have been. But Jackie, my dearest—you are *off the fucking point.* The point is: WE DON'T DO THIS SORT OF THING! Oh, I *will* be relentless busting dust and guarding your ass—I'd've even blown Randy Culligan's weenie off for you. Well, *maybe* I would have. But this is something else again. This is hurting someone else. This SUCKS. You want to know exactly why this sucks? Because YOU TOLD ME SO. You remember when, Jackie? Let me refresh your memory," and she dived into her leather satchel and produced three copies of an eight-by-ten black-and-white photo, which she handed to Jack, Susan and me.

It was remarkable. Jack and Susan both looked pretty much the same, but younger, fresher. They were dressed in turn-of-the-seventies clothes. Jack's hair was long and curly; he was wearing a ruffled Edwardian shirt with a laced drawstring top, sort of like Errol Flynn, and bell-bottoms. Susan's hair was long, straight and brown; she was wearing a bikini top and very short cut-off jeans. Both Stantons were wearing sandals. The real revelation, though, was Libby—who stood in the middle, an arm around Jack and Susan, towering over both, smiling with proud, parental satisfaction.

My first thought was, Why did Libby seem so tall? Then I realized: she was wearing heels. She was, in fact, very conventionally dressed and about a hundred pounds thinner. She had big hair (not yet gray) and was wearing a satiny sheath, and looked like a Kilgore Junior College Rangerette, or maybe one of Lyndon Johnson's daughters.

"Henry, weren't they just *gorgeous*?" She sighed.

"Yeah," I said, "but look at you."

"You little *shit*," she said. "I TOLD you I used to have a waist."

"Libby," Jack began.

"Oh hush UP," she said. "Don't ruin it. You remember when this was?" She looked at Stanton. "You *don't*, do you."

"The Miami headquarters in '72," Susan said.

"Well, of course," Libby said. "Henry, this was taken just after the convention. I'll never forget that convention—I was already running Florida, and Gary Hart finds me in a trailer, on the phone, whipping my delegation. And he has—*these* guys. 'O,' he said—he called me 'O'—'I brought some reinforcements.' And it was like, wow. They were golden, y'know? A different life form. I mean, it was just clear as day as soon as they settled in. They were geniuses at this shit. We had a crappy old subtropical piece of shit office in downtown Miami— and the Stantons were . . . Well, this picture was taken the day they reported to work. God, they almost turned it into a real campaign. Jack was out, talking to groups—all these old Jews and New Dealers, none of whom wanted to support George McGovern and the Forces of Drugged Fucking Anarchy. But Jack could recite FDR's first inaugural by heart, bring a tear to their eye. And then he'd say, 'The Democratic Party has given you a good life. Would you be here— would you be able to afford living here—without Social Security? Are you willing to gamble your future, your children's future, on the people who fought against Social Security and Medicare and the GI Bill and every other thing that has made your lives a little better?' "

"Probably swung six or eight dozen votes," Stanton said.

"And Susan—Map Woman!" Libby said. "She laid out the state, had every precinct organized, had the office running like a fucking harvesting combine. 'Course the Stantons brought along some sea-

weed and shit in their wake, Howard and Lucille—the Progressive
Labor Party's Fun Couple of 1971—but, with the Stantons, the deal
has always been: You take the bad with the spectacular."

"Libby, for Chrissake," Susan said. "What are you doing? What's
the point?"

"The point is—EAGLETON," Libby said. "You remember, Jack?
I must have known you—what, two days then? We hear about the
electroshock, and it's weird: That was the first time I actually considered the possibility that we might lose to that fuckbrain Nixon. Before that, I was *absolutely convinced* we would win. I mean, who would
ever vote for Tricky? No one *I* knew, 'cept the idiots I escaped from
back in Partridge, Texas. Can you imagine, Henry? We were so *fucking* YOUNG. And this one, this one"—she nodded over toward Stanton—"he takes me out, we go to this little open-air Cuban joint, and
I've got my head in my hands. Life has *ended.* And THEY did it—the
CIA. It had to be the CIA. I couldn't believe that Tom Eagleton
would really be a nutcase. They had to have dragged him off and
drugged him and made him crazy. It couldn't have been that
McGovern was just—a COMPLETE FUCKING AMATEUR. No,
they did dirty tricks. And I said to Jack, 'We gotta get the capability.'
You remember, Jack? 'We gotta be able to do that, too.' And you said,
'No. Our job is to *END* all that. Our job is to make it clean. Because
if it's clean, we win—because our ideas are better.' You remember
that, Jack?"

Libby had tears in her eyes now.

"It was a long time ago," Stanton said gently.

"Libby, you said it yourself," Susan said coolly. "We were young. We
didn't know how the world worked. Now we know. We know that if
we don't move on this Picker situation, two things will happen. The
first is, we're dead. Everything we've worked for since Miami twenty
years ago dies. And fast. It will die tomorrow. The second thing that
happens is, someday—someday soon—when the bloom is off the romance, when they've gotten sick of Freddy Picker's quiet, righteous
act, when they want to pull his *wings* off, some enterprising journalist
will stumble onto this. And if he doesn't, the Republicans will lead
him to it, on *their* timetable, next fall. It'll be another Eagleton—only
it'll be *our* fault this time, for letting it happen. Your fault, Libby."

This was, I thought, a pretty strong argument. Libby didn't. "Honey," she said, "you may be right, but it just ain't who we're supposed to be."

"Maybe," Stanton said, "we could leak part of it, the Sunshine stuff—we *know* the Republicans have that."

"Oh Christ, Jack," Susan said, angry that he was softening. "You don't think they're gonna have the rest soon enough? You don't think Eddie Reyes is gonna do a *whooops* with someone else—you don't think he's gonna spill it all? I mean"—she riffled through Libby's file—"Libby, he *did* call Picker a *maricón* cokehead, didn't he?"

Libby and I exchanged a glance: yes, he had. We'd just dismissed it as another stray expletive at the time.

"So, you'd even give up the Renzo angle?" Libby asked. "What fucking *difference* does *orientation* make?"

"It'll mean something to the *National Flash,*" Susan said.

"Ohhh, Susie," Libby moaned. "*You,* of all people."

Libby caught my surprise. "Oh come *on,* Henry—*you,* of all people. Remember what Eddie Reyes said: you should always assume everyone did everything back then. And, Henry, surely *you* are *familiar* with Mrs. Stanton's need for physical solace in times of spousal despair."

Now it was Jack Stanton's turn to be shocked. He shot a furious look at Libby, who smiled; then at Susan, who was blushing; then at me, too stunned to blush. We had all betrayed him—and he, of course, us. Evidently, everyone *still* did everything.

"Children, children," Libby said, shaking her head, surveying the room. "Ain't we got fun."

"This has gone far enough," Stanton said. "We have to decide."

"What's to decide?" Susan asked.

"Keee-RECT," Libby said. "There is NOTHING to decide. A decision has been made, by me and Henri. This dies here."

"I don't think so," Susan said.

"I'm sorry, sweetheart," Libby said, "but it does. And here's why." She dived down into her satchel again and pulled out another manila file, which looked very much like the first. "I won't distribute this one. . . . I didn't want to make copies," she said—nervously, I thought. "But I'll tell you what it is, and Jackie here can vouch for its accuracy. Silence, Governor, will signify assent."

Susan glanced at Jack—a what's-*this*? look. "I guess life is still simple in the small towns of America," Libby began, quietly. "A doctor's
office isn't very hard to get into after hours. And, Susan, when you
told me I was on the McCollister case, and when I heard that Jack had
had his blood taken, I figured I had no choice but to investigate the
matter fully."

Stanton paled; his right hand came up, he didn't know what to do
with it, so he put it flat on top of his head. "Doc Hastings kept very
detailed notes about your case over the years," Libby said. "I guess he
had . . . a rooting interest. I mean, he was a *full-service* family practi-
tioner, wasn't he? OH! I never thought to ask: Does Susan know?"
Stanton nodded yes. "Well, then, it's only Henry—and he knows everything else, so why not this?" She turned to me. "Doc Hastings is
Governor Stanton's natural father. Momma used that Kansas City
nonsense as a cover, and it worked real good, since Will Stanton never
came back from Iwo to say otherwise. Momma told Jack about it—
when? Doc's records say that you and he had your heart-to-heart after
you graduated college. And being thoughtful folks, Jack and Momma
kept it quiet—out of respect for Doc's wife and his two *other* boys. And
also out of respect for Momma's reputation." Stanton stared at his lap.
Susan stared at me. I stared into space. This was . . . Dogpatch.

Libby read my mind. "Yeah, Henry: this is who we are, Jackie and
me. Piney-woods pigpokers—right, Jack? Rule Number One: If it
moves, shoot it. . . . Or fuck it, 'specially if it's *family*! It's a wonder
Momma wasn't Doc Hastings' *cousin*."

"Libby!" Susan said. "You're out of control."

"Yeah, yeahyeah," she agreed, taking a deep breath, calming herself.
"I'm sorry. Where was I?" She moved forward and squatted directly
in front of Stanton's wing chair. "So, Doc Hastings did have a rooting
interest, didn't he? And root he did. Lord, Jackie! The machinations
he went through to keep you out of the draft! But the part *I* like best
is the most recent stuff: having Uncle Charlie take that blood test for
you. I mean, would you actually have gone through with it—letting
Uncle Charlie take the fall as the daddy? You think that would have
been CREDIBLE? What kind of shit is that?"

Stanton moved his right hand from the top of his head to his brow,
shading his eyes. He was *embarrassed*. I'd never seen him like this be-

fore. He was always so unabashed, so aggressively *in* the world, dominating every conversation, every room, even when he was just listening. But Libby had punctured that. She was in control here; the
governor was in full retreat. He appeared to squirrel down deeper into
his chair, trapped—with Libby in hot pursuit, down on her knees in
front of him, peering up, trying to make eye contact. "What kind of
shit *is* that, Jack?" she chided him gently, but with an edge of impa-
tience. "Oh, excuse me—I forgot: it's the *same old* shit. There's always
been a Doc Hastings or a Senator LaMott Dawson—or Uncle Charlie, or Susan—ready to fix your tickets whenever you fucked up. You
have *never* paid the bill. Never. And no one ever calls you on it. Because you're so completely *fucking* SPECIAL. Everyone was always so
PROUD of you. And me too. Me the worst."

She pushed him back, deeper into the chair, his knees jutting out.
She leaned forward, rested her arms on top of his knees, rested her
head on top of her arms. She perched at the edge of his lap, staring up
at him, torturing him. "It just makes it a whole lot easier for me," she
sighed. "I mean, it's totally depressing—What have I been *doing* this
for, my whole pathetic fucking life?" She seemed to wait for him to
say something. "Well," she said softly. "A situation like this does clear
the *sinuses* now, doesn't it?"

And Stanton finally looked up, looked at her—pleading silently, but
Libby wasn't buying. "So, here's the deal," she said. "You move on
Picker, I move on you."

"You wouldn't," said Susan, whose eyes were red.

"Try me," Libby said, turning toward her, breaking off her pursuit
of Jack Stanton.

"You would end his political career?" Susan asked.

"I bust dust," Libby said, getting to her feet now, moving toward
her satchel, getting ready to leave. "My job is to prevent people from
hurting you—including you. To my mind, you would hurt yourselves
grievously if you acted to destroy Freddy Picker, who—I think we all
agree—is a flawed but decent man." She hesitated, wiped her eyes—
once, then again—but the tears were flowing now. "And so, yes,"
Libby concluded, "I *will* destroy this village in order to save it."

And she dashed out of that room, faster than it seemed possible for
a big woman to move.

I raced after her. People were gathering outside now for the last meeting of the Stanton campaign—Brad Lieberman, Dwayne Forrest, Laurene, Leon, Howard and Lucille. Libby pushed past them, teary, hair flying through the smoke from Fat Willie's barbecue, toward her Jeep Cherokee.

"You drive," she said, tossing the keys over her shoulder toward me, never having looked back—*knowing* I'd be there. She rode shotgun, sobbing quietly, tears streaming. "Drive yourself home."

I did. I parked next to the river.

"So, how'd I do?" She smiled thinly through the tears.

"Just fine," I said. "More controlled than with Randy Culligan, more *nuanced*."

"But the gun was just as big." She smiled and sniffled. "Henry, you *are* outta here, right?"

"Not much left to stay here for, is there?"

"Look up there," she said. A pale full moon had appeared in the still-light sky. "That's me," she said. "Beautiful, huh? Very impressive to the earthlings. But Henry, honey, it's only reflected light. It needs the sun. And I lived my life drawing light and warmth from the Stantons—and, God, they were so good and glowing, I could go for years without remembering I wasn't producing any warmth myself, any *light* of my own. But the day does come when you look in the mirror and all you see is a dead rock. You know what I'm saying, right?"

"Hoo-HAH!" I said—a sorry, third-rate attempt at a Libby impersonation. "You a dead rock? You a lackey? HOO-FUCKING-HAH! *I'm* a lackey. You're the French Foreign Legion."

"Well, idiot boy," she said, shaking her head. "How the fuck do you think I earned placement in that booby hatch? It wasn't an *up* thing, y'know? It was a *down* thing. You know what I'm saying, right? I look in the mirror and see the dead rock. Without them, I'm dark and black and cold and dead and empty and airless for eternity. And they don't fucking need *me* at all, all they need is to *glow*. Drove me nuts. I was so bummed, so deep, deep down. I got trapped in the bathroom. On the floor, just below the mirror where I saw the moonrock. I couldn't get up off the floor. For several days, apparently. Susan found me. She put me—can you imagine?—into an *asylum* for *lunatics*. Moon people. What a hoot! All these unplugged folks and me, with a busted solar heater. So I figured, it must be *okay* now: You are now an *official* lunatic. Go for it! Turns out, though, that act—howling at the moon—has a limited shelf life. It's also kind of schizy if you're a moonrock yourself. You caught the best part of the show, Henri. But it's over; I quit."

There was nothing I could say to that. I put a hand on her shoulder; it was an awkward gesture. "Henry," she said, not looking at me, but staring straight ahead, mesmerized by the dashboard. "I can't bear the thought of going deep, deep down again. You look straight up, and there's a tiny point of light, way up there, and that's where the world is, and you don't have the energy to start moving toward the light, you don't even have the energy to assimilate Brahms, or chew your food. I don't ever want to be there again. I just won't risk that."

She stopped, shook her head. "They didn't even fucking hesitate just now—you saw that. Not a lick of humanity, not a thought about Freddy Picker. Fucking glowworms."

She put out her hand for the keys. I gave them to her. What an idiot I was.

"See," she said, weeping again, streaks down both sides of her face, "the deal is, Henry: don't let it happen to you. You still have something of an *atmosphere*. Don't worry about light. Think about oxygen depletion. Find yourself a life. Okay?"

She leaned over and kissed my cheek, and I threw my arms around her—and we stayed there for a while, both of us snuffling and hanging on for dear life.

Finally, she pulled back and put her big hands on my shoulders: "Now, get gone. Go find Daisy."

"And what about you?" I asked, opening the door, moving out. She slid into the driver's seat.

"When you're in limbo," she said, pulling away. "There are only two ways you *can* go. 'Bye, sweetie."

IX

What an idiot I was.

They found her body the next day. They found her on a dirt road, deep in the piney woods, southwest of Mammoth Falls. Two hunters poaching deer out of season found her. She had taken a director's chair out of the Cherokee, taken her leather satchel, taken the gun out of the satchel and shot herself—not in the head, which would have been too obvious and messy for Libby, but neatly through the heart. She had done this, apparently, after making a small fire; the remains of a manila folder were found there.

Stanton called several times, left messages on my machine; Susan called once. This seemed an appropriately halfhearted effort on their part. If they'd really wanted me, they would have sent someone over or come themselves, as the governor had the day we'd gone to Grace Junction so Uncle Charlie could get his blood pulled—or as the police did that Monday evening. I was the last person to have seen Libby alive. They asked me why I thought she had done this. They asked whether she had seemed distraught. They asked if I believed there was any possibility of foul play. They did not press too hard. Jack Stanton *was* still governor, the Stanton campaign had come upon depressing times, and Libby was a well-known, and certifiable, lunatic. "I know," I told them, "that the normal thing for me to say would be, 'I wish I had known. I wish could have done something to stop her.' But with Libby you never knew, and when she decided to do something, there was nothing you could do to stop her." And then, unexpectedly, I experienced a flood of intense, disorderly images of Libby in action—her charts of Loretta McCollister's classes; Randy Culligan's head between her breasts, her gun in his crotch; her gray hair flying out from under her Australian bush hat; that ridiculous satchel—and I began to cry. "She was," I told the police, "a very close friend of mine."

Libby's death made headlines, of course. It made the front page of *The New York Times,* lower-right-hand corner, two paragraphs jumping to Section B, page 10: STANTON AIDE TAKES LIFE. My reflexive reaction was to go to work, to do spin—not from the campaign headquarters but from Libby's little white frame house, where Jennifer Rogers and the rest of the Dustbusting staff had barricaded themselves. I spent the next thirty-six hours answering their door, shooing reporters away. I spent the night with Jennifer—chastely; we didn't even talk much—lying atop the bed she shared with Libby, with our clothes on and our arms around each other.

Libby, who rarely spoke anything but the truth, had been totally full of shit that last night. It was sort of shocking to see her so deluded. It was probably the only time I'd ever actually seen her crazy. And *I'd* been full of shit when I told the police you never knew with Libby.

You *always* knew with Libby.

I knew that night. But I didn't quite believe it. She was, I figured, just implying the *possibility* of suicide. It was subtext, part of the role she was playing, part of the number she was running on the Stantons. She had been a great actress. I was furious with her, furious with myself. And bereft.

"It wasn't gonna be a permanent thing with us," Jennifer said at one point, deep in the night. "She knew that. In fact, she *told* me that. She said, 'I can't say I admire your *proclivities,* honey, but who am *I* to judge?' She said I'd meet a guy after the campaign and fall in love—and maybe she'd get to be a godmother again. 'You'd be *amazed* the number of godchildren I have,' she said. 'And I am a *righteous* fucking godmother.' Henry, we all loved her so much—why did she feel she had to do it?"

"I don't know," I said. But I sort of knew—and I wondered why Jack Stanton hadn't yet withdrawn from the presidential race: was it out of respect for Libby, or because he was getting ready to act on what we'd given him?

I accompanied Jennifer Rogers to the funeral, which was held in a prim white clapboard Presbyterian church in North Mammoth Falls. (Libby had been the world's least likely Presbyterian.) We sat in the front row, right-hand side. The Stantons sat in the front row, left. Libby's body, in an enormous walnut coffin, stood between us and the altar. The church was full—and I was distracted, uncomfortable, and angry with myself for not being able to devote all my attention to Libby. But I *sensed* Daisy was somewhere back there, I *knew* she had to be there, and during the organ playing and the opening hymn, I would awkwardly half twist my neck and try to scan the audience. I saw Richard but not Daisy. It was driving me nuts. I was thinking that if she actually was there, and took off before I could get to her, I would (a) quickly check the downtown hotels and then (b) go to the airport and try to intercept her. Of course, (a) would probably be a waste of time—the best thing would be to go straight to the airport and wait. I'd have to get someone to take care of Jennifer. I began to scan for an appropriate muffin. Where was Peter Goldsmith, from the dustbusting team?

The windows were open, and the church was filled with late-spring smells, renascent dogwood and azalea—their petals littering the path to the little church—and a clean, dry breeze from the west; there was a distant lawnmower in action, the weekday sounds of panel trucks, handymen going about their business. And I drifted that way, becalmed by the normality around us—unable to get any closer to Daisy—until Jack Stanton rose to speak.

"Olivia Holden was the older sister I never had," he began, with an ineffable sadness in his voice. "I hope it doesn't sound too presumptuous when I say that she loved me—us, Susan and me—like family, and we her." He chuckled a little. "'Course, any y'all knew Libby, you know that meant a lot of yellin'. She never was satisfied with any of us, she demanded *perfection* from family. She wanted us to be bigger—" His voice broke here. "But none of us could be as big as she was"—a chuckle—"in any way."

He stopped, searched the audience—and found me. "I feel personally responsible for this," he told me. "I guess I probably shouldn't. I guess I could say—rationally—that I could never live up to Libby's expectations. I live in the world, a pretty rough world, and I play by *its* rules. But"—he was still looking at me—"she was right. I could have been better. And it seemed that whenever I had a moment of weakness, she was always there. She wouldn't let me get away with *anything*."

And now he looked at the full congregation again. "I guess that's what big sisters are for. Libby didn't leave any burial instructions. Susan and I had to think about what would be appropriate—and the choice seemed obvious: she will be cremated. *She* would have demanded a final flameout"—the audience laughed—"rather than a slow, sapping diminution in a field of daisies. She did not live a moment of her life at anything less than supersonic speed. She should leave the world as she lived in it—in a blaze of glory, throwing heat, dazzling us with her brilliance, her warmth, the amazing suppleness of her spirit. I feel—" and he stopped here, unable to go on. Tears rolled down his cheeks—different from the first tears I'd seen him shed, that day in the Harlem library, or any other tears since. The corners of his mouth were drawn down, his lower lip was quivering—like a child trying to keep composure, a boy trying to be a man. "I feel," he said, "as if a part of me has died. The bullet that exploded in Libby Holden's heart broke *all* our hearts." And then he whispered, "I cannot imagine life without that heart." He fled the lectern, collapsing in the front pew, across from me, head in hands, as the choir rushed into "Amazing Grace" in a vain attempt to exorcise the anguish, to smother pain with glory.

I was up quickly, scanning the crowd. I couldn't see Daisy. I saw a lot of other people I knew, and then Susan was next to me, tugging me gently into a small room behind the altar, handing me an envelope with my name on it. "She left you this," she said. "It was inside the one she left for us."

It was a small envelope from the hotel in New York that we'd stayed in during the primary, the note inside scrawled in scratchy ballpoint: "Aw shit, Henry. It was an empty threat. I coulda never given them up—and I think I would've had to. But you were an *inspired* partner in crime, most fun I ever had (with a guy). So my run is done. Remember: Oxygen. Big Love, L."

I handed it to Susan. She scanned it and then hugged me. "Jack's wrong," she whispered in my ear. "He isn't the one responsible for this. It was me. I was prosecuting a case, being a lawyer—being a hard-ass. I was making the case for politics as usual. I kept hoping someone would rise for the defense."

"You're so good," I said, pulling back from her. "You should *never* be the one who makes the case for politics as usual."

"Henry," she said, but I was out of there, out into the church, which was empty, except for the crowd around the governor, shaking his hand, consoling him. Richard was there, but I didn't stop to say hello. I raced down the aisle, out the door—and there she was, halfway down the path, in the dappled shade of a loblolly pine, arms crossed, in a black silk blouse and black pleated skirt, sheer stockings and low black heels, waiting for me. I was terrified.

"So what happened?" she asked, coolly.

"It's a long story," I said. "And I promise, I will tell it to you, tell you every last bit of it, and then I'll answer every one of your picky, acute questions. I'll do it until you are completely satisfied. I'll do it for years, for *the rest of our lives,* if that's how long you want. But only if you agree to several ground rules. First, I have to have the same rights as you do. And the most important is, I get to be as candid as you—and that means if I think the positives you did in Florida were just *okay,* I have a right—"

"But that wasn't—"

"—I have a right to say it without my life—our lives—crashing down around me. And second, the second ground rule has to do with what really *was* going on in New York: I will not fuck around with this anymore. The world, our world, moves just too fast to guarantee anything. But, Daisy, I am just totally fucking in love with your eyes, the way you see things—no. *Shit!* I am so *bad* at this. It's more than that. I'm in love with . . . whatever it is . . ." She was beginning to frown, but not her eyes. ". . . with the thing that makes you who you are. Your heart. With *you.* Okay? I'm in love with you. . . . Daise, look, I'm kind of a mess. I have no idea who I am anymore. And this—I realized this the last few weeks without you—this is the thing I'm most certain of in my life: the way I feel about you. So those are the two ground rules."

"Deal," she said immediately, and threw her arms around me. "Did you actually think it was gonna be a *hard* sell?"

"Oh God, Daisy," I said. "Thank you."

"You think," she whispered in my ear, "maybe we could go somewhere and continue this conversation with fewer clothes on?"

Perhaps I was wrong about sex and anticipation. There is also love. What we did that afternoon was neither campaign sex nor *non*campaign sex. It was something different entirely. It filled my heart with joy. I shouted at the ceiling, "I would like to dedicate this afternoon to the memory of Olivia Holden."

I told her about Libby. I told her about Freddy Picker. I told her about our adventures in Miami—except for Claudia-Gloria, and I made a quiet vow to myself that I would tell her about that, too, someday. I told her about the scene with the Stantons.

"They're right, you know," she said. "Picker will never survive this."

"Someone will," I said. "There *is* going to be a president of the United States—but that's gonna happen without me."

"Really?" she said.

"I guess."

"Henry, we're political animals," she said. "You're going to want to do this again."

"Maybe, but differently," I said. "Without—it's not the *conviction*. Maybe it's without the ambition. Maybe it would work if I did it humbly. I don't know. You think it's possible to do it gracefully? Look, Daisy: I don't want to even think about that now. I want to go find that beach we used to talk about in New Hampshire and just have my hands all over you for a very long time."

We were facing each other in bed, each up on an elbow. "You know," she said, "I don't think I was ever so happy as I was at that stupid Hampton Inn in Manchester—getting our three hours of sleep each night."

"So let's go there," I said. "Forget the Caribbean."

"You think?"

I thought about the dreary parking lot, the probability of bumping into Danny Scanlon, the last week of that campaign. It was getting on toward mid-April: there probably weren't any leaves on the trees up there yet.

"How about Bermuda?" I said.

"A little early for Bermuda," she said. "Might not get perfect weather."

"Okay, Jamaica. Ibiza. I don't care. Wherever." I jumped out of bed, throwing on clothes. "I'll tell you what: you get on the phone and start making arrangements. I've got one last piece of business to do here."

"Which is?" she asked.

"Stanton was looking directly at me when he talked about being responsible for Libby's death," I said. "He was apologizing. The least I can do is look directly at him when I quit. I'll be back soon. Maybe we should round up Jennifer and some of the other muffins—Libby's crowd—for a last, ceremonial dinner."

"Henry." She was up, out of bed, an arm around my neck, a hand on my cheek. "*You* may be all fucked up and confused about yourself—but *I* know who you are. And Libby did. And I'm sorry I was too damn proud to answer all your phone calls the past few weeks, and I'm sorry I wanted to hurt you after New York. And I do love you—but you've always known that."

"Daisy, this is the best thing that's happened—"

"Since we kissed in front of the hotel on the day we held Harris under forty in New Hampshire," she said. "That was the first time you told me that you loved me, even if you didn't actually say it."

"Henry, it must be mental telepathy," Jack Stanton said, when I found him in the kitchen of the Mansion, rooting around in the refrigerator, fixing on a package of Oscar Mayer bologna. He was wearing jeans, a purple western shirt and running shoes. "I just sent Tommy over to find you."

"Look, we need to talk," I said, in a tone of voice he understood immediately.

"I know that," he said. "And we will. But we've got some business first. Let me tell you what I've done. I've called Picker. I am going to

fly down there in about fifteen minutes and hand him Libby's file—
and apologize for compiling it, and tell him that I am pulling out of
this race tomorrow. I've called a press conference for eleven A.M., out
the backyard here. I figure that's what she would've wanted me to do."

I nodded.

"You know what her note to us said?" he asked, with a smile. "It
said, 'I am so fucking disappointed in you. SHAPE UP!' What did
yours say?"

"It said she could never have given you up."

"Henry, look. I know what you think, and what you're intending
to do—but could you just do me one last thing? Come with me now
down to Florida. You were with her last week. You did the interviews. Picker may have questions. I figure we should make all the information we have available to him, and you represent a big part of
that information."

"All right," I said. "Let me make a call first."

"She okay? Daisy?" Stanton asked. I nodded. "Tell her I'm sorry
about blowing her off in New York, too."

And so it was back to first things, Jack Stanton and me in a small
plane, flying from dusk to darkness across the South. There was an
airstrip in Capps, just north of Tallahassee, and a wood-paneled station
wagon with "Pickerwood" painted on the side waiting for us there.
The driver was an ancient redneck whose name also was Henry. It
was a perfect Deep South night, wet and wild, steambath humidity
and flying insects; the windshield was stained to the point of opacity.
Henry tried the wipers, which only made things worse. "Flyin'
scum," he said. "We're almost there."

We turned down a dirt road flanked by live oaks draped in Spanish moss. A quarter-mile in, there was a white fence and lawn behind
it. In the distance stood an elegant white plantation house with three
thick pillars and two curved, embracing wings. The dirt road turned
to gravel beyond the fence, the gravel became a vast circular drive
with a large plaster fountain in the middle, dripping gently, crystalliz-
ing the wetness of the night. Ancient yellow lights burned in the
plantation house. There was the sound of a viola: Picker's younger son

working on *Sinfonia Concertante* in his room upstairs. Every sound, every sense, seemed augmented—the slam of the car doors as we got out, the chatter of the insects, a distant owl. There was a misty moon, several days past full—Libby waning.

Picker's older son, Fernando, greeted us at the door and promptly disappeared. Picker stood just behind him, dressed casually—jeans, a striped, button-down dress shirt with the sleeves rolled, bare feet. He was deeply tanned, the wrinkles around his eyes paler than his skin, and pronounced; his hair was slicked back, as if he'd just gotten out of the shower. He ushered us into a den just off the main hall. There was a large console television in a corner, a dark green Chinese Art Deco rug, two flowered chintz sofas at right angles facing the television; the walls had bookshelves most of the way up, with a strip of plaid wallpaper—the sort of thing you'd find in a cocktail lounge with a hunting motif—above them, interrupted occasionally by brass sconces, which provided most of the quiet light in the room. Picker snapped off the television, asked if we wanted a drink. Stanton said Diet Coke, I nodded and Picker pulled a couple out of a small refrigerator in a cabinet below the bookshelves. He drank Orangina.

"So," he said.

"Well, I've pretty much decided to get out of this thing tomorrow," Jack Stanton said. He and I were sitting in one of the couches; Picker in the other, his bare feet up on a lacquered oak-log coffee table.

"That's what CNN is saying," Picker said.

"And I wanted to come and apologize," Stanton said. "You heard about my . . . friend—the one who died?" Picker nodded. "She and Henry here spent last week compiling this," and he took the Picker file out of a brown envelope and handed it to him. "She died because she thought I was gonna use it against you. And I might have, though I hadn't made up my mind yet. I might have. And so I wanted you to have it—that's the only copy left. We destroyed the others. I wanted you to have it because it might help you to know what others are gonna be digging after, and maybe finding—and because I probably shouldn't have sent these folks off to do it in the first place. I'm really sorry."

Picker had been scanning the file as Stanton spoke. He flipped it aside now. "You're a musician—right, Governor?" he said, nodding upstairs. We could hear his son stop and start, stop and start, working hard at the Mozart. "You know how when you're learning a new piece, you'll hit a passage—a little thing, a bar or two—and say to yourself: 'Shit, I'll never get that sucker.' And you work at it, you sweat over it, you become a little crazed by it. Then, suddenly, it *falls into place*—and you're still a little crazed by it, you can't stop doing it. You're in love with your ability to do it. It feels so damn good. You may even start neglecting the easier parts of the piece and search for other tough passages to master. It's sort of an addiction. I've warned Felipe about that because . . ." He paused, gathered himself. "Because that's how *my* life has been. It's what speculating in oil leases was like, what politics was like. I did it for the pleasure of the challenge, and things always seemed to fall into place. I'm not so sure it's a particularly admirable way to live."

Stanton nodded cautiously. "Yeah, it's a danger—when you do it for *it,* and not for them."

"Jack, I *never* did it for them," Picker said, his dark eyes fierce on Stanton. I was stunned by the harshness of this; it was a startling thing to say. It appeared we were in for an interesting evening. "That was why I quit the first time—part of it, at least. Because I knew that everything up until then had been all about me." He got up from the couch, came around in front of us. "And *I* could do *anything.* I could handle any passage. I could make a fortune, I could win an election— and the thing about cocaine was, it only reinforced that. It made me feel that anything *I* wanted to do was the *right* thing to do. You ever try it?"

"Yeah, once," Stanton said. "Freaked me out. Made me too speedy. Also I have a kind of screwed-up, sensitive nose."

"I loved it," Picker said, then looked at me. "Reggie Duboise was wrong, though: I couldn't handle it, either. It was the first thing I'd come up against I couldn't handle. That was really what fucked up my marriage—not . . . anything else. I knew, after Reggie saved me, after he found me and Renzo together, that I had to quit being governor. Truth was, I wasn't doing a very good job of it anyway. I had to quit and get my life together. And I did. My sons saved my life. It's the most basic lesson, right? Giving to them saved me from my own selfishness." He paused, looked at me again. "So is Renzo pretty far gone?"

"He's hangin' in there," I said.

"Good," he said. "I can't say I ever knew him very well. It was just a coke thing. I mean, the stuff made you feel so—like the hair on your arm was a sexual organ. He touched my arm. And, you know, since I could do *anything,* since everything was permitted—I did that, too."

"You don't have to—" Stanton interrupted.

"No, I'd better," Picker said, sitting back down. "I have to. I did do that, and I still don't quite know what it means. It wasn't a high-brain activity. It was something my body did when stoned. I walk along a street, and it's women I look at. I've been dating a really nice—I suppose I'll have to tell her now, too. A helluva price to pay." He shook his head.

"No one needs to find out," Stanton said. "Reggie won't talk. Renzo won't talk."

Picker eyed him closely. "I had no intention of ever taking this as far as it went. I felt an itch. I figured I'd put a toe in. I liked what Harris was doing. He was closer to right than you were, or so it seemed—although, I realized when it got going, that *that* was mostly appearances. He was still doing his Poli Sci class. It was a vanity campaign. But I figured: I'll do it for a week. I missed politics—the rush when you move them. Right, Jack? It's better than making money." He paused, leaned back, began to drift away from where he was headed. "That's why a guy like Larry Harris couldn't ever be president. You need someone who knows the emotional part of the game, the symbols, the theater, how to use the power. And you also need someone who *really* knows the issues—not like Larry, not academic fantasies. Someone who knows what's doable."

What *was* this? I had the sense it was some sort of valedictory. I wondered if Stanton was picking it up—undoubtedly he was. But I couldn't see his eyes, only the side of his face. He had the big ears on, that was clear from the intensity of the silences; he was pulling the story out of Freddy Picker, who had his knees back up on the coffee table now and his hands clasped around them.

"Could I have said no when Martha Harris asked me?" Picker continued. "I guess I could have. But I saw how vulnerable you were—and it was very tempting. I could see the whole scenario laying out, just perfect, for me. Though I guess, on some unconscious level, I still wasn't perfectly secure that what was past was past—and that's probably why I did the blood thing."

"It was great politics," Stanton offered.

Picker laughed. "Amazing, wasn't it? I just blurted it out. I really hadn't planned it. And it worked for me on a lot of different levels. I figured, Okay, if I'm gonna do politics seriously again, this time I've got to give something, instead of just getting that rush from them. But there was that *other* level, too, the one I wasn't quite aware of—but I found out soon enough."

He unclasped his hands, pulled down his knees, leaned forward. "In fact, I was jolted by it—by reality, I guess—as soon as they put the needle in my arm. It's amazing, the tricks your mind can play. All those years out of the business, I'd watch as politicians made fools of themselves—Gary Hart, John Tower, you—and I'd wonder: What *ever* could they have been thinking about? And then, there I was." He shook his head. "There *I* was. I hadn't really 'blocked' the past. I'd just refused to consider it. The things I did . . ." He paused, he shook his head again—in amazement, it seemed. "The things that would be considered 'scandalous' if the press got hold of them, those things were so far in the past, so distant—not quite real anymore, just barely remembered—and they had so little to do with who I'd become. It was, like, *silly* that I could be . . . destroyed by them. They weren't me anymore. They'd only been a moment. And that moment was less important, less a part of my memory, than—what? Than the years I spent on the board of the North Florida Art Institute. But this was potentially lethal. And so humiliating—everything I . . . And when they put that needle in my arm, it was like an electric shock: *Why am I doing this?*, I thought. *This is nuts.* And then I began to obsess about the blood. I added up the years since Renzo. Fourteen years. That's a long time, right? I searched my mind: hadn't my blood been tested a dozen times since then? Wouldn't they test for *that?* But maybe they didn't do it if you didn't ask them to—maybe it was a privacy issue, given gay rights and all. Was it possible that I'd never actually been tested for AIDS?"

The word had an impact. He let it hang in the room. He got up, got himself another Orangina, brought us Diet Cokes. "I tried to push it aside," he said. "I smiled for the cameras. They took that stupid picture of me giving blood. But I couldn't push it aside. I guess it symbolized a whole bunch of things—I mean, what *right* did I have to be running for president, anyway? What had *I* ever done to earn a seat at the table?" He stared at the ceiling; he shrugged up at heaven, then looked at his hands. "Then again, what did anyone else have going for them? Unknown politicians catch fire all the time. Who was Jimmy Carter? Who was Michael Dukakis? Who were *you* three months ago? Why *not* me? I did seem to be pretty good at it."

Picker shook his head and frowned. He sat back down again and leaned forward, anxious to explain himself—and almost relieved, it seemed, that he was finally getting the chance. "But the blood thing kept eating at me," he said softly. "I assumed they'd test all donations. Even"—he laughed—"from presidential candidates. But how long did it take to get results? And what if I *did* test 'positive' and some orderly decided to get rich by selling the scoop to the tabloids? Can you imagine? Yeah, I guess *you* can. But I was around the bend. I was sort of like Lady Macbeth—obsessed by the blood. I had to find out. But how? You couldn't just call up and say, 'Hi, this is Fred Picker. Gave a pint the other day. Could you check and see if I've got AIDS?' It wasn't anything you could really ask *staff* to do, either. I knew I was being nutty. I knew I wasn't being reasonable. And it kept building: Just before the rally in New Haven, I really freaked out, a total anxiety attack. I mean, I hadn't had one of those since—since the day Reggie Duboise saved my ass in Coral Gables. But there I was, shaking, hyperventilating, in the car heading over to the Yale Bowl. I was three-quarters convinced I had AIDS . . . and the other quarter was furious I was acting like such a weakling."

"Lordamercy," Stanton said. He had to say something.

"I stood up there in New Haven," Picker said quietly, "and I didn't know what to do. Did you see it that night?" Stanton nodded yes. "You know what I was thinking about, standing up there? I was thinking about *you*. Well, sort of. I was thinking: They're gonna find me out. Even if I *don't* have AIDS I'm fucked. They're gonna find me out—and then they're gonna do to me what they're doing to Jack Stanton." Picker wiped his brow with the back of his hand. The room was gently air-conditioned—it wasn't the usual arctic Southern over-compensation—and he was beginning to perspire. "It suddenly seemed so cruel, what they were doing to you. I mean, I haven't been a great person in this life. I've done a lot of stupid, selfish things, and running for president may have been one of them—but I didn't think I'd done anything that might remotely merit the humiliation, the viciousness . . ." His voice trailed off, his eyes clouded over. "It was like some sort of pagan ritual, the way they were ripping you apart. And I'd been kind of getting off on it, *feeding* it even. At least, until that moment in New Haven, and that's when I realized: *Stanton probably doesn't deserve it either.*"

Well, I thought—he deserved it some.

Stanton glanced over at me quickly, sensing that I was betraying him. I may have been, but Picker wasn't in any shape to notice. He was staring off into space, running a nervous hand through his hair. He was still back in New Haven, lost in his story: "I didn't know what to do. It was unimaginable—all those people waving posters with drops of blood. I mean, can you imagine? Drops of blood? I wanted some room, some time to think. So I tried to calm them down. And, of course, the exact opposite happened: Every last thing that came out of my mouth got them even more worked up. It was an order of power I'd never even imagined. It was like some stupid fairy-tale sort of curse, a King Midas thing. Everything I tried to shut it down only made it bigger, and I didn't have the courage to *really* shut it down. They were so . . . easily led. I began to think that even if I was okay, even if my blood was clean—I wasn't sure I really wanted to *do* this. I could never live up to their expectations. I could never give them what they needed."

He lowered his head and wiped an eye. I had come to expect that any politician I admired would be like Jack Stanton—larger than life, as formidable in the flesh as he appeared on television. But Freddy Picker wasn't. He was, resolutely, life-size—in every respect but one. He had a parlor trick; he could perform—brilliantly, instinctively—for the cameras. He didn't seem to have any higher purpose than that; he didn't seem to know much about politics. What Picker realized in New Haven—about the desperation of the crowd—Stanton had known from the womb. Jack Stanton also understood, intuitively, that the real challenge was far more difficult than simply meeting their expectations. It was about *exceeding* their expectations. It was about inspiring them. If you couldn't do that, you were Millard Fillmore. It was a *very* tough game. There were only two or three winners per century, and a fair number of the losers were burned at the stake.

Or disappeared from memory—and the Picker phenomenon was evaporating before my eyes. "So I called the hospital the next day," he was saying now. "I told them I'd been anemic in the past, and was feeling a little tired, and I just . . . I just wanted to see if the blood had been tested, y'know? They put me on hold." He laughed. "As if I were a normal human being. *You* know how it is, Jack: when you're governor, they never put you on hold. But I waited—and waited, and it was awful. Finally, the nurse came back on and said that, yes, they'd checked it and, no, there was nothing unusual about my blood, everything was fine."

I think I exhaled.

"But everything wasn't fine," he said. The words were coming faster, just cascading out of him now. "In fact, it got worse. I felt even more trapped. I began to obsess about the drugs. I drove myself crazy, making a list, trying to think of all the parties I'd been to down in Dade—parties just crawling with jerks who might give me up. And then there was Renzo. Who *was* Renzo, anyway? Had he told anyone? Would he tell someone now? Would he tell the *National Flash*? I got up every day wondering if *this* would be the day they found me out. It crowded out everything. You saw how much trouble I had keeping up with you during that Geraldo debate, right? It became impossible to think seriously about what I was doing—I was running for president, and all I could think about was my imminent national embarrassment."

"Tell me about it," Stanton said.

"But, Jack, the difference was: I was in over my head," Picker said. "You'd been preparing for this forever—least that's what I read. I just jumped in. It was more than a lark—but it wasn't quite *serious* either, if you know what I mean. I hadn't prepared. I didn't really know the issues. But most important, I hadn't thought about—all this stuff. And after New Haven, it became the *only* thing I could think about. So when we won New York, I made the announcement that I was going to come home and consider what was 'best for the country.' *Hah!* I was trying to come up with a way to get out before they found me out. And, Jack, I'd like to thank you for coming here tonight the—the honorable way you did." He turned to me—"Henry, I'm not even angry you went snooping around my past. Better you than most anyone else. . . . Anyway, you've given me the excuse to finally do what I'd been trying to get up the courage to—"

"Whut?" Stanton asked—impatient, finally.

"I'm dropping out," Picker said.

"Jesus," Stanton said, not surprised. "Are you . . ."

"Sure?" Picker laughed. "Yeah. You know how I said that all the things they'd hang me for—all my sins—were so far in the past that it seemed they'd happened to a different person? Well, I've come to believe that my political ambition is part of that, too. Something dangerous that should have been left in the past, like cocaine and the rest. The idea that I could be invincible, that anything *I* wanted to do was okay—that's an adolescent thing, right? I look at my boys and they . . ."

He stopped. The thought of his boys seemed to stop him cold. "I figure the press'll still find me out. They'll be all over this story, right? But maybe I can preempt them a little, give them part of it—and they won't go find the rest. I really don't want them to find out about Renzo. But, Jack, the bottom line is still: I'm a national joke, right? I don't see any way to get around that. And I still have to explain it all to my boys." He frowned, then stared down at his hands. They seemed paralyzed, palms up, futile on his thighs. He looked up at Stanton, his dark eyes sharp again. His tone hardened. "No matter what I do, those motherfuckers are *still* going to find the rest of it, aren't they?"

I couldn't see exactly what Jack Stanton did at that moment, it must have been something with his eyes—a twitch, a wince, a premonition of a tabloid headline, a glimmer of the agony to come. Whatever it was, Picker caught it—and seemed to implode, shriveling on the couch, knees up, shoulders shaking slightly, uncontrollably, arms over his head.

Stanton was up and across the room before I fully realized what had happened. He gathered up Freddy Picker, who curled in, burying his head in Stanton's chest. And he rocked Picker for what seemed a very long time, occasionally kissing him on top of the head—until, slowly, the former governor of Florida regained his composure. All of this transpired without a word, with barely a sound.

"Governor," Stanton finally said, "I don't know if you're a drinking man—I'm not much of one—but I think we could both use a small jolt of bourbon just about now."

Picker disengaged himself from Stanton's embrace, went to a cupboard and brought out a bottle of Jack Daniel's and three glasses. There were napkins in the cupboard, and he blew his nose with one. His eyes were wild and bloodshot, his hair was all over his forehead. But, somehow, he hadn't lost his dignity. "Jack," he said, "I hope you don't take this the wrong way, but you seem so *impervious*. Not sitting here. Here, you seem like a normal guy. But how do you wake up in the morning—like in the middle of New York, when they were pulverizing you—how do you just get up and face the world, knowing they're gonna tear your lungs out today, make you seem a crook and a fool and a liar, same as yesterday? I'm curious because it's a skill I'll probably be needing."

"I don't rightly know," Stanton said. "There just doesn't seem to be any other option for me—nothin' else I really *can* do. And yeah, I'm sure a part of it—a big part of it—is ego sickness. You called it an addiction. You're right. But that's not *all* of it. I do *love* it—the part you talked about, moving a crowd. And the strategy, too; the game of it. But I don't think I'd be baring my butt for random whipping by that self-righteous, hypocritical pack of shitbirds if I didn't believe that you can, on occasion, make people's lives a little better. I know it sounds corny, but I still get all excited when I come across some program we've done that actually works," he said, with genuine enthusiasm. He stood up, getting ready to go. "I mean, have you ever been to an adult literacy class? Grown-ups trying to learn how to read? You talk about New York. You know what comes to my mind? Not the primary. I already *forgot* that. What I think about is this little adult literacy program up in Harlem, Henry and I visited once." He turned to me, eyes glistening. "It was the day we met—right, Henri? It was just pure glory. It was like going to church."

Picker stood too, now. "Jack"—he smiled—"you may want to reconsider dropping out tomorrow."

"Yeah, well . . ." Stanton paused, blushed. "I've been thinking 'bout that."

"Truth is," Picker said, leaning against the door, hands scrunched in the pockets of his jeans, "this wouldn't have lasted much longer even—even if I hadn't been carrying around all this extra luggage. I'd pretty much run out of things to say. I didn't know what else to tell them." He laughed. "I'll bet that never happens to you."

"Freddy, you know what *I* was thinking, watching you that night in New Haven?" Stanton said then. "I was thinking: That's what *I* should have been about. That's the campaign I should have run. But *I* didn't have the courage." He paused, then, needing some physical punctuation, put his arm straight out on Freddy Picker's shoulder and looked him hard in the eye. "See, it doesn't really matter why you did what you did: you raised the game a notch. You created a standard—of, yeah, candor—the rest of us are going to have to deal with now. That's a real good thing for the country."

"I appreciate that, Jack," Picker said. "Even if it is unadulterated bullshit."

They hugged in the doorway. "Bullshit'll grease a lot of doors," Stanton said. "The real test is what you do when you walk through 'em. . . . Anything I can do to help you through this, Freddy. Anything. Right?"

"I know, Jack," Picker said. "I'll remember that."

The governor whistled a sad country tune as we walked down the gravel path to the station wagon. He didn't say anything as we drove to the airport—but as soon as we hit the tarmac he asked, "So, Henry, you still want to have that meeting?"

"Yeah," I said.

"Ten o'clock at the Mansion tomorrow."

He whistled his sad song again as we walked toward the plane, drifting through the voluptuous north Florida night. And then—in his effortless, understated way—he sang the chorus:

> *"I can still feel the soft southern breeze*
> *in the live oak tree*
> *And those Williams boys, they still mean a lot to me—*
> *Hank and Tennessee . . .*

*I guess we're all gonna be what we're gonna be
So what do you do with good ol' boys like me?"*

"You know why I love that song?" he asked.

"Probably the line about the Williams boys," I said.

"Not bad, Henri," he said, tossing a big arm across my shoulders, gathering me in. "Not bad at all. See, the rednecks'll always pretend otherwise, but everyone who comes up from around here knows: It's never just Hank. The picture ain't ever complete without ol' Tennessee."

I was awakened by the smell of coffee. Daisy was bustling about the place, at ease—at *home*. She saw me stretch and came over to the bed. "I don't want this taken as a precedent," she said. "You're gonna have to make coffee, too. Whoever is up first, okay? But I guess you had a rough night."

"An *amazing* night." And I told her.

"So Stanton lives for the umpteen-fortieth time to fight another day," she said. "You think the term *dumb luck* might apply here?"

"He probably sees it as perseverance," I said. "But Libby was *so* completely right: he *never* has to pay the bill. Even when he *wants* to. He was ready last night. He was gonna quit the campaign—and Picker just wouldn't let him."

"You think this is what people mean when they talk about *destiny*?" she said, and laughed. "Pretty pathetic stuff. You sort of want destiny to be something grander." She poured me a mug of coffee and brought it over to the bed. "So what are *you* going to do?"

"I'm packing for . . . where? Jamaica?" I asked. "Wherever destiny ain't."

"You sure?" She asked. "Henry, don't do it for me. It's okay if you want to see it through."

"Naww," I said. "Too much water under too many bridges. It could never be the way it used to be."

"Maybe that's all to the good," she said. "Maybe you'll be better at this if you don't do it so worshipful."

"You *want* me to do it?"

"I want *you*," she said. "I don't care what you *do*. But it would be nice if we had some politics to talk about, in between all the mushy stuff."

"There's all kinds of politics," I said. "I might be better off spending my time helping Bill Johnson run for attorney general over in Alabama."

"I could help, too," she said. "I could do some killer *positives* for him."

"I love you, Daisy," I said.

"Love me," she said, "love my ads."

Stanton was upstairs in the Mansion, a sanctum I'd rarely penetrated. He had a small office up there—a desk, a television, pictures of Susan and Jackie, a picture of himself taking the oath of office, a bookcase filled with the classics of Southern politics—V. O. Key, W. J. Cash, C. Vann Woodward, T. Harry Williams on Huey Long, many others. There was a gray loveseat just off to the side of the desk, facing the television. Susan was sitting there, and I joined her.

"Thanks for last night, Henry," the governor said. He was dressed for success, wearing a blindingly white shirt and his red-and-blue-and-gold striped tie; his navy pin-striped suit jacket hung on a doorknob. Susan was ready for prime time, too, in a blue cotton suit with a beige crepe blouse. "Meant a lot to me, your being there. Pretty incredible, huh? Freddy called me this morning. He said he talked to his boys after we left—batted .500. Older one seemed okay, younger one took it pretty rough, slammed the door on him. But I'll bet you anything they smooth it over. He'll be on the air soon," he said, glancing at the television—CNN, muted. "So what's on *your* mind?"

"I'm resigning from the campaign," I said.

"I don't accept your resignation."

"Look, I just don't feel comfortable about this anymore."

"About *whut*?"

I couldn't quite say.

"I spoke to Richard," he said. "He's back on board. And I'm putting him in charge: campaign manager. He'll be right here, in this office, within the hour. Howard's goin' back to being *consigliere*. I'll keep Adler around—peripherally. He has his uses, but he'll answer to Richard. And look, we can bring Daisy back if you want, too."

"That's not what this is about," I said.

"Then what is it?"

"Libby—Libby's test," I said, searching for some concise way to tell him it had all been just too much. Even after all the time we'd spent together, I still found it difficult to just cut loose, speak my mind. My chest was tight, my throat constricted. "You flunked it."

"Oh, for Chrissake, Henry," he said. "This ain't the Boy Scouts. This is— Wait a minute, here he comes."

Picker had gone to Tallahassee. He didn't look too good, but his body language was determined, proud. He stood there alone. His boys weren't with him. He was wearing a dark suit, a blue button-down shirt with narrow stripes that didn't work too well for television, a muted tie. He took a yellow piece of legal paper out of his pocket, but didn't read from it.

"All right," he said. "Today, I am ending my surrogate campaign for the presidency." There were groans. People were shouting, "Why, why?" Susan got up from the loveseat and moved around behind her husband, an arm across his shoulders, her cheek resting atop his head.

Picker tried to smile. "I know some of you are thinking this is déjà vu. We've been this way before. And we have. And I was right the first time—back in 1978: I'm not cut out for this work. I'm not qualified to even *pretend* to run for the presidency." Someone jostled the CNN camera; there was mayhem, people seemed to be rushing everywhere. "When Martha Harris asked me to continue her husband's campaign, I was so honored—I didn't stop to think about the consequences. That was thoughtless of me. I'd like to apologize—"

"Why *aren't* you qualified?" Someone shouted.

"Because I knowingly broke the law when I was governor." He sighed, and plunged ahead. "At a time when a lot of people were experimenting with drugs, I did too. Actually, it was more than experimentation—if I'd just been messing around, that might have been forgivable. But I lost control of myself. I—"

"What sort of drugs?"

"Cocaine," Picker said. "That was the real reason I quit in 1978. That's what caused the problems in my marriage. But I cleaned myself up. I put it behind me. I put it so far behind me that I almost forgot it ever happened. But it did happen, and it seems obvious that it would be wrong for me to continue this campaign. I was a fool to think I could ever . . ."

There was a fleeting, barely discernible patch of silence. The reporters were nonplussed, disarmed by his apparent candor once again. Picker sensed it and seemed to gain confidence. He moved to fill the dead air: "So anyway, I don't think there's much more to say. I'm pretty embarrassed," he said—but he didn't *seem* embarrassed. He was back performing his old parlor trick, more alive on television than off it. The pack would be after him soon enough; they'd muck around the Picker scandal and pull every last morsel off the bones of his candidacy. But he wouldn't be humiliated on camera, and that represented no small triumph. "God," Stanton said, "it's frightening how good he could have been."

It was almost as if Picker heard him. He'd been starting to move away from the microphones, but stopped. "There's one more thing," he said. "I want to thank Jack Stanton for being aware of this situation and not taking advantage of it. I know I'm not in a position to make a recommendation here, but I've gotten to know Governor Stanton a little better these past few weeks—and, maybe, you should try to do the same. He may be the most misunderstood man in American politics. But you can come to your own conclusions about that. And that *is* all I want to say. Except that I'm sorry. And good-bye."

There were six lines into the phone on Jack Stanton's desk and, instantaneously, every one of them lit up. The intercom—connected to Annie Marie at the statehouse—buzzed. Stanton cupped the phone, spoke to me: "Are you *still* having doubts about this?"

"Yes," I said.

"Take messages," he said to Annie Marie. Then to me, "I thought you got it, Henry. I thought you understood. This is about the ability to *lead*. It's not about perfection. Okay, I probably would have leaked the file to someone—and I'da felt real slimy about it, but you know what? The bottom line wouldn't be any different. Picker was going down. It was only a question of when."

"And *how*," I said. "He might not have been so kind this morning if you'd been the one who pushed him off the cliff."

"Okay. Fair enough. But, Henry, what are we doing here?" he asked sadly, shaking his head. "We're arguing over how many politicians you can fit on the head of a pin. Are you trying to say you've suddenly discovered there's such a thing as hardball, and you don't have the stomach for it—and you're squishing out on me? Come on. I know you too well for that. We've been through too much together."

"Too much," I agreed. I looked over at Susan. She was, for once, leaving the heavy lifting to Jack. She knew it was the only way to close the deal.

"The question *you've* got to ask is, what are the options?" He said softly, almost warmly, still patient with me, his blue eyes locked into mine. "Only certain kinds of people are cut out for this work—and, yeah, we are *not* princes, by and large. Henry, you know this better than anyone. You've watched Larkin, you've watched O'Brien, you've watched me do it. Two thirds of what we do is reprehensible. This isn't the way a normal human being acts. We smile, we listen— you could grow calluses on your ears from all the listening we do. We do our pathetic little favors. We fudge when we can't. We tell them what they want to hear—and when we tell them something they *don't* want to hear, it's usually because we've calculated that's what they really want. We live an eternity of false smiles—and why? Because it's the price you pay to lead. You don't think Abraham Lincoln was a whore before he was a president? He had to tell his little stories and smile his shit-eating, backcountry grin. He did it all just so he'd get the opportunity, one day, to stand in front of the nation and appeal to 'the better angels of our nature.' That's when the bullshit stops. And that's what this is all about. The opportunity to do that, to make the most of it, to do it the right way—because you know as well as I do there are plenty of people in this game who never think about the folks, much less their 'better angels.' They just want to win. They want to be able to say, 'I won the biggest thing you can win.' And they're willing to sell their souls, crawl through sewers, lie to the people, divide them, play to their worst fears—"

"You played to their fears in Florida," I said, trying to stop the torrent.

"You did too," he said. "You never said, 'Ohhh, *dear,* we're not being *fair* to poor Lawrence Harris.' You never said, 'This is morally repugnant to me.' You know why? Two reasons. First, your blood was up—like it or not, Henry, you're a warrior and we were at war—and you wanted to *kill* that pious fucker, just like I did. Only not *literally,* which shook all of us up—made all of us doubt ourselves a little and gave Picker the impetus for his move. But the second reason is more important: You knew I'd make a better president than Harris. You knew it. You may have had your doubts there, for a few days, about whether I'd be better than Picker—but you *saw* him last night. A very decent guy, smart, good instincts. But a *president?* No way. He's just barely a politician. I mean, in the end, Henry, who can do this better than me? You think there's anyone out there who'll do more for the people than I will? Think about all those other *wonderful* possibilities. Consider Larkin. And Ozio. And ask yourself this: Is there anyone else out there with a chance to actually win this election who'd even *think* about the folks I care about?"

"I care about the McCollisters," I said.

"I do *too,*" he said, glancing quickly over at Susan—and calculating that there was no concession to candor he could make here, nothing he could do but tough it out. If I stayed with him, I would have to live with that.

"I was thinking," I said then, "about maybe going over to Montgomery and helping Bill Johnson get himself elected attorney general."

That stopped him. But only for a heartbeat. He was, as always, much faster than me. "All right, if that's what you want," he said. "But do you know how long Billy's been talking about running for A.G.? You know how totally convinced he is those peckerwoods'll never vote for a black man? And say he does run, say you help him win—what, then? You know what the attorney general of Alabama *does?* He gets unsightly billboards removed. He sues the power company—unsuccessfully, always. And he sends Snopeses to the electric chair for knocking over convenience stores and sodomizing their granddaughters. Henry, we are talking about the presidency of the United States here. *Are you with me?*"

"He might also keep the trees clean," I said, with some heat. "Might keep some black kids from getting lynched." Stanton was surprised by my stubbornness. So was I.

"Look, Henry," Susan interrupted—gently. "We're gonna have to go out there in a few minutes and do this thing. The whole country is going to be watching, so we better spend a minute thinking about what Jack should say."

I nodded. "Henry, come on," Stanton said, stretching his arms out across the desk toward me. His voice caught slightly. His eyes narrowed, burrowing deep, searching my consciousness, desperate to make a stronger connection. His brow, his nostrils, the veins in his neck, his arms, his fingers—everything was reaching out, everything was focused on me. I knew this moment so well; I had seen him do it so many times. He could talk all he wanted about an eternity of "false" smiles: His power came from the exact opposite direction, from the *authenticity* of his appeal, from the stark ferocity of his hunger. There was very little artifice to him. He was truly needy. And now he truly needed me.

"We've worked so hard—*together*, Henry—to get here," he pleaded. "And it's there for us now. It's right there. We can do incredible things. We can change the whole country—not just Alabama. If we win this thing, you don't think Bill Johnson's gonna want to come to Washington himself? He can be attorney general of the United States—not at first, maybe, but down the road. That's why he came up to New Hampshire. To make sure I'd remember him when the time came. And it's gonna come, Henry. I can win this thing. We are going to make history. Look me in the eye and tell me it's not gonna happen. Look me in the eye, Henry—and tell me you don't want to be part of it."

"I . . ."

"Jesus, Jesus, Jesus, Henry," he said. "You want me down on my knees? I can't *do* it without you. Don't leave me now." He hesitated, searched my face for an answer. "You're still with me, aren't you? Say you are. Say you are. *Say* it."

He stopped, and suddenly smiled. I had trouble reading the smile. He was nonplussed, but confident. He wasn't conceding anything. "Aw c'mon, Henry. This is *ridiculous:* you've *gotta* be with me."

ACKNOWLEDGMENTS

I would like to thank some people who don't know who I am. This was a remarkable leap of faith for Harold Evans and Random House. I particularly want to thank Daniel Menaker, whose enthusiasm and insights were invaluable during an unusual—and very lonely—editing process. He seemed to understand what this was really all about before I did.

I'd also like to thank Kathy Robbins, who is remarkable in every way. This never would have happened without her.

And, of course, my family. You were very patient, and just terrific.

ABOUT THE TYPE

This book was set in Bembo, a typeface based on an old-style Roman face that was used for Cardinal Bembo's tract *De Aetna* in 1495. Bembo was cut by Francisco Griffo in the early sixteenth century. The Lanston Monotype Machine Company of Philadelphia brought the well-proportioned letter forms of Bembo to the United States in the 1930s.